THE EDGE OF IMPROPRIETY

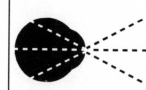

This Large Print Book carries the
Seal of Approval of N.A.V.H.

GALE
CENGAGE Learning

LIBRARY OF CONGRESS CATALOGING-IN-PUBLICATION DATA

Rosenthal, Pam.
  The edge of impropriety / by Pam Rosenthal.
    p. cm. — (Thorndike Press large print romance)
  ISBN-13: 978-1-4104-1729-9 (alk. paper)
  ISBN-10: 1-4104-1729-8 (alk. paper)
  1. Women authors—Fiction. 2. Italy—History—19th century—Fiction. 3. Large type books. I. Title.
PS3618.O8434E34 2009
813'.6—dc22   2009011064

Published in 2009 by arrangement with NAL Signet, a member of Penguin Group (USA) Inc.

THE EDGE OF IMPROPRIETY

PAM ROSENTHAL

THORNDIKE PRESS
A part of Gale, Cengage Learning

GALE
CENGAGE Learning™

Detroit • New York • San Francisco • New Haven, Conn • Waterville, Maine • London

For Penni Kimmel, with gratitude

PROLOGUE

Italy, Lake Como
Spring 1818

The baronet's rented villa faced the shore. Light from the lake's surface bounced and rippled against the drawing room's painted ceiling. A tiny child crooned a nonsense song as she wove her way among the other four figures in the room.

An English lady and gentleman — she elegantly willowy, he lanky, broad-shouldered, rumpled — gazed wordlessly at a pair of beautiful adolescents, while the younger couple — they were Greek — bore the scrutiny with the same patience they'd exhibited since having been carved from marble some twenty-odd centuries before.

The child traced curious fingers over the fluted draperies of the girl statue's tunic. The lady sighed. As one ought, in the presence of antique glory.

"Lovely," she breathed. "So austere, so

7

pure in their marble whiteness, so *civilized.*"

The gentleman laughed. "So cheap."

"Cheap?"

"Indeed. Marble's cheap in that part of the world. These are copies of bronze originals. The Greeks preferred their sculptures in bronze, colored and set with jewels for eyes. Very flash, the ancients were."

"You're teasing me."

"Upon my word I'm not."

His eyes were an intense blue in a sunburned face. His thick brown hair, bleached a dark sandy color by a relentless Mediterranean sun, was in serious need of cutting.

"The bronze was mostly melted down for nails and cannonballs — oh, and coin: A Roman general might pay his soldiers in melted statue. But they had such an abundance of marble, we find it everywhere — with its paint washed off, of course — and we've made rather a cult of classical white purity. The marble of the Parthenon was very likely painted in red and blue."

She pouted, partly from disappointment and partly — he knew — because the expression was as becoming to her as it had ever been. He watched the pout relax itself into a smile, heard it bubble into a laugh. "Still the scholar. And now a teacher, an authority."

Her voice deepened now, as she moved forward to stroke the long, tense line of his jaw. "I remember you as rather more the student."

Her eyelashes cast scalloped shadows over beautifully smooth cheeks as her bright hazel gaze moved along the length of his body. "An apt one. Alert, ready . . ."

"Fifteen years ago," he murmured.

"I'm pretending I didn't hear you say that." The eyelashes flickered downward. "Ah, yes." The caressing voice had dropped to a low-pitched whisper. "Well, *some* things don't change, do they?"

Some things did not. He sucked his breath through his teeth. No point denying the obvious.

No matter, either. He'd go take a long, brisk walk by the shore of the lake, and that would be the end of it. Still, no reason not to enjoy the moment. The best consolation for the loss of one's impetuous first youth must be this connoisseur's appreciation of the pulls and tightenings, quickened sensations, thrilling pathos of unsatisfied desire.

Her skin had flushed to a dark pink. Damask rose. No — he felt his nostrils flare — *musk* rose. The passing of fifteen years had rendered his sister-in-law's beauty earthier.

9

She must feel the same slow, aching pleasure he did.

At least, he hoped so. Because it was the only pleasure they'd be taking from each other this time.

She dropped her hand and he took a step backward.

"You've been avoiding me all week," she said. "This is the first time I've been alone with you since your arrival."

He inclined a square chin in the direction of the child, who'd walked around behind the girl statue. "We're *not* alone."

"No, of course not. But Sydney's so excessively capable of amusing herself, I'd almost forgotten she was with us. Odd, isn't it, in one so young?"

"Not so odd. I was like that."

"And still are. Whereas both John and I require constant attention and novelty."

"I can remember," Jasper said, "how very prepossessing John was as a boy — precisely the sort of young gentleman a baronet would want for an heir, while I was quite content to remain in the background in the event of inconceivable calamity. The arrangement left me lots of time for reading, long walks, and wild fancies." He grinned. "That was before I learned that a second son had to make his own way in the world."

The grin remained upon his face perhaps an instant too long before he began to speak again. "Yes. Well. So. Have you and John succeeded in amusing each other for this past . . . hmm . . . this past unspeakable number of years?" Perhaps he shouldn't have asked. What he'd observed between them this week hadn't been encouraging.

"Sometimes. Not very often. The amusement comes and goes. I expect it needs to for there to be any novelty in it. We spend a good deal of money on novelty. More than we can afford, I fear — on things, and on people as well."

Her eyes flashed for a moment — with shame, he wondered, or a certain pride in having gotten what she could from the situation she'd found herself in?

"Perhaps," she continued, "I *should* have run away with you back then." She shrugged. "I do enjoy travel — Constantinople would have been lovely. Of course, no one traveled during the war years but a brave few like you. Yes, I *should* have. . . ."

He welcomed the laughter that had overtaken him. "Be reasonable, Celia. You're imagining yourself a Lady Elgin — caravans of baggage, tents like miniature palaces, torchlit regattas on the Bosporus. It wouldn't have been like that for us; I was a foolish boy to propose it, with no notion whatsoever of the . . .”

Danger, he'd been about to say. Pirates, brigands, petty and not-so-petty chieftains setting up their own little island or mountain kingdoms in rugged pockets of a sprawling Ottoman Empire.

Leave it alone, he told himself. Her modish popular misconceptions of antique art would be nothing compared to her Byronic Oriental fancies — especially these days, with her life settled into routine and her husband running to fat. The Albanian costume Jasper had brought would never fit his older brother; he'd make him a present of a nice old rug instead.

Jasper wasn't accustomed to attending much to his own looks. A revelation then, to see himself this week through Celia's veiled and not-so-veiled glances, to contrast the person she seemed to see with the confused, love-struck young scholar of fifteen years before. Catching his reflection in a pier glass, a window against a night sky, or the lake in a moment of glassy stillness, he'd wondered at the rangy, brown, tousle-headed fellow staring back at him, long bones and attenuated nerves sheathed in lithe muscle. A stranger even to himself.

A romantic adventurer. A novelty.

No, Celia, not this time.

John would soon be back from the boat dock. If Jasper were to ask the important question, he'd have to do it quickly. As Celia was very well aware, even as she made him work to get the opportunity, in her eagerness for his attention. Or had Jasper been courting *her* attention more than he liked to admit?

Pensively, she gazed at the pair of statues. "Well, they're lovely, in any case. The boy's an archer, I gather, or some sort of athlete. And the girl?"

"A young Aphrodite. But as for the boy . . . Oddly, he's her son, Eros — Cupid, if you will, though not a chubby, simpering Italian version. The nubs on his shoulders are the remnants of wings — he's not running; he's flying. Yes, I know he appears the same age she does. But then, the gods don't age as we do."

She looked away.

"I think," he said, "that they're the work of the same hand. It'll be a great pleasure to send them home to Athens, much as I've loved having them with me. They're the achievement, I suppose, of all my wanderings."

"How strange," she said. "I've never gone anywhere, and yet my achievement is also a girl" — she nodded at Sydney, who'd squatted down to examine the kneeling Aphrodite's sandal — "and a boy."

A boy, yes.

Yes, finally. A boy. He'd be fourteen now.

Jasper willed himself not to let his voice tremble. "I must own that I'm not able to picture what he looks like. A pity you have only that single old miniature with you, of him still in petticoats."

Her smile had a hint of mockery in it. "He's as beautiful as your statues. When we had a family painting done last year at Wheldon Priory, the artist had to restrain himself from making Anthony the center of the composition. I felt sadly neglected — quite the unnatural mother in my vanity."

"The miniature is accurate, then. He looks like you."

"As I've looked in certain moments. I expect you'd recognize something of that in him. I wonder how you'd take it. Anthony has your family's height, though."

Anthony. Anthony John Leigh-Carrington Hedges, as John's overjoyed letter to his brother had had it in emphatic underlinings. *An heir!!*

The mail had taken some months to find him. Jasper had celebrated the birth of the son — *his* son, though no one but he and

14

Celia would ever know it — with a four-day debauch in the best brothel in Smyrna. There'd been hashish; he couldn't remember much of what happened, but since then he'd always gotten extraordinary service when he patronized that establishment.

"Anthony." He repeated the name, pronouncing it aloud for the first time in memory.

The little girl sitting on the floor raised serious blue eyes. "I want Anthony to come," she said.

As did Jasper. Every bit as much as he feared it.

Celia smiled. "He was very sweet with her when we saw him in London, just before we came away. How clever she is to remember — it was only a few days; we had to pack him off to spend the remainder of his holiday with a school friend if we were to catch the good weather for embarking."

She lowered her voice. "A pity, though, that she's the clever one and he's the beauty. I mean, she's well enough. . . ."

"More than that, I think," Jasper said.

"Really."

"At first glance," he said, "all one sees in her is my family's serviceable looks."

"Oh, yes, she's John's."

"But I can make out hints and glimmer-

15

ings of you. Perhaps it's for the better that one must look to discover the ways she'll be beautiful."

"You have a sharp eye."

"I've been sharpening it on the most magnificent artifacts mankind has ever created. But about Anthony." Would the name ever come naturally to him? "What sort of boy is he?"

She shrugged. "A boy. Boisterous, spirited, impatient. Indifferent scholar, excellent horseman. John likes to take him hunting. They get on very well together."

As they should. What had he expected? Stoically, he waited for the spasm of guilty, helpless longing to loose its hold on him.

"Perhaps you'll come to England and meet him." Her smile was mischievous. "Well, you'll have to come home sometime, Uncle Jasper."

"Uncle Jasper." Sydney repeated it carefully before adding the syllables to the song she was singing to the sculptures.

Uncle Jasper was what Anthony would call him.

"Someday I'll come," he said. "Not now. You know I'm going to be accompanying these back to Greece."

"Without being paid for it." That was John at the doorway, red-faced, genial, but refusing as a matter of principle to accede to what he called his brother's widgeon-brained political illusions.

Jasper hadn't heard him approaching. He stepped farther away from Celia, and then wondered if it had been necessary to do so. Or even wise to act as though anything were amiss.

He glanced at her. She remained serene, unruffled, mildly diverted by the spectacle of the brothers' predictable sparring.

"Dr. Mavrotis will pay my expenses," he said. "It's all I ask. The sculptures will belong to the Greek nation — when they seize their independence from the Turks."

John harrumphed. Peaceably, Jasper spread out his hands.

He'd make no further argument. He and John had had it out more than once through the week preceding.

Yes, Jasper had repeated, he'd happily show the sculptures to anyone who wanted to see them. For there were collectors here at the lake: After all those years at war, Englishmen couldn't buy up enough antiquities once they got to the continent.

But no, neither Eros or Aphrodite was for sale.

And no, he repeated to himself now — firmly, to convince himself of it. Nothing was going to happen between himself and Celia.

Nor would he ever return to England.

He wasn't sorry to have made this visit, but he wouldn't be doing it again. Leave his past sins to themselves. Oldest story in the world, or near to it: a son not knowing his true father — the stuff of tragedy if ever it were to be revealed, but in this case, at least, it never would. Jasper had sworn it numerous times these past years, even as he'd begun to conceive how he'd spend the rest of his life.

For while there'd be no redeeming his sins, he'd come to consider that other wrongs might be more liable to rectification. One *could,* he'd begun to think, try to help a dispossessed people find their own destiny. Return a fledgling nation's patrimony to them, in the small but not insignificant way of two beautiful statues.

"Well, Jasper?" John must have asked him something while he'd been woolgathering, but the moment had passed. Evidently too impatient to care for an answer, the baronet had turned to his wife. His voice had taken on a querulous edge; Jasper listened warily.

"We should hurry if you want to go sailing as you said you did. I did ask you to be ready. And is Berridge's party for Lord

Gorham really tonight?"

Celia's reply was bland as milk. "The party for the earl and his wife is tomorrow; you needn't concern yourself. And I *am* ready — or shall be once I get a maid to bring Sydney to the nursery. Do come with us, Jasper," she added. "John's a wonderful sailor."

"Can't today," Jasper said. "Sorry. I've got correspondence to do, my monograph to attend to."

The perfect, perennial excuse: Always have a monograph to work on, at least in conversation. An English gentleman like John wouldn't know quite what a monograph was, but it sounded scholarly, important, and demanding of attention. And anyway, he did owe Dr. Mavrotis a letter, and one as well to the friends organizing a Greek emancipation committee in London.

As though needing to prove his intentions, he patted his pocket for the spectacles he'd recently taken to wearing at his writing desk.

But what was that tugging at his coat? He looked downward to see that Sydney had finally tired of the sculptures.

"Don't bother the maids," he heard himself saying. "I'll take her upstairs."

He picked her up and they exchanged companionable if rather solemn smiles.

"Hullo, Sydney," he said.

"Hullo, Uncle Jasper," she returned.

Grateful for the easy reciprocity of her company, he gave her a squeeze, and she returned the favor with a kiss.

He was holding her again at dawn, when she'd woken up crying for her mother. The maids told him she'd slept calmly through the storm, awakening only in the eerie, empty calm that followed — after the bodies had been recovered, taken away to be prepared for burial.

The sudden squall had surprised everyone, British travelers and Italian natives alike. Gathered by the shore in the livid light just before sunrise, a little mixed group repeated in sonorous chorus that Sir John Hedges had been a wonderful sailor.

It must have been fate.

Misjudgment.

Tragic accident.

No answer.

In which case, they might simply cease their chatter, Jasper thought. But they wouldn't. The English would repeat comforting commonplaces until their jaws tired of it, in praise of the baronet's bluff manliness and his wife's beauty. The Italians invoked the will of God, and especially the

20

Madonna, to help them grieve for *la bambina.*

Jasper suggested he might go see to the little girl. The little crowd nodded respectfully and parted to allow him to trudge back up the path. Receding behind him, the chorus of dirges mercifully became one with the sound of the wavelets lapping on the shore.

There was also a boy, someone said after Jasper disappeared into a grove of cypresses leading to the villa. At Eton. Poor young chap, asleep in his hard, schoolboy bed. He was the baronet now.

Sir John's younger brother was doubtless the guardian, someone else said. A bit of an eccentric, the men agreed; most interesting, the women returned. Those who knew reminded those who didn't that he'd been abroad for a good many years, doing something somewhere in the eastern Mediterranean.

He'd probably be going back. A guardian needn't be physically present; the lawyers could see to most of the business, and you could always find someone to care for the property — oh, and the children — if you paid.

The more immediate question was

whether Lord and Lady Berridge would still be having their reception for the Earl of Gorham. Was it proper, in light of the recent tragedy?

A pity not to have *something.* Perhaps a more subdued gathering, no dancing. Which was finally what the Berridges agreed upon, the night before the Gorham party was to move on to the Amalfi coast. Life must go on. Tragedy or not, there was no reason not to have the pleasure of introducing the earl, his young second wife who everyone said was such a dazzler, and the silent, almost indecently handsome Frenchman who kept so close to the couple's side.

Did Monsieur What's-his-name even speak English? The general consensus was that with his looks, he hardly need speak at all.

Almost everyone attended the party. The stout, balding earl shepherded his ravishing companions about as though they were willful children. But as to who played exactly what role in the little traveling comedy — *that* remained deliciously unclear to the rest of the guests, allowing them to imagine whatever they might. It was part of the pleasure, the looseness of being out on the continent after so many years of war and confinement at home.

Privately, a few people tried to imagine what the evening would have been like had Lady Hedges, the English community's hitherto undisputed beauty, faced off against Marina, the exuberantly gorgeous young Countess of Gorham. It would have been a close thing, but the edge probably would have gone to youth. The earl had extensive estates in counties Wexford and Waterford. People said Lady Gorham was Irish, though you wouldn't know it from how she spoke. She was reputedly a bit of a bluestocking. Difficult to imagine, but the earl was said to find it diverting.

Not that one could believe everything one heard.

Nor should one gossip *too* much, in the face of the sad events so lately visited upon them.

Anyway, the earl and his party were gone.

And Mr. Jasper Hedges was closing up his brother's villa in preparation for his own speedy return to England.

CHAPTER 1

Mayfair, London, eleven years later
March 31, 1829

    The footmen set platters of lobster down upon the table. *Homard à l'Orringer* was the kitchen's pride, bright white flesh and crimson claws veiled by a velvety sauce of green and pink peppercorns and gracefully arrayed over watercress pulled from the banks of the duke's Hampshire streambeds that morning at dawn and rushed by fast carriage to His Grace's house in town, overlooking . . .

The next few words were difficult to make out, rendered nearly illegible by an uneven, raised splotch on the paper. Their author, Marina, Countess of Gorham, frowned and bent her head closer to the page proofs. The print swam before her eyes; the moisture that had dripped from somewhere onto the page only made matters worse.

25

Wait, she thought. *Wait, I've got it after all.*

Not impossible if you squinted at the paper from a certain angle. She nodded; the blurred print *did* say *Green Park* rather than *Grosvenor Square,* as it had seemed at first. She *would* get through this thing on time, even with an hour less to do it than she'd originally planned.

Not that she was sorry to have woken at six instead of five. Last night had been worth it — especially in light of her recent difficult decision not to take the young baronet Sir Anthony Hedges as her lover for the Season.

The guest she'd entertained in his stead wasn't nearly as handsome. But how could he be? Sir Anthony was handsomer than the Apollo Belvedere. Still, the discreetly managed encounter with a lover of two Seasons past had served as consolation and also proof of her late husband's philosophy: that for the greatest possible pleasure and the minimum strain on the emotions, nothing beat a certain sort of handsome, shallow, grateful young man.

Harry Wyatt, Earl of Gorham, had liked to call the world a pleasure garden. And so it was, Marina thought, for anybody with the means to afford admission and the wisdom to follow Harry's advice not to confuse pleasure — in all its variety — with heartfelt, uncontrollable passion. *Avoid passion, Marina,* he'd told her. *No one needs the yearning emotional stuff. A little genteelly administered pain can be diverting on both sides, but stay away from anything you can't control.*

Given her own experience of what she couldn't control, Marina had had to agree with him. And she was sure he'd commend her for the control she'd exercised in passing up the handsomest young gentleman in London. Because despite his perfect manners, splendid waistcoats, and sunny good nature, Sir Anthony Hedges had turned out to want love — the passionate, heartfelt stuff — in a way that touched and rather baffled her.

Nor would it hurt, she expected, if he had someone to help pay for the waistcoats.

But as Marina couldn't give him either thing — and as she'd surprised herself by discovering that she liked him — she'd offered her friendship and advised him to make the best use of the Season by achieving a good marriage.

Rejecting his advances had been surprisingly exhilarating. Making her own choices was still a new thing for her, after all her years on the receiving end of other people's

— of men's — choices.

Glancing up at the bright green ivy twining 'round the windows, she preened in the sunlight filtering through the tiers of Belgian lace. Still in her loose chintz morning gown, she allowed a deep, uncorseted breath to sweep through her waist and belly until it made shuddery little aches in her thighs. Souvenir of last night's encounter. Reminder of the pleasures and independence she'd achieved. Good to keep it that way.

Even if, now that she'd reached thirty-six, pleasure and independence came at the cost of constant petty bargaining: with the body that threatened to show the consequences of eating just about anything worth eating, the eyes that bruised for lack of sleep. All a matter of work and discipline. If choice was a luxury she could afford these days, the leisure in which to contemplate it still lay beyond her means.

She forced her gaze back to the page in front of her.

The typesetters had done yeoman's labor to make coherent sense of a manuscript written in her difficult hand, its native uneducated scrawl so inappropriate to its subject matter: of princely carriages and palatial residences; witty, fashionably dressed people posed in flattering attitudes;

faceted chandeliers shedding their light upon fine linen; glittering cutlery ranged in military precision next to platters of superlative food.

No doubt about the food: the Duke of Orringer's fictional lobster salad had even caused its flesh-and-blood lady authoress's mouth to water. The page was smudged because Marina had *drooled,* as one would never say in one of her books. Hungering for an imagined dinner, she'd dribbled a little puddle of all-too-real spit, right there upon the page proof of *Parrey, A Gentleman.*

Ah, well, she'd leave it to better writers to wring tears from their readers.

Blotting her lips, she took a sip of water from a cut-glass goblet and cast her eye down the paragraphs.

Taken straight from life, that business about having the duke's chef *unwrap the fine linen cloth* from around the watercress . . . *with surpassing care, crumbs of rich black Orringer earth and droplets of the estate's crystalline stream water still clinging to its delicate roots. . . .*

When Lord and Lady Gorham had returned from the continent, the watercress they'd eaten had in fact been plucked at dawn from the Hampshire estate's stream banks and whisked into the hands of their chef in London. Delightedly admiring the kitchen staff, Marina had flirted and flattered her way into their confidence, unwittingly accumulating the knowledge that had become her writerly stock in trade.

Harry'd left her fixed comfortably enough when he'd died six years ago. But naturally the children from his first marriage had gotten the real property. How fortunate that she could draw on her memories to buy back a little luxury for herself.

Her mouth was growing moist again. All she'd eaten this morning was an apple, in preparatory penance for the luncheon she'd be serving at midday — if midday were ever to come.

It was ten now. She needed to get through the rest of the pages in time to dress. The apple still had a bit of flesh clinging to its core. She nibbled at it. Shrugging her shoulders, she devoured it, seeds and all, up to its stem. Swallowing it down with a big gulp of water, she took what sustenance she could before plunging into the love story that finished off her book — her readers' moral price of admission to the witty, wealthy, wicked, and highly exclusive world they trusted Lady Gorham to guide them through.

A pity, she thought, that she couldn't skip

the next few pages of prosy sentimentality — or cut its sweetness by sipping a mug of porter as she worked.

How long had it been since she'd drunk anything like that? A decade? More like two.

Count the pages instead of the years, she exhorted herself. *Divide them into the number of minutes. . . .*

She bit her full lower lip, sighed, and corrected her way through the duke's dinner party, Miss Randall's brave declarations of hopeless love, and Mr. Parrey's lengthy, belated discovery of his better self. The lovers swore their troth while their author deleted a comma, corrected two misspellings, expunged an extraneous repetition, and thanked her personal gods for the comforts of grammar and orthography — learned at about the same time she'd dropped her accent and drunk her last mug of porter.

She rubbed the back of her neck. Just a very few pages to go.

Why had Sir Anthony insisted upon seeing her today? *As a friend,* he'd insisted. For some of the advice and counsel she'd offered.

All right, she'd told him, they could talk about it — whatever it was — over luncheon, before her publisher, Henry Col-

31

burn, joined them for coffee and to discuss how best to puff and publicize what one hoped would be the most widely read novel of the upcoming Season.

Anthony ought to stay for that discussion as well, she'd added. Because in some ways he was part of the puffery, since — physically, at least — she'd modeled her current novel's hero upon him. Making Mr. Parrey the handsomest gentleman in her fiction, *all glowing skin,* as her book had it, *sparkling eyes of a fine, tawny hazel, windblown hair of bright chestnut, a splendid set of shoulders held lovingly within the embrace of Stultz's best superfine.*

And leading the reading public quite reasonably to assume that the model for Mr. Parrey was the author's current lover.

Marina wondered if Colburn had set a date for publication. It would depend upon the balls and other great events scheduled through spring and summer. As the owner and editor of several gossip sheets, he would have been gathering intelligence like a spymaster. His rule was that the *writing* of a society novel was the least of it. The real work lay in publicity and placement, the rumors in his lesser publications, and reviews in his literary journals.

But that was *his* job, she told herself. Hers

was to write as well as she could; to maintain herself in moderate luxury and gratifying independence; and, today, to make her last weary assault on the proofs.

The bells of several west London churches chimed their contending elevens. The light at the window grew brighter as the pile of finished pages continued to grow. A favorable omen: The last of them was perfectly without error. With a flourish, she placed the virgin sheet of paper atop its fellows.

Half past eleven. Marina Wyatt, Lady Gorham, stretched shapely arms above her head, rolled her shoulders until her back was tall and straight once more, and allowed the lids of her large gray-green eyes to droop and her full lips to fall into a lopsided, exhausted grin. The proofs of *Parrey* were corrected and its authoress not yet perished from starvation.

CHAPTER 2

"Adored Marina."

Windblown hair and sparkling eyes, perfectly sculpted jawline, thighs one couldn't
help running one's eyes over (in lieu of
one's fingertips), splendid broad chest
beneath perhaps a bit *too* charming a waistcoat of pale green faille. The young baronet
strode into her sitting room as though
emerging from a heroic painted backdrop.

But would a painter have caught the vexed
expression in his eyes? She rather doubted
it, in light of how long it had taken *her* to
recognize the tentative half-grown boy at
the core of this affable, elegant, perfectly
turned-out young Corinthian of four or five
and twenty.

She led him in to luncheon. More fun
even than eating to watch him devour the
food she gave him. Anyway, he'd take his
time before confiding in her. So there was
no point asking why he'd come, except in

the way of polite inquiry after everyday matters.

His new phaeton? Topping, he replied promptly. So light, well sprung, and perfectly balanced for all its height. He'd gotten quite the knack of driving it since that first, rather hair-raising outing he'd taken her on.

And had he taken out any other ladies in it? Here he shook his head and looked deliciously mournful. Yes, he knew he should marry. And he would, too, since Marina had commanded it. She had his word that he'd make some sort of choice by the end of the Season, which after all had barely started up. But the other ladies he'd observed had such an air of sameness about them, especially in contrast to . . .

She laughed, shook her head, and let him natter on — the happy truth being that his flirtatious overture was harmless. It had been a struggle, but by now they both recognized that they made better friends than lovers.

And did Marina know, Sir Anthony asked, that Mr. Crockford had offered to let him dine and drink for free at his gaming establishment, so long as the phaeton remained parked at the curb to advertise Sir Anthony's presence within?

To dine and drink, she repeated. But he must remember that the gaming debts would still be his own. And when one had inherited an ancient estate . . .

His bright eyes widened, darkening at her chiding. He replied with uncharacteristic sharpness. "Could you think I'd put Wheldon Priory in jeopardy? Or do anything to hurt Syd?"

Odd. He never spoke to her of his family. The subject was clearly a painful one, though he seemed to think she knew a good deal more about it than she did.

No, wait. She did know, in the tangled way that one knew these things. He'd been orphaned a decade or so back. A carriage — no, a *boating* accident. Shocking: The poor drowned couple had left a boy at school and a much younger child.

She and Harry had been in Italy with Monsieur . . . But there was no point trying to remember the name of any of those gorgeous, interchangeable boys. Nor what game of Harry's devising they'd played that night, or whether it had been she or the young man who'd bounced about the carriage the next morning on a sore bottom. Though she did remember that it was she who'd seen to their mounds of baggage. Good job that Harry hadn't been able to

36

buy the sculpture he'd wanted, from the noted connoisseur Mr. Jasper Hedges, who — now that she was putting it all together — must be . . .

"My uncle." Sir Anthony's narrative had run parallel to her thoughts. "And erstwhile guardian. Come to spend a few months in London and quite ruin the Season for me.

"I disappoint him. Don't know what it is," he continued, "but we're never together five minutes before he manages to make it absolutely, abundantly clear that I'm not — never was and never will be — what I should be, that I'm still a stupid schoolboy, and that he won't be satisfied till I'm some version of *him*. Queer, ain't it? Especially since by and large people seem to like me as I am."

The understatement would have been humorous if his anxiety weren't genuine. And yet it was clear that he was too good-hearted to cut a family member. Though young men of fashion, Marina reflected, did so every day. Ah, she remembered, but in this case there was the younger child to be considered — the one he'd never hurt.

Still, it didn't stop him from prattling on, which seemed to be why he'd come.

"The old gentleman's a crab, a curmudgeon. A skinflint, a cranky, crotchety, reclusive eccentric whose only amusements are digging up rusty old Roman coins on the estate and penning tedious monographs. Only comes to town to set the British Museum straight on some fine point pertaining to antiquities. This time he's here to assess some gentleman's collection. He's taken a house near Russell Square, don't you know — he's a stickler for old-fashioned family honor, but he wouldn't dream of dwelling among fashionable people.

"The letter announcing his arrival managed to take me to task for my debts, my frivolity and lack of purpose, and the infrequency of my company — though one wonders why he'd want the company of one so worthless as he makes me out. He'll dog me through London, hectoring me every chance he gets. I endeavor not to show how much it nettles me, but surely he knows it. And enjoys it."

Poor Anthony. Parents — and their surrogates as well, it seemed — could be a burden. For an unguarded instant Marina allowed herself to wonder what sort of mother *she'd* have made, if she'd been able. Not that Harry'd wanted more children . . .

They shared a consoling silence as the footmen cleared the table and brought in the coffee service. "You have my sympathy," she said then, "but I'm not sure what I can offer in the way of help. I don't expect that your uncle would approve of the talk about your supposed liaison with me, and the *on-dits*. . . ."

"He hates gossip, and he's too high-minded to read anything penned during the last two millennia."

Her mouth twisted. "No novels, then."

"Never. And as for women, I think he cares only for those carved out of marble."

She had to laugh. "You make me envision him in rusty breeches and a moldering periwig."

He laughed too. "Well, he's not very elegant, with dirt on his shoes and ink stains all over his cuffs. But" — he lifted his chin, to great decorative effect — "there's nothing for it. I shall simply have to limit our meetings without severing our ties. And you *have* helped me, Marina, by sharing my confidences and making sport of him with me, and I expect . . ."

He trailed off at the appearance of her butler announcing Mr. Colburn. And by the time coffee was served (very light and very sweet for Sir Anthony, black for the others), the discussion had passed to matters of business — the sort of business that depended upon a Season of pleasure.

Colburn would be releasing Marina's new book the same day as Lord and Lady Drayton's ball, and following it up a fortnight later with a major work of puffery, *The Key to Parrey: Concordance to the Personages and Events, by a Friend,* a few days before the Season's first major assembly at Almack's.

"Which will have the desired effect," Marina reminded him, "only if I actually receive my Almack's voucher."

For the patronesses of the famous Assembly Rooms were London's version of the Fates. Twice as many of them and quite as powerful, at the start of every Season these ladies met to sort the applications for admission into three baskets. Whereupon Marina's application would languish for a few weeks in the *undecided* basket, in yearly commemoration of the fact that the Earl of Gorham's Irish second wife had been his mistress before he'd married her, and he'd spent a fortune to get her into good Society.

"Don't fret," the publisher said. "The voucher will come. A patroness's niece fancies herself a poetess and wants a place in an anthology."

While the *Key to Parrey* would reveal her characters' true identities, plucked straight from *Burke's Peerage* and *Baronetage —*

which indispensable tomes it happened that Colburn also published.

"I'll put some eager young fellow, perhaps Disraeli, onto it," he told Marina, "so you can move right onto the next novel. Of course, you two will figure in it, Sir Anthony as the model for Parrey and Your Ladyship for the worldly Marquise of L— . As well as a host of other august personages, both those who enjoy the publicity and those who throw entertaining little fits over being included."

"And the innocent Miss Randall?" Marina asked, "Mr. Parrey's inamorata?" She gazed significantly at Sir Anthony, who gazed significantly into his coffee cup. "Of course there *isn't* one at this moment," she said. "But there *will* be," she added firmly.

"The *Key*'s author will have it that he's not at liberty to say," Colburn replied, "except that she's very wealthy and very sheltered."

Which allowed, Marina thought, for the possibility that Anthony might court the wealthiest young lady making her debut this Season: Harry Wyatt's daughter, Lady Isobel, fresh from school in Switzerland. More than allowed for it, in truth — as Colburn had worded it, the text rather hinted at that interesting possibility.

41

She suppressed a sigh. Harry's children had never approved of their father's second marriage. Anthony would probably have to drop her friendship. Still, it would be a wonderful match for him. And think of all the gossip it would generate, the additional publicity for her novel.

Irksome. Confusing. Profitable.

"Which brings me," Colburn continued, "to the delicate question of when my *on-dits* may have it that you two are no longer *à deux*. I propose we do it earlier rather than later; what do you say? Do you suppose you could be cold and civil to each other at the Draytons' ball?"

Both of them laughed and supposed they could.

"Good. By the time Almack's opens, all the eligible young ladies will be wanting to be of as much consolation to you, Sir Anthony, as Miss Randall was to Mr. Parrey."

Marina smiled. So be it.

"And that concludes our business, I think," she said. "My proofs are finished and wrapped in brown paper, and I'm eager to have my walk on the Rotten Row while this fragile sunshine still holds."

Colburn returned her smile. "Yes, that's everything." He paused. "Except for a favor

I'd like to ask of you, my lady. For I wonder if you might invite Mr. Jasper Hedges, Sir Anthony's uncle, to your dinner party later this week."

Sir Anthony blinked.

"I want a book about antiquities," Colburn said. "And Hedges's monographs, privately printed and scholarly, are also devilish clever and entertaining. Opinionated, acerbic — the man's not afraid to make enemies. With a little puffing, a touch of judicious editing . . ."

"And with its unworldly gentleman author paid at a moderate rate," Marina couldn't help adding, "by a canny publisher, the first to see his commercial possibilities . . ."

"You're an intelligent woman, Lady Gorham," the gentleman replied. "No wonder we work together in such blissful accord. Nor has it escaped my notice, Sir Anthony, that you and your uncle do not enjoy such harmony. Or perhaps you don't remember your eloquence on the subject at Crockford's last night?"

"Oh, lord. How loud *was* I?"

"Not excessively so, after I pulled you into a dim alcove — don't thank me; delighted to be of service. More to the point, though, why shouldn't *you* incur your uncle's gratitude by helping him find a larger audience

43

for his erudition? Why not be the dominant male in the herd, if I may so put it, and lead *him* into the sparkling literary Society where *you* are a favorite, the protégé of beauty and brilliance both?"

Colburn bowed his head in Marina's direction before addressing himself once more to Sir Anthony.

"Why not . . . ?" His voice faded to a suggestive whisper, the remainder of his sentence left to its subject to finish as he might.

Why not face *Uncle Jasper instead of avoiding him? Give him reason to be beholden to* me? *Show him a world where* I'm *at the center? And a lady . . .*

Or so Marina supposed her young friend must be thinking. And though he continued silent, she could see his eyes responding to Colburn's challenge.

After all, the London reading public still thought them lovers, and would continue to do so until the opening ball at Almack's. If it helped his amour propre for him to show off a bit for the fear some ancient uncle in his moldering periwig . . .

She lowered her eyelids to signal her acquiescence.

"Bring him along, then," she murmured, and he nodded his thanks with an engaging boyish laugh.

"Why *not* bring him along?" he said. "Why not indeed?"

CHAPTER 3

As she'd predicted, the sunshine hadn't held. The next day dawned gloomy, skies steadily darkening. Toward midday the heavens opened, but by afternoon the rain slowed to a pale drizzle from a pearly sky over Bloomsbury.

A few birds chirped in the budding plane trees overhead; fat droplets of water gathered on the branches to splash atop her umbrella and into the puddles at her feet.

The soles of her half boots were hardly waterproof. She'd be glad to turn the corner at Great Russell Street. As at the moment she found herself glad of everything, and everything seemed to glow with misty possibility.

Her first errand of the day — to a shabby office in the City — had brought its usual humiliations: insults from her principal creditor (as she thought of him), her own responses in kind. Still, she was done with it for the month. She'd handed over the bank draft for April, pulled her skirts about herself as the door squeaked closed behind her, and breathed more freely with every step down the steep stairs, out to the narrow street, and into her carriage.

After which the visit to her modiste in Bloomsbury had almost been a pleasure. The green sarcenet was nearly done. Madame Gabri would be sending it to Marina's house in Brook Street in time for tomorrow night's dinner party.

And what a lovely surprise that the modiste would be charging last year's rates, in thanks for the mention of her name in Lady Gorham's last novel, *The Tale of Lord Farringdon.*

The bon ton's *best ladies look all the better for the work of her magic needle,* Marina had written. Which was certainly true of Marina herself, even as the styles grew more horrid with each Season: cumbersome, overdecorated skirts continuing to widen; challenging tight bodices that madame assured her would only become lower and tighter; and puffing about the upper arm, what the fashion magazines most appropriately called the "imbecile sleeve" — a yard of fabric for each arm at least. The only good thing about the general effect being the illusion of a smaller waist.

The modiste had disagreed. "Not the *only* thing, my lady," she'd told Marina over tea. "Remember that it isn't everyone who can carry off the wide swath of shoulder and bosom it reveals."

Pleasant to be reminded of her better features, even as she regretted the passing of the fluid, Grecian-inspired white muslins of her youth. And she'd certainly come to the right place to mourn the passing of style *à la Grecque.* Passing through the courtyard to the venerable portals of the British Museum, she snapped her umbrella shut and entered the building.

It was the first collection of precious old objects she'd seen besides Harry Wyatt's own. At his estate in Hampshire she'd wandered about feeling more like an artifact than a viewer — for wasn't he always telling her she was the most beautiful thing he'd found on his travels?

If left to herself during the trying period just after she'd become Lady Gorham, she likely would never have come near this museum. But everyone had to see the great marble sculptures Lord Elgin had taken from the Parthenon in Greece. Counterfeiting an excess of delight, she'd expected to be bored beyond imagining. Surprisingly, she'd found it thrilling — the splendor of the marbles; the bewildering accumulation of other objects intrepid travelers hauled home to Britain; the multiplicity and variety of animal and plant life, fossils caught in rock or amber and displayed in the trays, drawers, and cases divided into what seemed an infinity of little compartments with their tiny, laboriously scripted labels affixed.

Thrilling yet oddly reassuring: the earnestness, the utter absence of dash or *ton* in these galleries a welcome relief to a young woman striving for acceptance in the dashing, *ton*-ish world in which she'd found herself.

And when she'd begun writing little sketches to amuse herself, it had been in these galleries where Marina would sometimes catch sight of an arresting, anonymous face or figure and think of a suitably expressive or humorous name to be affixed. She still salted her novels with amusing minor characters — a shopkeeper, perhaps, or a country parson — before moving on to the main plot in the heroine's drawing room.

No new face caught her imagination today. Only a familiar mocking grin and a pair of bright black eyes peering at her from the other side of a glass case.

"Mr. Disraeli." One of the most successful, amusing, and outrageous of Colburn's novelists: Just look how the impish young man had gotten himself up today; he must have danced between the raindrops in his sapphire velvet and narrow, beribboned shoes.

When his novel *Vivian Grey* had been published last year it had rivaled her *Farringdon* in sales — no mean feat, for as a Jew, he'd experienced nothing of the Society he wrote about, concocting his fantastic tale of high life and political intrigue out of the vapors of passionate ambition.

Her smile softened now as she gave her hand to his father standing at his side. "How good it is to see you, sir. And how does Mrs. Disraeli do?"

"Quite tolerable, my lady. She often speaks of how she enjoyed your call upon her."

"I shall come once more, if I may, now that I've finished my latest." The mother was mystified by her son's adoration of a world that didn't want him, but Marina — who understood it completely — had been pleased to assure Mrs. Disraeli that her odd, brilliant boy was bound to make his way.

She must make time to call again. She'd have to find a shortcut to that next novel. Perhaps Mr. Parrey could discover a long-lost identical twin. . . .

Recalling herself, she allowed the elder Mr. Disraeli to lead her among the cases of Persian and Macedonian coins, while his son babbled on about *his* next novel. They'd take their leave of her, they said, at the hall that held the great Greek marbles.

"We've already visited them today," the younger man added. "I insisted we go directly upon our arrival. Papa wanted to save them for last, but I've spent all my patience waiting for the patronesses of Almack's to discover how indispensable I am. And here you are," he now said with a flourish. "The Elgin Marbles."

Pausing to bid her friends farewell, she stood aside to allow a trio of other viewers to enter the gallery ahead of her.

Botheration.

It wasn't as though she'd expected to be alone. One often saw scholars, students, and artists bent over their sketchpads, heard their civilized, respectful murmur of informed or fatuous commentary.

But sharing the Elgin Marbles with a mama and papa and their noisy, fidgety, half-grown child was another matter. Her eyes swept quickly and impatiently over the trio, with their unmistakable air of being up from the country. The tall gentleman with his unusually upright figure had the look of a clergyman.

Odd that he'd bring his child into this hall of naked statuary. Inconsiderate too: The little beast would doubtless be emitting gasps and giggles, sighing with boredom and demanding to be taken out for cakes and ices.

Marina would simply have to close her ears until then — and remain on the side of the hall where the centaurs did battle.

But as if to spite her by proving her wrong, the next minutes passed exceedingly peacefully, with not a gasp, giggle, or demand for more thrilling amusements to be heard. The girl from the country — how old might she be, certainly not thirteen yet? — conducted herself more quietly than had the younger Mr. Disraeli. An occasional raindrop pattered down upon the skylight. And when the child did ask an occasional question, it was in so soft a voice that Marina found that she couldn't make out the words.

If she'd wanted to make out the words. In which — it hardly needed saying — she had absolutely no interest whatsoever.

She moved a bit closer to inspect a group of large standing pieces.

How might a youngster respond to these

epic works of art? Marina couldn't imagine. Guiltily, her thoughts strayed to Harry's children. She might have asked to have them visit more often; Lady Isobel must have been sad to lose her own mother.

She hadn't asked. The earl hadn't needed to make it any clearer: Not only didn't he want more children, he had very little interest in the two he had. His nobody of a second wife was in no position to ask for anything; it was astonishment enough that he'd wanted to marry her, rather than simply keep her as his mistress. In truth, she'd counted it excellent luck that people were calling her a *nobody.* They could have been calling her a sight worse — and might still, she thought briefly, if she fell behind on her monthly bank drafts.

But what were the girl and her father whispering about in front of that group of sculpted horsemen?

Now that she'd come around a mass of broken pillars, including the remarkable one shaped like a woman, she had a better view, and could hear a few words as well. "Xerxes . . . Persians . . . Panathenaic Procession." Odd to hear such weighty syllables so eagerly whispered by a child.

A nicely dressed child, she'd give the family that — quite sweet how simply but elegantly and expensively she was turned out, in contrast to the rusty (oh, dear, even slightly shiny) black that contained her father's excellent shoulders.

(But when, she wondered, had she found the time to take note of his shoulders? Or to consider — for it seemed she had considered it, in some sly, hidden part of herself — whether the legs in their shapeless trousers might be good as well?)

His hair was thick, cut more closely than was fashionable — as though he couldn't be bothered with anything but the simplest arrangement — its color of a metallic brightness. One could see that it had once been a sort of sandy brown, now brindled, tipped with silver. Pale gleams from the skylight shone down upon it.

Perhaps she might add a country clergyman to the ensemble of minor characters in her next novel.

Perhaps the clergyman could disclose the mystery of the twin brothers' birth.

Perhaps . . .

Enough perhaps, she chided herself. It was one thing to catch sight of an interesting face, quite another to be making patent excuses for ogling strange, even if well-built, gentlemen behind their backs.

It must be the proximity of the exquisite

bodies the ancient sculptors had rendered so perfectly, she thought. Or perhaps some not so pleasant memories stirred up by her visit, earlier today, to that baleful office.

What ever the mix of confused affect that had caused her to stare at him so shamelessly, she'd better stop it immediately. Had she forgotten that his wife was also in the hall? For all Marina knew, the lady could be entirely aware of the attention her husband had been attracting — and would most likely, and quite correctly, have found it outrageously impolite.

She peered down the gallery: Where *had* the lady taken herself? There she was — in front of the formidable, recumbent Dionysus from the temple pediment, done in the glorious round. But upon closer scrutiny it had become clear the tall, plain, angular creature, gown drooping where it ought to cling, was far too young to be the child's mother.

Silly of her. One hardly needed an author's powers of observation to discern that the woman gazing so avidly and unselfconsciously at the god's splendid, muscled torso (and downward too) hadn't celebrated very many birthdays beyond her twentieth. And that she was too completely, naively fascinated by the masculinity sprawled out before her to be *anyone's* mother, or, for that matter — one dearly hoped — anyone's wife.

A governess then, quite as the unbecoming gown and austere bonnet proclaimed her. An unusually well treated governess to have leave to wander among the antiquities as her fancy dictated, while the gentleman took his daughter about and answered her precocious questions.

Impatiently, Marina moved past a row of marble panels, turning her eyes back to the gentleman and to the child by his side, the dress of pale blue cotton that was only a little spattered about its hem from the rain, the white apron, good boots, bonnet dangling at the back of the neck, and sky blue grosgrain ribbons in the girl's thick fair hair.

One of the ribbons was coming loose.

Irksome. She found herself wanting to fix it before it slid to the floor.

She needn't have concerned herself. Because even while the eager murmur continued — "Athena . . . handmaidens . . . goddess's ritual garment rewoven every year . . ." — the gentleman reached down to retie the ribbon. The bow he made was merely serviceable, but his gesture was so quick, so sure and practiced, so quotidian, plain, and entirely to be taken for granted by a girl lucky enough to feel herself so cherished, that his daughter might not have been quite aware of it.

Marina felt herself go short of breath. But the child didn't change the tilt of her head. Continuing to stare above her, at the figures raised in low relief upon the slab of marble fixed onto the wall, she whispered something that Marina supposed must be another question.

Impossible to hear: The girl must have been carefully schooled not to disturb her fellow knowledge seekers within the sacred confines of a museum.

And so it was the gentleman who finally broke the silence, when it seemed that he couldn't suppress a low rumble of laughter that suggested pleasure rather than ridicule.

Less restrained in the wake of his outburst of mirth, his voice came a bit louder now, the words at long last audible to Marina. "But that's a very good . . . my word, that's a most *excellent* question, Sydney. The best kind of question, the kind no one knows the answer to — well, not *these* days, anyway, perhaps someday if . . . But let's move on, shall we, to the parts that originally faced east? It'll make more sense if I show you. . . ."

He swiveled his long body at the waist to

point to some figure on the frieze directly above Marina's head. Catching sudden sight of her, he halted in midgesture, his smile apologetic and a bit self-mocking, his surprise evidently quite genuine. It seemed clear enough that he'd thought himself and his family group alone in the gallery.

Which meant, Marina thought, that until this moment he hadn't been in the least bit cognizant of her presence. While she'd been rather making a cake of herself tiptoeing about the room with her eyes on him and an ache in her chest.

She might have found the situation more humiliating still if his smile hadn't been so engaging.

Odd — she'd expected a scholar's pallor. Perhaps his skin seemed browner than it really was, in contrast to the brightness of the hair at his temples, the gleam of copper-rimmed spectacles.

No, he really was that dark: The hand that had fixed the hair ribbon had been burned by the sun and hardened by some sort of labor.

A light on the wall caught the glass of his spectacles, rendering them opaque. Breathing calmly (yes, that felt better), Marina inclined her head to change her angle of vision. The large blue eyes behind the lenses were warm, friendly. A sunburned hand moved to the bridge of his nose to bring the spectacles into a different alignment.

The young person had begun to fidget and now to glare. Jealous, possessive, moving a step closer to her father, she stared smugly up at Marina.

We were very well by ourselves, thank you, her expression seemed to proclaim, even as she dipped and bobbed back up in a polite enough curtsy, while the gentleman continued to gaze at Marina from above the rims of his spectacles — and while Marina did her best to assure that he continued to do so.

Unworthy, she'd reflect later, amid a twinge of guilt and a glow of satisfaction. She'd acted most unworthily.

If you could say that she'd really acted at all. If you could call the merest of smiles an *act.*

Except that it hadn't been the *merest* of smiles that had stolen across her face. Useless to wonder why and pointless to deny having done it: Marina had returned the gentleman's casual, affable smile with one of a brightness last seen when Sir Thomas Lawrence had painted her portrait fourteen years earlier — and taught her to put the whole of her body behind what might seem like a momentary flicker of pleasant emotion.

And damn anyone, she thought now, who might find the body behind the smile too old or too fat; they were the only smile and the only body she had. And if she were to put every bit of candlepower she had into a flirtatious glance at a country gentleman she'd never see again, among Lord Elgin's collection of marble sculptures in the British Museum on a rainy London Wednesday afternoon, well, what of it?

Except that he'd held her glance with a keen, critical, highly amused one of his own. If they'd been gamblers one might wonder if he might still hold a trump card.

She'd wonder later how much time had elapsed. Ten seconds? A minute?

But if she didn't care to see his hand . . .

"I beg your pardon," she murmured. "I expect I'm in your way." Whereupon she quitted the hall in a loud swoosh of skirts, and left the family group to sort themselves out among the marbles.

The gentleman with copper spectacles murmured something to himself, the words too soft to be discerned, his eyes still fixed upon the exit doorway, spectacles pushed higher onto his nose.

The governess, Miss Hobart, raised reluctant eyes from Dionysus's torso in time to see the last of Marina passing out to the hallway. Hastening now to her employer's side, she asked, "Is there a problem, Mr. Hedges?"

The girl tugged at the gentleman's hand. "Uncle Jasper?"

The gentleman remained silent, rubbing a calloused hand across the curve of his lower lip. The child and governess stared at him. And so, it almost seemed, did a number of blank white marble eyes from about the room.

The marble faces brought him back to consciousness of the human ones in need of his attention. *How very singular,* he thought vaguely, and gave another low rumble of laughter.

Well, *that* was an unexpected pleasure. One didn't see ladies like *that* back home in the country. One had almost forgotten. . . .

In any case, he was glad of his appointment tonight.

The physical sensations would keep — would only add to the mild anticipation he'd been feeling all day.

Laughing more heartily this time, he was able to collect himself.

"Yes, well, where were we? The eastern

section of the temple frieze. As I was saying. Look . . ."

The trio took a few steps closer, situating themselves now where the lady had stood. Eyes turned upward toward the figures in marble, child and governess settling themselves to attend to what the gentleman would say.

Jasper James Hedges cleared his throat.

But he couldn't help but feel himself first hesitating, then hurrying through the fine points, even slurring the Greek words once or twice, and generally giving short shrift to what he'd intended as the culmination of his argument.

Which annoyed him. For when you were explaining things to a young person as clever as Sydney you were honor-bound to deliver as good an argument as to the gentlemen of the Dilettanti Society, if not a better one than those self-regarding gentlemen could be bothered to hear. Or in any case, a much better argument than he was managing to deliver right now.

Sighing, he gave it up. "I'm making a muddle of it. The Parthenon's too big a subject for one day." He smiled apologetically. "And I expect that too much beauty can be exhausting."

Miss Hobart had murmured something

that sounded like an assent. Mr. Hedges glanced at her. She looked flushed, he hoped with exhaustion rather than some sort of illness. The too-prominent bones in her cheeks were bright pink, the lips of her wide mouth in need of moisture.

Definitely exhaustion, he decided. For it couldn't have been an easy task for Miss Hobart to get herself and Sydney settled in as quickly as she had — and also, he reminded himself guiltily, to have done so much to get his papers, coins, and other artifacts in order, while he'd been unpacking his books and overseeing the business of having a very modern cabinet installed, with an even more up-to-date lock.

How much time had they spent in this hall, anyway?

He glanced at his pocket watch.

Long enough.

Too much beauty . . .

Had they been disturbing the lady? He'd always insisted that Sydney speak quietly in a hall like this one, and she'd learned to take the proscription seriously.

More likely the lady had found them amusing, even eccentric. Yes, *eccentric* was how he was often described; *eccentric* was probably the best thing Anthony ever said about him; no doubt *eccentric* had been *her* impression as well. If she'd even bothered to find a word for him and his household during that briefest of instants when the three of them had passed under the scrutiny of her knowing, heavy-lidded eyes.

A gray sort of green, he thought. Color of stormy northern seas. Irksome that he could remember so perfectly, when she'd doubtless forgotten all about *him* directly after quitting the room.

"We'll come here again," he said brightly. "Well, of course we will — we'll be living so close by, this institution might as well be our drawing room. But if we stay any longer today," he continued, "we'll be singing the wrath of Mrs. Burroughs." The excellent woman he'd engaged to keep order in the house on Charlotte Street was rather a martinet.

"I ordered an early dinner," he told the girl. "There'll be time for me to say good night and read you something before I go out."

The governess smiled gratefully at him. He nodded. Yes, he could see that she needed a rest.

Sydney was tired too; he could recognize the droll expression that had taken hold of her face — eyes widened, mouth contorted by a mighty effort not to give way to a yawn.

He stroked her hair.

"What shall I read to you?"

CHAPTER 4

Sydney had chosen Mr. Lamb's version of the story of Ulysses. An old favorite of hers: Jasper had watched her lips shaping the words along with his as he read, a bit sonorously, until her eyes drooped shut while the hero was still in the land of the lotus eaters.

She must have gotten a good sleep, for this morning she was full of her accustomed energy. Miss Hobart looked a little better as well. The two of them were chattering happily over breakfast.

While *he,* after an expensive night out . . .

Which had been worth the price, in the obvious, palpable ways of the body. First time in a while: His life in the country was hardly that of a dreamy, sensual lotus eater. But if you had to transplant yourself to London, he thought — hell, and in the midst of the Season, too — you wanted something of what London did best, didn't you?

Especially after yesterday's inspiriting encounter among the Parthenon marbles.

He'd engaged the girl through an introduction house he patronized when in town, and he hadn't been disappointed. Skilled at her trade. Pretty, cheerful. Generous.

And awfully talkative, at least afterward.

He hadn't minded. He enjoyed the serendipity of female chatter. Nice to know something of the person inhabiting the body, gratifying to satisfy one's curiosity after the fact, himself listening relaxed against the pillows, wine and biscuits near to hand.

She'd let slip that she had a young man she cared about. Good luck to them, Jasper thought, so long as the fellow was kind and the girl not given to sneaking the house keys out of a customer's pocket so that her young man might steal the family silver.

But what really engaged this young woman's imagination was fashion — learned from the ladies' magazines but cultivated to studious perfection, it seemed, during her afternoon walks to see what the ruling beauties of the *ton* were wearing.

" 'Specially Lady Gorham," she said. "The novelist. But even if you're up from the country I warrant you'll recognize *her* name, sir. The Beautiful Bluestocking of Brook Street, people call her, with that thick black hair, greenish eyes with the heavy lids — the *on-dits* in the papers always comment on her eyes, you know, her posture, and, of course, her costumes. She's not quite young anymore, but it don't seem to matter, what wi' her elegant, haughty expression and voluptuous figure what makes others' seem a bit skimpy. . . ."

He'd begun to stare. She hadn't noticed, prattling on about some dressmaker. A modiste — she'd pronounced the word carefully, enjoying the French sound of it. "Lady Gorham recommended Madame Gabri — well, not exactly *recommended* her, sir. More like she wrote about her."

Oh, yes, the little courtesan told him in response to his question, the lady wrote quite wonderful — about clothes and food and manners; you could learn a bit of everything from her. . . .

It had taken him some effort to turn the conversation away from the lavender twill she'd bought cheap and would be taking to that same modiste. And why not? she demanded. Wasn't her money as good as other people's? Assuring her that it was, Jasper slowly — carelessly — brought the talk back around to Lady . . . well, actually to *Lord* Gorham.

"Oh, him — he's dead. And her, she keeps company with the famous young society beaux, takes up with a new one every Season. This time it looks like it's this Sir Anthony something, a baronet from Essex, I think, and oh, my word, but *he's* a handsome one, quite the crack of fashion. . . .

"But what's wrong, sir?" she'd asked hastily.

Nothing at all, Jasper'd assured her. Only that the hour grew late. He must be going.

Home to the rented house in Bloomsbury, a night spent tossing in bed, an icy morning bath, and now — couldn't break custom — a most trying family breakfast.

He took another swallow of the new housekeeper's coffee. Quite as strong and scalding as he'd requested, it was bracing enough to distract him from the breakfast congealing on his plate, the irritating chirp of female voices across the table. Coffee to bolster him up for today's call upon the gentleman whose collection he'd be appraising — and as armor against this most plaguing letter in front of him, which had spoiled any last chance of decently digesting his eggs and sausage.

He'd recognized the seal's imprint as soon

as the footman handed him the morning's post. The noble head of a hunting dog — he was accustomed to vainly searching for its image when the post arrived in Essex. It had been his brother's seal; now, of course, it belonged to the young gentleman known by all of London as *quite the crack,* even among the *famous society beaux* she took up with.

Never mind that at home in the country, weeks and months might roll by without that particular canine appearing on the seal of a letter. Here in London, when they were almost within shouting distance of each other, the footman had brought in two communications from Anthony all at once.

Sydney had torn into hers immediately, shards of wax skimming across the table while she read aloud in the piping voice Jasper usually thought delightful, but today found entirely too high-pitched for his taste.

Impossible to muster the concentration to listen. Jasper tried to lose his attention in the other letters he'd received.

"And what of *your* letter, Uncle Jasper? What does it say?"

"News from a German antiquarian trying to sell a sculpture. And a report from my friends in Greece." He pocketed the communications to read more carefully.

"Not *those* letters, Uncle Goose. The one Anthony sent you."

"Nothing of importance. He tells me that a friend of his would like me to make an additional guest at a dinner party tonight, and that it would be 'good fun' " — he allowed himself a grimace — "if he and I could attend together."

Written in an innocent, sloping, schoolboy hand, as though no one were "taking up with" anyone, much less the lady who'd haunted his intermittent sleep and whom he'd come to breakfast determined to forget.

My friend Lady Gorham . . . jolly dinner parties . . . Brook Street . . . Thursday . . . well, tonight, actually, beg pardon for suddenness . . . literary types . . . enchantée *to make your acquaintance.*

Hell.

"But it *will* be fun." Sydney wrinkled her nose in response to his grimace. "Because he'll drive you there in the high perch phaeton he's just purchased. Very . . . um . . . bang up to the mark, he makes it sound."

Bang up to the mark? Where had she learned so idiotic a phrase? Or half learned it: She was still trying to fit her mouth around it, pronouncing it carefully, as though it were Latin. As always, he found

71

himself charmed by her attempts to take in new knowledge, even of a canting, fashionable way of speaking.

"But you still haven't answered my question."

Had she asked a question?

Miss Hobart sent Sydney a reproving glance and Jasper a sympathetic one.

Thank the gods for *her* assistance. Extraordinarily well educated in the classics, she was also doubtless responsible for whatever manners Sydney had. *If left to myself,* Jasper thought, *I'd have probably spoiled her beyond redemption.*

Turning his attention away from today's annoyances, he allowed himself a long, consoling gaze over his spectacles at the fair-haired child across the table: adequate regular features and keen blue eyes of the Hedges family; hints of her mother's beauty glimmering out when one least expected it.

He waited until the wave of pain (lighter these days, but never entirely eased away) broke over him.

Her beauty would brighten in the next years; it would be soon enough that everyone saw it. But, thank the gods, not yet.

"Wipe the spot of jam from the corner of your mouth, Sydney." Miss Hobart spoke while pouring cream and shoveling sugar into her coffee cup. Jasper shuddered as she lifted the hideous concoction to her lips.

"Over there on the right, toward your chin," the young woman continued. "And now why don't you ask Mr. Hedges your question once again, more slowly this time, for he must be terribly tired out from all the effort he's expended" — she barely hesitated here — "in moving us and our belongings up from Essex."

Another advantage of her classical education was her ability to balance worldly knowledge and domestic tact. He nodded to her and turned an encouraging eye toward Sydney, who sat straighter behind her glass of milk, and — eyes very wide and blue — asked if she might go driving with her brother in his new phaeton this afternoon.

She'd be quite safe, she insisted.

Which was true enough. For not only was Anthony excellent with horses and carriages, he'd been remarkably protective of his sister from the moment Jasper informed him of his parents' death — stiffly, clumsily. . . . *Damn.* Jasper hated remembering it.

Ruddy cheeked from the cricket field, hair wet and slicked back from a hurried brushing, a bewildered half-grown stripling with his mother's lovely face had been ushered into the headmaster's study to speak to an uncle he'd barely known the existence of, come to tell him of his parents' death in as few words and with as little affect as possible. *According to your father's will I'm guardian to you and your sister.*

Anthony had wept, and Jasper — *damn my soul,* he thought — had stood stone-faced and silent, as though he'd felt nothing at all, while he'd felt so much, but how even to begin to express any of it? And if he'd dared to speak — if he'd put out a hand, an arm — who knew what he'd have said or done if he'd lost control of himself?

And so he'd said nothing — just hovered in his mourning like a crow and listened to the young stranger with the too-familiar features grieve for *my mama and papa.*

His papa, especially, who'd liked to take him hunting.

A relief when the boy had sniffled back his tears to ask after his little sister, a greater relief to report that Sydney was doing extraordinarily well; she hadn't understood much about the accident and had stopped crying for her mother. And that she'd accepted her uncle's care and was happy to be home with her nurse at Wheldon Priory, where Jasper would be looking after her until she was of age, and taking care of Sir

74

Anthony's property until he came of age as well (the boy had jumped to hear the *sir* in front of his name).

What Jasper hadn't reported was that the little girl had rather taken to him. Nor could he have told a fourteen-year-old boy that he found it surpassingly wonderful to have someone to look after; one might even say that he'd fallen in love for the second time in his life — an innocent, redemptive sort of love this time.

So instead he'd said that he was duty-bound to respect the terms of his brother's will and to return to England to undertake the responsibility of a guardianship of the children and the property, after all those years wandering Greece, Italy, and the Levant, earning his way by means of his knowledge of the great ancient civilizations.

How dreary he must have sounded.

"He must be very tired indeed." Sydney's whisper broke in like a ray of light through oppressive clouds. "For it's almost as though he were sleeping with his eyes wide-open. I shouldn't have guessed he'd be so ex-hausted, when at home he's able to dig such large piles of dirt when he's out looking for coins — the steward calls him a veritable Watt and Boulton earth-moving engine."

Relieved to be recalled from his memories,

and pleased to think of himself as an engine rather than a crow, Jasper laughed gratefully. "Yes. All right. I surrender. You *may* go driving this afternoon. And I expect that I shall attend the dinner party as well."

For it wouldn't hurt to find out what, if anything, was going on between Anthony and his "friend," Lady Gorham. For purely disinterested reasons. Duty. Responsibility. Anyway, he'd seen the lady only once, and for no more than a minute. How could he possibly have imagined . . . ?

Impossible to imagine anything now that Sydney had jumped from her chair and run to his side.

"So long as you do your lessons," he protested from amidst the barrage of hugs and kisses, and promises of eternal gratitude, prodigious scholarship, and perfect behavior that threatened to smother him and upset the coffeepot.

"And I mean *do* your lessons," he repeated, "with care and attention, and no more discussion of that velvet spencer or whatever it is that the two of you have been going on about while I was pretending — *merely* pretending, as you see — to be sleeping with my eyes open."

Sydney scampered off to the schoolroom. The governess had turned to follow her when Jasper called her back.

"But you have to make it absolutely clear to Sir Anthony," he said, "how exceedingly careful he must be while driving with Sydney. And he should have her back no later than half past five so she can have an early supper."

She nodded somberly, and he felt an embarrassed rush of sympathy. He'd always suspected she disapproved of Anthony — if truth were told, rather more than Jasper did. She had no tolerance for shallow, meaningless fripperies. Daughter of their excellent vicar back in Essex, she'd run her father's house for him, visited the district poor, read and studied with him in the evenings, and bravely and competently nursed him through his final illness.

She'd never complained about any task Jasper had set her. But when Anthony had come down to Wheldon last year, Jasper had noted that the boy's frivolity seemed to nettle her. He hoped she wouldn't be too discombobulated by this sojourn in London — worse luck for all of them that it had to be during the Season.

"I regret that I won't be here this afternoon at three when he comes. I shall send him a note, though, accepting his invitation to Lady Gorham's dinner party."

The lady we saw in the museum yesterday, he'd almost added, merely as a point of interest, before stopping himself. No good to be gained from mentioning Lady Gorham. Marina. Lady Gorham. No reason on earth why Miss Hobart should be interested. No matter that his lips and tongue had wanted to shape her name again.

"In any case, I shall endeavor to be back here upon his and Sydney's return, after examining the Viscount Kellingsley's collection of sculptures. You might tell Sir Anthony to stop a few minutes in my study in case I'm late — help himself to a drink — but of course you needn't sit with him."

Miss Hobart twisted her long, narrow hands about each other uncomfortably. If he could, Jasper thought, he would have saved her the necessity of meeting a person she found objectionable.

But there was no putting off the discussion with Kellingsley. It would be a long day's meeting; he'd set off as soon as he could after responding to the German collector — exciting news; he must try not to get his hopes up. And, of course, he must write to Anthony, and he knew from experience how long it would take to pen a few dry words to *him*. Oh, and send a note to the Brook Street address, to Lady Gorham who "wrote quite wonderful." Well, he doubted *that*. Hmm, perhaps he could stop at a bookshop on his way out.

He smiled (even if a bit frantically), nodded at Miss Hobart, rose from the table, and turned away.

"Mr. Hedges." Had he missed something? She sounded as though she were repeating herself.

He turned back to face her. "Beg pardon, miss. What is it?"

"I merely meant to point out, Mr. Hedges, that Sir Anthony will probably not have time to stop here after he brings Sydney home. For he'll have to return to his lodgings in order to change his clothing for the dinner party."

She was right. And oh lord, he would probably have to talk to Mowbrey about which of his own coats would serve — and linen, that sort of thing.

"I could speak to Mr. Mowbrey for you if you like."

"You're a treasure, Miss Hobart. Please do speak to Mowbrey." His manservant probably had the easiest job in England, except when it came to carting about old bits of stone and iron.

And how silly of me to think Anthony might have time to see me before leaving for the dinner party. Silly and stupid — the veritable crack of silliness, absolutely bang up to the mark when it came to stupidity. Of course changing one's clothing came before seeing one's stiff old erstwhile guardian. Or even perhaps having a drink, a few words together — a conversation, as he believed it was generally called, and as he might be forgiven for desiring to have.

Ha, as though we two have ever had a conversation.

Grimacing — needless to say with disdain rather than disappointment — he turned away again and quit the room.

And not an instant too soon, Helen Hobart thought, if she were to maintain her composure. Another moment and she should have burst into rueful laughter or dissolved in tears. Lord only knew which. Perhaps both. The laughter, of course, because Mr. Hedges was so excessively transparent when it came to his hurt feelings about Sir Anthony, and yet so entirely incapable of speaking to his nephew in any way except the sternest and most forbidding.

Well, it wasn't for a governess to comment upon her employer's muddled affective life — especially when there were her own unruly feelings to be managed, tears to be

80

kept at bay, plaguing memory to be suppressed.

The memory. She'd thought of little else since yesterday's visit to the museum.

The autumn afternoon had been unseasonably warm at Wheldon Priory. Too warm for lessons. She'd taken Sydney for a ramble, and they'd discovered Sir Anthony asleep on the riverbank with his coat spread beneath him and his waistcoat by his side, a sudden breeze pressing the linen of his shirt against the ripple of muscle above his belly.

Sydney had giggled and wanted to wake him up. But Helen had silently and forcefully waved her away, staring as long and hard as she dared, to try to *memorize* him, to have that precious intimate view of him for her own whenever she wanted it — in the privacy of her own imaginings and her own bed at night.

It had doubtless been a terrible mistake, but it was too late now to laugh or cry about it. She had a list of tasks. She was fortunate to be able to keep lists in her head.

Speak to Mowbrey.

Set Robert the footman to delivering Mr. Hedges's letters.

Tack up a torn hem — well, that was easy enough, and relaxing. The challenge would be to take the blue spencer down to the kitchen and hold it over a steaming kettle to remove whatever stuff her charge had gotten stuck on the velvet.

Prepare Sydney's Latin dictation. Virgil, Aeneas in the underworld: *regions of sadness . . . groves of myrtle . . . paths where roamed the victims of unrequited love.*

And go find herself a new situation.

Not today. But it should be easy enough during a London Season — so many great families here, and herself so impeccably capable, plain, and serviceable. A treasure, Mr. Hedges had said: It would be a pity to let him down, and also to leave Sydney, who was rewarding to teach, and funny and lovable into the bargain. Like having a little sister, if one didn't mind envying one's little sister almost past reason.

For it was Sydney whom Sir Anthony would swing around in his arms when he came this afternoon, before peering at her with great solemnity through his quizzing glass, eliciting embarrassed and delighted giggles while she waited for his pronouncements on how devilish pretty she was getting. And only then — as always and just the slightest bit belatedly — would he straighten up and remind himself of his manners, absently bidding Miss Hobart good day and asking how she did.

Leaving it to Miss Hobart to mumble an indistinct reply and to voice a prim and dutiful reminder that he must have Sydney home by half past five and drive most slowly and carefully in his phaeton. In response to which he would shrug his shoulders (such shoulders, she'd have to restrain herself from staring) and make a little grimace — odd how when he grimaced he bore so strong a resemblance to Mr. Hedges — before solemnly agreeing to the entirely unnecessary strictures his uncle had made her deliver.

"Yes, I know you'll be careful," she'd say while tightening Sydney's bonnet strings. "And do have a lovely ride in the phaeton."

Phaethon, son of the sun god Helios, had lost control of the immortal, fiery horses that drew his chariot. The earth would have been destroyed in the conflagration if Zeus hadn't killed Phaethon with a thunderbolt.

"A lovely ride," she'd repeat, her voice all ashes, as though she'd already been destroyed in a conflagration. Which would be a better fate, she thought, than the life she was enduring these days, and which could only get worse now that they were in London with him so close by.

She would have to find a new situation, because this one was killing her by degrees.

And as he and Sydney drove away in the phaeton she'd stand on the front steps and wave to them — which they might or might not notice — when what she really wanted was to call out to him, implore him not to drive too close to the sun.

CHAPTER 5

Damn tonight's dinner party anyway, Jasper thought. How could he have been stupid enough to agree to attend? For one thing, he wasn't dressed appropriately — even if an hour ago he'd somehow convinced himself otherwise. The suit that Mowbrey had brushed and aired for him had looked well enough in front of the pier glass, but it had taken only one glance from Anthony to dispel *that* sad illusion.

Two glances, actually: one at a worn, shiny spot on his coat, the other at the smudge of ink on his right cuff.

And not a flicker of an eyelid directed toward his face. But then, he and the boy rarely exchanged more than a wary handshake.

How had he managed to soil the shirt cuff?

He'd arrived home late, his mind on Lord Kellingsley's collection and the interesting questions some of the objects had raised in his mind. He'd wanted to consult his files of engravings, but there hadn't been time. And certainly no time to open the package he'd ordered this morning from Hatchard's. Too bad: Lady Gorham's most recent novel would probably have set him up for the evening with a laugh at its fashionable vacuity.

He'd barely had a moment to jot down a few notes from the afternoon's meeting — which had gone extremely well, if you didn't count an unfortunate contretemps with Mr. Ayleston-Jones of the Dilettanti Society. For that gentleman *would* interpose some entirely outdated notions about how to reconstruct a statue from surviving fragments. Jasper hadn't intended to turn his response into a quip at the pale, plump, exceedingly wealthy gentleman's expense. But his enthusiasm had run away with him, a few sharp, well-chosen words getting tangled up with the technical details. No great harm done, he supposed. Lord Kellingsley had evidently found it instructive as well as amusing, because some moments later he'd suggested that perhaps Mr. Hedges might like to catalog his library too.

And so he'd just wanted to make a few memoranda for his next meeting with Kellingsley, during which they'd be negotiating a fee for his services. A pity for a gentleman to charge money for such a thing, but he'd put off the necessity long enough.

He'd dipped his pen in the inkstand at the very moment the house keeper had hurried into his study to tell him that Sydney was feeling sick. Which had doubtless been when he'd splashed the ink on himself, though in the worry and excitement he hadn't noticed it until Anthony's arrival, when the smudge had drawn the boy's fine bright hazel gaze like a moth to a flame.

"Your sister has been sick to her stomach. What did you feed her?"

"Why, the usual thing. The rout cakes and ices from Gunter's that she likes so much. Oh, and perhaps a few chocolate nonpareils . . . but she seemed quite fine when I left her. Is she all right now? It isn't one of her earaches, is it? I can't imagine —"

"*Can't* you? Imagine that you might have fed her more than was good for her?" For Sydney, in the midst of her weeping, had admitted that everything had been so lovely and delicious they'd had difficulty choosing, and so Anthony had ordered a great many things.

Typical, Jasper thought. And typical, too, the boy's muttered response that he should have remembered that his poor little sister wasn't used to sweet things; she got little enough of *that,* he warranted, nor any fun at all from her stick of an uncle and that fearsomely excellent governess.

Which had set off the stick of an uncle in outraged defense of the "fearsome governess" who'd so patiently and selflessly murmured words of comfort as she rubbed Sydney's back and held her head over a basin. Excellent Miss Hobart had gotten the worst of things, as she always did, while certain thoughtless creatures — Jasper had declaimed in his loudest, most aggrieved voice that *certain* spoiled, thoughtless young fools, hardly older than the young woman — gadded about London without a care or consideration. . . .

The gods on Olympus only knew how much longer he would have continued in that vein as he and Anthony strode side by side down the hall to the front door. He might still be at it if he hadn't caught a glimpse of the young woman in question, white faced except for a spot of bright red high on each prominent cheekbone, quickly making her way to the staircase.

The new phaeton had been parked at the curb with an admiring little crowd gathered about it. Emerging from his side of the angry silence, Anthony had grinned as he took the reins from the boy who'd been holding them and gave him a bright big coin.

At least he was generous as well as extravagant.

And Jasper was bound to admit — if only to himself — that the light, high-sprung little carriage was a thing of beauty.

Not that he had anything but the most horrified suspicions of what it might cost. But he did know the amount of Anthony's income. Better not to ask the price — of the phaeton or, for that matter, the brocaded ivory waistcoat hugging a torso grown broader since last autumn's visit to Wheldon Priory. Better to climb wordlessly aboard, settle onto the soft leather seat, and stare in wonder at the beauty of the young man working the reins so skillfully to move the carriage into the line of traffic in the street.

Forget the last botched quarter hour. Forget all the times and all the ways he hadn't known how to show . . . well, what must be silently, painfully admitted to be love. Leave aside the years of bitter rows; the boy's debts, scrapes, rustications from university; the man's lack of sympathy. Just take the opportunity, Jasper told himself, to gaze, to marvel, to forget there was such a thing as mortality — except, of course, one's own.

The moment passed. The silver-threaded embroidery on Anthony's waistcoat glimmered as the phaeton moved through pools of yellow gaslight. For extravagant, showy flash, they might have been traveling down Oxford Street atop one of Alexander of Macedon's elephants.

Jasper turned his face forward, eyes on the space between the horse's ears as it picked its delicate way through the chaos of cabs and carriages; the quizzing stares of gentlemen, painted smiles of ladies; jewels and velvet, plumes and turbans; smart and shabby vehicles jostling for place along the crowded thoroughfare.

One could almost hear the rustle of inky pages, the rumor mill churning away. *Sir Anthony. Lady Gorham. Marina.* Silly, affected name; upon acquaintance the lady would doubtless prove herself equally silly and affected.

The traffic crossing Regent Street was appalling, but the phaeton wove neatly through it. Anthony drove with impressive skill and restraint, handling the reins like an infant's leading strings, as if he still had Sydney next to him.

As if I were a child, Jasper found himself

thinking, rather ungratefully. *Or a cracked old vessel needing to be packed in cotton wool.*

Sydney would be fine. The pity was to have inflicted all that mess and bother upon Miss Hobart. Perhaps, Jasper thought, if Lord Kellingsley paid him enough, he could hire more help as well as pay the tradesmen back in Essex.

He let his imagination wander to this morning's letter from Germany, the sculpture it described. He thought of the cabinet he'd had built and the lock installed on it, and what he might put into it beside his portfolios of engravings. He thought of the letter from Greece, of an idealistic dream long put aside.

The traffic was moving more swiftly now, pushing his thoughts along with it. What did it mean, "the young men she takes up"? Did it have to mean what he supposed it to mean?

Stupid, what else *could it mean?*

They were slowing down once more. Jasper opened his mouth to curse the traffic but shut it again. For they'd stopped in front of a nice, trim little house — good ironwork, door and shutters shiny black against the neat brick, well-dressed people approaching the front steps.

Brook Street. An unendurable journey come to its much-too-sudden end.

Anthony had leaped down from the box. "Allow me to hand you down, Uncle Jasper." *Fashionable London is* my *world, not yours.*

Jasper stared at the impeccably gloved hand held out to him. *The bloody hell you'll hand me down. Just how ancient do you think I* am, *anyway?*

Landing lightly yet squarely on his feet, he felt himself smiling for what felt like the first time all evening. The boy blinked. Jasper smiled more broadly. One took one's triumphs where one could.

"Shall we go in, Anthony?"

It was well-known, even among those who'd never been invited, that Lady Gorham received her guests while seated in a yellow brocade armchair below the famous portrait Lawrence had painted of her. *Like the brand mark on a cask of wine,* Colburn had once described the arrangement, and Marina had to admit the worldly wisdom of his observation. People liked to associate you with some unchanging representation of yourself; oddly, they didn't seem to tire of it.

The effect remained good, tonight's green gown quite striking against the yellow upholstery. She might sometimes protest how wearying she found it, maintaining the sameness of her persona through the ebb and flow of fashion, but in truth she was very well satisfied with her place — beneath the portrait and in the World as well.

"Lord and Lady Summerson, how very nice."

"*Grazie,* Contessa. Yes, it's been far too long."

Satisfied to have earned her situation and proud that she could afford to pay for it — even to a dinner party whose premier dish was an enormous salmon cooked with four bottles of champagne and a pound of truffles.

"Mr. and Mrs. Colburn, how delightful. Yes, thank you, Mrs. Colburn. It's Madame Gabri's creation; I'm excessively glad you approve of it. And the diamond pendant you're wearing — new? Just this evening? My dear young lady, you've got a veritable jewel of a husband. No, Mr. Colburn, I haven't seen him yet, nor the uncle, of course, but I'm confident . . .

"Ah," she murmured. For as the Colburns drifted off to join the Italian countess, she caught sight of a new group at the door, with Sir Anthony in a splendid — and splendidly expensive — cream waistcoat at its center, laughing at some sally of Mr. Disraeli's.

Given the young baronet's tastes, she thought absently, it was a pity one couldn't marry him to a Rothschild. Still, the Season was bound to offer excellent possibilities. Someone had mentioned a fabulously rich young woman arrived from America. And there was always Lady Isobel.

She caught Anthony's eye and sent him a questioning glance. He smiled from across the room as though to reassure her that, yes, he'd brought the uncle.

She smiled back — good, excellent — and he inclined his head in the direction of a gentleman standing a bit behind him. He was as tall as Anthony: She could make out a good pair of wide shoulders, a taut energy, a wary reserve — the cumulative effect oddly familiar.

In a moment, she told herself, she was bound to remember who this interesting personage was. But as for now, where was the funny old uncle in breeches and periwig?

A footman in her mustard yellow velvet had steered his way through the knot of people. A number of gentlemen followed in his wake — or that of the tray of champagne he carried — awarding her a perfect view of

Anthony and the gentleman from the British Museum.

For that was who he was. The amused eyes behind the spectacles. The close-cropped hair. The hands, now gloved: From time to time during today's hectic party preparations, her inner vision had flashed images of quick fingers around a blue ribbon, the gesture so casual, her response to it so charged with reluctant longing.

How ever had he come to be here? She didn't even know his name. He wasn't anybody at all. His evening dress was barely presentable — those gloves. And yet here he most indisputably was, hovering unwillingly at the threshold of her drawing room.

How? And who?

A too-observant guest inclined his head toward her. Marina supposed she must have said something aloud to herself. Or perhaps she'd gasped in amused surprise, when the answer to her questions had come like the solution to a riddle — a double meaning laying itself open and bare, confusions suddenly comically and reassuringly explicable.

Could you think I'd . . . do anything to hurt Syd? She'd assumed *Syd* to be a little brother rather than the girl with ribbons in her hair and a formidable knowledge of Greek sculpture. *Ah, well.* She smiled, shook

95

her head, waved the nosy guest back to his conversation, and kept her eyes on the gentleman who'd turned out to be Uncle Jasper. Mr. Hedges. Jasper.

The corseting about her waist must have caused a momentary shortness of breath. Marina usually found such a thing unpleasant, but tonight she found herself reminded of one of Madame Gabri's maxims: that a certain constriction about one's center was worth it for the effect it created. There was something to that; giddily, she allowed herself to feel the rise of her breasts above the gown's décolletage.

Wait, though. Someone else was staring at Mr. Hedges from across the room. Not merely staring — Mr. Ayleston-Jones was *glaring, fairly glowering;* she wondered why. As a hostess, she'd have to keep a watchful eye on both gentlemen. Though she'd rather give the lion's share of her attention to the one of them whose presence was causing her to sit up so very straight in her yellow chair.

And who was also, she reminded herself with some severity, a gentleman who hated fashion, gossip, and much of what made her who she was. A scholar, a *stickler for old-fashioned family honor . . . too high-minded to read anything penned during the last two millennia.*

Which would seem to leave out such popular entertainments as she was paid to write for strivers, mushrooms, and lord knew whom else. And which — she reminded herself defiantly — she wrote with all the wit and intelligence she could muster.

The younger and the older gentlemen were making their way to her chair: Sir Anthony smiling, casting the sort of glow about himself that a public personage did, striding through the room secure in his knowledge that everyone knew who he was and wanted him to know them; Mr. Hedges close behind, face expressionless, posture — it seemed to her — mildly combative, rangy shoulders held well back to expose an expanse of old black waistcoat.

She sat up even straighter, smiled the smile she'd presented him with when she'd thought him a quaint country clergyman, breathed as deeply as she could, and waited for him to smile in response. As he must, she thought, when introductions were made.

CHAPTER 6

But the murmured greetings had gone rather too quickly, all else overshadowed by Anthony's evident delight in making the introductions. Not, Marina reflected, that subtlety had ever been his strong suit. Tonight, however, he'd rather outdone himself, managing to call her by her first name some half dozen times in fewer minutes.

Well, what had she expected?

Mr. Hedges's face remained expressionless. Though his eyes flickered behind the spectacles, perhaps in an effort to make sense of things.

Or perhaps not. Perhaps he found it all rather a bore.

And then — and all too soon — it was time to go in to dinner.

The plan had been for Sir Anthony to escort her while Mr. Hedges led pretty Mrs. Colburn in. Marina had watched the publisher's young wife smile and dimple as she gave the gentleman her arm. The diamond pendant had doubtless been intended as a reward for a task that had turned out less onerous than expected.

Rather a good joke on all of us, Marina thought, *for having accepted a green young gentleman's view of what constitutes* cranky *and* crotchety.

She glanced down the table. The menu was clearly a success; she hadn't much appetite for the salmon, but at the rate it was disappearing it must be worth the price of its ingredients. Mr. Ayleston-Jones seemed to have found particular solace in it, only occasionally pausing from his energetic chewing and swallowing to glare up the table at Mr. Hedges.

She turned to Sir Anthony.

"The bear hasn't such sharp claws after all," she said. "After all your worrying, it seems that the dragon doesn't breathe fire at a Mayfair dinner table."

He laughed. "I expect you're right. In the country, he and our vicar used to make their dinner table jokes in Latin — quite the romp, I assure you. The vicar's fearsomely superior daughter would make me feel a complete booby, for *she* would always know the right moment to laugh."

He paused as though struck by an uncomfortable thought, caught himself, and continued. "Tonight, though, there does appear to be a human side to Uncle Jasper, at least when he smiles, as he's doing right now at Mrs. Colburn."

He *was* smiling, wasn't he? What interest could he possibly take, she wondered, in that spoiled little chit ablaze in gems? She awarded Sir Anthony a dazzling and highly visible smile of her own.

"He lives such a retired, unfashionable life," he told her. "And he's been so awfully strict and pettish with me." He put his hand on hers and she squeezed his fingers. As she often did, she told herself hastily.

"But tonight," Sir Anthony said, "I'm willing to grant you that he's surprisingly like everyone else, the proof being that for a moment earlier on . . . do you know, Marina, that I was quite convinced he'd fallen in love with *you?*"

He laughed merrily, and after a moment she joined him.

Did they have to incline their heads quite so close together? Mrs. Colburn having turned her attention to the Italian count, Jasper'd taken the opportunity to sneak a long glance at the head of the table.

What could she and Anthony be whispering about?

Again.

The boy had touched her hand again too, while she . . . They *must* be lovers, he thought. There was a palpable aura of intimacy, a level of comfort. . . .

Hold on.

Comfort. Anthony had been trying to create an impression of intimacy — the gods only knew for whose benefit. *For surely the boy wouldn't care what* I *think — about her, or about anything at all.* No, it must be for the sake of the accursed *on-dits,* even if it went quite beyond Jasper's understanding why one would want one's personal affairs served up in print for general consumption.

But then, he understood so little of what went on west of Regent and south of Oxford streets, in the little plot of English property the estate agents called Mayfair and its inhabitants called the World. He'd been stuck in the country for too long to feel confident of anything but coins and sculpture, poetry, and his own rapturous, shameful memories of uncontrollable love for a beautiful woman.

Still, comfort wasn't passion. He took another surreptitious glance at the boy — at *her* — just to be . . . well, *almost* to be sure.

Almost was all you ever got — but if it were a question of artifacts he'd stake his reputation on it. What was missing from the tête-à-tête at the head of the table was the cold fire that accompanied passion and desire, the paradoxical, thrilling sense of reaching and never completely having. All the stuff that, with every glance he took at her, was suffusing his senses while emptying him of his own good sense.

The footmen were bringing in the dessert course: cakes with spun sugar, pineapples, ices flavored with muscadine and bergamot. A pity he couldn't have worked up more interest in that very good fish dish. On his other side, the conte had begun another story; it seemed to Jasper that the Italian gentleman wanted Mrs. Colburn's husband to publish a memoir.

Perhaps it happened more often than he knew, this business of threadbare aristocrats peddling their thoughts if they had them, or their lives if they didn't. In fact, now that he thought of it, it seemed Mrs. Colburn had been hinting that her husband could possibly print something Jasper might write. How very odd. Lord Byron might have gotten rich if he'd accepted payment for "Childe Harold" — which of course, as a gentleman, he hadn't. Lady Gorham, on the other hand, seemed to have no problem with this very modern way of doing things.

Not that Lady Gorham or any of her business — literary, pecuniary, or otherwise — was any affair of his. No matter how lovely she was, set like a jewel in this house encrusted with art objects. Nor how stormy her eyes or how devastating the haughty, upright posture that made one yearn to know what she'd be like in other poses, without the strictures of clothing or corseting.

He did his best not to stare too sharply at the head of the table. Were she and Anthony laughing at him, making jokes about what an old stick he was? Had he guessed correctly, after all, about the limits of their friendship?

Beautiful . . . yes, yes, he'd gladly admit it. Bluestocking, on the other hand . . . was all the more provocative for its unlikelihood.

Give it a rest, he urged himself, and found himself almost grateful to have his attention wrenched toward the other end of the table, whence a familiar, plummy voice was pompously issuing forth.

Oh, lord, Ayleston-Jones. Well, certain things couldn't go unanswered.

Marina had missed the beginning of the

little fracas, but it was easy enough to catch up.

"And if Napoleon was a great art thief, Mr. Ayleston-Jones, what was Lord Elgin? What was *I*, in my small way," Jasper Hedges continued impatiently, "and the other English gentlemen who roamed, explored, and yes, *plundered* the eastern Mediterranean?"

Opinionated, acerbic. Colburn had said the man wasn't afraid to make enemies. Which might be all very well between the covers of a book, but not at a Mayfair dinner party.

Ayleston-Jones was sputtering. The decanter in front of him was almost empty, the footman at his shoulder distracted.

"I'll grant you," Jasper Hedges continued, "that it's wonderful for your ordinary Londoner to walk down Great Russell Street, pop into the museum, and see the greatest sculptures the world has ever produced. But for your ordinary Greek . . . for your Greek *citizen* . . . well, they're *almost* citizens nowadays, the people who invented the very idea of citizenship. I hate to think how they lost their patrimony because they were weak and subject to the Ottoman Turks, and because Elgin wanted those sculptures to decorate his house in Scotland. While as for Elgin's consideration for our national cultural life: Remember, he offered to sell them to the government only *after* he lost all that money in his divorce suit."

People at both ends of the table had begun to drop their conversations to listen in to this one. In a moment they'd start taking sides. Mr. Hedges's blue eyes had lit up, his chin lifted. Strong, square chin. But there'd be time, Marina promised herself, to contemplate his chin later. While as for now . . .

"Ah, yes, the Mediterranean." She spoke quickly, liltingly, and rather randomly, directing her most glowing smile toward the Italian aristocrats and letting the warmth drift down the table as though on a southern breeze. "How happy the earl and I were on our journeys in the Mediterranean, and how gratified I am this evening to have both Mr. Ayleston-Jones *and* Mr. Hedges among us, not to speak of the conte and contessa. . . ." Drawing out the cadences in the hope that her wit might catch up.

She knew so little of this stuff. A coherent argument was clearly beyond her capabilities. Her charm would have to serve, because otherwise Jasper Hedges was going to say something coherent enough to set the entire dinner table at odds.

"And what a privilege to be able to ask my brilliant guests to unravel a conundrum from the great Mediterranean mythologies."

Ah, she had it now. Best to continue speaking slowly, though. Her guests had had an excellent dinner; there wouldn't be a lot of blood going to the brain.

"The conundrum being," she continued, "why, when choosing the objects of their . . . *affections* — their *physical* affections, I mean, the great classical gods we see cut from marble — and sometimes the goddesses too . . ."

Expectant laughter rippled down the table: How like Lady Gorham to bring the conversation 'round to the generally interesting subject of the physical affections.

She smiled. "After all, it's not obvious, is it, why the great, mighty immortals so often chose frail mortals to, ah, *spend* their passions upon. When they themselves were so perfect, so limitless . . ." She liked *limitless*.

"So bored," Jasper Hedges said.

Well, that's *a bit harsh.*

But now that she looked, she could see that he meant it sincerely and impersonally. She bent her head in his direction; his eyes were bright against the weathered brown of his skin. *Please continue, sir.*

"They're bored with perfection," he said, "and certainly with immortality."

His voice came in quick, staccato bursts.

"The gods, you see, are like big spoiled children who like to sneak down to the servants' hall — or the wealthy young dandy who'll stand his coachman to mug after mug of ale, in return for being allowed to take the ribbons now and again. Like all of us, the gods want what they can't have."

The copper wire of his spectacles had caught the light. "And what thrills them, what torments them with curiosity and desire, Lady Gorham, is the possibility of death. Mortality. The fragility of our bodies, their vulnerability to the passage of time. Human limitation is something the gods can never truly know, but they find its pathos quite beautiful. And the only way they can experience death's pathos is through a human's touch."

A shiver passed through her. Followed by a flood of warmth.

Gazing at him for a longer moment than she'd intended, she noted that a few idle conversations had started up around them. His logic had been too paradoxical for many, the pace of his speech too quick. But for a woman who was no longer young — for whom words like *touch* and *pathos, fragility* and *desire* seemed to shimmer with mystery — one might almost think he'd intended his remarks expressly for her.

107

While as for wanting what one couldn't have . . . But that was too complicated for now.

At any rate, unpleasantness had been averted. Ayleston-Jones was too foxed to reply. Colburn was watching with some interest. Sir Anthony Hedges had turned his attention to the admiring lady on his right. Most of her guests were engaged with other chatter.

The general mood was of contentment. The food had been excellent, the women pretty, the conversation diverting, if you liked that sort of thing.

"Ah, yes, quite so," Marina heard herself say to Jasper Hedges. "And how clever of you," she added, "to understand so well that the gods of the Greeks were as bored as the elegant young Corinthians I choose as the heroes of my novels."

His eyes widened. The corner of his mouth moved.

She felt a small triumph. "You might try one of my books someday, Mr. Hedges," she said, "if you think my sensibility wouldn't bore you."

He smiled. For a moment she thought she'd finally evoked the smile — the one from the museum — that she'd wanted for herself since he'd entered her drawing room. But it was another sort of smile. Of challenge or of response, she couldn't quite tell.

Nor was she quite certain which of them had issued a challenge to the other.

His surprised laughter was like a river flowing beneath the after-dinner tinkle of silver and glass. When next he spoke, his voice was almost too soft to be discerned among the rustle of many desultory conversations.

Somehow, though, she'd managed to make out what he was saying.

"Bored, your ladyship? No, I shouldn't think so. No, hardly bored reading *you,* Lady Gorham."

Chapter 7

The principal detritus of the evening swept away, she'd come back down the stairs in dressing gown, soft slippers, and shawl to thank the servants for their splendid work and bid them leave the rest of the cleaning for tomorrow.

"Let the fire burn down of its own accord," she told the footman. As she sometimes did when too keyed up to sleep after a taxing dinner party, she'd be stopping for a while under the dimly lit lamps downstairs before going up to bed.

Usually on such nights, she'd kick off her slippers and curl up in a deep armchair with her feet tucked beneath her. But tonight she found herself pacing between her sitting room and the library, now and again throwing herself down onto one particular settee, moving herself about against the cushions, imagining she could feel a residual warmth, the impression an angular body would have made in the deep, plush velvet.

"Come, Mr. Hedges," she'd said when Colburn had approached him after dinner. "I'll get you two settled in the library, where you can have some peace, and some good brandy too." She'd wanted to stay, but instead she'd taken Anthony with her to her reception room, he to turn pages at the pianoforte while the contessa sang and played, while Marina herself led her guests in praise between arias.

So she didn't know what sort of business agreement the gentlemen had reached. Although by the look on Colburn's face as he'd bidden her good-night, she suspected that Jasper Hedges had held out for more than what he'd at first been offered.

While as for the offer *she'd* made . . . ?

Of herself. Done subtly enough, she supposed, under cover of the murmur of other conversation. She hadn't caused a spectacle. He wasn't the sort of gentleman anyone would think to link with her in the public eye. He was, she'd dared to think, something new for her. She shook her head. He was probably nothing at all, as she'd doubtless come to realize tomorrow morning, after a good night's sleep and a productive morning at her writing desk.

Still, the fact remained that offering

111

herself was exactly what she'd done.

You might try . . . my books . . . my sensibility.

The younger, slimmer, richer Marina gazed down at her from the Lawrence portrait. With disdain, or perhaps a touch of pity.

She'd better get herself to bed. It certainly wouldn't do any good to wait up any longer. *Admit it,* she chided herself, *you've been waiting for him* — and for Lord only knew how long. She'd been waiting, hoping, and wishing for a rapping at her front door.

Had she merely imagined the promise in his eyes when he'd bowed, thanked her for an exceptional evening, and taken his leave of her?

Hardly bored, he'd said, and she'd thought she'd known what he'd meant by it. She'd supposed she had an instinct for such things.

Her instincts must not be what they'd once been.

Worse still, it seemed she'd begun imagining the sound of rapping at her door.

Quite accurately, too. The sound she fancied she heard was quite as he *would* knock, exactly that series of quick, loud bursts — unwilling and embarrassed all at once.

The consequence of earning one's living by the work of one's own imagination was one's ability to get the little details right — down to that final, softer knock. It was time to go upstairs to bed.

Barefoot, she padded down the hall to the staircase, pausing there for a moment before grimacing, shrugging her shoulders, and continuing to the entryway.

The night air had turned cooler since Jasper had told Anthony he'd rather walk home; a pale fog had descended upon the streets. He'd encountered a watchman twice now — the second time the man had peered suspiciously at him. He wondered how long he'd been prowling Mayfair's meticulously tended, iron-gated squares. The tolling of church bells was of no use what ever; he'd been incapable of counting the chimes, the passing quarter hours dissipating into the mist that stung his cheeks, his mouth, and his lungs.

Bracing air: He was well in need of it. As for his walking about in circles, it must be the effect of the brandy, if not his astonishment at having negotiated a substantial sum of money for a book on ancient gods and Greek antiquities, illustrated with some dozen engravings copied from Jasper's collection. Jasper had insisted upon the engravings, and Colburn had finally agreed.

A successful business negotiation accompanied by an unusually excellent brandy: No wonder that his head was spinning, and that he'd found himself back on Brook Street instead of on his way home to Bloomsbury. Undoubtedly the brandy had sent him north and west when he should have gone east and south.

Undoubtedly, my arse. His lip curled; he bit down on it. His little self-deceptions were pathetic.

The street was devoid of pedestrians. Her house wasn't entirely dark, but perhaps it was her custom to keep a few lights burning. Perhaps the servants were still clearing up.

Perhaps.

Had she truly given him reason to think he might be expected? When he'd left the house he'd been quite certain that an understanding had passed between them, but now he wasn't certain of anything. How could he be? How many years had passed since he'd had *any* understanding with a woman that wasn't contingent upon payment?

No choice but to risk looking like an idiot, knocking upon her door and braving the inevitable surly night porter, for milady was surely long abed.

Still, there were worse things than looking like an idiot. One of them would be going home without having taken his chance. While as for the other thing, the worst of all: A frieze of images drifted across his inner eye — Anthony whispering to her; Anthony touching her hand, laughing with her, smug and secure in his place at her right near the head of the table.

Earlier this evening he'd assured himself it was merely a friendship. But now?

Might Anthony have circled his phaeton back to Brook Street?

The thought of *that* possibility had caused him to rattle the knocker loud and hard enough to dispel the plaguing images — and to frighten away any ghosts who might be haunting the streets.

No answer. Perhaps the porter was dozing.

I'll leave in a moment, Jasper told himself. *Time to shake off this plaguing obsession. Go home, forget about her.*

After one final, quiet, and excessively civilized rattle of the knocker.

And when the door opened, when he saw her framed in the doorway . . .

Somehow he hadn't expected to see her

hair floating about her shoulders and her body free beneath her dressing gown. Nor to find himself so moved by the patterns of dark and pale she made.

Hitherto he'd seen her heavy, dark hair only swept into an imposing chignon at the back of her head.

Loosed about her neck and shoulders, the wild profusion of little curls seemed to soak up what small light there was in her hallway. Her skin looked fragile against the flat blackness, shading to violet beneath her eyes, in the hollows of her neck and the spaces below the finely shaped bones of her clavicle.

He'd hoped to think of something clever to say. But his throat was constricted by the vaporous night air, and all he could manage was a rough, whispered request that he be allowed in.

She'd nodded silently and waved him into the green marble foyer, her shawl and wide, lace-trimmed sleeve falling away from a rounded forearm. He didn't know why a length of ivory skin below the elbow should make him understand that she was naked under her dressing gown, but he was suddenly quite sure of it.

The door had fallen shut behind him; he no longer felt the night air at his back.

Was he still feeling the brandy? Was time passing too quickly or too slowly?

When one was endeavoring to rid oneself of an obsession, one wanted it all over quickly. But he found he didn't see it that way. On the contrary, he felt himself possessed by a need to notice — to comprehend, to possess everything that was happening. Life was too short not to own this moment, to hold it, to weigh it in his palm.

But all he could get his senses to register was the speed of the pulse in her wrist when his hand encircled it, the shine and shiver of the fine pale hairs on her arm as he ran his fingers up to her elbow, her chest rising and falling as he drew her against his own, her mouth and his pressed together as though to devour each other.

Yes, like that.

No, not until he found out what he needed to know.

Grasping her shoulders, he wrenched her away from himself, the separation like the opening of a wound.

"One question," he said.

She nodded, her eyes almost black beneath their dark, heavy lids.

He'd intended to ask it more elaborately, but it turned out that "Anthony?" was all he could manage. Thank the gods that she appeared to understand.

"No," she said. "I swear it." Her voice was low, slowed by a sort of wonder, even of triumph. "No. Never. You must believe me, Jasper. People think it happened, but it never did. He wanted it, but I simply . . .

"No," she repeated. "He's too young. Too immortal."

They both laughed then, not because anything about the exchange was so awfully humorous, but because they both found it singular to discover — even so harshly and abruptly — that, whatever their differences, they clearly shared some sort of idea of decency and responsibility.

As well as an understanding that if this one particular responsibility to decency were to be observed, every other responsibility could wait.

And every other sort of decency as well.

Everything could wait while they hurled themselves at each other a second time. His spectacles had gone a bit askew; her hair got tangled in his calloused fingers as he lifted it from her nape. He kissed the back of her neck; she arched beneath him as his lips traced the bumps of her spine.

Silk rustled against skin, against wool and linen and more silk. Her shawl slid down her back as she reached her hands beneath his coat, his waistcoat, and his shirt now. Her fingertips were soft, dry, devastatingly light, and cold as ice against the skin at the small of his back. He shivered — rather deliciously — and then glanced downward.

Her feet were bare and bluish white against the pink marble tiles. "You're freezing," he said. Eyebrows raised, he inclined his chin toward the hallway, in the direction of that damn little throne room of hers, where she held court among her guests under her portrait.

He wanted to have her in there.

She shook her head. "Upstairs," she said.

But there were so many stairs, Marina thought distractedly. She passed up and down this same staircase a half dozen times a day without giving it a thought, but tonight the simple ascent was taking altogether too much time.

And when they'd paused — panting a bit — at the landing and she put out her hand to lead him to her bedchamber, he grasped her to him instead, crushing her and himself against the wall as though he couldn't or wouldn't go any farther.

For a moment she considered simply pulling him down to the floor. Right here, in the corridor. But that wasn't how Lady

Gorham did this sort of thing. With a great, gasping effort of will, she turned her head away.

"Come on," she whispered. "It's the second door on the right. This way. Please, darling, let's not waste any more time."

They jostled each other into her bedchamber. He kicked the door shut behind them; she dragged him to her bed and they fell upon it most inelegantly — grasping, groaning, thrashing about. There was some pulling of hair, more than a little banging of knees and poking of elbows, and an excess of clutching at what ever could be clutched at.

How very singular, she thought. *Lady Gorham usually manages this part of it so much more gracefully.*

Oh, Lord, he thought, *she'll think me an utter barbarian.*

For in their unseemly impetuosity, each of them had tried to take hold of the same button on his trousers.

Jasper slapped her hand away.

She gasped, stared haughtily at him for an astonished moment, then shrugged her shoulders and laughed.

For the life of him, he couldn't imagine

why he hadn't simply let her open the button.

Too proud? It would seem so, but too stupid might be more accurate. He let himself imagine for a moment how delicious it would have been to submit to her lovely, quick fingers. A better idea in any number of ways — after all, he wouldn't be able to hold off forever.

But by the look of her, it was clearly too late to take it back, plead that when in extremis he was clumsy with buttons and ties.

She'd given a last low laugh and moved away from him.

"All right," she said. "Fine. But I want you to remove every item — I don't take a gentleman to bed with his stockings still gaping about his ankles."

The corner of her mouth twitched. He thought there might be a dimple in her chin.

"Go ahead," she said. "Please, I shall be more than content to watch."

Gorgeous. Green-eyed. Impertinent and imperious. The dimple merely adding insult to injury, and leaving him no choice but to swing his legs over the side of the bed, sit with his back to her, curse, and wrestle with the buttons.

He yelped when he stuck his hand with the foolish pin Mowbrey had insisted on putting in the lapel of his jacket. And she did help him once — in truth, she saved him from choking when he endeavored to pull his shirt over his head before the cravat was unknotted.

He could hear her chuckling about something. Glancing quickly over his shoulder, he saw that she was holding his shirt in her hand and shaking her head over the ink-stained cuff.

"You have a beautiful back," she said. "Quite wonderful, given the leanness of your waist, how the muscles slant outward toward your shoulders — rather in the shape of a chevron. You *could* consider putting better, newer linen against such a back."

"Thank you," he said, not at all graciously. "Perhaps I shall."

Her voice was burnished irony and maddening self-possession. "My pleasure."

Returning his attention to the job of pulling his trousers down over his legs, he reached for the string that closed his drawers and pulled it open.

"My . . . pleasure," she repeated, in a different tone of voice entirely.

She forced herself to roll her hands into fists at her sides. Because much as she wanted to touch him, she'd be damned if she'd allow herself to slow things down any more than he'd managed to do already.

Still, the view from over his shoulder was definitely . . . hmm, *engrossing,* might one say? — his upcurving cock really quite lovely to look at for the sculpted elegance of the distended veins. It would, of course, be vulgar to pay undue attention. Quite all right, she assured herself; she was merely giving it what attention it was due.

And if she could feel her mouth loosening, if she'd had to bite down upon her lip not to sigh for the spectacle of his flesh continuing to lengthen and harden as it rose from his half-removed drawers, she could always divert herself with the comedy of the situation they'd found themselves in. For he *would* curse and mutter in his awkward haste to peel the old black fabric of his trouser legs down his thighs, kick off his shoes, and finally to rid himself of the last of his accursed clothing.

Oh, Lord, *almost* out of it. Yes, he'd finally tugged off the last stocking, which action she had determined to be her signal to take a few quick steps around the bed. To stand in front of him, allow her dressing gown to fall to her feet, and step over and out of it, toward him, in the freedom, elegance, and power of her nakedness.

■ ■ ■ ■

He had been intending to say something, in a self-parodic, mock-comic sort of growl, about how she could bloody well have gotten the clothes off of him herself.

As he'd tossed aside the last of his garments, he might even have opened his mouth to begin speaking. Some distant part of his mind might even have been aware that he was smiling, which was odd, given how confused, overwrought, and painfully aroused he was — and that her taunting had only made it worse.

Or perhaps *not* worse — for he *was* smiling, wasn't he? Yes, he could feel it. *Give it up, Jasper,* he told himself. *Allow yourself to own that this desperate, passionate business is turning out remarkably funny, nice, even friendly.*

But as he looked up, words and smile faded on his lips, dissolving in a new and even more surprising rush of feeling: the same tenderness he'd felt at the sight of her at the doorway — but also a sort of wonder. One narrow white foot planted slightly in front of the other, she stood nearly motionless: lips parted, breasts rising and falling with each breath, a black corkscrew of hair at her temple aimlessly adrift on a current of warm air from the grate.

Breathing flesh, tinged with pink, tipped with inky black and earthy brown. The curves of her body swooped from heavy breasts to narrow waist: a shadow of convexity at the belly, another at the triangle of splendid black curls below it, and then the heart-stopping curve outward to a lushness of hips, long but rounded thighs.

He reached out a hand, both hands, to take hers, to draw her slowly toward him, to lay her down on the bed, where he could lean above her and brush his lips, his tongue, his fingertips against her. He didn't know how long he could hold back, but for as long as he could he wanted to taste and touch, trace and hold and learn to comprehend the lines and volumes of her.

She arched her back; her belly had become a shallow bowl. Her breasts overflowed his hands, the nipples hardening, areolae darkening between his fingers.

It was worth the patience, the effort of will, to watch her coming to her arousal that way.

Well, very nearly worth it. *Just a little more time,* he told himself.

He nudged her up farther toward the headboard so that he could dip his head down over her breasts, take one nipple between his lips and then the other, feel each of them in turn hardening against his tongue and between his teeth. Very lightly with the teeth: He forced himself; he didn't want to challenge her unduly — not yet, anyway, not until he got to . . . well, whatever he was sure he'd find in her.

Right now it would have to be enough simply to tongue and nibble and tease while he moved a hand into the space beneath the arch at the small of her back, fingers tracing the curve of her arse as they crept downward in search of the secret, sensitive place where the cheek met the top of her thigh. Because he thought that if touched there she might — oh, yes, she'd let out a strangled moan, a gasp, and a small but gratifyingly helpless exhalation. The fraught sounds of her breathing would have been nice to hear from any bed partner, but most particularly from a lady too fastidious to take a man to bed while he was in his stockings.

He worked a finger up inside her to feel the wetness, the trembling that echoed the pulse quivering in her throat. He moved his eyes to her face — he'd intended to smile at her encouragingly (and triumphantly too, he supposed). Except that she'd shut her eyes. *Damnation.*

■ ■ ■ ■

Beguiled as she was by such excess of sensation, Marina hadn't been able to entirely ignore the sound of a little critical voice. Oddly, it resembled the inner voice that sometimes savaged her writing, though in this case observing (rather disapprovingly) how uncustomary it was for Lady Gorham simply to lie back and give way to a man's caresses.

Hadn't she done enough of that when she'd been younger? the voice demanded. If, of course, one could describe the gropings and forcings she'd been subject to during that period as caresses.

While men like her husband were another matter entirely.

In any event (the voice continued), wouldn't it be safer to treat this gentleman as she'd been managing the series of young lovers she taken since Harry's death? Approach the business in the same spirit as mounting a horse: Assert her will and everything would proceed quite nicely, if, it must be admitted, with not very much novelty.

Admonitions buzzed in her ears; judgments and comparisons flitted behind her closed eyelids. Pests — she wanted to chase them away. But if she were able to banish all the thoughts and memories, it would be only him and her alone in her bedchamber.

And the truth was that she found herself a little afraid of that possibility.

The problem (but how singular to be calling it a problem!) was that he didn't seem to have the slightest interest in taking her abruptly or finishing with her quickly — though, from the feel of his cock butting up against her thighs and belly, he'd lost nothing of the urgency she'd glimpsed over his shoulder a little while ago.

The confusion was that she couldn't quite make out where her pleasure ended and his began.

At least, up until this moment. Because although he was still employing his fingers so beautifully, he'd taken his mouth away from her breast.

Damnation.

She opened her eyes to see him raised up on one arm, gazing down at her.

"And now," he whispered, "I want you to *keep* your eyes open. Because now that I'm out of my clothes, I enjoy being looked at as much as you do."

She almost bridled at being told what to do. But he was right: She did like to be looked at. She always had, and there'd been a time in her life when it had made things a damned sight easier for her.

And why — now that one thought of it — shouldn't a man also enjoy the pleasures of scrutiny, the embrace of admiring eyes?

"Could you do that for me, Marina?"

She laughed, nodded her head, and put her hands about his neck to draw him down into a kiss.

Of course, an open-eyed kiss hardly counted. But she kept her eyes fixed upon his as he raised himself above her; she couldn't help but smile to share her pleasure in drawing her legs up about his waist and tilting her hips toward him. She breathed a deep quiet "ah" when he entered her, and they continued to gaze at each other as they moved.

She could see in his eyes that he liked it when she hugged his hips as tightly as she could with her thighs, even as she felt herself stroked so firmly, filled so definitively, taken so emphatically.

Damn, was the nasty little critical voice really going to intervene again, at *this* moment of all moments? It wasn't fair — and yet the little voice wasn't stupid. Because what it was telling her was, *To hell with milk-and-water words like* taken, *Marina; the* correct *word for what this gentleman is doing is* fucking *you, and if you can't call a fuck a fuck you shouldn't call yourself a writer.*

She giggled. He grinned and dropped a light kiss on her nose. Together they helped each other find the rhythm once more.

Her inner critic had spoken the truth — wonderful to have the right words when you needed them. Moving with him and yet coming to meet him as well, she grasped him to her with all the little muscles inside her: to welcome, to hold, and then to bid him a tiny farewell with every arc and thrust of their bodies. To fuck and be fucked, in all the word's plainspoken glory.

She loosened her thighs a bit — so he could help her raise her legs about his shoulders now. Deeper, better, tighter, thanks. Better for him too, she thought. She could see his lips tremble, and he knew that she could see it.

He'd begun to groan. He *did* like to be looked at. He liked to be known — in bed, if perhaps nowhere else, he was generous about revealing himself.

But that last thought had come fleetingly to her, during the last moment when it would even be possible to have a thought, before there was only flesh and flash and thrash and motion, the wet darkness and heat lightning of sweat-slicked bodies locked together in a rocking and a heaving, a lifting and a holding and a blissfully thoughtless letting go.

Some time must have passed. She had no idea how much; she had very little idea of anything except that he was still lying atop her — heavy, in the awfully nice manner of masculine muscle and sinew lying agreeably on top of a deeply, happily satisfied female body. She'd have to move herself, move *him* a bit too, if she were to get a view of the clock on the mantel.

Later, perhaps, she decided. Because at this moment she couldn't muster the requisite curiosity about what ever the bloody time might be.

Wait, he was stirring, groaning, trying to pull away from her. She tightened her arms around him.

"That was . . ." His voice came rough against her ear. "That was . . . hmmm . . . that was . . ."

Delicious to have rendered such a very articulate gentleman at a loss for words. "Yes, it was," she whispered. "Exactly," she said. "Quite." And they both laughed.

"Am I too heavy? You must feel crushed."

"No, I like it."

"Mmm, I like it too, but fair's fair."

He rolled over and took her with him. She was lying atop of him now as they kissed. The movement had knocked his spectacles awry; she had to straighten the earpiece. Which somehow set them laughing again, this time so deeply — their bellies heaving and quivering against each other — that he had to put her down on the bed next to him.

Catching her breath, she wiped an eye with the corner of a bedsheet. "What did *you* find so funny?" she asked.

"I don't know exactly," he told her. "Perhaps something about how excessively frightened I was of coming back to your house after I'd left." He kissed her chin. "Yes, there *is* a dimple there — a sweet, shallow little one. Did the painter notice it? I don't think it's in the picture."

If anyone had ever noticed it, she thought, they'd never mentioned it. Not even Sir Thomas Lawrence. "You're very observant."

He shrugged. "I've learned to be. And what made *you* laugh?"

"Perhaps the memory of you all tangled in your clothes as you tried to divest yourself of them. How old is that shirt, anyway?"

"I haven't the faintest idea; I've never much cared what I wear, and these past few years there hasn't been money for such things, especially after the . . ."

But why had the expression on his face changed so suddenly and so radically?

What she could see of it, before he'd turned his head away from her.

CHAPTER 8

Under no circumstances would he go on prattling about the trials of managing an estate on next to no money. And if she thought him rude, Jasper told himself, so be it. He'd almost blundered into telling her things that weren't anybody's business but his own. Well, and Anthony's, legally speaking, but in that way it was lucky that Anthony rarely came down to Wheldon except to hunt a few times a year, and that the boy was happy to leave the household accounts to his dry old stick of an uncle.

His brother and his wife had spent a great deal on novelty, Celia had told him that last day in Italy. *More than we can afford,* she'd added. At the time, he'd thought it an exaggeration, voiced to gain his sympathy.

Back in England, he'd learned she hadn't been exaggerating in the slightest. And that in truth she'd done her best in the face of the inevitable, insisting that John put something in trust for the children before the money really began disappearing. By the time Jasper got a look at what he could expect to maintain the estate on, it was pretty much gone.

The solicitor had described it with a sort of reluctant admiration. He'd been in his profession a long time, he'd said, and had rarely seen a fortune evaporate with such stunning rapidity.

In all the horrid confusion following the deaths, Jasper hadn't found time to send the sculptures back to Greece. A lucky thing. Stoically, he'd sold them to the highest bidder. And the money had gone a long way toward helping, at least until these past few difficult years, when it had run out too. Perhaps he shouldn't have bought back those parts of the estate that had been lent in mortgage — or anyway, not so soon, with the roof still in such bad shape — but it had felt so good to redeem the property for Anthony and those who'd come after him. A father ought to be able to do that much . . . even if the boy would never know that the man who'd done so was his father. Or that the man he *thought* was his father had made it necessary through his extravagance.

But Jasper hated the moments when his

resentments got the better of him. Such moments came suddenly — sometimes inconveniently. Never quite so inconveniently as now, however.

He sneaked a look across the pillows at her surprised and worried face. At moments like this one, he probably looked rather like some desperate character mounting the gibbet on his way to his execution. *Swallow back the resentment,* he told himself. *Pretend it doesn't exist.*

Because it was one thing to lie back and enjoy the entertainment of a woman's post-coital chatter. Quite another for a gentleman to disclose his own secrets.

Surprising that he'd even let things come to such a pass — that he'd even come close to talking about it. But there was so much about this evening that was surprising; he'd have to puzzle it out later.

He nodded apologetically and did his best to calm his facial expression.

Her voice was gentle. "I hadn't meant to pry," she said. "I hadn't known that teasing you about a worn old shirt *was* prying. I simply found it so amusing, you see — the two of us together as we are, the . . . unlikelihood of it, and yet the . . ."

The two of us together. As. We are.

Simple present tense.

Until this moment he'd assumed that they'd taken each other to bed in order to satisfy, to slake the disturbing passions that had overtaken them. Indulge themselves, get it over and done with and into the past, and move on.

But when *was* such a thing over and done with? Suddenly the present tense didn't seem so simple.

But perhaps they didn't have to decide that just yet.

A long tress of her hair lay across his chest. Carefully, he wound it around his finger, and then again so he and she would have to move an inch or two closer together, and then another few inches, and then . . .

By the time he'd removed his finger from the ring he'd made of that lock of hair, she'd turned herself about in his arms, so that he could feel the weight of her breasts in his hands and stroke himself against her arse. And so that she could move her hips forward and back, making tiny arcs against him, chuckling every so often as his cock jumped against her, crooning to feel it hardening in the curves and hollows of her thighs and bottom.

"Ah." He sighed.

She laughed — a bit evilly, he thought.

"I thought you enjoyed being looked at,"

she said.

"I enjoy being . . ." He felt his voice come out a bit hoarse. "Oh, wait, slower, Marina, yes, like that — umm, yes, I enjoy being . . ."

But he never got to specify what it was he enjoyed being, it having become quickly and unavoidably evident what each of them and both of them enjoyed *doing.* They scrambled to their knees. And this time — or perhaps from this angle — the coupling was quicker, louder, bawdier, and suggestive of other possibilities as well.

Collapsed atop her back, he lifted the tangled knot of black curls to nuzzle at her nape. Delicious to listen to her purr under his lips. Catching a glimpse at the tall window across the room, he could see through a narrow verge above the lace at her windows that the sky wasn't black anymore, but an inky blue.

It was late. It had been an extraordinarily long and tiring day. How nice it would be to stay the night, wake up with her breasts against his chest or her arse against his belly. He wasn't sure which he'd prefer; it might be nicer still to find himself surprised upon waking, by how their bodies had sought each other in sleep.

He felt his jaw go stiff. Had he seriously considered staying? After moping about so rudely because he hadn't wanted to speak to her?

Still, there was no denying it: He'd quite spontaneously imagined himself not appearing at the breakfast table at Charlotte Street. Which would be the first time in . . . Well, the truth was that he *always* came down to breakfast, had done so unfailingly for more than a decade. Even when Sydney'd had her bread and milk in the nursery, he'd always popped in to say good morning and see how she'd slept.

At first it had merely seemed to him the sort of thing an orphaned child ought to have. Her mama and papa having disappeared, she might find it a comfort to be assured of her guardian appearing regularly. But as time went on, he'd begun to own that he liked having a child across the table, even if it might mean spilled milk, willfulness, and the occasional fit of temper — and no chance what ever of his getting through his book or newspaper.

He hadn't stayed the night with a woman for eleven years. Not that he'd ever particularly wanted to; there'd always seemed to come a point in the proceedings when he felt himself ready — even eager — to settle accounts, brave the elements, and get himself home. And if he didn't feel that way tonight, all the more reason why he ought to be going.

He didn't want to insult her, though. Reluctantly, he murmured that he needed to go.

She forced her eyes open, rolled away from him, pulled herself up against the pillows. Her breasts swelled as she laughed, a bit ruefully. "Yes, you *do* have to, I'm afraid, if I'm to get anything done tomorrow — my obligations to Mr. Colburn keep me on rather a tight rein, you know."

Well, *that* was ruddy cold-blooded. Hadn't she even *wanted* him to stay?

Because it was one thing for him to overcome temptation for the sake of duty and family. It was quite another to find that he wouldn't have been allowed to stay even if he'd asked.

But this was absurd. How many contradictory things could one think, could one *want* at the same time? If only, perhaps, her breasts hadn't moved just then, if she hadn't voiced that vulgar little commonplace about herself being kept on a *tight rein,* the phrase suggesting other, provocative, disturbing images . . .

Hell, would his feelings this astonishing night ever cease confusing and confounding him?

In silence, he pulled his drawers on, tied them closed, and with some difficulty found the rest of his clothes, lining up his shirt, stockings, trousers, and cravat on his side of the bed, the orderliness of the procedure in absurd contrast to the poor pieces of clothing. She was right about the shirt; it would do as a pen wiper. He should use some of Colburn's money to buy himself some new linen. And where the bloody hell was his right shoe?

Enough, she told herself, *of all this confusion. Someone* needed to speak plainly.

She narrowed her eyes and leveled her gaze. "You must forgive me, perhaps, to have supposed that you'd rather enjoyed yourself this evening. It had appeared to me, at any rate, that you were as entertained as I, and as eager to continue the connection. Was I mistaken?"

She'd intended to say *moved* instead of *entertained.* But now she was glad she hadn't, for the gentleman who'd insisted she keep her eyes wide open continued to avoid her gaze.

Her fault, she supposed, for not keeping to her avid, grateful, and not awfully challenging young men. She ought not to say anything further. If she opened her mouth again she'd sound shrewish.

So be it. "I'd expected we'd be occupying ourselves with kisses and compliments at these last moments, and making the necessary scheduling arrangements. Forgive me if I misinterpreted the course of the evening's events. I'd rather thought we were agreeing to be lovers for this Season."

At least he was looking at her again, eyes glinting beneath his spectacles. She met his gaze squarely.

"Is that how you do it?" His voice was grudging, she thought, but also genuinely curious. "Measure it out by the Season, I mean."

"No one's ever before asked me to spell it out. But yes, I expect it's become my custom. The span of time between early spring and midsummer seems as long as one needs to plumb another person's depths, learn his desires, explore what pleasures —"

She stopped herself. "Whereas you're an unmarried gentleman. And allow me to observe that *you* clearly haven't been going without, these past years. Well, how do *you* do it?"

"I pay. It's my single luxury. And I find that the span of time between ten in the evening and one o'clock in the morning is usually long enough for one to . . . well, explore a bed partner's depths, or what ever it was you said."

"Cynic. Rake. Who would have thought it?" She was breathing entirely too shallowly, she thought, even without any corseting about her. But there was nothing for it but to continue. "And so, was the time we spent together tonight sufficient for you to have had enough of *me?*"

And what would she say, she wondered, if he answered *yes?*

He laughed instead. "I've never been called a rake."

"A rake," she told him, "is a gentleman morbidly intent upon demonstrating his need for erotic novelty, his intolerance for repetition."

"*Morbidly,* eh?"

"Rather."

He raised his eyebrows. "Well, it's a clever observation. Quite good. Accurate in some ways, I expect. Who said it?"

She essayed to keep the triumph out of her voice. "Lord Farringdon said it in my last Season's book. Which is to say . . ."

He had the grace to show his appreciative surprise. "Which is to say that *you* said it, Lady Gorham; I shall have to find out what else you and your bored Corinthian heroes have to say about the ways of the polite world. But I must inform you that by Lord Farringdon's lights — and consequently by yours — I'm not a rake at all, because *I* have a taste both for novelty and for repetition."

Some eager, exuberant part of her would have liked to squeal out something like, *Ooh, good, I do too.* But she merely lowered her eyes in polite agreement.

Though a little of that *ooh, good* might have shaped the curve of her lips.

"While as for the end of this affair," he continued, "I find it impossible to estimate how long it'll take me to have had enough of *you.*"

She let out her breath as slowly as she could. "Oh, the length of a Season, I should think. You'll have had enough of me — we shall each have had enough of the other — before autumn."

He laughed. "Well, it's good to have come to an understanding, anyway."

"And is an understanding an agreement?" she asked.

"It seems so."

"Because a lady likes these things to be official, you know. A lady likes to be convinced."

Something like a smile tugged at the corners of his mouth. He leaned down over the pillows to embrace her, and she pulled him down next to her on the bed.

"Convinced?" he asked after a time.

"Not entirely. You'll find that I'll take as much convincing as I'll take . . . well, everything else I'm sure you'll be giving me, novelty and repetition both."

"Oh, yes. And may I come back tomorrow evening to continue trying to convince you?"

"The night following. Tomorrow night I won't be able to come home early from . . . hmm, a rout and then a reception. But the night following . . . yes, I'll manage. I can leave at eleven."

The disappointment that flashed across his face made her smile as much as the little tightening she'd felt in her thighs. "We *couldn't* meet every night — though I'm flattered, delighted, and . . . impressed that you should wish to." The tightening in her thighs had spread to her belly.

"But my life," she continued, "as I live it — well, there's rather a lot of puffery involved. A lot of being seen with a certain sort of people."

"Not the shabby, scholarly sort."

Her smile twisted, became rueful. "Alas, my most faithful readers have no admiration whatsoever for *shabby* or *scholarly*. And as they adore the exclusive Society that doesn't adore or even welcome them, my life and my books make up a sort of substitute version they can buy for themselves."

How sure of herself she sounded, she thought. As though she were revealing everything there was to be told.

He nodded thoughtfully.

"You don't approve of it," she continued, "but I'm afraid that's simply how it is. The place I've made for myself depends upon an ongoing *public* story that's mostly exaggeration and lies. You can read about it in the newspapers if you like — I should imagine it might be like deciphering the Rosetta Stone."

"Well, then," he said, "we have something in common, at least in our mutual needs for privacy. Even if we follow different paths, you in the World . . ."

"At its edge, just this side of scandal . . ." she murmured.

"And me outside of it, a sober, straitlaced guardian to innocence."

An image flickered in front of her inner eye, of his sunburned hand on a blue ribbon, a blond head. The mildest twinge of envy, of sadness and dissatisfaction, passed through her core. She wouldn't give way to it.

"So long as you agree," he said softly,

"how important it is that we keep the separate parts of our lives completely separate."

Meaning most especially, she thought, his family. *All right, so be it.*

"Utterly separate. In neat little compartments." She smiled and shrugged away the last of her dissatisfaction. "Like those trays of insects and bits of bone and mineral in the British Museum."

"Exactly so."

"You needn't worry," she told him. "I'm as good at secrets as I am at puffery and publicity." Better at secrets, she resolved, than he would ever know.

"Well, then," he said, "shall I come around night after next at half past eleven? Quietly, secretly. Merely to convince a lady in need of convincing. It will be a most selfless act on my part, I assure you."

She smiled to dispel the remaining tension in the air, and for this evening's pleasures as well as those to come. "Yes," she said, "or anyway, to spend the remainder of the Season attempting to convince me."

CHAPTER 9

And so another London Season was launched, quite as Lady Gorham, in an early novel, had described the busy interval between spring and the middle of summer: a "rich tapestry of event and festivity." A fabulous, closely woven pattern — particularly for those persons placed highly enough to be received in exclusive drawing rooms; dance in ballrooms lined with silk and flowers; jostle one another, spill drinks, and gasp for air upon the great town houses' crowded staircases; clutch a prized Almack's voucher in a finely gloved hand; and read all about it in the *on-dits* the next morning.

While in other houses, perhaps at less good addresses, there were quite as many dinners, balls, routs, and receptions to attend — sometimes quite extravagant ones, because of late there was a lot of money to be made in trade and manufacturing. But though a great many hands were kissed, dinners digested, and marriage contracts sealed at these middle-class festivities, for many in attendance there lingered a stale scent of the second-best, a sense that this really rather tiresome business of pleasure must be done better by the personages known only through the *on-dits* and the Society novels. In consequence of which, London's cits and mushrooms read Lady Gorham's chronicles of the *haut ton* with the same earnest application they directed to the prices of cotton and coal.

Parrey had been released to universal acclaim. The reviews placed it high in the firmament of English fiction, for what Mr. Degustibus called its "wisdom, wit, and taste" and Sir Ignis Fatuus its "wit, sensibility, and exquisite discrimination."

A small but elegant pyramid of the handsome volumes had appeared in Hatchard's window on the day of publication, and the following evening Lady G— wore violet silk and black pearls to Lord and Lady Drayton's ball, most exquisitely indeed. But most surprisingly and shockingly, the *on-dits* reported that the lady had not danced with Sir A— H— even once, no matter how splendid his looks, how perfect his linen or his peach satin waistcoat. And she'd left the ball early, perhaps by half past eleven.

And so it must be true, the *New Monthly Magazine* concluded a few days later, that — as hinted in those pages last week — her ladyship and the baronet were no longer *à deux,* though they'd bowed once, most cordially.

Or, as the *Atheneum* had it, twice but coldly.

Prompting the gossipmonger for the *Literary Gazette* to remind his audience that this handsomest of London's young beaux was nonetheless still believed to be the model for the hero of Lady G—'s most current fiction, which had gotten such splendid notice from Fatuus and Degustibus both. And to point out that two large tables holding nothing but stacks of *Parrey: A Gentleman* had been seen at the Temple of the Muses, Finsbury Square.

While several other papers, at the beginning of the next week, took care to admonish their readers that a familiarity with *Parrey* would be de rigueur for anyone expecting to take part in civilized dinner conversation — or perhaps even to serve a good dinner — in the coming months. Happily though, obtaining a copy could hardly be easier, as the window at Hatchard's was displaying no other book, and readers might be relieved to know that the quarrels raging about the identity of the principle characters would be resolved soon enough in the forthcoming *Key to Parrey.*

The *on-dits* neglected to mention that Lady Gorham's Almack's voucher had been delivered to Brook Street only a week before the opening ball, and that the nods and greetings between the lady and the assembly room patronesses were brief and rather chilly. But the writers might be forgiven the omission, because the real news of *that* evening was that although Sir A— had danced with a certain handsome American heiress, he'd stood up twice with one of the Season's most fascinating debutantes, Lady I— W— , about whom the public might expect to read more, the young lady possibly being the model for Miss Randall in *Parrey.*

Not bad, Colburn thought when his clerk brought him the first fortnight's receipts. Quite good, the mentions of Lady Gorham at Almack's. And even better, he told himself, that the *Gazette* had picked up the story of Sir Anthony and Lady Isobel, which he'd told his own writer to divulge over a pint of ale, as though too inebriated to keep a secret. Nice when you could get the competition to do your work for you. His writer would be getting free drinks for the rest of the Season. And in a few days, if the young people were still speaking to each other (or perhaps even if not), it would be time to print the next item, about Lady I— being Lady G—'s estranged stepdaughter. Not bad at all, Colburn thought.

"Pas mal." Madame Gabri gave a happy shrug of the shoulders as she counted the orders for evening costumes she'd received. Not bad indeed, even if a distressing number of the customers had requested gowns patterned after Lady Gorham's violet silk. Which could be done easily enough, the modiste knew, if with less than imposing results.

She scowled. How few were the London ladies who truly knew how to dress: for every intelligent customer — like the new little one who'd brought that excellent lavender twill with her — there were ten wanting nothing more than to copy Lady Gorham, even if they had nothing of the countess's complexion, posture, or figure. Still, it was good business and good publicity — for the countess, and for those tradespeople like madame herself, who earned their livings in her reflected glow.

■ ■ ■ ■

It could have been worse, Lady Gorham told herself determinedly. At any rate, the persona the reporters made of her could hardly be sillier.

No matter. She set the newspapers aside, resolving to set to work at what was still a desperately confused attempt at a novel about Mr. Parrey's twin brother, lost at sea off the coast of Ireland. (No, not Ireland — she should stop thinking about Ireland and put away those little sketches she'd been writing too. Make it Illyria; much better, no one even knew where Illyria was.)

It *would* have been worse, she thought, if Jasper hadn't bothered to read *Parrey.* And *much worse* if he'd thought the book was bad.

But he *had* read it. "There aren't any other books to be had in London this week," he'd said at first. "Sorry, Marina; I'm teasing you. It's good. There are bits that are as good as the rake in *Farringdon.*" After which he'd begun moving his head downward, enumerating the book's virtues between kisses as he went: *clever, graceful, accomplished, witty, intelligent. . . .*

She'd ceased listening after *intelligent.*

Which might just prove, she thought now, that an authoress's vanity had some limits, if her other appetites did not. For at seven in the morning — even after having succumbed to the hitherto unthinkable act of eating a little something with him after midnight — she was as hungry as ever.

It was as though she could still taste a residual sweetness on her tongue. He enjoyed cakes and fruit and wine — to fuel his engine, she'd joked, after he'd confided that his steward had compared him to a Watt and Boulton earth-moving machine.

They'd laughed together at that, and she continued to cherish the memory of it, for (just as they'd promised) they'd shared very little information about themselves, of course excepting some reasonable inquiry about the need for possible precautions.

The discussion had been brief enough. Disease wasn't a problem, and he seemed to understand without tedious explanation that years of certain expediencies could make a woman barren. Good not to have to fret about it, anyway. More delightful to fuss over whether to eat the morsels of food he kept offering. *Just a tiny bite, Marina, one grape — no, have two — here, from my fingers, before I have a quaff of wine myself, from a most exquisitely modeled drinking cup.*

She needed to get back to her writing. Which meant that she needed to stop the vulgar, delicious thing it seemed she was doing in her chair. When, she wondered, had she begun rubbing her thighs together and moving her bottom about like that while she recalled particular moments of the past few nights — the shivery feeling of his pouring claret into the declivity her belly made when she lay on her back, the marvelous roughness of his tongue as he drank it up and licked her belly clean?

The bills for laundering her sheets had become prodigious. She was getting less sleep than ever.

None of which seemed to matter. Not while *Parrey* was selling. Jasper actually liked it, and she liked Jasper's attentions very much indeed. Her life was in perfectly good order — or would be, if the Season weren't flying by so quickly. And if only she could apply herself to the dreadful, superfluous manuscript about the stupid twin brother, and not find herself scribbling useless little vignettes about *Ireland,* of all places.

With a dreamy, satisfied smile, she chewed a big bite of apple and turned her eyes to the sheet of foolscap on her writing table, putting both Ireland and her wonderfully energetic lover out of her thoughts. Reality would intrude soon enough; just let her sweep that knowledge to the margins of her consciousness, leave the dead to their rest for just a little while longer.

Coming down the stairs for luncheon, however, she could see reality's rude intrusion in the lines of her butler's worried countenance.

But this was *too* soon. Oh, well, no matter.

"Begging your pardon, my lady. But there's some sort of tradesman waiting for you in the library."

"In the library, Merton?" The servant had been with her only a year or two and had consequently never seen the "tradesman" before. But he had a sharp eye for trouble.

"He insisted on waiting there, madam, even after I tried to send him down to the kitchen. He said Lady Gorham would understand."

The important thing to remember was that she *was* in fact Lady Gorham, and that she'd deal with this visit as Lady Gorham — as a countess — would. "Yes, you did right; thank you, Merton."

She walked slowly down the hallway to the library, Lady Gorham's wide poplin skirts rustling about her as she went.

■ ■ ■ ■

The "tradesman" — the one she thought of as her principal creditor — stood with his back to her, facing the bookshelves on the other side of a long oak table. The air smelled sweetish and sickly — tallow, from the pomade he'd visibly slathered onto his thinning hair. It would leave a stain, she thought, on the velvet collar of his too new, too flash, slightly too tight brown coat.

Her nose prickled. She could feel it wrinkling in disdain. Even without a penny in his pocket, her father would have wrinkled his handsome nose exactly the same way, in response to some crony's lapse in dress or etiquette.

But hadn't she promised herself she'd leave the dead to their rest? She'd think only of herself, of what she had and wanted to keep, and all she feared to lose.

"Do you find my library interesting, Mr. Rackham?" she asked.

Slowly, he turned himself about to face her. "I do indeed, Lady Gorham. I find your library interesting indeed."

He held an open copy of *Parrey* in a pale, plump hand. The hand had a moist look about it; she tried not to shudder for her poor little book. "Always a pleasure to dip into your writings, dear — the silks and the superfine, the excellent company, and" — flicking a quick, sharp tongue over wide lips — "oh, dear me, yes, those delicious, delightful dinner parties, no doubt reported straight from your own table. You must have *me* here to dine sometime, you know. I fancy a good trout quite as much as your hoity-toity Mr. Parrey."

He paused, as though to give her time to resolve that she'd see herself in Jericho before he set foot in her dining room.

But she and Rackham had been having the same conversation since his first visit, soon after Harry's death, and by now it had begun to feel like reading lines from a familiar play written in verse. He bobbed his head up and down a few times as though counting the meter, before concluding with a lugubrious sigh that "in the end, though, there's nothing like those salmons we ate in Ireland. Savory is what I calls 'em. Sssavory."

His eyes bulged like a toad's — Captain Sprague had liked to call him "Toady" when he'd sent him scurrying out to do an errand. Perhaps, she often thought, if her erstwhile lover had treated this most junior of his officers with less contempt, the former junior officer wouldn't feel himself endlessly compelled to make her suffer for what should be long past and dead.

Still, did it really matter *how* he went about extorting money from her? Her past had become his property, captured lurid and alive in the papers he maintained. She thought of his airless little office, the ledger books on the shelves, monthly payments lovingly and fastidiously recorded in a code of his own devising. He'd read to her once from one of "her" pages. Taken together, he'd boasted, the information could constitute a hidden parallel *Peerage* and *Baronetage* — of those of the *ton* who had something to hide.

The money mattered to him, of course; it would to anyone. But the power must be more important to him. What ever mean, miserly delight he took in recording each payment and computing the interest on it must pale beside the glee with which he invariably informed her (though she never asked) that he was "doing exceeding well, dear, wi' my best compliments to *you,* for having gave me my start."

And what wouldn't the Almack's patronesses give to hear what Gerry Rackham could tell them about the Countess of Gorham?

Raising her chin, she spoke as though looking down upon him from a great height. "My payment to you isn't due until tomorrow, May the first. It's not like you to get a date wrong, Mr. Rackham. Nor the points of our agreement, which is that *I* come to *you.*"

"The bank draft." As though it had slipped his mind. "Ah, quite right, the draft upon your account. Well, that's it in a nutshell, dear — you've hit the nail on its very head, Lady Gorham."

He grinned, and his eyes bulged. "O' course, some might take it as a courtesy, me coming all this way to inform you o' the unavoidable rise in the rates I find m'self obliged to charge you. When it's only what I does wi' all my clients, when I observes their fortunes heading in that nice steep arc toward the heavens. The new book's a stunner, and Colburn's doing quite all right by us too."

By us. She suppressed a shudder.

"Though I should be most particularly grieved," he continued, "was you to forget the offer I made you once."

Would that she could.

"You're welcome as ever, you know. The possibility still stands of your receiving my patronage . . ."

160

As he liked to call it . . .

". . . at a discount rate. We aims to please. And who knows, maybe you *would* be — pleased, I mean, after all them mere school-boys you takes up wi'."

She wanted to sneer, but somehow managed not to.

"You and I," he continued, "could work out the particulars at our leisure, perhaps over a sip o' claret. There's a rattling good inn I know, and not too far away either."

Should she shudder, sneer, or laugh so long and hard that he'd never dare make the offer again? She maintained a condescending seriousness. "Thank you, no. I shall pay off my obligation to you financially and in no other way. There's no need, Mr. Rackham, for any change to the terms of our agreement. Just tell me how much more money you want."

He shrugged. "Another twenty-five a month'll do it for now."

"You shall have it." She'd have to redo her accounts: no more elaborate salmon dishes at her dinner parties. Still, what choice did she have?

"Need you have come to inform me of the change in what you're pleased to call your *rates?* The post is very good in England, you know. You might try it sometime."

"I find, *Lady* Gorham" — he drawled out the syllables, as though to point out that one could call a thing, or a woman, anything one liked — "that my clients remember the particulars o' their obligations a sight better in the context o' a bit o' *personal* reminding, in a *personal* setting. Jogs the memory, see."

He looked around him. "Fixed up the place very smart, I *must* say. It were a bit bare when I come calling the other time, directly after the poor old earl knocked off and his heir kicked you out of the estate in Hampshire.

"Reminds me of another library — this one's more splendid, o' course, but the general effect . . ." He breathed out a wet, ostentatious sigh. "Such happy memories for all of us, the drinking, the gaming, the big oaken table the captain had 'mongst his own volumes, his long-legged Irish tart dancing atop it to the tune of a fiddler playing 'Rule Britannia,' and her wearing nothing more than a pair of red shoes and stockings with green gaiters."

"Garters." She'd spat out the word before she could stop herself. His eyes narrowed in petty triumph.

"Well, *you'd* know, wouldn't you?" His high whine of a laugh rose as she struggled to dam up the flood of memory he'd un-leashed within her. Ireland; Papa; Captain Sprague among his men, their eyes fixed hungrily upon her as she danced.

For a moment she thought she might drown in the memories.

She'd do no such thing. *Just bear in mind,* she told herself, *that little Gerry Rackham finds this . . .* ritual *as taxing as you do.* Sometimes she wondered what he'd do if she took up his offer of a "discount" in return for favors. There was always the pos-sibility that he'd run away panic-stricken from what once had been so humiliatingly forbidden.

But there was always the possibility that he wouldn't.

The long-legged Irish tart might have risked it. But Maria Conroy — for that had been her name — had been young and fear-less.

Maria Conroy had also had nothing to lose.

At any rate, he'd returned *Parrey* to the shelf. He must be satisfied that he'd gotten his own back — for today, at least — against his commanding officer and the pretty girl in her green garters, whom he'd been al-lowed to look at but not to touch.

"I'll make out the bank draft right now,"

she told him. "You can have the extra day's interest, and it'll save me a trip to the City."

His lips had moistened at the mention of a day's more interest on the money; she might have gotten him to agree to take the check if she'd kept quiet about saving herself the trip. Of course he'd want her to make an inconvenient extra trip to the City.

With maddening slowness, he took his time writing something in one of those battered memorandum books he was always carrying. Did it mention her name? Was it written in code or frighteningly plain English?

She stared. He wrote more slowly, finally looking up to grin at her. "Can't do it, my lady. Rules is rules. The money's due tomorrow. First of the month, quite as you had it before."

The grin, she thought, was in anticipation of tormenting her tomorrow as well as today. Still, he *was* putting the book back into his coat pocket — rather jamming it in, and his pencil too, for the tightness of the coat. The little ritual signifying, at least, that the end of *this* interview was in sight.

"And now, till then . . ." he drawled, "I'll be taking my leave of you, Maria."

The final weapon in his arsenal. Mar-EYE-ah. In his ha'penny English accent the name sounded common; she could hear the voices of British soldiers — "Ho, Paddy, a mug of ale, and be quick about it." While on an Irishman's lips *Maria* would sound like flute music.

"Begging your pardon, o' course, Lady Gorham, for an old friend's lapse into familiarity." Rackham could always tell when he'd scored a hit.

Stupid, she supposed, that she still hoped someday he'd let the old resentments go.

Or at least take comfort from the miraculous fortune that had saved his life when Sprague and the rest of the men had lost theirs — for he'd been out running the captain's errands when a band of Irish rebels had trapped the captain and the rest of his officers in a barn and set it afire.

She herself had been in England at the time, safe and pampered as never before and on her way to a new life. Sprague had passed her on to the earl of Gorham, in return for the earl paying his debts. On the deck of the packet boat, she'd breathed in the air off the Irish Sea and rechristened herself Marina.

She and Harry had read the newspaper accounts of the conflagration together, their untouched toast and coffee growing cold in the morning light, through the windows of the sweet little house in Marylebone she'd lived in before they'd been married.

It had been *her* great good fortune to get away before she'd had to go searching for a new protector. And as no one had yet known of Rackham's survival, it had appeared there'd been no one left to tell about her last year as Maria Conroy. And so a huge obstacle to the earl's wanting to marry her had fallen away.

Great good fortune indeed.

If you could call it good fortune that half a dozen men screamed in her dreams some nights. And that this slavering little toad of an extortionist bade fair to be plaguing her into perpetuity.

"My footman will let you out, Mr. Rackham," she said.

And it was only after she'd heard the front door close behind him, after enough time had passed to assure that he'd disappeared down the street on his way back to his office, that she allowed her head to droop forward into her hands, body curled inward to the extent that her stays and the tight-waisted poplin of her gown would allow. And only some time after that when she came to realize that her inner eye had fixed on a rather singular image — of a glass case full of dead, dry insects and bits of bone and crystal, each object strictly segregated into its own tight little compartment.

Like a life — like *two* lives — caught and held, trapped and divided by their deepest secrets.

CHAPTER 10

And so, Jasper thought with some wry amusement the next morning, *I find myself reduced to this.* Scanning the *on-dits* for London, the first of May of the year 1829, when his head was supposed to be in Athens, centuries before the birth of Christ.

Closeted in his study, surrounded by shelves of books and small, quaint antique artifacts, allowing himself a final few moments to fritter away before setting to work on the manuscript he was writing, it had become his habit to look for mention of Marina. Always easy to find her in the pages, at Mrs. Somebody's rout, the Duke of Something's regatta, or dancing with the Honorable Mr. Whosis at Lady Whatsis's ball.

One of the gossip columnists wondered if Whosis might be Lady Gorham's latest lover. But the gentleman who wrote for a competing newspaper rather doubted it — offering the convincing evidence that Her

Ladyship had left the ball early and alone.

Here Jasper had to smile a little at what he knew and the *on-dits* didn't — his smile, however, quickly followed by a sigh and a shake of the head. For, given how little the gossipmongers really knew and how much they simply made up, it would clearly be foolish to trust the other newspaper accounts he'd been reading of Sir Anthony Hedges courting this or that prodigiously wealthy young lady.

Disheartening that here he knew no more than the rest of the British reading public, even as to whether the stories were true.

And if there *was* anything to the reports, equally disheartening to own himself entirely incapable of judging whether marriage would be a good or bad thing for the young man he knew so little.

A good thing, he supposed, if it paid his debts (for Anthony *must* have debts — the cost of the phaeton alone . . .). And good as well if it kept him away from the hazard table at Crockford's. Who could say? It might even give him a sense of purpose and responsibility.

But very likely a bad thing if . . . Jasper thought of John and Celia, their bored toleration for each other so patent, so palpable, just hours before their deaths. And *theirs* had been considered an excellent marriage: the Hedges family's ancient pedigree and modest fortune enhanced by Celia's splendid marriage portion and equally splendid looks.

The looks and pedigree had survived into the next generation. Thusly equipped, Jasper thought dryly, Anthony ought to do quite well in the London marriage mart. Doubtless the boy'd be able to make the most of the short, festive span of months devoted to the serious lifelong business of match- and alliance-making. Perhaps he'd marry somebody very rich indeed.

If such a thing might be deemed "doing well."

Might the boy be capable of doing anything better?

He might have been, Jasper supposed, if he'd ever gotten the opportunity to pattern himself upon a better example than his parents. Or his guardian.

Perhaps Uncle Jasper might initiate a conversation about it. Find out what the boy was thinking. Try to be a confidant, an adviser, even a sympathetic listener.

Impossible to imagine it: Since the dinner party, their relations were strained as ever and rather more confused. These days when they bumped shoulders in the hallway at

Charlotte Street, the boy might gaze at Jasper in perplexity, as though in search of the predictable old recluse of an uncle. The current citified Uncle Jasper might be more socially acceptable, but no more appealing or forthcoming — in truth, more tight-lipped than ever.

Well, he replied to himself — for his thoughts seemed to have aligned themselves into two opposing factions — well, but he had to be tight-lipped, didn't he, with all the secrets he was keeping these days. As gratifying, even thrilling, as his affair with Marina had made his life, it was perforce and completely a private, personal matter — as little to be known by his family as his family was available to be discussed with *her.*

Enough, he chided himself, of this time wasting. He needed to return to his notes about reconstructing sculptures. He had to search for clues in his collection of engravings — some hundreds of years old — of precious old Greek works or Roman copies. He'd work it up for a chapter for Colburn, later today to put the information to use when he met with Kellingsley. After a meeting at a warehouse in the City with the German who wanted to sell a statue.

He turned both sides of his attention to

his desk, to the few words idly scribbled on the blotter. Prepositions, mostly. He had no memory of scrawling them down, but he supposed there was no mystery what he must have been thinking.

Beneath. Atop. In and *out.*

The case structures of classical Latin and Greek might be more elegant, he thought, but what a good job vulgar, sturdy, hybrid English did in putting a body — or two bodies — precisely where they should be. Where he and Marina *would* be — tonight? No, not tonight; she had engagements tonight. Tomorrow night, then, after he was finished with all the tasks he'd set himself today.

He grinned — good to have a reward in view. At one with himself again, he happily set himself to work at the mysteries of piecing together old statuary.

The work went well, the meeting with the German collector even better. The statue that man had to sell *was* the lovely kneeling Aphrodite Jasper had had to sell more than a decade ago. Thrilling that he could afford to buy it back now. There was something to be said for this business of writing for pay. Perhaps, all these years, he shouldn't have been so old-fashioned about it.

The deal was struck, compliments exchanged, and cigars shared. Leaving the warehouse, the German gentleman offered to share a cab. But life in London was so awfully sedentary; Jasper needed to stretch his legs. His mind worked better when he walked. He wanted to plan what he'd write to Dr. Mavrotis. The Aphrodite returning home at last: He wanted to savor it, anticipating the telling of it.

He'd take a shortcut toward Lord Kellingsley's house through some little backstreets he'd happened upon recently. Though in *this* rough neighborhood he must make sure not to get so immersed in his thoughts that he'd lose cognizance of his pocketbook.

Which was why, he suspected, he'd happened to be alert enough to catch sight of a familiar, finely cut profile at the window of a handsome carriage.

How singular to glimpse her in this rabbit warren of sad, sagging buildings, moldering brickwork, and soot-blackened windows. Marina's coachman must have taken a wrong turn. Or perhaps he also used these streets as a shortcut on his way to better venues.

Has she seen *me?* Jasper wondered. Difficult to tell what she could see with all that dark veiling about her bonnet. He'd surprised himself by recognizing her so readily. In the daytime her face had a different kind of loveliness; there seemed to be a pensive sadness about it. But that was probably a trick of the light, or a mood suggested by this melancholy little thoroughfare.

No doubt the carriage would drive on before her eye fell on *him*.

But wait, it wasn't moving. Because a cart-load of apples was tipped over on the cobbles just ahead, the apple vendor howling as a swarm of street urchins made off with as many of her wares as they could carry.

The overturned cart blocked the road; there was no room for a carriage to turn around in such a tight space. Marina would be stuck here until the street was cleared, her coachman endeavoring to calm the horses amid the urchins' hue and cry, the vendor's helpless wails and loud imprecations against her tormentors. The apple seller wasn't a young woman. It was a wonder, Jasper said, that she'd been able to haul the clumsy conveyance after her. No chance she'd be able to turn it right side up.

He could take advantage of the disturbance in the street to go over and say a few words to Marina.

His mouth twisted. Yes, right. He could avail himself of the opportunity to have a few words with his beautiful mistress by exploiting the misfortune befallen a broken-down old woman selling apples in the street. . . .

"Guv'nor, ye'r a ruddy angel sent fro' heaven." The woman croaked out the phrases more than once to cheer him on as he pushed and heaved, tensed his thighs, and finally got the cart balanced on its wheels again.

He thanked her now for the compliment, and she presented him with a shiny, golden yellow apple for his troubles.

At least he hadn't strained his back. You were safe if you knew to lift from your center; the technique worked as well, it seemed, with carts of apples as with marble. But his muscles would ache tomorrow, perhaps most especially the ones he'd employed in catching a last few of the little apple thieves before realizing he'd do better to hand out pennies to the more civilized children loitering about if they helped the woman retrieve what of the fruit had not been crushed, stolen, or eaten.

"And give her this as well," a voice rang out from the window of the carriage; a gloved hand held out a pound note to him.

"I enjoyed watching you," Marina told him when he came to the window. "But then," she added softly, "I know you like to be looked at."

"I hadn't thought about it that way." Even if suddenly he could think of little else besides her eyes fixed on him while he pushed and strained his muscles and successfully lifted a heavy object. If one could describe the ensuing rush of consciousness and sensation — this deliciously involuntary conjuncture of mind and body — as *thinking.*

The problem with this mode of *thinking,* though, was that it tended to knock every other kind of sense out of one's head.

"A surprise, though, to be meeting you in this odd hidden corner of the metropolis," he said now. "Bit of the middle of nowhere, I expect, which is why I use it as a shortcut to where I want to go . . . well, because sometimes, you know, *nowhere* seems to connect to a thousand *somewheres . . .* and you . . . well, I expect that *you* also . . ."

The hell of it — besides the fact that he was babbling like an idiot — was that he must leave her directly if he wasn't to be late for his afternoon with Kellingsley. What time was it, anyway? Rude to take out his pocket watch. Uselessly, he glanced up at a clock set high in the wall of a decrepit old building, its hands stopped at half past eight several decades ago.

She smiled at that. Her face had lost its mysterious sadness. More like mystified, he thought, by the nonsense he'd been spewing.

"Nowhere . . . ?" she said. "Shortcut? Ah, now I see what you meant. Yes, of course . . . my coachman taking a shortcut through these streets. Quite."

For a dazed, silent moment, they simply continued to smile at each other.

"And in truth," she said now, "I also have an engagement this afternoon."

Of course she did. More than one engagement, and well into the evening. He'd be reading about it all tomorrow morning.

A pity, she said, that she hadn't time to drive him where he was going.

A pity indeed, he agreed. He bade her good day, and she called out to the coachman to drive on.

His mind muddled, his hand absurdly continuing to grasp the yellow apple, Jasper could hear nothing but the rumble of her carriage on the cobbles as he walked on.

Well, *that'd* been something to see.

Gerrald Rackham rubbed his neck where

it ached him from craning to peek down at the street through the little corner window of his office. A bit mean, he expected, to laugh at the poor old apple seller, even if the way she'd kept up her howling had been something wonderful.

But more to the point was that the upset had kept Lady Gorham in view a few minutes longer. Her carriage, anyway.

Bugger that schoolmaster, though, or that parson. Or whatever he were in his spectacles and black coat, who'd set the cart to rights so speedy-like. Bloody Good Samaritan: without *his* interference, the old lady might still be caterwauling and the lady in the carriage — the one Rackham cared about — would be waiting down there even now.

Lucky thing for the gent, though, he thought a bit condescendingly. For Rackham would wager that it weren't every day a straitlaced personage like that one might be squinting through his specs at a woman such as *her.*

Not that I gets all that many squints at her myself.

Shivering like a dog emerging from an icy stream, he shook his head back and forth as though to extricate himself from the chilly melancholy that threatened to engulf him.

Only natural, he thought. After all the excitement of meeting her face-to-face — twice in as many days — it were no surprise to feel himself sinking into a slough of despond now. Even if she did torment him so dreadful with her accursed pride, her refusal to be brought down low by anything he said.

Today he'd almost thought he'd got her, when he'd ragged her about her newest boy, meaning, of course, that Honorable Mr. Somebody in the *on-dits.* For a moment she'd looked startled, even (he'd dared to fancy) a bit distressed. But then she'd only lowered her eyelids in her haughty way and given a light, superior laugh — like to demonstrate to him he didn't know nothing about it.

So more than likely it wasn't Mr. Honorable in her bed these nights. Perhaps, as that other report had had it, there weren't another lover yet.

Strange the way the question ate at him, given the gut-twisting hatred he was wont to lavish upon whatever lover she did have.

But hating was something Gerry Rackham knew how to do. Made the whole thing bearable, somehow, when there was some elegant young gentleman with a name and usually a title, to make pictures of in his mind. The pictures, of course, with *her* in them as well.

Because over the years, he'd come to need those pictures, late at night especially.

With a sudden spasmodic motion, he pulled open a drawer, swept a pile of newspapers from it, and tossed them into the stove that heated the room (*overheated* it, as she would have it, but he liked it that way, even if it sometimes got a bit smoky in here).

He read the papers first thing every day, to keep track of his clients. And then he read them again, for his own private purposes. And again, if he needed to — as many times as he needed to, to fill his mind with pictures of her. Marina. Maria.

Pouring some gin into a cup, he stared into the grate until he thought he could make out the image of those long legs of hers — dancing, kicking, as quick and bright as the last licks of flame from the newspapers. The gin eased his mind a little. The situation couldn't last, he told himself. Not with her and her ways. She wouldn't be leaving them big fancy festivities early and alone for *too* much longer. He'd bank on it.

Unless . . . But *that* was a cruel notion; he should've tossed back the gin faster, to keep such wicked ideas at bay. *Unless* she was leaving the parties to meet up with somebody on the sly. A man who'd have her all to himself, the affair selfishly hid away from her admirers among the populace.

And hid away from myself, he thought, *what deserves to know* everything, *if I can't have her any other way.*

It wouldn't be fair. She'd never done it before. Why would she now?

But with her, you could never quite be sure. And you couldn't get nothing out of her servants neither. She paid them too well for that; probably learned to do so from the old earl.

A last burning shred of newspaper shot sparks before its flame died. Rackham refilled his cup and took a nice big gulp.

He drew his coat closer about himself. Cold-blooded, he must be, for he was always glad of the heat — nice to warm himself inside with gin and outside with the heat from the papers burning in the stove. Coat pulled tight about his hips, he felt the bulge of the memorandum book in his pocket, a goad to make his latest entry in his ledger. In his words, anyway, she was all his, and even more so once he'd transferred his latest notes into his own secret code.

His ledgers, his code, his dreams . . . and

perhaps, Gerry Rackham thought, some evening soon he might also take a midnight stroll down Brook Street.

CHAPTER 11

Marina had to smile at the picture Jasper made the following night when she opened her front door to him. He was silent, but the pained little wince at the corner of his mouth spoke volumes as he stepped slowly into her front hallway. His muscles *were* stiff and sore, she thought, from helping the old lady yesterday.

How charming he'd been; how resolutely he'd put his shoulder against the clumsy old cart to move it. Softly, she put her arms about his neck to draw his head down for a kiss.

Usually they'd hurry each other up the staircase, but tonight, in the pool of moonlight coming through the high window, they kissed gently, tentatively.

"Oh, Lord," he whispered, "what must you think of me, so broken down and rickety? Perhaps I shouldn't have come."

"On the contrary," she replied, "I'm

delighted. And especially that you arrived so promptly."

He groaned. "Took a cab. First time. Other nights I've walked. Well, other nights I've *run,* actually, at least part of the way."

"Good for you to indulge yourself in a cab for once. You can run again some other night, and I shall enjoy imagining it. But if you can get yourself up the stairs to-night . . ."

"Of course I can." He thrust out his chin. "And you needn't think —"

"I don't. I shouldn't dare. But first, there's a bath for you. Come on. Here, take my hand. Let's get you into the water before it cools."

Jasper had already seen the room where she bathed, the capacious enameled tub standing upon tiles of green marble amid a little forest of waxy green plants and large potted ferns, and lit by a bank of candelabra set with thick, creamy tapers.

But seeing it — briefly, by way of a tour of her rooms — was one thing. Experiencing it as it was meant to be experienced — tub nearly overflowing with fragrant, soapy water; candlelight flickering through clouds of moist air — was quite another. Having all this voluptuous luxury devoted to the matter of his comfort another thing still.

She was brisk and businesslike in the matter of undressing him — if you didn't count a stifled giggle when she came to the trouser button that had once been such an object of contention between them. After which — and after gently removing his spectacles and putting them safely aside — she led him to the tub and helped him lower himself into it.

"Is the temperature all right?" Her voice floated to him through the fragrant steam as she bustled about the room. "Because we can adjust it if you like: I've got a few buckets of cold water over there in the corner, and more water heating in front of the fireplace. I imagined you'd want it quite hot, though."

Yes. Very hot. He sank down more deeply into it, almost up to his nose.

"Lady Gorham," he murmured, "has anyone ever told you you're a ruddy angel sent from heaven?"

The giggle rang out a bit more freely as her flushed face appeared amid the steamy air at the side of the tub. She'd taken off her dressing gown and pinned her hair into a careless knot at the top of her head, but curling tendrils were already loosening themselves about her neck and in front of her ears. The air smelled of the burning beeswax tapers; the water was scented with something he didn't recognize.

He sniffed curiously.

"Lotus," she said.

Closing his eyes for a moment, he sniffed more deeply. How singular that until this moment he'd never known what lotus actually smelled like. He smiled his astonishment, his pleasure. She was wearing a very plain, wholly untrimmed muslin shift. When she leaned over to kiss him, he could see her stiffened nipples, the flesh around them dark and distinct beneath the cloth's gauzy weave.

She ran her finger up his arm now, to his shoulder and around the back of it, where it felt as though a great many muscles must attach together. He thought of men sculpted from bronze and marble, reaching back to throw a javelin, bending over to hurl a discus. . . .

She pressed a fingertip — hard — against one particular spot, and he stopped thinking of anything.

"Ouch."

"I thought that might be one of the sore places."

Her face, her breasts, disappeared back into the steam. He felt himself bereft. *Don't go, Marina,* he wanted to call out.

But he was glad he hadn't said anything when he felt her hands upon his back, her fingers suddenly slippery against the painful spots at the bottom of his shoulders. She must be using some sort of oil: It smelled of pine, like the resin the Greeks used to flavor their wine.

There was another smell too. He took a long, astonished breath. "Wild thyme," he whispered. The stuff had been growing everywhere over the rocks the day he'd found the Eros and Aphrodite in a remote Achaean village. There'd been a broken shrine; the statues had been buried for centuries beneath mounds of earth. Somehow he'd known where he and the other men must dig. The moment of discovery had been thrilling, but for too many years since he'd looked back upon it as theft, as one of his greatest shames.

And now he didn't have to. Because now — soon — he'd be making restitution. This morning he'd locked the Aphrodite away in the cabinet in his study and posted his letter to Greece. The little kneeling goddess would wait at Charlotte Street until Dr. Mavrotis's arrival in London this summer. And after he met with Parliament and with Jasper and the other gentlemen of the Greek

Emancipation Committee, Mavrotis would accompany the goddess back home.

Her fingers paused for a moment. "What did you say just now?"

"The scent. Wild thyme. In Greece. But please don't —"

"No, after you said that. I thought I heard . . ." She chuckled. "No matter." She resumed her probing and kneading of the knotted muscles and tendons.

It hurt a bit.

"Oh, yes, that's it exactly, Marina."

It hurt quite wonderfully. As though the warm blood had once again begun coursing through his back and shoulders.

Perhaps it had — as indeed the blood seemed to be coursing more quickly to other parts of his body as well. He opened his eyes, glancing down past his belly to his knees rising out of the suds. And then finally to another perturbation of the water's surface.

If *perturbation* it could be called.

"I think," she said, "it's time to give you a bit of a wash."

On her knees again at the side of the tub, Marina lathered up a large sea sponge. Pretty, she thought, all the little rainbow bubbles, a few of them floating upward until they popped from the heat of the candles.

She'd wash him slowly, beginning with his hands, lingering over the fine bones in his wrists. "No ink stains today," she murmured. She moved the sponge up each arm in turn — to his shoulders and now down his chest, following the dark, smoky line of hair down his lean belly. . . .

The head of his cock showed itself above the water's surface. She watched it dreamily. *Like a lotus,* she thought, *rising from the water where it grows.*

She bent over to brush her lips against it. Her lips, and then the tip of her tongue. And then, not quite intending to, her lips again.

But — she chided herself — she needed to stop, groan as he might in protest.

All innocence, she sent him a mildly aggrieved glance — *I simply can't imagine what might be troubling you* — and cleared her throat.

"Ahem. Let's see to your feet, shall we? Of course, you already know I'm rather particular as to a gentleman's feet. . . ."

He groaned again. "Did anyone in these environs call you an angel? Because if *I* did, I was sadly mistaken."

She returned a suitably evil laugh. Fun to tease him, and in truth, she did rather like his feet — long, narrow, with high arches and straight toes. Not too hairy, either. She lifted one out of the water to wash it carefully, especially beneath the toes. One and then the other one before she moved up to his shins, knees, thighs.

Eventually — and happily — she'd get around to where he wanted her to be.

But not before she worked a little at the muscles in his thighs. She thought of how stiffly he'd stepped into her hallway, and she remembered how he'd tensed his upper legs yesterday when he'd lifted the cart. Surely he could use a little massaging *there,* to work out the achiness. She put aside the sponge to use her fingertips.

The problem was that she didn't want to hurt him by putting too much weight on the hurt places.

He was watching closely. "Careful," he muttered.

She promised herself she would be. Wonderful, she thought, a man's lean limbs, the finely defined shapes of the separate long muscles.

He grimaced. *Oh, dear.* She rose higher on her knees to get a better angle. Balancing on her haunches, she leaned over him, intent upon keeping her touch firm but even.

Careful . . .

But how could she be careful when suddenly she'd been immobilized? She tried to pull against him, to twist out of his insistent grip.

When had he grasped her forearms so tightly, one in each large, sun-browned hand?

Why was he grinning, his blue eyes gleeful, alight?

And *how* — with a cry of triumph on his part, some choking and sputtering on hers, and amid great, splashing tides of sudsy water — had he managed to tumble her into the tub on top of him?

"*Much* better," he told her, "but move your left leg, won't you, Marina, over to the other side of me. Come on, climb up; don't worry about squeezing me. I assure you that a little muscle ache is *nothing* compared with those well-intentioned discomforts you've been inflicting upon me. In fact, *please* squeeze, ah, yes, *that*'s right, that's . . ."

"That's . . . perfect," she whispered, as best she could through her gasps and giggles.

"Perfect." He whispered the word back into her ear and crooned it against her neck as he entered her, and as she slipped and grasped and tightened herself around him, and then straightened her back to sit astride him.

And it *was* perfect, she thought. No matter if soapy water were in truth a highly imperfect lubricant of a woman's private parts; she seemed to have done quite well for herself while she'd been fondling and massaging and admiring his body.

Perfect even if he did seem to be groaning a little with every spirited upward thrust of his hips. Still, if it was pain he was feeling, it was of a very particular sort, for he was also gazing up at her in evident delight. She squeezed her thighs about him, and he laughed aloud amid his groaning and amid the sounds *she'd* begun to make as well, at the feel of his hands about her breasts, his calloused fingertips tightly pinching the sopping wet muslin, chafing her nipples beneath it. Chafing, almost hurting her — though it couldn't exactly be hurting because she didn't wish him to stop, and because what she was calling out was, "Yes, yes," as she rocked her hips in rhythm with his thrusting.

"Yes," he whispered in response.

Oh, yes.

And oh, no — there was absolutely no need whatever to tell her to keep her eyes open this time. Nor any chance that she or he — that either of them — might forgo the spectacle of the other's pleasure. Nor to miss an opportunity to exhibit one's own delight, for now she was calling out in loud, joyous whoops above the miniature crash of what she'd come to think of as the waves, the tides, the sloshing and splashing of water out and over the rim of the tub.

She called and cried and laughed for the sublime silliness of it as she rode his cock, his hips — and, oh, dear, his poor, punished thighs — to the crest of her excitement. And then she let him pull her down against his chest, that she might embrace him with all her body — and with much affection as well — as he thrust and rocked and bucked, laughed and groaned his way to the pinnacle of his own pleasure, the easy delight of his release.

"But you must be cold," Jasper heard her voice murmuring against his chest, calling him back from wherever his mind had been wandering. "It's been a while, I think. The water's become so tepid. Your poor hurt muscles will stiffen up in the chill. . . ."

They both sputtered with laughter at that, though, at the silly little double entendre of *stiffening up*. Scholar and bluestocking, he thought — at times like this it was nice to share a feeble little joke. They held each other tightly as their bellies rippled with their guffaws and giggles.

Still, she was probably right, at least about herself. *He* was actually warm enough, but the rounded arm she'd flung across his chest was all gooseflesh. No doubt that the wet — the wonderfully sopping wet and almost entirely transparent — little cotton garment she still had on was chilling her. He moved his hands over her to feel how the shift had ridden up her rump to her waist, even as it still clung most thrillingly about her breasts.

She'd begun to shiver. "Come on," he said, pulling himself up and dragging her along with him.

Once out of the tub, he peeled the wet shift from her body and regretfully tossed it aside.

There were puddles everywhere, rainbow bubbles still rising out of some of them. She cautioned him to take care not to slip on the wet marble, and they made their way arm in arm to the fire, to the rack of soft Turkish towels warming in front of it.

He chuckled with surprised delight. Of course she'd have such towels, rare enough though they were in England. The height of luxury to dry oneself — to dry each other

— with cotton worked in this thick, loopy weave, and then to drape their bodies in the large sheets of the soft, absorbent material. The Ottoman Turks might be almost forgiven for their empire over his beloved Greeks, Jasper thought, for this excellent contribution to the comfort and well-being of all humanity.

Chewing thoughtfully on a fig from the platter set between them, he took a sip of wine. "What a lot of water your servants are going to have to mop up into buckets and haul away," he remarked.

"Not so much as you think," she returned. "There's a drain in the floor among the tiles — there, do you see it? It leads to some sort of a leaded pipe, and thence to the gutters outside. The architect who suggested it — it's rather an advanced design, I gather — said I could splash about as much as I liked and not have to worry about leaks or mess. Though I doubted he'd have imagined just how much splashing it's possible for a person — well, for *two* people — to do."

Jasper laughed. "Never in his wildest dreams . . . and certainly never in *mine.* The baths I visited in the East were segregated by sex. While as to the drainage here . . . Yes, I see now — quite, quite excellent. Nothing like what the Romans had, of course . . ."

Pulling out what pins remained in her hair, she smiled affectionately at his pedantry.

". . . but I expect we British will catch up eventually," he said.

"This room," she said, "cost nearly all the money I made from my first novel." The pins gone, she was shaking her hair dry in front of the fire. He couldn't see her face behind it. "I imagine you find it a shocking extravagance," she added softly.

"I should be a most ungrateful fellow if I did," he told her.

"Yes, but I know you think it a bit disgraceful for a gentleman — and certainly for a lady — to write for money."

Odd, he thought. It was as though they'd somehow traded positions across an unspoken gap of custom or propriety — or across one of the many that separated them.

"Not so much anymore," he said now. "Times change, and even a crusty old gentleman scholar ought to be able to change along with them. The bigger change, though, was the blow to my prejudices, my surprise that a Society novel could have been written as well as yours. . . ."

She shook her hair away from her face, tossed it back over her shoulders, and moved closer to him. "If you continue speaking thusly, I shall have to drag you into bed right now."

"Soon enough. While as to money earned for writing," he heard himself saying, "do you know that today *I* spent every penny Colburn is going to pay me on something I've wanted to buy for . . . well, for a very long time indeed."

He hadn't told anyone in his household about the Aphrodite. Sydney and Miss Hobart had been out shopping when it had been delivered, and when they'd returned he'd found himself unable to mention the little goddess he'd brought to the villa at Lake Como.

You saw the sculpture once, Sydney, when you were a very small child. . . .

The day you last saw your mama and papa.

The memory had clotted his throat. He hadn't been able to speak about it.

But he wanted to tell *someone* — share the beauty of the object, the joy of doing justice at last. He thought suddenly of how Marina had looked just a little while ago, kneeling to towel off his hips and his loins. He could still hear the even, matter-of-fact tone of voice in which she'd spoken. "Part your legs just a bit more," she'd told him, "so I can reach better."

And so he had, trembling beneath her calm, careful hands, breathing with wonder as he gazed down at her. Posed, though of course unwittingly, in the same position as the goddess, she'd spoken with a sweet, earthy, erotic reasonableness that had something ancient and eternal about it.

"You're woolgathering," she said now.

How long had he been silent? "I'm considering whether to drag *you* into bed."

"After you first tell me what marvelous object you purchased today. Well, if you *want* to tell me, of course. But please do, Jasper. Have you bought yourself a new coat?"

Actually he'd ordered one of those last week. But he was saving that as a surprise for her.

"I bought a sculpture of the goddess Aphrodite. Fifth century. For a friend, a Greek patriot, to bring home to his nation."

Her eyes widened. "How glorious."

And then she laughed, her face growing flushed over some sudden thought. "I *thought* you said Aphrodite, back there in the tub. But at the time I was vain enough to think you meant . . ."

"I did as well. Which makes it all the more wondrous."

"Ah." Her hand crept into his.

What a lovely smile she had. How delightful it would be to tell her all about the sculpture.

And he would.

Soon.

While as for *now* . . .But really, was there any need for anybody to drag anybody to bed? With the fire still burning so nicely right here, and all that soft Turkish toweling spread out beneath them?

She was wearing one of the larger towels wrapped about herself like a sarong, tied above her left breast. He pulled at the little knot that held it together, and caught his breath as it fell away.

"Ah," she said again. A very long, soft, happy *ah* indeed, as she and he sank down to the floor.

Though it were almost half past three, Rackham could see that there was still a light burning in her bedroom window.

Stupid still to be waiting here at the corner, more difficult all the time to avoid the watchman. She must've fallen asleep with the candle still burning. Or reading, he reckoned, improving her bluestocking-ish mind.

Or not.

He'd got here too late to see any gentleman who might be going in. For there'd been a spot of business for him to attend to, and after that an interview with a new client. Well, he couldn't help be gratified it was so well-known that if you wanted to find out anybody's secrets, you went to Gerry Rackham — that was, of course, if you could afford to pay more than them what was paying Gerry Rackham to *keep* their secrets in the first place.

The job he'd been offered weren't all that interesting, though, especially in contrast to seeing who were visiting *her,* but he'd get on it tomorrow.

Time to stroll about a little — the watchman was on his way back. He should pack it in, try again another night.

But hullo, what was that? Her front door slowly swinging open, a pale slice of light shining out from the hall. Widening. And now a gentleman's boot stepping out though the doorway.

It must be Mr. Honorable Whatsis after all. . . .

Except the tall, thin sort of gentleman buoyantly, if a bit shakily, making his way down the steps and now the front walk was clearly not the Honorable Mr. Whatsis.

Oh, Maria.

For it were the schoolmaster with the specs from yesterday coming through the iron gate.

Maria, how could *you?*

Easy, like he'd done it before, like he bloody owned the place, the gentleman what'd righted the old lady's applecart had shut the gate behind him — a gentleman not at all like them usual pretty boys that Rackham were so like to hate, and so practiced at hating.

Not *her* style of gentleman at all. At least, not the kind she was like to be going about with, anyway, at them routs and balls and receptions.

Which meant . . . well, you didn't keep notes and files about a lady for half a dozen years — you didn't think and dream about her every night since Ireland, and how many years was that? — without knowing what it *did* mean. That this gentleman wasn't for show. This one must mean something to her. *This* one . . .

Moving himself behind a plane tree, Rackham stood frozen, fists opening and closing at his sides. The gentleman with the specs weren't young. He walked a bit stiffly — from heaving the cart yesterday? Bugger that, he were walking stiffly because he . . . because *she* . . .

I'll kill 'im.

But not tonight, it seemed, because the

201

gentleman had hailed a cab and stepped into it. And as this cab had disappeared before another cab had come by, Rackham had clearly lost sight of him. But not forever. There'd be other nights.

Other nights and other ways to get to him and — finally and most importantly and after all these years — to *her.*

CHAPTER 12

The Season continued to weave its tapestry through the next weeks of May, as the hawthorns grew heavy with creamy blossoms, the rhododendron blazed forth in London's parks and gardens, and the smallest, sweetest rosebuds were gathered to line the walls of this or that sumptuous ballroom.

Lady Gorham was seen everywhere. *Parrey* continued to sell, and the model for its handsome hero to provide the gossipmongers with material. For a while the press couldn't make up its mind whether Sir Anthony's friendship with a certain wealthy American lady would bloom into a courtship. But lately (and none too quickly, given how little time there was for these things to develop between April and July) they'd come to agree that the object of the young baronet's intentions was most probably Lady Isobel Wyatt. For the two were often and unambiguously seen together — at parties, in ballrooms, along the Rotten Row in Hyde Park.

And a good thing too — his tailor, his hostler, his boot maker, and especially the proprietor of Crockford's Club thought. A good thing, and rather a relief when you were looking at it from the point of view of unpaid bills. Not that they didn't wish the young fellow all happiness — and many more good years of custom too.

While gazing up from his own morning newspaper, however, Jasper Hedges wasn't sure this impending alliance was such a good thing at all. *Don't marry for money, Anthony. It didn't help John. If only I could tell you . . .*

But, of course, he couldn't tell him any of it. Nor had he even tried to find a way.

Not, he supposed, that he'd ever *really* tried to find a way. More accurate simply to say that nothing had changed between the two of them.

Except that keeping his distance had been one thing, Jasper protested to himself, during his lonely years of scrabbling the estate together and digging up old artifacts in the fields. For then it had seemed there was little enough he *could* do to help a young man grow into a happy maturity — since what, after all, had he been able to do for himself?

But mightn't he do better these days, now that he'd surprised himself with his recent relative prosperity in London? Not to speak of having interesting work to do, a challenging book to write, and a gorgeous, fascinating mistress with whom to occupy his secret evenings. It didn't seem fair, somehow, that during such a gratifying period of his own life, he couldn't find a way to offer his help or counsel — at any rate to offer *something* — to Anthony.

And yet he couldn't, and it nettled him so deeply he'd even considered asking Marina for advice on the subject. And then squelched the idea immediately.

Yes, right, he'd told himself. Oh, yes, that would be bloody perfect, wouldn't it, after his having made it so primly, icily clear to her that their intimacy didn't extend to matters of his family. What had he called himself, *guardian to innocence?*

Well, anyway, it was still accurate when it came to Sydney.

No choice, he told himself, but to continue cutting himself in two.

Coming home at dawn from Marina's bed, Jasper the sensualist might stagger up the front steps like a drunkard, muscles trembling from a night's glorious exertions and face still wearing a happy, exhausted, and not at all intellectual grin. But by the time he came down to breakfast (and he always did come down to breakfast), he'd once again become the high-minded if loving gentleman who'd made his little niece tremble when he'd demanded to see her copybook yesterday.

Marina's besotted lover and Sydney's quaint, straitlaced guardian might inhabit the same body, but they had very little to say to each other.

And Anthony's father was as confused and useless as ever.

Enough, he told himself. *Put down the damned newspaper and go buy yourself a new blotter for your desk* — a blotter that didn't have those suggestive little prepositions, *atop, beneath,* and the rest of them scribbled over it. Because he wouldn't be seeing her for hours yet, and the waiting was difficult enough as it was. Ten hours, plus or minus ten or so minutes — he hadn't realized he kept so accurate an inner clock, but there it was; in ten hours, more or less, he'd be lying back and allowing her quick, slim fingers to manage the buttons and ties.

Sometimes the undressing part was hasty,

sometimes not. Sometimes they laughed and played, as in the bathtub. Or played without laughing; most recently they'd taken to acting out little dramas of power and submission; he'd been surprised that he'd had to coax her to that sort of thing, but when it worked it was splendid, shuddery fun, even to be on the receiving end of things.

Your humble servant, he'd called himself.

A pleasure engine, she'd said, smiling, licking her lips, and flicking a fingernail over the tip of his cock. My *pleasure engine.*

He'd winced, even as he'd stiffened as though in attendance. *If milady wishes it.*

That night he'd wished it every bit as much as she had.

Sometimes they negotiated — though not in so many words, perhaps — for pleasures, liberties not yet taken.

Soon, soon, he told himself.

And sometimes they were merely coarse, bawdy, and energetic. Just last night — to his immense delight — they'd had a monstrous good time fucking each other nearly silly while he wore nothing but his stockings.

"Vile," she'd told him between giggles. "Such dreadful taste, no *ton* at all about you, I don't care how long your . . ."

She'd paused, leered a bit. He'd raised his eyebrows.

". . . lineage or how ancient your ancestry." She'd grinned, and he'd nipped at her ear.

"I mean," she continued, snuggling into his arms, "can you imagine the Apollo Belvedere —"

"A most overrated piece."

"Hush. Can you imagine the Apollo Belvedere or . . . oh, all right, the great Dionysus from the Parthenon, if you prefer, clad in nothing but a pair of . . ." But she'd dissolved in giggles, flushed and confused, warm and girlish and giddy, and he still found himself absurdly charmed by the memory of it.

And how nice it was that since he'd told her about the little kneeling Aphrodite, he and she had been able to speak about sculpture. She'd been awfully patient with his enthusiasms about telling originals from copies, deciding how to reconstruct old pieces. And she'd been more than patient — enthusiastic, even — about his opinions as to returning sculptures to their original homes.

"Well, yes," she'd said one evening. "Absolutely. Empire *is* like theft. But then, I'm Irish."

Which, as he'd been about to respond,

wasn't the same thing at all, Ireland simply being a part of Britain. But before he'd been able to say any of that, she'd packed him off home, pleading the lateness of the hour, her own unalterable routine of rising early. Between smiles and kisses, she'd threatened that if he didn't go he'd be liable to a lecture from *her* about her opinions as to the writing of novels.

Her self-discipline was admirable. He ought to be getting to work himself. Just as soon as he put the blotter atop the *on-dits,* and a blank piece of paper atop the blotter.

Because there was Sydney, pounding upon his study door. And there was Miss Hobart's murmur, chiding her for bothering Mr. Hedges when he was at his heroic labors.

"Come in, ladies," he called.

"The plan for this afternoon," Sydney said, "is for Miss Hobart and me to walk to Hyde Park — yes, Uncle, with a footman; don't worry. And then to meet Anthony there, at the Rotten Row. He's at his tailor's today, you see, and can't spare the time to come get me."

"His boot maker's, I believe, Sydney."

"You're right, Miss Hobart. I was forgetting."

Helen Hobart suppressed a sigh, because

she herself would have found it impossible to make such a mistake about anything whatsoever that Sir Anthony had said. No matter how meaningless or trivial, her flawless recall was crammed with idly dropped remarks about tailors and boot makers, gambling, boxing, and simply larking about, which, when you thought about it, was the only sort of thing he ever said in her presence (of course excepting the remark about the "fearsomely excellent governess").

She'd hated him for calling her that. Or anyway, she'd believed she hated him for some three days after the event, until he'd come again to call for Sydney, his face all meekness and chagrin as he apologized handsomely for Sydney's illness. His very waistcoat had looked somehow subdued and of a paler hue than usual as he spoke — though perhaps it was simply a new one. And although she tried to accept his apology graciously, she expected that her response hadn't come out that way.

Probably it had simply come out *fearsome.* For even as she'd owned to herself that she didn't hate him and couldn't even be angry at him, she had to admit that she probably had no choice but to be what he'd said she was. Because in truth she *was* a fearsomely excellent governess, governessing being the only thing she knew how to do, and *fearsomely excellent* her way of doing nearly everything.

In which case, she told herself sternly, she ought to devote some of that excellence to ignoring the stupid, insinuating talk in the newspapers about his paying court to the richest young ladies in London.

A pity she had to know this as thoroughly as she did. And once again, she had only her own excellent competence to blame. For when Sydney had been sick to her stomach, the housekeeper, Mrs. Burroughs, had conceived an admiration for Helen's management of the affair. "No high-and-mighty, too-good-for-the-rest-of-the-household governess *you* are," the woman had decreed. Mrs. Burroughs had seen governesses come and go, she told Helen, but it was a rare one that wouldn't be too proud to hold a child's head while she brought up them treats she'd stuffed herself with.

The household staff had become Miss Hobart's friends and advocates. And as Miss Hobart had once in an unguarded moment expressed an interest in the newspapers, Mrs. Burroughs was only too glad to pass them to her before they went into the rubbish bin. The consequence being that Helen had access to the hateful *on-dits,* and that she read them with a passionate, unfailing devotion late at night by the light of a guttering candle.

She hadn't wanted to go on today's excursion. It was difficult enough to bear it when he came to Charlotte Street to fetch Sydney for one of their outings — and somehow even worse since his apology.

But Sydney had been remarkably well behaved lately, even applying an unusual amount of effort to the hitherto detested subject of arithmetic. She deserved a treat.

"I've already seen the royal menagerie," Sydney had firmly informed her, "and Astley's Circus as well, of course. And it's more fun to view the antiquities at the British Museum when Uncle's along — you don't mind my saying so, do you, Miss Hobart?"

"Not at all." She'd laughed.

"We can peek in the shop windows on our way. And even go into the bookshops."

"Of course."

All of which Sydney was now describing to her uncle with great aplomb. "And if I notice Anthony's paying attention to any fascinating young ladies in the park, Uncle, I'll be sure to tell you about it when we get home."

Eliciting a bark of embarrassed laughter from Mr. Hedges. For it was plain to see,

Helen thought, that he was also curious about his nephew's comings and goings. Though of course he wouldn't mention it — not to Sydney and of course not to Miss Hobart, who was so evidently above that sort of flummery and frivolity.

Absurd the sort of secrets people who shared a household thought they could keep from one another. And thank goodness, Helen thought, that *she,* at least, could do it successfully.

It all came down to who people thought you were and what they expected of you. Which at least meant that she needn't fear for earning her living. With her good French and German and Latin (she hadn't even mentioned what Greek she had), her graceful dancing, fine sewing, and adequacy at the pianoforte, the clerk at the employment agency had told her she'd have no difficulty whatever in finding another situation. Even with her one inadequacy (for she'd been entirely can did on this point: She simply could *not* paint china), he was sure he could place her in a better-paying job, and an easier one too, perhaps in a school — there was a good one in Hampstead for young ladies — or in a wealthier, less eccentric household, where (he'd added, as though to tempt her) she wouldn't have to use her Latin.

She'd felt a sinking in her stomach at the thought of a wealthier, less eccentric household. She'd told him she'd be back in a few days, but that had been a week ago.

And so it would be a good thing if today in the park she *should* see Sir Anthony paying charming court to some wealthy young woman. At least it would goad her back to the employment agency. Perhaps they could find her a new situation that was so far from London, or even from England, that she need never again —

"No spying or reporting, please, Sydney," Mr. Hedges was saying. "Just enjoy your walk out in the fresh air with Miss Hobart. Oh, and your copybook's quite excellent. Here it is."

They bade him good-bye, Sydney urging him to write a book so splendid and famous that the whole world could come to know his brilliance, and learn what the great sculptures were about as well. And it was only after they'd walked down Charlotte Street, Robert the footman looming over them protectively a few steps behind, and after they'd turned westward, that Helen thought to ask Sydney where the copybook was.

"But I thought you took it, Miss Hobart."

"Of course I didn't, dear. I remember most expressly that you had it in your hand."

"Yes, of course, I remember it too now. I must have put it down when I sneezed into my handkerchief, so it's still in Uncle Jasper's study. But it's all right; we can fetch it tomorrow, and anyway, I've begun another copybook for lessons."

The plan might work very well, Sydney thought. For although her uncle's study was a most private, sacrosanct retreat, to be visited only in his presence, she didn't think anyone would mind too awfully much if she were caught there in the act of retrieving a lost copybook. Which would remain lost — for no one would find it wedged behind the Essex estate registers — until such time as she needed it, should she ever be found having sneaked in to read *Parrey.*

What a surprise to have espied the novel she'd so wanted to read — and *Farringdon* too, which was one of her favorites of those she'd already read — on the shelves a few days ago.

While as to how they'd gotten there — for Uncle Jasper was too much the scholar to read novels — she could only suppose that some dim-witted, well-meaning admirer had sent them as a profoundly misconceived gift.

But what wonderful luck. For she preferred Lady Gorham's novels to all the others her friend Alice Crofton's mama had been reading when Sydney had joined them for a holiday in Bath last Christmas.

The holiday had been enjoyable, at least at first. Not that Sydney would ever trade her brilliant, straitlaced, devoted old uncle for any other girl's more fashionable and indulgent mama, papa, or even a mama and papa both. She quite liked the life she and Uncle had at Wheldon Priory and here in decidedly un-*ton*-ish Bloomsbury; in truth she even enjoyed her lessons with Miss Hobart. Alice's family hadn't a clever bone in all their bodies, dinner conversation was as predictable as their dining room was well-appointed, and Alice's older sisters were really quite silly with all their talk of bonnets and trimmings.

But it seemed to Sydney there'd been a sort of excitement, a breathlessness to life in Society an odd challenge to keep at it — for *ton* wouldn't stand still and wait for you — an ever-increasing obligation to be admired. She'd found it fascinating to watch, and then she'd found it exhausting.

And finally she'd found it rather frightening, and had retreated into Mrs. Crofton's sitting room to read her way through the shelf of Society novels she'd found there, wherein she'd discovered (at least in those that of them that she'd liked) that eventualities in life might be resolved through wit and intelligence. Thank heaven, she thought, that at least in certain of these novels, a woman might be valued for her intelligence. And among these most comforting of the volumes on the shelves, Lady Gorham's had been Sydney's favorites.

Because as she approached her thirteenth birthday, Sydney had come to feel a certain despair, a *need* for comforting, about the baleful responsibility confronting herself — of growing up to be a lady, and most particularly the sort of lady her beautiful mama had been.

Not that she could remember her mama, but the family portrait still hung in the place of honor at Wheldon Priory. And since Sydney'd been a very little child, she'd stared up at the graceful, willowy woman with the charming hazel eyes, holding the plain, pasty-faced baby that had been herself. For it was Anthony, and not Sydney, who looked — who had *always* looked — like the beautiful lady in the portrait. One glance at Anthony and one at herself in the mirror put the lie most readily to all his canting talk about her growing up to be most "devilish pretty."

She'd never be pretty. Or graceful or elegant or anything that the lady in the portrait was. In truth, she wouldn't be a very successful lady at all; nor did she want to be.

Not that there weren't good things about being a baronet's daughter, chief among them that you didn't have to worry about earning your living, as Miss Hobart did. But being in Society, having to be admired and doubtless failing, seemed a quite wretched fate. Sometimes it seemed to Sydney she'd be better off if she did have to earn her living.

The trouble was that that there was very little a baronet's daughter *could* do. Except write novels, like Lady Gorham. Which would seem to solve the conundrum rather neatly, Sydney decided. One wouldn't have to feel frightened of the polite world if one became an observer and chronicler of it, controlled it by applying one's wit and intelligence to it.

One could use words to mock — but also to have and hold, for wasn't mockery also a way of containing it all? Wasn't elegance of wit a way of grasping the very things that might be too overwhelming if one relied only upon one's emotions and senses?

One could create worlds of splendid-looking men and brave, intelligent, honest (and also rather splendid-looking) women who held their own with them in conversation.

One could, in short, prepare for the onerous, looming, impossible prospect of becoming a lady by training oneself to do the best thing a lady could do — which was to be a novelist like Sydney's admired Lady Gorham.

And so, what excellent — and entirely unexpected — luck to have espied *Parrey* on Uncle Jasper's bookshelves. Not only had she wanted to read it since she'd seen it in the windows of Hatchard's, but she could study it as a model for the novel that she herself had begun writing just a fortnight ago. Just as today she wanted to amass a store of observations of the London Season, seen from the ideal vantage point of the Rotten Row.

What a lot there was to do, Sydney told herself, when one was lucky enough to have found one's vocation. Crossing Oxford Circus on the arm Miss Hobart offered, she smiled affectionately up at her governess.

CHAPTER 13

But when they got there, Anthony was nowhere to be found about the Rotten Row.

Sydney wasn't entirely surprised. If *she* were a young blade on the town, *she'd* be late. And so would the hero of her novel. Though in the case of the story she was contriving, she hadn't yet decided if her duke had won a fortune at a gaming club, smashed someone's face in while boxing, or gotten himself challenged to a duel. From a narrative standpoint, any of these might serve. And while of course she hoped it wasn't a duel that had detained Anthony today, she *was* rather hoping her brother owned one of those lovely boxes of pistols lined in sapphire velvet, and might show it to her if she asked.

But either boxing or gaming would do well enough, if she could get him to describe it.

While as for waiting, in truth she was grateful for the opportunity to watch the gentlemen and ladies on horseback and in their carriages. Most of the ladies sat at their ease in broad, low, plush-upholstered barouches that moved as stately as Cleopatra's barge. But a few drove their own phaetons and curricles, sitting very upright to hold the ribbons — which, of course, was what Sydney's azure-eyed, flame-haired heroine, Lady Philippa Dorinda d'Arcy Deveraux-Demarest, would do.

At this moment, though, she most needed to keep her ears open to the talk swirling about her. Wonderful how much you could learn while casually circling a small area of lawn. A girl and her governess might be invisible; people said all sorts of instructive things in their presence — even about Anthony.

At first she'd considered sharing some of this information with Miss Hobart. But as soon as they'd approached this area of the park her governess had assumed what Sydney called her Athena look: head high against an overgrown stand of rhododendron, eyes fierce and distant all at once. It wouldn't do to disturb her; doubtless she was meditating on something very improving and Greek. In any case she was obviously oblivious to all the recherché conversation — to use a word Sydney had only recently learned.

Nearly learned it, anyway. *Reh-sher-SHAY.*
Silently, Sydney shaped her lips about the
syllables, as though tasting an exotic new
ice from Gunter's — kumquat, perhaps, or
lychee nut. Savoring the word rather than
gobbling it, she listened for its echo in the
leaves rustling overhead while she essayed
to find a precise shade of meaning to assign
to it. She did know that it often came up in
sentences where people said *ton* and *exclusive,* though she thought there must be a
little bit more to it than that.

But there were so many fashionable words
and phrases, and it was particularly difficult
to use them well when she got so little
practice at home. For Uncle Jasper *would*
insist upon speaking plainly. And not only
did he not indulge in gossip, but when he
spoke of money it was most likely a matter
of boring household expenses.

Rather than as it was done here, which
was to assign a mystical, magical number to
a person passing by. Somehow everyone
seemed to know that this gentleman had
ten thousand a year, that lady a dowry of
twenty-five.

It had taken Sydney a while to understand
that when people said *twenty-five,* the remaining three zeros were to be understood,

but now she took it as much for granted as anyone else. How quick with numbers fashionable people were, and what a bother that Society required you to be such a good cipherer. Up until now Sydney had detested arithmetic, but lately she'd begun to apply more effort to it. Miss Hobart had been gratified, and Sydney saw no reason to explain that it was in the service of her vocation as a novelist.

Not, of course, that improving her skills at multiplication and even long division had made her any more capable of performing the conjurer's trick of reading, as if from an invisible placard hanging from this or that elegant neck, exactly how much money a personage riding, driving, or strolling along here possessed. Though it seemed to work only for fortunes of a certain magnitude.

"At least forty," the gentleman with white hair was saying, while he nodded at a splendid barouche landau rolling down the path. "Lady Isobel Wyatt, sister of the young earl, don't you know, just out of school in Switzerland . . ." Interesting. The lady looked little more than a girl.

"And don't think Sir Anthony don't know it too," the gentleman continued, "for all that he keeps his counsel, puffing out his chest to display his latest waistcoat and set

off his fine jawline. It's clear that he's directing his attention there and not to the
American fortune."

Whatever could they mean by *the American fortune?* But the bit about the waistcoat
and especially the jawline was funny for being so accurate. Miss Hobart would probably find it humorous as well.

If Sydney could find her, that was. For
she'd wandered a bit afar in pursuit of useful information. Lucky that her governess
and the rhododendron were both so spindly
— there she was: Sydney spied her in
conversation with two ladies. One of them
was almost as tall as Miss Hobart though of
course far more elegantly and expensively
dressed, and speaking in a very singular accent — for a breeze had struck up, and Sydney could hear the sounds and cadences
before she'd quite caught the meaning of
the words. The voice came so slow as almost
to be a drawl, its nasal, flat *a*'s and long *i*'s
like vistas against an endless horizon.

". . . a proper English governess could set
her own terms and PAY-tronize her social-
climbing American employers rather than
the other way around. . . ."

"Are you an American, ma'am?" *Oh, dear.*
The accent was so interesting that Sydney

had spoken before she knew what she was about.

"Sydney!" Miss Hobart exclaimed. "You gave us a start. Where are your manners, interrupting like that? And what were you thinking of, to speak when you hadn't been introduced?"

Fortunately their new friends were most polite and forgiving. And yes, the tall one *was* American. Sydney wondered if she had anything to do with that *American fortune* she'd heard discussed, but soon became too interested in the lady herself to care. For Miss Edith Amory, as she introduced herself, here to pay an extended visit to her cousin Lady Withers, came from a place with an almost unbearably beautiful name.

Cincinnati had a most noble Roman ring to it, Sydney commented admiringly. The observation seemed to please the ladies; Miss Amory nodded approvingly at Miss Hobart, and Sydney felt proud of herself and her governess both.

But it was the *Ohio* part of the name that practically tripped off the tongue. It came from the Iroquois Indian, Miss Amory told her, for *good river.* "You see, Miss Hedges," she explained, "my family has been there since I was a little girl, when Pa helped finance the first paddle-wheel steamboats."

Which made Sydney sorry to have to report in response that *her* family came from dreary old Essex — and that except for Uncle Jasper they'd barely budged from Wheldon Priory since King Henry VIII had made them a gift of it three hundred years earlier. But Miss Amory was too polite to let on that she must find them all most hideously stodgy.

"I've been doing the London Season, you see," the American lady said. "It's such fun, and your brother, the baronet Sir Anthony, has been so awfully kind."

And so Miss Amory *must* be *the American fortune* after all. No doubt her pa, as she called him, had sent her off to marry as well as she could. Well, a baronet wasn't a bad catch, especially when he was extraordinarily handsome, and kind and pleasant into the bargain.

Of course, Sydney would miss her brother dreadfully if he went off to live in Cincinnati, Ohio, but perhaps she could visit him. Uncle Jasper might not care to go, but Sydney and Miss Hobart could cross the ocean, ride paddle-wheel boats down the Ohio River, meet Iroquois Indians. Perhaps Sydney could write about their handsome, ruddy bare chests and painted aquiline faces while Miss Hobart had improving conversations with governesses who plied their trade in America.

Until this moment her dreams had been of traveling to Greece and Constantinople. But America sounded equally fascinating, especially in the way its citizens didn't seem to stay put in one place.

"I was born in Boston," Miss Amory was saying, "but my pa could see the need for people getting down the Ohio River, so he moved us seven hundred miles west."

She laughed then at the sight of Lady Withers's raised eyebrows. "Forgive me, Emily. I'm always forgetting that it's not the done thing here to speak of money made in trade."

Which *was* — well, yes — just a little bit out of the way. Sydney had to admit it, even if unwillingly. Perhaps someone should change the subject to one of more general interest.

"Oh, look," she heard herself saying, "my brother's over there. I'd forgotten to be keeping my eyes open for him, and now it seems he's stopped to talk to . . ."

But diverting the flow of a social conversation might take more skill than she'd supposed. Perhaps she might have better pretended not to notice Anthony shedding the brilliant light of his smile upon the young lady in the barouche — the earl's sister, whose forty-thousand-pound portion had most definitely *not* come from trade.

"Lady Isobel Wyatt," Miss Hobart said in her coolest, best-modulated governess manner. "Sydney, you oughtn't to begin a sentence you don't know how to finish."

"Yes." Miss Amory's voice came out a bit abstracted. "I see him over there with *her.* . . ." She paused, and Sydney found the pause most piquant. The American lady *must* be in love with Anthony; how interesting it was when people were in thrall to their emotions, the conversation ebbing and flowing about its moments of silence. In a certain situation what was left unsaid might be as important as what was on the page. There were bits in *Farringdon* where Lady Gorham had rendered just such conversations; Sydney resolved to go back and study them.

"I've made Lady Isobel's acquaintance already." Miss Amory's voice had become uncharacteristically soft, her drawl almost glacial in its slowness.

"And of course," her British cousin said briskly, "we'll be inviting Her Ladyship to the ball the family will be giving in dear Edith's honor. We're getting the invitations together now, a bit late, I fear. . . ."

"Fancy dress, it'll be." Her former buoyancy restored, the American lady smiled encouragingly at Sydney. "If the guests care to, of course — it won't be mandatory. But I insisted upon the possibility of fancy dress — I argued for it until I prevailed, and so you see that it's my fault the invitations are a bit tardy, though Emily's too good to say so."

Her oddly accented voice took on a note of conviction, though she continued to smile. "I wanted to give our guests an opportunity to be what they dream of being, instead of what birth has decreed. A most un-British sort of notion, don't you find it so, Miss Hedges? Keep an eye out for your invitation in the post, Miss Hobart."

Sydney blinked and then nodded firmly. A wonderful idea to dress as what you wanted to be — though easier in her case if she'd ever actually seen a lady novelist. And why *shouldn't* Miss Hobart be invited, even if (as Sydney suspected) Miss Amory had said it partly to tease her cousin? Still, Mr. Hobart *had* been a vicar. Sydney decided she quite liked Miss Amory.

"Good day, Sir Anthony," the lady was calling out, for he was on his way over to speak to them at long last. "How nice to see you. I've been having *such* a good time meeting your sister and Miss Hobart."

"Will you marry her?" Sydney gazed up at Anthony as the phaeton set off. "Or will you marry Lady Isobel?"

It took him a moment to get his sputtering laughter under control, and another for his hands to reassert their authority over the reins. "My word, you *are* growing up quickly. And so you're reading the *on-dits* in the newspapers? I shouldn't have thought Uncle would permit it, or the formidable governess either."

"I don't even know what *on-dits* are. Oh, yes, wait a moment, I do — I forgot. Alice Crofton's sisters used to read them aloud to each other at Bath. Days when they found themselves mentioned were like half holidays. *On-dit* — hmmm, French for *one says* — is that right? And no, I haven't been forbidden to read them. At Uncle's house no one would ever read something so unimproving, and so no one has thought to forbid me to do it."

"Well, you should be forbidden. *I* forbid you. You're much too young. And I expect I needn't ask whether you're permitted to read novels."

She raised her eyebrows primly, refusing to nod or shake her head, and trying to think of an answer that wasn't exactly a lie. "No, of course you needn't ask me about *that.*"

"So how *do* you know what people say about me?"

"Oh, I hear bits of conversation in the park. Perhaps my ears are unusually sharp."

He awarded her a brief chuckle. After which he peered searchingly and rather dolefully at her, as though imploring her to tell him what she'd heard without actually lowering himself to ask.

What fun to know something he didn't. "Well, I don't know if I can remember it in any detail. . . ." Pretending to catch sight of an especially picturesque stand of trees in the middle distance, she gazed poetically at it until he muttered something about there perhaps not being time to go for ices this afternoon.

"But I've just suddenly recalled," she said, "that there was a gentleman speaking about Lady Isobel and Switzerland and her fortune. The gentleman says you affect not to know about it, but that of course you do."

"Ah, yes? And what else did this gentleman say?"

"That you're keener on her than on Miss Amory."

"Hmmm. Which of them would *you* like

me to marry?"

"It's not fair to ask me, as I haven't met Lady Isobel. But you'd be very rich either way, and I'd like *that,* for then you could afford to fix up Wheldon Priory as Uncle can't. I don't really understand what mortgages are about — though of course *you* must — but now that he's finally paid them off I heard him telling the steward there's still the roof to pay for. Well, and the improvements the kitchen needs . . ."

But Anthony's facial expression had sharpened. He looked suddenly — and quite atypically — angry, uncomfortable. Sydney couldn't account for the change, but she supposed it must be her fault. Miss Hobart had told her it was bad manners for a child to speak of financial matters, and as always her governess had proved correct, even if every adult on the Rotten Row spoke of little else.

He oughtn't to blame Syd, Anthony thought. With her sharp ears and clever head, not only had she picked up the gossip about the park, but she quite evidently understood the financial state of affairs at Wheldon Priory better than he — or at least than he had until quite recently.

He hadn't comprehended a bit of it, actually, during the infrequent dreary discussions he'd been subjected to in the years since he'd come into his inheritance. Uncle Jasper and the solicitor would drone on and on, while it fell to Anthony to try to hide his sullenness and not to fall asleep in his chair. Good enough to know that *he* could live in relative style and comfort, and that Sydney had a respectable portion set aside for her.

But after that it all got very tangled, though the solicitor always ended the discussions with some remark like, "Well-done, Mr. Hedges, to get that paid off, and not easy, I shouldn't think." Which only proved, Anthony would think at those times, that Uncle Jasper was clever where Anthony was stupid.

Or that Uncle Jasper was dull enough to care about those interminable columns of numbers.

Because after all, what gentleman of spirit could really give a rap about numbers — so long as the beloved old house still stood on its foundations and one could come down and hunt once in a while?

He certainly didn't care, Anthony had thought. Or hadn't cared, anyway, until a week or so ago, when he'd gotten the idea of perhaps borrowing against the property

— just in a small way, to cover a few debts that had gotten a little out of hand. Or to see if he could, anyway.

To see, before he made any *really* serious decisions about his future, just where he stood in terms of property. To try, for the first time in his life and hopefully the last, to get some understanding of the whole boring mess.

And so today he'd gone to speak to the family solicitor, enjoining him to promise on his life not to tell Uncle Jasper about the meeting.

Though why *should* he keep it secret? he'd wondered. Wasn't the property his own? Didn't Uncle just manage it for him according to the terms of his father's will, as the old coot had so sonorously put it?

The solicitor had given him an earful, after pledging Anthony in his turn not to tell Mr. Hedges a word of it. About how Mr. Hedges had lived such a cheeseparing life these years (*Well, he has his indulgences, like all of us, but not so often, I warrant, as a gentleman might want*) in order to pay off, out of his own very small fortune, those very *mortgages* that Sydney had spoken about so blithely. And how Mr. Hedges had wanted the information kept from Sir Anthony — exactly what bad shape the estate had been in at one time.

And Anthony expected that there had been more that the man could have told him, if he'd asked.

But he hadn't. He'd been too ashamed to. Of course, he'd felt a measure of gratitude. He expected he should have felt very grateful indeed, but in truth the gratitude had mostly been overpowered by a sort of angry, coruscating sense of shame that not only had his stick of an uncle been paying the bills out of his own pocket, but he hadn't thought Anthony — the baronet, after all — intelligent or capable enough to be told of it.

But then, Uncle was able to see that about me from the beginning, that I'm a trivial, featherheaded sort of man. Man now and boy then — the boy trying so very hard to be the charming, happy son his mama and papa might love, though they patently hadn't loved each other, and yet failing, for all his efforts, to keep them alive.

Uncle Jasper had been protecting him all these years, rather than according him the respect a better boy, a more substantial man might have deserved.

Odd how shame made you angry with everyone, and not just at oneself.

But it was too late now to worry about

any of that.

And so Sir Anthony and the solicitor had promised to keep each other's confidences, and Sir Anthony had left the office without inquiring any further about whether he might borrow against those recently redeemed properties.

He wouldn't. He couldn't. Which, he supposed, meant that he knew what he had to do next.

He had to marry well. Not for love, because he wasn't sure what love was all about. But he couldn't afford to wait around to find out. He didn't want to hurt anyone by doing this, but he didn't see why he should. Uncle Jasper wouldn't care one way or the other — no need to worry about him or his opinion of the thing. But certainly Anthony could carry it off in an agreeable, gentlemanly fashion that would make life as easy and pleasant as possible for everyone concerned.

Agreeable was clearly the key.

Which was rather funny, because Sydney, who'd been doing her best to keep the conversation going, had just used that very word to describe Miss Amory.

"She's very agreeable, don't you think?" she was saying. "I like her awfully, and she's going to give a large party and invite a great many people, including Miss Hobart."

He smiled at her. "Your highly superior governess dressed for a ball. How singular."

She wrinkled her nose in return. And she was right, he thought. He oughtn't to make sport of the governess. He was about to beg pardon, but Sydney's mercurial thoughts had moved on, and rather too quickly for him.

"Oh, but I forgot," she told him now. "Did you know that one could meet Iroquois Indians in Ohio?"

He had to laugh. "I hadn't considered the Iroquois angle. Still, Miss Amory *is* agreeable. But then, so is Lady Isobel. Both of them agreeable to speak to. And to look at as well, if of a certain sameness."

"How silly you are, Anthony. There's no sameness about their looks whatsoever."

Not really their figures or their physiognomies, he wanted to explain. But there was something about being on the marriage mart — a pressure to compete, to shine — that seemed to tax a young woman's resources and harden her expression into that sameness.

In truth, the two young women to whom he'd paid his attentions were less afflicted by it than most. It was one of the things he liked about both of them. Perhaps in consequence of their own large fortunes, both of them seemed relatively unharried by their situations.

But lately even *they'd* begun to betray the strain of needing to outshine a rival. Try as they might to hide it, both Lady Isobel and Miss Amory had come to seem increasingly offended, almost distressed, by the sight of the other. All of which was too difficult to explain, though, and hardly encouraging news for a girl who'd sooner or later have to put herself on the same auction block.

And anyway, Sir Anthony thought with a shrug, it wasn't only young ladies who were depending upon their chances in the marriage mart.

He doubled the phaeton back upon the path to return to where they'd begun — to the very superior governess herself. Catching sight of her against a stand of graceless, leggy shrubbery, he was surprised to find himself oddly comforted by the picture she made. Perhaps because *she,* at least, had nothing of that forced, husband-hunting brilliancy about her, as she stood tall, lonely, and pensive in soft, spring afternoon light.

CHAPTER 14

The weather turned warmer as May neared its close.

Delightful if you were among the company at Lady Something's garden breakfast, or the Duchess of Anyshire's boating party to Greenwich. Less delightful if you were either of those ladies' upstairs maid, squinting by candlelight to thread a needle or spitting to test the heat of a flatiron.

Or if you were a kitchen slavey at Gunter's in Berkeley Square, hauling ice and rock salt, cranking the handles of ice-cream machines, ladling out the cold, sweet confections in every flavor, including kumquat and lychee-nut. Porters were dispatched with hampers of little sandwiches, tarts, and oyster patties. *Carry it quick,* they'd be told, *or it'll go bad in the heat.* They bumped their hampers down the stairs to the tradespersons' entrance, the delicacies to be set out on gold salvers for midnight suppers.

Ink-stained wretches in Grub Street produced their own confections, and Henry
Colburn rushed them into print according
to the same logic: Wait too long and an item
would become spoiled, useless, and indigest-
ible.

While in the neighborhoods just off St.
James's, the dolly birds were busier than
ever. The girl Jasper Hedges had visited
upon first moving to London had done
quite well for herself these past few weeks
— found a steady protector, and a rich one
too. Not that Mr. Ayleston-Jones was a very
pleasant gentleman: She frowned as she tied
her lavender bonnet strings for her walk out
to see what the ladies were wearing. No
matter, she told herself. It wasn't like she
didn't have her own young man to see when
she could.

Modistes and milliners sewed deep into
the night. Tailors, boot makers, mercers, and
haberdashers worked as hard as their female
counterparts. They were paid better, of
course, when they were paid at all. The man
who did Sir Anthony's exquisite waistcoats
remained grateful for the custom it brought
him, even if his wife made disagreeable
noises about when the young baronet might
be paying all those bills. "Read the papers,"
the besieged tradesman retorted. "He's set

to marry the richest debutante in London; it says so right here."

Courtships wended their way to proposals or evaporated in the hot air. Matches were made, betrothals announced; happy couples strolled in the parks and gardens while as yet unmatched young ladies redoubled their efforts to shine in the dwindling time remaining to them.

Shopkeepers stayed open late; hackney drivers jostled for place in front of the opera. Bow Street Runners did their inadequate best to police a metropolis most people didn't believe needed policing. Parliament was debating the possibility of an actual police force, though there were still some who thought the idea too foreign, too *French* a notion for London.

By the end of May, the most gratifying part of Mr. Gerrald Rackham's work was over and done with. Because by now anybody who was going to get an Almack's voucher had gotten one, in consequence depriving Rackham of the opportunity to deliver his speech about, "what a pity if your lovely daughter should be left out o' a Wednesday evening, missing the possibilities she deserves, all them young swains what could be paying her court.

"Shouldn't wonder," the speech went on,

"if Her Ladyship your wife might take it a bit hard if word of that one little youthful indiscretion should find its way to the ear of the patronesses."

He loved giving that speech. But by this time in the Season it had far outlived its usefulness. Like the Almack's patronesses who must now content themselves by dismissing a late-arriving guest or anyone not dressed up to standard, Gerry Rackham would have to take his satisfactions where he could. Most Seasons, just around now, he might be feeling a twinge of malaise. But lately he had more important things on his mind.

He'd found out nearly everything his newest client needed to know: about that gentleman Jasper Hedges having bought a statue, and stashing it as safe as you could these days — the men who'd delivered the statue said they'd put it down in a room with a great many books and portfolios.

No one knew where he kept the key to that excellent Bramah lock on the cabinet, though. In which case, Rackham had informed the client, it might be wise to bring in a specialist in such matters. Yes, he knew one, a good one. For an extra fee he could make the introductions. It had worked out very well; with this new client, money didn't seem to be an object.

Interesting how things developed. Of course, it wasn't the first time during a Season that different items of business got tangled up together. But it *was* the first time in Rackham's memory that the target of his investigations had turned out to be a gentleman Rackham himself had business with.

The very same detested Jasper Hedges who'd come out through *her* gate that night. And several nights to follow too.

He'd followed him home a few times by now. Kept a little *too* close to him one careless night — he'd almost gotten himself beaten over the head for it, had to scuttle away fast, down an alley. Since then he'd been lying low.

But he'd get his own back. He need only wait until *her* next visit to his office, June the first. Just a few days more now.

He scanned the newspapers, taking his time over Lady Gorham looking lovely as ever in vermilion silk at Lord High-and-Mighty's rout a few days ago. Nothing else of interest, nothing but oohing and ahhing over the big party Lord Withers's family would be having for the American lady. He shook his head, pulled his coat tight about him, and threw the papers into the fire.

Dull bunch, the Withers family. Couldn't

get nothing on them.

And damn all Americans anyway. Bad as the Irish, or almost.

"*You* look amused," Marina said. The few syllables had come through her lips in small, panting gasps. For she'd only just let Jasper into the house, and they were both still catching their breath after a heady first embrace.

"*Do* I?" His voice was similarly rough; he paused for a moment to calm it. "Well, yes, there *was* something, an invitation I received. I've been wondering. . . . But first . . ."

Putting a hand up against the wall to steady himself, he forced her closer to him, parting her legs with one of his so she couldn't escape, she thought happily, even if she'd wanted to. She made a feint at wriggling away, as much for the pleasure of feeling his grasp tighten about her as from her conviction that he oughtn't to take everything for granted. And also because . . . well, there were a few piquant, possible *because*s, like signposts pointing to alternative destinations for the two of them tonight.

Or had the course of the evening's journey already been charted?

Pretend as they might, didn't they both

know the way quite well enough already?

Hadn't they been hinting, teasing, playing, promising — for long enough?

Odd how you knew when the time was right for some new venture into pleasure.

The day had been unseasonable, the warmest they'd had so far. Even at midnight the air was heavy, a bit damp, hardly any breeze at all. She'd managed to get through her obligations well enough — of course, she always *did.* But today only by moving slowly, as though through a haze of shimmering fancies, and by having her maid pour spicy rosemary water through her hair.

Would he find the scent too strong?

Lifting his lips from hers, he sniffed appreciatively. "Oh, Lord, you're delicious. Let's get ourselves upstairs. I'll tell you about it afterward. Unless . . . ?" He nodded in the direction of the room with the yellow armchair, the Lawrence portrait.

"No."

"Well, then, upstairs, my girl, and be quick about it."

She shook her head and stood firm against the cool stone of the entryway's wall. "Your girl, am I? *Yours,* my arse."

So much for hinting or teasing. So much for any subtlety whatsoever. She couldn't help but laugh at herself.

He laughed too, while he inched a hand around to the small of her back, drawing her a few inches closer while his fingers gathered up the muslin of her peignoir until he could probe and fondle. *Vulnerable* was the word that floated through her mind. Vulnerable and at the moment very much his indeed — and by gasping as suddenly and helplessly as she had just now, she'd quite neatly proved his point.

His laughter fading, his gaze intent, he moved a leisurely finger up and back until it had made its way between the cheeks of her arse. Immobilized, she stared back at him, struggling to keep her equanimity as he continued to touch her with slow, light fingers.

It seemed to go on for a very long time, but it had probably taken only a moment. Quickly now, as though after a briefest of pantomimes, he let the fabric drop, like a curtain, to cover her again. Light from the gas lamp bounced off his spectacles. He made his face a blank as he stroked her through the muslin, his hand moving down to the bottom of the curve of her derriere. He held it there now, cradled its weight, held *her*.

"Yes," he said companionably. "Precisely. And soon enough too. How very prescient of you."

Prescient or desiring? But this wasn't the time to think her way through a conundrum. He'd pinched her — hard — through the fabric. The best she could do was restrain herself from yelping. She thought she could feel the weave of the cloth; despite the fineness of the muslin it felt scratchy, the hard pads of his fingers pressing beneath it.

Or had she been responding to the sound of his voice instead? No time to sort it out — and not much space between their bodies. He'd lifted her chin with his finger to bring her face close to his. His eyes were keen. He spoke softly and extremely clearly. "But surely you understood me when I said I wanted you upstairs."

An image wafted across her vision: of peaches in a silver basket, so ripe one could hardly touch them without bruising them. She'd set them aside for him for later; the juice would trickle down his chin, near the corner of his lip, that new glint of whisker. She might dissolve into liquid just thinking of it. Or was it the sound of his voice that was making her feel that way?

But she wouldn't dissolve so soon. "Oh, I *understood* you well enough. It's just that I'm not your girl."

"My Lady Gorham, then." He bent his

head down over where the top of her breast overflowed the peignoir, bit down into the roundness of her breast, sucked hard, and lifted his head.

A blue mark remained. "*Mine,* you see? Now upstairs with you."

He took a step backward, folding his arms across his chest as though appraising a piece in some gentleman's collection, not touching her anywhere now — unless one counted the lingering feel of his mouth on her breast, the warm, wavery air charged with his proprietary gaze.

She moved her hand to the bruise he'd made, fingers pressing to make it throb a little. Her skin marked easily; a mark would take its time to heal. For the next days she'd always be thinking of the blood he'd drawn beneath her skin, wondering if it were well enough hidden beneath a gown's décolletage.

Where had she been invited? What had she planned to wear? She'd have to make some changes.

When all the time she'd be wishing she wore the most revealing of her gowns, to show off the mark like a jewel.

She felt her lips soften, tremble. "Yes." Breathing the word rather than saying it. Her eyes were equally soft, she expected, and her thighs, her belly. She pressed her fingertips more deeply against her breast and gazed at him as she spoke. "Oh. Yes."

The sounds had come out clearer now. Long, round *o*. Liquid, sibilant *s*. Clearer but hardly English — the language, rather, of a body opening, flesh relaxing its tensions.

An answer that obviated the necessity for any further questions.

If he'd noticed any of that, he pretended not to. "There, you see how easy that was? Now, up the stairs with you, and no more of your insolence."

A beam of pale light had just now come slanting through the window, across the entryway, and onto the staircase. A cloud must have drifted away from the face of the moon.

Her peignoir was of a muslin similar to that little shift he'd been so keen on — in truth, of a stuff that was even thinner. Madame Gabri had raised her eyebrows when she'd first seen the bolt of fabric; Marina had told herself the modiste must be scandalized by the expense of it. When she'd chosen to wear it this evening, she'd told herself it was because of the weather.

Because there were times when one told oneself anything rather than the truth of one's desires. The moonlit staircase was bathed in cold, bluish light — rather as she'd pictured it, but in truth more beautifully. He'd be able to see clearly through the fabric as he climbed the stairs behind her.

No more of your insolence. She put a foot on the bottom stair and lingered for a moment. For surely one couldn't call it insolence if a lady took the staircase a bit more slowly than her lover might have intended her to, and with a hint of sway to her arse as she made her ascent.

The stairs were thickly carpeted. Hardly breathing, he and she walked so quietly that she fancied she could hear his callused fingers tugging open the buttons of his trousers — which it seemed he *could* do perfectly quickly when he wanted to badly enough. She laughed silently to herself and felt herself reassured and emboldened by the humor of it. Because for some time now — she wasn't sure since when — she'd been learning how laughter gave one the courage the extremes of pleasure demanded.

A bit late in life to have learned all this, perhaps, but better than never. How fascinating at long last to feel a measure of control over these matters of mastery and voluntary submission.

There'd been no chance of it when she'd been younger. And after the years with Sprague and then Harry Wyatt, there'd been nothing she'd wanted less than to be told what to do. No wonder she'd kept to her grateful, docile young men: their eagerness to please, their simple, predictable gratifications. A few years of having them at her beck and call hadn't been a bad thing. Perhaps it had given her the confidence for nights like this one, games where one made up the rules as one went.

Games where one didn't always get it right. The only games worth playing.

She paused for a moment at the top of the stairs.

"Is there ointment?" His voice came muffled from behind her.

"Ointment? Let me think." She paused.

"Don't stop walking." The voice had lowered almost to a growl. He was close behind her, hard against her thighs. She could feel the open buttons pressing through her peignoir into her flesh.

She moved a little more quickly. "The ointment," she told him, "is in its little jar, in the drawer in the bedstand."

"Good."

They'd passed through the door to her bedchamber. His hands were around her waist now. Half lifting her onto the bed, he moved her onto her knees, raised her hips, raised the peignoir, and tossed it up over her back and head — like a tulip shedding its petals, she thought, an umbrella blown open in a storm.

More naked this way. Exposed, anonymous, animal. You needed a certain sense of who you were, she thought proudly, if you were willing to risk losing it this way.

She buried her head in the pillow, dug her knees into the mattress. He nudged her legs farther apart, pressed her shoulders downward. She moaned to feel her breasts crushed against the bedclothes. Like a shadow of lightning in a darkened sky, the shape of the mark on her breast hovered blue against the black velvet of her closed eyelids. An electric shudder traveled down the curve of her spine. She arched and bent, spread and opened to him.

"Good, good . . ." The sound issued like a groan from his lips. Perhaps, she thought, she'd overdone it a bit by taking the staircase as slowly as she had. In any case it was clearly excessive to expect him to undress. In her mind's eye she could see him up on his knees between her parted legs, trousers open, cock in his hand as he rubbed himself with the ointment (she'd heard the drawer's hasty rattle; she suspected he'd left it slightly agape).

No time to heat the stuff, turn it to liquid. When she'd imagined tonight, she'd always supposed something more leisurely, one and then the other of them holding the little jar in front of the grate as they sat naked on the floor in front of it with their arms about each other.

But there *was* no fire in the grate tonight. No matter: His hands were hot and dry enough to melt the stuff; she could imagine it becoming liquid on his fingertips. Not simply imagining it, she could feel it now — quite liquid, wonderfully thick and richly unctuous, exactly the stuff you wanted in this situation — as he parted the cheeks of her arse and began to rub it into her, roughly and gently too, pressing, opening, entering her with his fingers.

Roughly, to remind her that there was a limit to what he could do to help her. That when it came down to it, it was *she* who'd have to moan and breathe and shudder herself to the proper, open, obedient soft-ness, to take herself past pain or perhaps (she'd have to choose) to linger at its por-tals.

But gently as well — to show her, she thought, that he understood, that he was grateful and adoring, delighted, impatient. Well, mostly impatient now, and steadily moving past gentleness — if much more slowly, she expected, than he wanted to — in order to allow her to learn it anew. A pedagogical streak was a very good thing in a man, and particularly in a lover. He clearly understood that she'd have to discover for herself — this time, and (*surely!*) the times to come — how to exercise this dark art of shaping the most hidden part of herself around him.

He'd entered her with his cock; she'd breathed and opened and found the way to let him in, to fill her — was there any fullness like it? — and now to move with her, and she with him.

With or against him? A bit of both perhaps: She might never know completely. It was amusing in its way — or would be, if at such a moment she'd been able to spare the time for amusement. As though there *could* be a tick of extra time or a scintilla of superfluous space with him moving so hard and deep and quick now within her. (Had he really been gentle just a few moments ago? Had there really been anything ever before besides this arching, this spreading and opening and filling?) As though there were any reality aside from the darkness spreading within her and the harsh, deep, unseemly noise it seemed that she was making.

His cry, when it came, was higher, as she and he drew each other closer together and drove themselves beside themselves with pleasure. A blank moment now — blue, black, and then hot white against her eyelids — before she collapsed flat and wet and sticky onto her front, with him spent, gasping, exhausted atop her, both of them enmeshed in a gauzy, scratchy, sweaty tangle of hard, provoking buttons and half-removed clothing.

"I'll wash you," she told him.

And a good thing, he thought, that she could muster the energy, especially with all his clothing that she had to get through first. But it seemed that she'd managed it. Sighing and stretching, he gave himself over to the soft cloth, scented soap, and cool water around his cock and balls, between his legs, and up around his belly.

Revived by then, he took a turn at washing her, trying to be gentle, as soft and yet as thorough as he could with her really quite miraculous bottom, its thrilling cleft, the pair of dimples above it.

"You're *sure* I'm not hurting you?" She'd

given a low laugh in response. Yes, well, he supposed he could see the humor in it, him asking her that *now.*

He sighed with satisfaction and well-being, with the achievement of something so long, so deeply desired. And then, inevitably — humanly, he expected — with frustration that none of this was going to last forever. And that when it came to an end it would be bloody difficult to give it up.

How much longer did they *have,* anyway, before she went to Brighton to puff the damn book? You'd think it had been enough of a success already; did she really *need* to live so extravagantly?

But that was selfish of him, and unreasonable too. He'd rented the Charlotte Street house only until the end of July. He'd contracted to finish his work for Kellingsley — and his book for Colburn too — by that time; the roofers at Wheldon Priory assured him he could move back home by then. He certainly wouldn't be able to afford keeping two addresses.

Not so bad a situation, he comforted himself. A few weeks of this extraordinary affair left before they'd each quit London. Time still for any number of pleasures — really *quite* extraordinary. The affair of a lifetime, probably. He'd certainly never had anything to compare.

"Wait," she'd whispered. "I'll be back." As though he'd be going anywhere just yet. She'd pulled away from him, gotten up to fetch something. He turned over onto his belly to watch her walk across the room, to see her as clearly as he could without his spectacles. By the time she reached the other side of the room, she would disappear in a blur, and his thoughts would become as hazy as his vision — the living woman, the goddesses of legend, the sculptures he'd dedicated his life and intellect to, all jumbled together in delicious erotic confusion.

He thought of a legend about a particularly beautiful statue — the Aphrodite of Cnidus, her marble thigh stained one night by some poor sod who'd stolen into the shrine and had his way with the goddess. Delicious to fall in love all over again with this mythology, inspired to it as he was by Marina's legs, her shoulders, the wild tumble of curls falling to the middle of her back, flare of hip and arse.

And equally delicious to feel, even now . . . oh, just some mild, random stirrings, of course, but gratifying nonetheless, as she emerged — as out of a cloud — from the beautiful blur at the edge of his vision.

Something bright in her hands. A silver basket.

"Peaches," she said. "Here, I'll cut you a slice."

Nice to be fed from her fingers. If only *she'd* eat something now and again. For the briefest of instants he allowed himself a forbidden and oddly homely fancy — of sharing a breakfast table. One ought to begin the day with something substantial in one's belly; he'd feed her porridge, eggs, sausage.

Absurd to be imagining it. He put it sternly out of his mind. But thoughts of the breakfast table had reminded him of something else.

"I received an invitation," he told her now between bites of peach, "this morning, to a most elegant party — or a big, expensive one anyway; I don't know if I'd be able to tell the difference after being such a recluse for so long. At any rate it's fancy dress, though not mandatory to attend in costume, the invitation said. My word, it's been years. Lord Withers was at university with me, but we haven't kept up. I was surprised to be thought of. They must indeed be inviting a huge list of people, just as it says in . . ."

He paused to take another bite of peach,

perhaps a bit uncouthly, but just in time: Another moment of his jabbering and he would have told her he'd gotten that bit about inviting everyone from the *on-dits* she thought him too high-minded to read. "Well, it's made for rather exciting news at my home, you see. My . . . um, niece's governess has also received an invitation. The young American lady is an acquaintance, I gather. Most kind of her to invite Miss Hobart, I thought."

She'd turned away at the sound of the word *niece. I deserve that,* he thought. But all she said, if a bit coldly, was, "Interesting. Of course, you probably don't know that your nephew has been linked in the gossip columns with the American lady, Miss Amory."

As well as with her stepdaughter, though that might be a delicate point with her.

But this was becoming ridiculous. Secreted away from the world as their affair was, did they really need to speak so circuitously to each other? How had they gotten themselves into such a muddle of private and public intelligence? Enough was enough.

"Actually, I did know. The truth is, I've rather taken to following the newspapers about Anthony's comings and goings," he said, "and about you too.

"Well, you *said* I might read about you." He mumbled it, shamefaced, and reached for the bedsheet — somehow he found himself wanting to have something to hide behind — but it seemed to have fallen to the floor. There was a pillow nearby, but that was silly to try to disappear behind a pillow. His spectacles, then — to put *something* between him and her. And when he'd adjusted the earpieces and peered out at her — when her image had swum back into sharp focus — it seemed that she was gazing at him with an unexpected sweetness in her eyes.

Probably just a trick of the light, a prismatic effect caused when he'd moved the lenses into position.

She spoke briskly. "Well, of course," she said now, "you realize that I shall be at the ball as well."

They both were quiet after that for a while. None of what they'd just said to each other really signified very much, he thought. And yet somehow it changed things between them. Gazing at each other across a bank of goose-feather pillows had suddenly become something different, in light of the prospect of gazing at each other across a crowded ballroom.

Public and private lives, segregated like little fragments of bone and mineral in an airless case at a museum.

"We needn't speak to each other at the ball," she said, "if you don't wish it." Her voice seemed to tremble a little here even as she laughed. "In *that* crush, it'll be difficult enough even to find each other."

"What sort of costume," he asked her, "will you wear?"

"I'd thought of Cleopatra — it's fun to paint up my eyes and wear a wig and chaplet, but . . ."

"But what?"

"Well, Cleopatra would hardly be Cleopatra without a certain modicum of décolletage. And you've made *that* rather an impossibility for me just now, you see. When I'm bruised, it takes a while for it to fade."

"I'm awfully sorry." Staring rather giddily where she'd pointed, he took another large bite out of the peach slice she'd offered him.

"No, you're not sorry. Nor do I want you to be." She licked the peach juice from his chin. "Do be careful; you'll get yourself sticky." After which she continued licking down his jaw and neck, where he was sure he hadn't dribbled at all.

"Thanks," he said after a time. "And you're quite right; I'm not sorry." He

261

fingered her breast — thoughtfully, even rather proudly — and then gathered her up into his arms. "I'm not in the smallest, slightest bit sorry. But in that case, what *will* you wear to the ball?"

"I'll be a Spanish lady, I believe," she said. "It'll be easy to hide the mark amid a profusion of black lace. And you?"

"I'll . . ." He knit his brow, tightened his arms about her, and swept her into a long kiss before continuing. "This business of costume balls and fancy dress is quite a novelty for me. Do you know, I believe I've changed my mind about what I'm going to wear. I'm still not sure; you'll simply have to wait and see. But meanwhile . . ."

He pressed himself against her, and she pressed back, laughing a little.

"My word," she said softly, and tightened her arms about him. Because at least for tonight, neither of them would have to wait for anything. On the contrary, they'd have to hurry if they were to finish before the sun came up what it seemed they'd started once again.

"It's the last of May. The solstice will soon be upon us. Curse these short nights," Jasper whispered.

"These short, *hot* nights." Marina mur-

262

mured her words somewhere in the vicinity of his neck. "Oh, yes, curse 'em indeed."

CHAPTER 15

"And may the devil curse you forever, Gerry Rackham," she snarled.

The first of June. She stood, fists clenched, in his horrid little office, staring down at him seated at his desk, with all the hatred she could muster.

Numbly, absently, she noted that her Irish accent had come back. Not in full force, but she could feel it curling — really rather prettily — about the edges of her voice for the first time in years. "Damn you to hell," she said, and turned on her heel.

Pacing nervously about the nasty little space as he watched, she reminded herself of a prisoner in a dungeon, if a most fashionably attired prisoner (her mouth twisted for the irony of it) in new, pale mulberry poplin.

She could hardly breathe. No wonder, furious as she was — and corseted too, to the full extent the costume required. And because on this dazzlingly warm day he was still burning coal in his filthy stove.

"You *could* open a window," she said.

Actually he couldn't. The rotting frames were sealed shut, probably held together by the soot and grime of decades. Cold-blooded little creature that he was in his too-tight coat, he seemed to find it comfortable.

"*You* could tell me a little something about Mr. Hedges," he returned.

"And *you* could f . . ." She searched her memory for the filthiest of insults that the English soldiers used to hurl at one another, and stopped herself just in time from speaking aloud. Still, he'd already won a little something from her, just by making her remember.

"I'd tell you nothing about him," she said, "even if I knew it."

He wasn't quite able to hide his disappointment that she'd managed to swallow back her bad language. "That's all right, though, at least for now. I'd actually prefer to take the payment another way, and this time it's not more money I want from you, Maria."

Sell herself rather than betray Jasper. Though by selling herself, wasn't she also . . . ? But this wasn't the time, she told herself, to work any of that out.

Or perhaps it was, since Rackham had begun to speak more slowly, for the pleasure of hearing himself say the words. "I'm obliged to levy this extra charge on you," he said, "due to inflation. *Inflation,* don't you know. My *expenditures* is *rising* something terrible these days." Wiggling his hips about in his chair, he had a good solitary laugh at his stupid joke.

"And then," he continued more seriously, "I'm not getting any younger. Well, neither of us is, Maria."

He'd be taking his payment from her, he told her, at that inn he'd told her about.

That was, if she didn't want her story told all around London, her position among the *ton* destroyed quite completely. Which was what *would* happen to her if he told the right personages all that he knew about her.

Who knew? Maybe the press might even send some scribbler to Ireland, to the village, after he told them where it was and how to get there, to ask someone still living there what they knew of her. Write it up for the papers: *Lady Gorham, the* Real *Story.*

Because, as he pointed out — slowly, patiently, in his rheumy voice — hadn't she noticed that people were becoming a bit less free in their ways these days?

He supposed they'd finally had enough of the fat, gouty old king and all his mistresses and horses and spending so free on his own pleasure when he were the prince regent. Britons were getting prissier, less like to put up with certain whispers of impropriety. And they especially enjoyed taking it out on a certain sort of woman.

Which were doubtless (she could see he was winding up to a conclusion) and most particularly true of a certain scholarly sort of gentleman. The sort who'd make his residence, say, in Bloomsbury. Because that sort of gentleman would have a respectable family to attend to, no matter how or with what sort of woman such a gentleman might choose to disport himself with of an evening.

She flung the inkstand at him at that point, missing only narrowly.

"Don't try that again," he said.

"But that's it, isn't it?" she said. "The point of all this is *him.* You couldn't bear for me to be happy for once in my —"

"I'm not getting any younger," he repeated stolidly. "I've waited bloody long enough for *my* turn."

"Then you can bloody well wait a little bit longer. Until after Lord Withers's ball a week hence. Reserve a room at your rattling good inn for the following night." She noted that the Irish accent was gone again. Just as well.

"And if I'm not there," she told him, "you're free to expose me and my past to all of London. Tell them every precious filthy thing you know about me."

She slammed down her bank draft before he could reply, and hurried out of the office down the stairs to her carriage.

Eight days hence, she told herself as the carriage rumbled out of the narrow street and onto a decent thoroughfare, *she'd* be in Calais, classic refuge for disgraced members of the beau monde when their debts or indiscretions caught up with them.

Wasn't Brummell still in Calais? Charming, sad, and poor — yes, one still heard reports from travelers who'd looked him up. She and Harry had given him a good dinner years ago. It would be pleasant to joke about all this with a gallant, witty gentleman whose life had had its own reverses.

Or course, with her widow's portion, she could certainly afford to live in Paris if she chose. She'd decide once she got across the channel.

Her finances were in quite decent shape — especially since she wouldn't have to be paying Rackham anymore. Her solicitor could let the house, see to the servants

268

who'd be staying.

It wouldn't be a disaster. Of course, she'd have to do a lot of planning this next week. One couldn't leave for a sudden unannounced tour abroad without being extremely thorough about details, papers, letters of credit.

As her carriage rolled into Brook Street, she found herself rather congratulating herself upon her clean-headedness, her lack of regret. Not that she hadn't enjoyed the life she'd built for herself this past half dozen years. Well, who *wouldn't* enjoy such admiration as she'd attracted? What girl from a remote Irish village wouldn't have liked to be known by everyone, invited everywhere in the great metropolis? Of course, her looks had had a great deal to do with it. Her looks, yes, and other things too. But she'd be damned if she wouldn't also take a little pride in what part of it she'd created through her own wit and work and discipline.

Not so bad, though, to be able to loosen the discipline a bit. At least — she laughed here as she swept her skirts up the staircase — she wouldn't have to finish the stupid book about Mr. Parrey's confounded twin brother. Perhaps she could even pick up some of those decidedly un-*ton*-ish little

269

sketches about Ireland she liked to noodle about with.

A pity, though, she thought as she entered her bedchamber and shut the door behind her, about her affair with Jasper Hedges. For she must admit she would have preferred if *that* had lasted out the Season.

The span of time between early spring and midsummer . . . as long as one needs . . .

Was that *really* all the time one needed?

She'd have plenty of time in France, to try to answer that question.

But as for the following seven days in London — and especially the nights — she'd just have to make the time as memorable as she could.

There was so much to do — oh, Lord, there was still her gown for the Withers-Amory ball. Holding lengths of black lace in front of her, she dreamily examined the effect in the looking glass. Yes, the lace would work; the blue mark at the top of her breast would look like shadow. She told the maid to send the lace to Madame Gabri to have the costume made up.

And perhaps, she thought, smiling as though she had nothing more vexing to occupy her mind, tonight she could finally manage to persuade Jasper to disclose what sort of costume he'd be wearing.

■ ■ ■ ■

While at approximately the same time, and some way across London, an exceedingly vexed Jasper Hedges scowled at himself in a pier glass and wondered what in the bloody hell he'd wear to the damned party after all.

It had been years since he'd tossed the Albanian costume into a cedar chest. But upon taking a look at it yesterday, he'd decided that the white embroidered tunic, tasseled sash, and slim leggings were still rather dashing, and that the cedar had done its job of keeping the moths away quite admirably. Dispatching his manservant on some fanciful errand, he'd shut his dressing room door tightly against possible incursions on his privacy before holding the pieces of clothing up to himself in front of the looking glass. Not bad, even if the spectacles looked a bit out of place. At any rate, it would still fit him well enough. And even in his tassels and embroidery, he probably wouldn't be the most absurdly or conspicuously costumed gentleman at the Withers-Amory ball.

Which had seemed a satisfactory enough notion yesterday, but far less satisfactory today.

271

What singular challenges life in Society threw one, he thought, when one had been a recluse for so long.

Because one of the new suits of clothing he'd ordered — the black one — had turned out rather becoming. And the tailor, Mr. Andrewes, had told him that it would be appropriate for a ball if one wore it with a good waistcoat.

She might enjoy that, Jasper thought. At any rate, she'd catch the joke of it if he appeared at Lord Withers's house dressed — *costumed,* one might say — as a properly appointed, even elegantly dressed English gentleman.

Rather fun, he thought, to have a private joke between her and himself, and in a public venue. Nothing more than that, he told himself. Well, except for a certain insistent and rather unworthy set of imaginings that it seemed he couldn't rid himself of. *Oh, admit the truth to yourself and be done with it, Jasper* — he rather liked the way he looked in the new suit of clothing and he wanted her to see him in it. In public. Odd how that worked, when he professed to loathe publicity, and when their affair was so secret. Odd that he found the whole idea of dressing up for her in a public venue so engaging.

It would be the first time since her dinner party that he and she'd be out in the world together. He quickly disclaimed the thought. They'd hardly be *together.* Except perhaps in *his* mind — naturally he couldn't speak for *her.*

He remembered how she'd looked the evening of her dinner party — green gown, yellow armchair, a roomful of gentlemen's desiring eyes upon her. Before he could stop himself, he thought of the little wound he'd given her at the top of her breast, the thrill that had passed through him when she'd pressed her fingers against it while gazing up at him.

Mine, he'd said. *Mine,* he thought now. *Mine if only (only!) in pleasure. Mine,* even if no one but he would ever know it.

Painfully, stoically, he forced his attention to the business at hand. The black suit of clothing hung in his sparsely furnished wardrobe; a few days ago he'd made an order for a black silk cravat, some good white linen — *you have a beautiful back,* she'd said. But he'd procrastinated, dammit, in the matter of a waistcoat.

When he'd asked Mr. Andrewes to advise him where to get a proper one, the tailor had laughed. "Sir Anthony Hedges is your nephew and you're asking *me* about waist-coats?"

No wonder he'd procrastinated. Ha, *pro-crastinated. Froze in terror* would be more accurate. As though he'd never faced a brigand or pirate, or even the sneak he'd encountered the other night. Had the fellow in the brown coat really been following him? He'd skittered like a rat into the shadows when Jasper had called him out.

It wasn't as though he was afraid of a fight; he'd have loved taking on the little brown rat. But this would be worse. Since his visit to Andrewes, Jasper had come to feel the most fearsome ordeal an English-man could face would be to appear a vain old fool in the eyes of Sir Anthony Hedges, the kingdom's unofficially anointed Knight of the Waistcoat. Especially when that young man had seemed even less forthcoming than usual these past few weeks, if such a thing could be imagined.

Leave it alone, he'd told himself; he'd wear the white tasseled costume and that would be the end of it.

But it wasn't the end of it. Absurd that he wanted to strut and display himself for her, but he did. Like the heroes of his boyhood, Leonidas at Thermopylae and the rest — egotistical as they were courageous, the great classical warriors would have understood what he was feeling. And so he called upon them as he rehearsed the few difficult words until he didn't sound quite so pitifully ridiculous.

Beg pardon for asking, but where might I find a good waistcoat that wouldn't be terribly expensive or look too flash, and which might be appropriate for a ball?

All of which, just a few minutes ago, he'd heroically managed to blurt out to Anthony.

Sydney was upstairs. She and Miss Hobart had been fussing about something all morning. Which was very good luck — Thermopylae or not, he couldn't have gone through with his little ordeal if it had meant looking like a silly old coot in front of Sydney.

And so he'd planted himself in the entryway to catch the boy alone before Sydney came down. Utterly out of character, the words he'd spoken. Jasper had barely recognized himself; no wonder Anthony had frozen in astonishment for a few seconds, stared, and then frowned (Jasper stopped breathing), before shrugging his handsome shoulders, smiling — well, *almost* smiling — and yes, offering his assistance.

"Well, there *is* a waistcoat that I ordered for myself. Not too expensive — the fabric's rather plainer than I usually wear. But it doesn't quite suit me, and I've . . ." The words came out a little muddled here. He might have been saying something to the effect that he'd been rather waiting to pay for it — or probably, Jasper thought, to find the means to do so. He should be taking the boy to task for that, he expected, but instead, he heard himself asking what color waistcoat it was.

"Blue," Anthony replied. "A shade I think would look very well on you. For Lord Withers's ball, is it?" The words uttered with no discernible curl of the lip, no angry boyish dramatics. Nothing more than an exercise of taste and judgment, a sharing of expertise between gentlemen: Jasper had rather had to steady himself under the force of it.

"Hmmm, yes, quite suitable," the young man continued, "after he nips it in at the waist, using the small seams toward the back. Half an inch or perhaps the smallest touch more. Be sure to tell him I said so." Voice dropped to a murmur, eyes narrowed as he gave the question his most serious and expert consideration. And if the application of such prodigies of mental energy might appear a trifle excessive . . . *Well, then,* Jasper told himself with a shudder, *I bloody well should have gone out and braved Bond Street* without *the benefit of the boy's advice.*

Could it be, he wondered now, that he'd never given Anthony an opportunity to show his own sort of competence? Had he really never asked the boy for anything before? Would it have been so impossible to admit he'd ever needed anything for himself?

"Thanks," he said now, quietly, doubtless almost unintelligibly, continuing to mumble about how he'd known Withers at university . . . kind of him to send the invitation, a surprise, of course, and to Miss Hobart in particular . . . But now that he thought of it, Withers had also known Miss Hobart's father. . . . Right, hadn't thought about it in years, but he'd heard, read, been told . . . perhaps it had been Sydney who'd mentioned it. . . . The American lady . . . rather nice . . .

All the while wondering whether Anthony wanted to marry the American lady, or that earl's sister — or someone. All the while wanting to do something — *anything* — to help, knowing he couldn't, and wishing to hell he'd never started this infernal jabbering, with the boy staring at him as though he'd taken leave of his senses and himself not knowing how to stop.

He didn't want to pry. No, that wasn't true. He *did* want to pry, rather awfully.

I want you to be happy. Happier than any of us *managed to be.*

Faces swam before his inner eye: John's, Celia's, and now another one. He blinked. *She* didn't belong in his thoughts right now. She oughtn't to be part of the *us* he'd been thinking about.

The boy was eyeing him most suspiciously.

"Well, anyway, thanks." At least it had come out audibly this time. "I'm exceedingly grateful."

The dizzy moment had passed. Anthony shrugged, nodded, and offered the tradesman's name and Bond Street address, repeating all the particulars about how the waistcoat should be altered. Jasper was busy noting it when Sydney came bounding down the stairway.

"I do beg your pardon, Anthony. I know you don't like to wait, but . . ."

The two men stared up at her in some surprise, both of them, it seemed, having forgotten about her. She stared back at them for a moment (*for it must be unusual,* Jasper thought, *for her to be seeing the pair of us even in physical proximity*), shrugged her shoulders with the enviable affective flexibility of childhood, and burst into a stream of chatter that was hardly more intelligible than Jasper's had been — something about a costume Miss Hobart was making for herself for Miss Amory's ball.

"You wouldn't believe it; she's got this old white muslin of her mother's, quite unwearable and old-fashioned. It probably dates back to the times when Uncle was young, it's so very Grecian-looking — rather an antiquity, one might say."

She paused for a gulp of air. "And she's ripped out all the seams and put it back together and made herself into Artemis the huntress goddess, and it's completely and utterly lovely. You'll both be so absolutely surprised when you see it. I'd love to see the looks on your faces — well, I *shall* see Uncle's, I'll be tiptoeing out of bed to watch, the night of the ball, before the two of you set off."

Miss Hobart sent her apologies for not coming down, but she'd just now had another idea for how to drape the muslin in the back and wanted to try it out. Sydney apologized once more for being late, but it had been so interesting, she'd found it difficult to tear herself away.

"So she sews as well as nurses the sick, comforts the afflicted, speaks Greek. . . . No, you're right, Syd, I'm bound not to tease anymore." But Anthony's careless drawl seemed very far away, as Jasper pondered the words *when Uncle was young. Hell.* He'd better straighten out one thing before they went any further.

"The waistcoat, Anthony. It's not a very *bright* blue, is it? It won't make me look like one of those rouged and corseted old gentlemen ashamed to be their ages?" For he'd rather be dipped in the River Styx, suffer the tortures of Tantalus, take on the labors of Hercules, than have Marina think him vain.

The boy stared for a moment and then gave a gentle smile. "An exceedingly gray sort of blue, Uncle Jasper, surpassingly grayish. Like slate, only paler. You'll be the very *dernier cri* of elegant sobriety." He winked. "You see, Syd, Uncle is going to go to Miss Amory's ball disguised as a supremely well dressed English gentleman."

Which had caused Sydney to ask a hundred impertinent questions and Jasper to shrug his shoulders in humility and confusion while Anthony expounded upon the mysteries of gentlemen's formal dress.

Still, he supposed it wasn't the worst thing, to be caught out in a moment of vanity.

And by the time the two young people

went out — for a much shorter drive than they'd intended at first, because it seemed that there was more to be said about these matters than Jasper could have imagined — Jasper had offered the loan of the Albanian costume, Anthony had looked at it and accepted it (with Sydney's enthusiastic approval), and they'd even laughed once or twice. Which was probably more laughter shared between himself and the boy than in all the years since . . . well, than ever before.

He gazed at his reflection in the entry hall mirror and narrowed his eyes. *Dernier cri* of elegant sobriety indeed.

And then he closed the door of his study and got down to work, because he owed Henry Colburn a manuscript.

CHAPTER 16

Marina had to laugh at herself — or at least to try *not* to — upon entering the Witherses' ballroom. No point pretending she hadn't been searching for Jasper from the moment she'd mounted the grand, curving staircase. But it was rather comical to be scanning such a large space filled with so colorful a crush of variously attired people, in quest of one particular gentleman who might be costumed any way at all.

Of course, she couldn't simply prowl about. Everyone knew Lady Gorham, and tonight she made a striking figure amid cascades of black lace, a high comb in her black hair. What good fortune that she hadn't dressed as Cleopatra, she thought as she exchanged brief greetings with Lady Isobel, imperious for all her smallness of stature under a black wig, brown eyes coolly gazing out from the lozenges of precisely applied kohl surrounding them.

For a while she found it impossible to disentangle herself from conversation, including an amusing one with a mismatched young couple, he Persian and she Elizabethan. "But I won't monopolize the pair of you any longer," she told them as Sir Anthony sailed by in his white Albanian finery — perhaps in search of Lady Isobel, Marina thought as she drifted purposefully and tactfully away from the young gentleman the World thought was her recent lover.

It didn't take much drifting to lose sight of him in this crowd. She needn't do much more than turn to her left to find Lord Withers, congratulate him on the splendor of the ballroom, and ask after Miss Amory.

The gentleman wasn't sure where his young cousin had gotten to, but he'd pass the compliments along to her and to his daughter when next he came upon either of them. The red and blue silk draperies and the masses of flowers had been *their* doing, he told Marina. His only contribution was the music. The orchestra wouldn't only be playing waltzes and quadrilles; he'd insisted upon the good old country dances and some reels in honor of their American guest.

His only contribution besides paying for the thing, Marina thought. She smiled affectionately at him and told him how fine he looked in his simple evening coat. Perhaps, she thought, he'd dressed so in order to make those who hadn't bothered to get themselves up in costume feel more comfortable. Take, for example, the tall gentleman in severe black evening dress — *ah, yes!* — who'd just now led a reed-slim young woman in a white Grecian costume out to dance.

How straight his back, how graceful his step (she wouldn't necessarily have expected that; she must look more carefully, to be quite clear). As he and his partner (and who *was* the partner?) took their places in the row of dancers and his grizzled hair caught the glimmer of the chandelier above him, she'd simply found herself staring.

Could one put the force of one's desire behind a stare? Could one communicate it across a crowded ballroom? She retreated to a sofa at the foot of the room to find out.

It seemed that one could, for he'd managed to return her gaze before reapplying his attention to the steps. It was a good thing, she thought, that he was proving a surprisingly skilled dancer, because she didn't intend to look away, no matter how it might cause him to feel.

And who *was* his partner?

Oh, good, it was only the governess from

the museum.

Nice to have such a good view of the dancing, from this sofa. Though until this moment she'd thought herself alone — until her thoughts had been interrupted by a loud, ostentatiously romantic, and boyish sigh.

How long had Anthony been sitting beside her? Where were Lady Isobel and Miss Amory hiding themselves?

"We oughtn't to be in such proximity." Eyes on the dancers, she spoke rather as an automaton would.

"Oh, hang that," he returned. "Can't we be friends again, after all this great long time we've spent being former lovers?"

Two months probably *was* a great long time at his age; at the moment she hadn't the wit to debate it at length. "All right. I suppose we needn't last out the Season so publicly cool to each other. But why have you chosen this moment to propose our reconciliation?"

"I've chosen this moment because you *are* my friend, because I have something to tell you, and because I need you to do me a service."

What he had to tell her was that he'd proposed to Lady Isobel, and that she'd promised to give him her answer later tonight. No, he hadn't told Uncle Jasper yet. He hadn't supposed it would matter.

She suspected he was terribly wrong about *that,* but it wasn't her business to interfere there. Still, congratulations were in order. She offered them warmly.

"Thanks," he said. "I imagine it'll go all right, if she'll have me. Make things easier, anyway. And one nice thing about her — when her abominable brother suggested that if we marry I mustn't ever speak to you again, she told him to go to hell, that she didn't intend to forbid me to see anybody. That if she refused me, it would have nothing to do with *you* one way or another."

Marina laughed. "So she turns out to be Harry's daughter after all. Good for her. And for you too." Not that they'd have to worry about whether to speak to her after she was gone to Calais, but it was still pleasant to learn that both young people had some backbone.

"Yes, she's quite agreeable. As I said. But as for what I wanted to ask you . . ."

Abruptly, his voice had taken on a new urgency. Forcing herself to look away from the dance floor at last, she turned to him in some surprise.

"Dear Marina, I want you to promenade with me. And when the dance ends, as it will soon, I want us to be standing next to Uncle Jasper — do you see him over there? — Uncle Jasper and that . . . that very unusual young lady, Miss Hobart."

Do you see him over there? It was difficult not to laugh aloud with relief to find that she mustn't have been staring *too* obviously. Although now that she'd turned to look at him, it was clear that Anthony had had *his* eyes upon the dancers the whole time they'd been speaking as well, and that Marina might have been crossing her eyes or sticking out her tongue for all that he would have noticed.

"Over there," he repeated. "The young lady who doesn't look like anyone else in the room."

Now that she looked more closely, the young woman *did* possess a rather original sort of attractiveness. Still, did the leading beau of the Season really need to lay strategies to meet her? Absurd to be getting himself in such a pucker.

But Anthony shook his head. "She's a very superior sort of person. Well, I've always known that; she's always made me feel like an idiot — worse than Uncle did, but of course it never mattered what *she* thought about me. But upon my honor, she makes me feel shy tonight.

"Still, if I happened to turn up near where she happened to be standing, she wouldn't wish to be impolite, when all I want to do is tell her how awfully nice she looks. Because a young lady likes to be told she looks nice at a ball. Even if it's an idiot making the compliments. But she *does* look nice, and she deserves to be told it. And as my life is likely to change after tonight, I shouldn't like to think I hadn't taken the opportunity. . . .

"Anyway, you *do* get on well enough with Uncle Jasper, don't you, Marina? I mean, it wouldn't be a terrible hardship for you to engage him in conversation . . . ?"

He looked away in embarrassment, and she turned her own eyes back to watch Jasper making his way down the row in good time to the music. The orchestra was taking the last chorus in a richer harmony and a more pronounced rhythm; the dance was coming to its end.

"A terrible hardship?" she murmured. "No, I shouldn't think so. Not for a friend."

She rose to her feet and gave Anthony her arm.

All of which — although none of the four people in question could have rendered clear account of it — somehow led to Lady Gorham and Mr. Jasper Hedges making a pair for the next country dance, while Sir Anthony Hedges led the interesting young woman in her Grecian drape of muslin to the far end of the row.

In the instant before the musicians struck the opening chord, Jasper felt himself suddenly transported back to childhood. Memory of a dance lesson: He couldn't have been more than eight when the teacher had quite humiliated him by singling him out from the other children to illustrate a principle.

Never cling to a partner's hand, Master Hedges. You must learn to balance force and weight, support and freedom.

Shy as he'd been, he'd gotten the point — forced himself to learn it, perhaps, rather than be made an example of again. *Yes, much better, Master Hedges,* the blowhard of a teacher had called out.

Odd what one remembered.

He bowed to Marina, and she swept down before him in an all-too-quick flash of white skin and black lace. If you didn't know the almost-faded little bruise was there, you wouldn't. Good luck, then, that he did know exactly where to look for it.

He bowed to the little lady costumed as Queen Elizabeth on his other side and then to her dark-haired Persian partner.

What a lot of business went on before a dance could quite get started. And what a surprise for a reclusive type like himself to find himself enjoying the formalities, the claiming of place and partner within the assembled participants. One didn't dance in secret, shamed, midnight solitude. One lined up with one's partner in everyone's full view, under the bright lights of the chandeliers. One smiled, nodded, gathered one's energies at one's center, and waited to be swept into action upon the beat of the music.

What a beautiful smile she had.

Was he ashamed of their secret midnights?

Moving *dos-à-dos* around her, he sought refuge in a more scholarly view of the matter. All civilizations danced: There was something touchingly human about the urge to create formal, graceful abstractions out of the business of meeting and parting and meeting again — as though each figure of the dance were a little love affair. Approach and retreat, turn and return, as though the mystery of human desire could be put in order and set to music.

Perhaps it could. Or perhaps it was simply a lovely fancy to feel confident, as you cast away your partner — as you and she moved away from each other on that small push of the hands — that the pair of you would meet again at the end of the row.

His dance master had been right about one thing: You couldn't cling. You moved through time. You moved *with* time. Moments counted: If you wanted to make a compliment, it couldn't take longer than the few beats needed to pass and circle — as he and she were doing now, paying precise attention to the measure.

"I like your costume very much, Mr. Hedges. Or is it a disguise?"

Join hands with the next couple, circle, and return.

"Whichever you like, Lady Gorham. I wondered if you'd enjoy it if I got such a thing up."

She returned a quick smile and nod.

Circle the other way now, with a new neighboring couple. Lucky he had a good memory for steps and patterns: lovely to contemplate the tilt of her neck.

Come back to meet your partner.

"And the exceedingly handsome waist-coat?" she asked.

Circling around each other, shoulders almost touching, timing their breath and measuring their steps to avail themselves of the fleeting opportunities to speak. Dancers passed around and among them; space shaped and reshaped itself as though through the lens of a kaleidoscope. But the music made it impossible to forget that time went in only one direction.

"I have Anthony to thank for it," he said. "And thank him I did," he added upon impulse, at the last possible moment before they turned away from each other.

"I'm very glad of it," she told him when next they met.

"Though I wonder . . ." But he'd said that too late to finish it before he had to turn again.

And so they took the next steps in silence, turning their attention as if by mutual agreement to the young couple in white who'd come up to be the neighboring couple on the row.

For there were an odd number of couples in the long row of dancers. So although Sir Anthony and Miss Hobart had begun on the other end of the line, the order of the couples had changed as each pair went down the center and then cast off to lead the line around.

Mr. Hedges, Lady Gorham, Sir Anthony, and the young woman in Grecian costume were now a foursome, making a most striking pattern of alternating black and white as they formed a star with their raised, joined right hands, changed directions, and repeated the pattern to the left: The dancers in black were all smiles, surprise, and delight at the novelty of finding themselves together in view of a thousand eyes and in the light of a thousand candles; the two dressed in white were serious, tentative, awestruck to find themselves together at all.

Marina had danced with Anthony before. In fact, it had been his grace on the dance floor that had first caught her notice at the end of last year's Season. How singular, she thought now, the similarity with which he and Jasper placed their feet, bore the weight of their bodies at their centers, and curved their arms as they took the steps of the dance. They didn't resemble each other much in other ways, but their movements, their gestures, the way they took your hand and circled past you — all of these were of a pattern and a sameness most agreeable to contemplate.

Uncle Jasper, Anthony had said, *manages to make it clear that I'm not what I should be.* And what Anthony was supposed to be, according to Anthony, was a version of Uncle Jasper himself.

At first she'd dismissed it as petulance on

the boy's part, insensitivity on the uncle's. But as time had gone on she'd begun to wonder. Even as enemies, they'd seemed to share a bond. This evening, in such close and measured proximity to the pair of them, she found herself wondering — once more and quite seriously — if there wasn't after all something more than a general family resemblance between them. For in a way she wasn't sure she quite wanted to contemplate, they seemed versions of each other after all.

None of her business; she wouldn't think of it.

She'd simply watch Jasper, his eyes full of wonder as he and Anthony circled each other, nodded, executed the steps neatly and respectfully, and returned to their partners.

She'd watch Anthony, his eyes full of Miss Hobart — that touchingly and quaintly elegant young lady who clearly loved to dance and just as clearly couldn't take her eyes off her partner.

He's only being kind to her, and surely, Marina thought, *she'll understand that. At least if she truly is the "superior person" Anthony supposes her.*

She turned back to bow to her own partner. The orchestra signaled the end of the dance, movement and measure came to a fullness and then a halt, smiles and applause were exchanged all 'round, and Marina and Jasper wandered away from the center of the floor.

They were silent as the orchestra struck up a waltz.

"I'm not awfully good at that thing," Jasper said. "I learned to dance before the waltz became fashionable, and I'd rather talk just now."

She nodded.

"Still," he said, as Anthony and Miss Hobart whirled by, "it gladdens my heart to see him being so good to her. I wouldn't have asked him to dance with her — he generally makes her uncomfortable with his frivolity. But there they are, and I can see that she's enjoying it. It's generous of him to take the time from his own friendships" — he paused here to shrug his shoulders — "to give her a little pleasure this evening. Poor, excellent young woman — I fear that our household makes a terrible lot of demands upon her."

"She's a lovely dancer," Marina said. "And now that everyone has seen that, she'll probably have more gentlemen asking her to dance, and he can go back to his own affairs."

At least, she hoped so — for the young couple did waltz beautifully.

"And do you know," Jasper was saying, "that I'm finding there's more to him than I should have thought? You were right about that, and I thank you for helping me understand how to see it."

She smiled, paused, thought of how she might want to reply to that, and found that she didn't know how to begin. "And so does Anthony dance very well," she told him. "And so do you."

He squeezed her arm — until that moment she'd almost forgotten he was holding it. Unconsciously, it seemed, they'd reverted back to the familiarity of her bedchamber.

But they weren't in her bedchamber, and she was beginning to become conscious of that fact — as well as of the stares attending them, even in a quiet corner of the ballroom.

"Do you wish us to be so public?" she whispered.

He lightened his touch, and she took her arm from his and backed up a few steps.

"Thank you," he said. "I'm sorry."

They exchanged a glance. The exuberance of the moment had passed, though the familiarity lingered.

And so she left in her carriage, and some minutes later he followed in a cab.

CHAPTER 17

"But I seem to remember," she said, "that, at least at the ball, you said you wanted to talk."

They were in her bedchamber.

"I do want to talk," he told her, "and we shall. But the problem, Lady Gorham, is that I found myself missing you so confoundedly all the time it took me to get here. . . ."

All the time it took me to get here . . . How long, she wondered, had she been waiting for him to get here? How many years since she'd supposed she might have an affair as enthralling as this one?

All the time it took you to get here, and tomorrow I'll be leaving for Calais.

Today, in actual fact, for it was after midnight already.

Forget today and tomorrow. The only thing that matters is now.

"You were actually rather quick about it,"

she said. "Must have found a good cab-
man."

Her maid had barely had a chance to
remove the black lace gown and hang it
back in the dressing room; she'd been about
to begin on the stays and petticoat when
Marina had heard his loud knock at the
door. Dismissing the maid, she'd wrapped a
silk paisley shawl about herself and hurried
down to let him in and fetch him back
upstairs. And so, although the shawl had
since slid to the bedchamber floor, her
corset remained as tightly laced as the black
Spanish costume had required.

Before tonight, she'd always greeted him
in the scantiest peignoirs she could manage.
Naked, for all intents and purposes: It was
simpler that way. Nakedness had its own
sort of power — she'd learned to make it
so, anyway, in her past, and she was glad of
the skill. Half-undress was riskier, showier,
a more precarious balance between the
worlds of the bedchamber and the ballroom.

Of course, he could always unlace her —
and surely she'd ask him to do so in a few
more moments — after she'd taken her full
measure of delight in his awestruck gaze at
the top halves of her breasts spilling over
the top of the corset, and her own pleasure
in feeling them crushed against the smooth

weave of his lovely waistcoat.

Constriction and freedom, skin and satin — for the moment she found herself quite amply engaged by the sly little satisfactions, the sneaky protocols of half-undress. Let him decide how to proceed. For the moment she found it diversion enough to be held against him, her breath coming sudden and shallow as he bumped an inquisitive fingertip along the crisscross ties that ran up the center of her back and moved his other hand along the strips of whalebone sewn into the heavy linen that gave her no choice but to hold herself so straight.

"Formidable," he murmured. "A great deal too formidable to bother with right now. And anyway . . ."

His lips were moving down her neck to her chest. She leaned back in the circle of his arms. He bent his head over her breasts as though he were starving and she'd brought him a tray heaped with figs and peaches and grapes.

Belatedly, she reminded herself that with all the fuss and bother of preparing for the ball, she hadn't thought to have a snack sent up for him tonight. He didn't seem to mind awfully much. His mouth was lively. The little wound on her breast had begun to ache most poignantly under his lips as she allowed him to guide her across the room toward her bed.

With their arms about each other it seemed almost as though they were performing another dance figure. Bow and bend; he placed her gently upon her back, slid to his knees between her parted legs. Pushing away her petticoats, loosening the tie of her drawers, he pulled the thin cotton lawn down over her legs — slowly . . . it was as though a breeze had caressed her thighs — and tossed them to the floor.

Her bed was rather high off the ground; the small of her back rested at the edge of the mattress. Until this moment she hadn't realized how she'd feel with her torso so rigidly corseted. Immobilized, for all intents and purposes, her legs dangling over the side of the bed, she could barely curve her spine; her toes only just reached the floor. Too late: There was no way to anchor herself. In some ways it would have been easier if he'd bound her to the bedstead; ties at her wrists or ankles would at least have given her something to strain against.

But as it was there was nothing she could do but lie back while he kissed her up and down the insides of her thighs, from her knees to the rise of her mons and then back again.

How clever of him. But by now he knew how intimate she found this sort of love-making, the most intimate incursion of any — the most challenging of all positions for her: to be held helpless and immobile, captive beneath his mouth.

He made a long, upward stroke of the tongue almost to her groin, nipping her very lightly and following the wicked little bite with a dozen feathery little kisses and then another long, catlike stroke of his tongue.

The sigh emitting from her lips had come from somewhere deep within her belly. He paused — perhaps he'd straightened his head for an instant, listening. *Yes, I'm ready,* was what the sigh had signified — to be opened, explored, discovered.

How many times, she wondered, could one be discovered by a lover? In how many ways? And when one had so much to hide.

When so much would be revealed. And soon enough too.

Stop it. Stay in the now.

He parted her with his tongue, and suddenly there was nothing *but* the here and now.

Ah. Yes. Like that. She gasped for breath at the tiny, seemingly careless first flicker of sensation against her flesh. It was as though he'd lit a twisted rush and allowed it to smolder.

Too slow. His mouth quivered against her cunt. She supposed he must want to chuckle at her discomfiture. But he kept himself in check — he had to, she thought, in order to attend to this business he took so seriously of making her seethe and simmer when she wanted to burst into flames.

Perhaps she could move a little, speed this up just a bit.

Couldn't she be allowed some tiny measure of control, at least of the rhythm? From within the carapace of her stays, perhaps she could arch her back, lift herself a half inch closer to his mouth. She doubted the movement would be perceptible except to herself.

Silly of her: Of course he'd felt it, and he wasn't going to allow it to continue either. He'd moved his hand to hold her firmly in place, his palms curled about her hip bones, calloused fingertips hard against her belly's soft skin while he continued taking his agonizingly slow time licking and lapping and nibbling at her, fanning the glow at her center as it pleased him to do. Until, when the brilliant flare of it finally came, it was as if a wisp of red silk had caught on fire.

Flame to ash to smoke to air — when it happened, it happened *that* quickly, leaving her gasping and astonished and laughing for the wonderful, warm, satisfied joy of release.

Gathering whatever strength she had left, she reached down to pull him from where he knelt, until he lay happily atop her while both of them tried to get their breath back.

"You shall have your turn soon enough," she whispered when she was able.

His reply was almost too soft to hear — a purr of anticipation or a growl of self-satisfaction, she could hardly tell which, and so it took her a moment to make meaningful syllables from the warmth of his breath at her ear.

"I shall be honored, Lady Gorham."

"So it's *Lady Gorham* now, is it? How odd," she murmured, "that you've begun calling me that this evening."

"It is a bit odd," he said. "I usually find *Marina* such a lovely name. But this evening I was quite taken with Lady Gorham, the public personage. It felt so strangely intimate to be dancing with you in front of all those eyes."

"Sometimes," she said, "the name Lady Gorham feels to me rather like a costume for a fancy dress ball."

Was she in costume at this moment? She wasn't sure. She didn't know what one could call this state in which they'd found themselves, somewhere between formal dress and nakedness. With so many layers of secrets still between them — so much to be unlaced, unbound, untied, removed.

He pulled at the strings at the back of her stays.

"Umm, yes, thanks," she murmured, and returned the favor by helping him out of his coat and off with his cravat. But the lovely waistcoat must stay on, she decreed; its satin was so cool and smooth against her finally, joyously bared nipples. Chuckling, he and she held each other more tightly now, until the moment passed and Marina felt the muscles in Jasper's arms and shoulders go tight and tense.

"I want to tell you something," he whispered, "but I'm rather afraid to."

The lights were very low. They raised their heads from the pillow and gazed at each other for a very long moment. As he had on their first night together, he was able to say only a single word — "Anthony" — followed, a long pause later, in a low, choked voice, by, "Do you understand what I'm trying to tell you?"

"Yes," she said, "I think so. I've been wondering, supposing it was merely my imagination, the subtle resemblance between the two of you — even when you weren't getting on at all. I'd wonder and then I'd remind myself to mind my own business. But tonight, dancing with the two of you, in that singular intimacy we shared among seven hundred other mortals . . ."

He smiled at the word *mortals* before making a choked sound and looking away. She thought his eyes might have been wet, but he'd looked away too quickly.

"It's been a very long time," he said. "I never thought I'd tell anyone. It feels like aeons." He laughed, a bit harshly. "But then, I expect I'm accustomed to thinking in terms of aeons. Of empires coming and going and leaving behind traces of their glories."

"We don't have aeons," she replied, "but I expect we have as long as you'll need to tell me about it. Please tell me, Jasper. I want to know how it all came to be."

And then perhaps, she thought, *I might tell you* my *secrets.*

For why shouldn't he hear it from her first?

If she were brave enough to risk the look on his face when she told him.

She'd decide that later, though, after he told her what he had to say. They'd entwined their bodies so tightly together, her lips were close upon his neck. As he spoke, she could

305

feel it vibrating in his throat.

Still, not much of it came as a surprise. In the years since Harry Wyatt had brought her to England, she had, after all, learned enough about the nation's upper classes to write novels about them.

Not that it took a very deep or subtle understanding to know that the quiet, thoughtful younger son of a baronet — much in the shadow of his prepossessing older brother — would need a career, and that the Church was the obvious choice. The *only* choice, so far as the boy's father was concerned, for although the old baronet was a good enough sort (Jasper was scrupulous about giving credit where it was due), he wasn't "awfully sensible of the inner natures of those about him."

She hadn't, of course, known much about the extensive knowledge of the classics one would have to amass in order to put one in the way of such a career. But she hadn't had to know any of that, the heroes of her novels mostly spending their university years lounging about their apartments between duels and debauches.

"You weren't so far off in most cases," he told her, "but in mine, it was possible to learn a lot and at least to debauch a little.

306

I'm a quick study — and I did have a little time for my fancies, for I'd taken inspiration from those great, sensuous stories the ancients told." And, of course, a university city might provide that sort of amusement, if one were circumspect — and if one were (he'd laughed here) "single-minded, curious, wildly energetic, even if rather awkward at first, and absolutely in awe and delight over what a pair of bodies could do for each other."

She pouted in mock jealousy; he laughed some more and kissed the pout away. "I'm glad," he said, "that we never had occasion to meet when we were both younger, me still so awkward, while you . . . But certainly you were never anything but beautiful, confident."

She looked away. He shrugged his shoulders and continued to speak.

"But I could hardly avoid my growing awareness that I could never be happy in the Church. The more I read about the ancient world, the more I wanted to travel there and see what was left of it. I wanted art, adventures — yes, and mysterious darkeyed girls with veils and bracelets 'round their ankles too. I wanted pirates too, and got them, but I'll tell you all about that some other time, Marina."

She tightened her arms about him.

"The main thing, though," he continued, "was that I didn't want to be buried alive in Essex, in the living that my father was waiting to bestow upon me, and which happily he gave to William Hobart in my absence.

"He might have sent me for a grand tour of France, Switzerland, Italy, but England was at war then — and he wasn't the sort of person to understand why anyone would want to go to 'uncivilized' places like Greece. I was in a quandary, and so the day after I took my degree I left Cambridge to confide in my older brother, John, ask him how I might face the inevitable conflict with our father."

Such, in any case, had been his intention. He'd traveled all night to get to Kent, where John and Celia had made their home. But when he got there he found that his older brother was in London.

" 'You can find John at his mistress's house, if you want,' Celia told me angrily. She'd had a stillbirth — premature — just a month or so before. I hadn't known about it, or how melancholy it had made her. For it had been the second of such episodes, and although John had been comforting enough at first, he'd grown impatient with her — there not being much basic sympathy between them."

Marina nodded rather reluctantly.

"They liked each other well enough," he continued, "when things were going well, but as she put it, 'He's not really awfully fond of me when I don't have the energy to make myself as beautiful as his mistress — and it makes him furious when I'm not as willing. And so he's gone to London until I'm ready, as he put it, to "be a good, agreeable, dutiful wife once more." ' "

It was Jasper's turn now to look away.

"But of course," Marina took up the story, "*you* found her quite beautiful enough as she was, perhaps more beautiful than ever in her pallor, her vulnerability and melancholy."

He turned back with a surprised expression on his face.

"I write novels," she told him. "I rather understand the points upon which a plot might turn. And *she* . . . ?"

He shrugged. "No doubt you already understand, then, that *she*," he said, "turned out quite willing enough to take *me* to bed, to dazzle me, make me fall in love with her. I expect it was rather a game for her to seduce me, and a little revenge against John."

"Something like that," she said, "would be

my understanding."

"Though of course," he said, "that wasn't how I saw it at the time.

"Surely, I thought, now that we'd shared such passion she couldn't possibly stay with John. I'd take her away, I thought. I forgot about my father and went back to Cambridge to ask everyone I might possibly know — tutors, school friends — until I secured an introduction to a gentleman sailing for Athens who wanted a secretary. He wasn't happy when I told him I wanted to bring a lady along, but he said I could if I paid her expenses. I thought, in my naïveté, that she'd sell a few jewels, come away with me. And who'd care, on the other side of the world, if we weren't married? What would be important was that she and I'd be together, seeing all the ancient glories."

His laugh had no humor in it. "I was twenty-one years old. I rushed back to Kent to tell her the good news, that I'd found a way for us to run away together — only to find her in the midst of packing herself up to go to London. Gowns and jewels were everywhere — open pots of rouge, jars of creams and ointments hugger-mugger on every surface. . . . I hadn't known cosmetics came in such a variety of hues — I'd barely known what cosmetics *were*. Her maids were running about in a stew of agitation, but she was deadly calm. For she'd ascertained that she was pregnant with our child, and she needed to go to London *now,* before John could come to know it. She needed to be a 'good, agreeable, dutiful wife' to him as soon as possible, and as convincingly."

He stopped. "And she did. She paused at the door of the coach that morning, turned once to wave at me, and was gone. She looked awful; I remember the dark shadows beneath her eyes. There could be no doubt of her condition: She'd been puking for a week — the ride to London must have been hellish.

"But when she'd got there she must have managed to hide all that, to be as ravishing as she'd ever been. No doubt John had begun to tire of his mistress. And when Anthony was born some seven and a half months later, John was so overjoyed to have a beautiful little heir that he barely counted the months — I remember the letter he sent me. Well, he wasn't the sort of person to let details get in the way, I don't suppose he would ever have suspected *me,* and, of course, by then I was long gone. Smyrna. It had once been Phoenicia."

There was a silence. It took him a long time to speak, and when he did his voice was almost a whisper.

"And all that time, and for all those years after, I wanted my son. I coveted him. It wasn't fair, I told myself, that John should have him. I know how that sounds; it was a horrid, guilty thing, and you must believe me that I never intended to do anything about it or even to tell anyone.

"I *didn't* do anything about it," he added.

She shook her head, because of course he hadn't, but he pulled away from her almost angrily.

"Don't be so certain," he told her, "because I'm not. When I came to stay with them at Lake Como, was I flaunting my life as a wanderer, a romantic adventurer? Was I revenging myself on the pair of them by making them feel dull, trapped in the repetition of their own unsatisfactory arrangements? Had I managed to make her want me — *really* want me this time — and to make John know it?

"I can't know. But I do know that they were angry at each other the day they went out on their sail. At the moment I hadn't thought I'd caused it, but since then I've had a great deal of time to wonder, to imagine what they might have said to each other in the hour before their deaths."

They were lying side by side now on her

312

bed, each staring up at the ceiling, the six inches or so of space between their bodies like a vast gulf fixed between them.

"You can't imagine," he said, "how it feels to get what one has wanted so desperately, at the expense of two deaths."

She held herself very steady, breathing slowly, biting the corner of her lip. Surely, she thought, he'd feel the shudder she hadn't entirely managed to suppress. But he wasn't attending.

"And so I had my son," he said, "and I had my punishment too when I saw him weep for his father — the one he *thought* was his father, the one he loved. Perhaps I added to the punishment myself by how stupidly I managed the thing. I wanted him to be like *me,* you see, and he wasn't, and I didn't know how to love him for who he was.

"Who he *is,*" he added. He reached across to her and took her hand. "But I learned to live with my stupid resentments and posturings," he finally said. "Until . . ."

"Until," she said, "tonight."

"Tonight's the upshot of it," he said, "but it's come upon me slowly these past weeks, this business of wanting nothing more than his happiness. Of rather liking him, you know, for who he is, instead of merely loving him so fiercely and hopelessly and unhappily. Of learning to be happy to have what of him I have — no need to resent the part of him I don't, to wish that someday he might know . . . But what he knows is its own kind of truth. It makes me happy even if . . ."

"You're not sure you deserve it."

His mouth twisted, he rolled over to face her. "I expect so. The thing about being a younger son, of earning one's way in the world, is that you're never quite sure whether you've earned all you should."

"You've been a wonderful guardian to your . . . niece. That might be thought of as earning your right to happiness with your . . . family."

She thought he might flinch at the sound of the forbidden words — *niece, family* — but he nodded gratefully.

"When I first saw the two of you in the museum," she continued, "I was . . ." *Consumed by envy,* she wanted to say, *for a girl with such a loving father.* But that was her story, and not his.

"I was charmed," she told him — warmly, graciously, as Lady Gorham might tell him — "by the sight of the two of you, so comfortable with each other, side by side, so sweetly scholarly among the marbles."

"I thought you found us quaint," he said.

She wanted to correct him, but she only shook her head and smiled until he had nothing to do but return the smile — or at least send back a faint reflection of it. And until they'd inched themselves back across the little divide between them on the bed.

"I shall have to think more about what we've said tonight," he said. "But not just now. Because just now, you know . . ."

"Just now you may still have your turn, if you want it."

If he wanted it . . . Could there be a possibility, Jasper thought, that he *wouldn't* want it?

Would there be any man anywhere who wouldn't want what she was offering?

The heartiness of his laughter must have been enough of a signal. She'd begun sliding herself downward, undoing the first of the buttons. . . .

But there seemed to be a pounding on the door downstairs.

He sat up. She did too. *It can't be about me,* he thought. *No one knows I'm here.* Unless Anthony had guessed . . .

Anthony . . . Oh, God, Sydney . . .

He had his coat on and his cravat in some distant approximation of a knot before the

315

polite rapping at her bedchamber door had begun.

Her butler, endeavoring to appear as respectful and disinterested as the situation demanded while visibly entertained by it.

"Beg pardon, my lady," the butler said, "but there's a man waiting downstairs, says he has an urgent message for his master, Mr. Hedges."

CHAPTER 18

"It won't be long, dear." Helen Hobart
spoke as soothingly as she could, arms
wrapped about the weeping child, while a
flannel-robed and curl-papered Mrs. Burroughs led the upstairs maid in a tragical
chorus of wailing about never being burgled
in all their years of respectable service —
well, never before tonight, anyway. After
which the housekeeper would perform a
solo turn of dark mutterings about certain
gentlemen being out on the town when their
families needed them, which led into the
cycle of wailings starting up again.

Each wail sent Sydney into a new fit of
trembling, and every dark muttering about
Mr. Hedges's absence brought on new tears.

Helen glared at the house keeper even as
she addressed her words to Sydney. "I'm
quite, *quite* sure," she repeated as slowly
and clearly as she could, "that your uncle
will be home in just a few more minutes.

Robert has taken a cab to go fetch him from the party."

Patiently, for what must have been the dozenth time, Helen reiterated that Mr. Hedges would already be with them if not for the density of traffic at the height of the Season.

And in any case, she continued comfortingly, he was surely well on his way by now, even with all the carriages and cabs jostling for place at Miss Amory's costume ball, because — brightly, confidingly — "you can't imagine what a crush it was, all those vehicles, more than anything I myself could possibly have expected."

After the fifth or sixth repetition it had begun to sound quite reasonable even to herself. Though in truth she'd only pretended to send Robert to Lord Withers's house, because there had been no doubt in Helen's mind as to where her employer really would be found.

Robert had listened calmly to her whispered instructions — "You do remember the house on Brook Street, don't you, where you delivered a letter a few weeks ago?" It had been good of him, Helen thought, to set off without so much as a conspiratorial wink, content to wait until tomorrow for the pleasure of revealing the true facts of the matter to Mrs. Burroughs and company. It would be a good story; Helen could hardly begrudge him the fun he'd have telling it. None of the household staff would have suspected Mr. Hedges, of all people, of a midnight assignation with the famous Beautiful Bluestocking of Brook Street.

Well, anyway, it's none of my affair, Helen told herself. It would be soon enough that she'd be putting the vastness of the Atlantic Ocean between herself and this troublesome family. Stupid of her, even for a moment, to worry about Mr. Hedges's reputation among his servants. Misplaced loyalty to have hesitated in sending Robert out to find him. It wouldn't be fair to make a terrified child wait until breakfast.

While as to reputation . . . had Mr. Hedges's nephew given a thought to *Helen's* reputation this evening?

"The burglar might have killed me." Sydney's tears were coming more slowly now, but her voice was very small and frightened, as though she were trapped in the terrifying moment, with no choice but to tell about it again and again until her uncle came home and made her feel safe.

"I fell asleep reading, and when I woke up he was pointing a pistol at me.

"A pistol," Sydney repeated. "I saw it,

though I didn't see much of his face — he and the tall one had their cravats wrapped around them below the eyes. I tried not to make a sound, but I think I cried a little, and when I did, he cocked the pistol and nodded to the other one to do *something* over by the cabinet, but I didn't see what; I was afraid to look. And then he said in . . . in . . . such an evil voice, 'I'll leave you alone this time, *and* the statue, but tell your uncle I'll be back, miss.' I hardly let myself breathe after that, and if it weren't for the other man — the *good* one, you know, and he was tall, with very dark blue eyes — hissing at him not to be a fool and put the pistol away, he might have killed me. And he might have killed *you* too, Miss Hobart, instead of running away when he heard you come home."

"But he didn't kill anyone, dear; we're both absolutely unharmed. Nor, I think, did they get a chance to open the cabinet, and I don't believe any antiquities have been taken from the shelves either. They got themselves back out the window, they left with an empty cart, we're all unharmed, we're all extremely lucky, and I think we should be all exceedingly, humbly, and *quietly* grateful for it."

Helen had intended that last as a rebuke to Mrs. Burroughs. But it had merely set the housekeeper off again.

"Bother the antique-ities. It's you I'm grateful to, Miss Hobart — thank the Lord almighty that *you* at least come home when you did, and scared the burglar and his thieving hordes away before they was like to murder the houseful of us."

There weren't *hordes of them, for lord's sake.* Helen bit down on her tongue rather than say it. Probably no more than two. Two and a cart, perhaps a wheelbarrow. She'd definitely heard some sort of scuffle out in the mews behind the house, them helping each other get out through the window, and then wheels rumbling on the stones. She might have run to take a better look, but at the moment she'd been too frightened and confused. She expected she ought to try to remember everything she could, to tell Mr. Hedges — who damned well ought to be home by now, the selfish wretch. Even if, as was probably the case, all men were selfish wretches, surely it was Mr. Hedges — and not Helen — who ought to be racking his brain for clues, logicking this thing together, and bearing the burden of his niece's and his servants' weeping and wailing.

Because Helen had her own weeping to do in the airless privacy of her little bedchamber, as well as her own thoughts to put in order, possessions to pack up, and final ill wishes to send in the direction of the dishonest, duplicitous, despicable nephew she hoped with all her heart never to see again.

"And as for *you*, you little imp . . ." The housekeeper was evidently undecided whether to smother Sydney in kisses or shake her; Sydney snuggled closer to Helen in case of either eventuality. "I hope to-night's disaster will teach you not to sneak down to your uncle's study in the middle of the night to read them wicked novels with burglars lurking about; let *that* be a lesson to you. . . ."

In response to which Helen could hardly help expostulating, as though in a classroom or court of law, that in the first place there hadn't been a disaster, in the second that Sydney could hardly have been expected to know that burglars would be lurking about, and finally, thank you very much, Mrs. Burroughs, but Miss Hedges and I shall discuss the young lady's clandestine perusal of novels later — and we shall inform Mr. Hedges of it at some more appropriate time.

She repeated the bit about waiting to tell Mr. Hedges what Sydney had been reading. Mrs. Burroughs nodded reluctantly, and Sydney sighed, the tears sliding down her cheeks more quietly now, more in guilty relief, it seemed, than in fear.

I didn't do it for your sake, imp, Helen thought. *I did it because I needed to calm myself by speaking in big long words like* clandestine perusal.

Because perhaps if she continued to speak — slowly, clearly, multisyllabically, and in such a logical, patient, fearsomely-excellent-governess sort of voice — she could forget ever having tried to be anything other but a logical, patient, fearsomely excellent governess.

Artemis in a pale, scanty drift of a white Grecian gown: If only there were a way to make it as though none of that had ever happened. She tugged her cloak tighter about her bare arms and shoulders. No matter that the night was sultry and the kitchen lamps were blazing; at least she could hide the gown from view, even as she tried to erase the memories . . .

. . . of herself standing at the edge of the ballroom.

. . . of Sir Anthony Hedges leading her out to dance. Twice. Though it had felt more like once, the dances blending into each other, theme and variation, different ways for two bodies (yes, bodies) to be together. A country dance and then a waltz, and then he'd walked alongside her down the terrace steps into the dimly lit garden. Both of them had found themselves rather flushed, but neither of them wanted to bother with refreshment. He'd smiled. *Waltzing,* he'd said, *can be warm work; don't you agree, Miss Hobart?*

She'd agreed quite readily — as though she spent all her evenings waltzing. For a moment it had felt like that; for a moment it was as though the two of them shared . . . opinions? Points of view? Everything. It had been such an agreeable conversation — so easy, as though they'd known each other for years.

But that was a stupid way to put it. For they *had* known each other for years, in a family sort of way. Years before she'd been Sydney's governess, she and her papa would sometimes be invited to Wheldon Priory. There'd been those dreadful dinner parties, the beautiful bored boy sitting across the table from her; she'd hardly known how to keep from staring at him.

And yet, at the ball he'd been so jolly about all of that — even remembering those horrid Latin dinner-table jokes. Helen supposed he must not have anyone to discuss family matters with. Because he'd wanted her to share his astonishment that after all

324

this time he was coming to find his uncle moderately tolerable, and to listen when he asked if she thought he were mad to suspect a *tendre,* or even something earthier — *can you credit that, Miss Hobart?* he'd asked — between Mr. Hedges and the Countess of Gorham.

She'd never considered the possibility until he'd mentioned it. But Mr. Hedges *did* come home awfully late these days, she'd told him. And she'd laughed then, and he had too — the laughter filling her with such generous goodwill, toward Mr. Hedges, Lady Gorham, and all the world, that she hadn't been bothered by what the *on-dits* said about anybody — including Sir Anthony and whom he might marry.

Because if one chose — as Helen had done — to consider this conversation as a sort of comfortable family matter, then one could permit herself to ignore what she'd learned from the gossip in the newspapers (at least for another little while, until they went back into the house, which surely they'd be doing soon enough).

And when they'd walked a little farther, and gone on to speak of simple, agreeable things — the fields and forests around Wheldon, the people of the village — it had gotten increasingly easy for her to forget that he was a famous figure of the *ton,* and to see him as nothing but a friendly, generous, and openhearted young man who'd been so kind as to dance with her at a party where she really didn't belong.

He missed Wheldon Priory, he'd told her; he really ought to come down more often. Recently he'd begun to wonder whether he enjoyed London and its amusements so much after all. Perhaps now that he and Uncle were getting on better, and now that he might be able to afford . . .

But then — he'd suddenly interrupted himself — the course of one's life could change extremely suddenly, before one quite realized the import of the changes — *Do you know what I mean, Miss Hobart?*

Which ought — if nothing else would — to have reminded her once and for all that all of London knew he was in search of a wealthy wife. But he'd looked so sad when he'd said it that she'd found herself oddly guilt-stricken instead, and filled with regrets about her own plans, the position in America she'd been offered, her sorrow to leave Sydney and even Mr. Hedges.

And that must have been the moment when she and he had ceased talking, stopped walking, turned to face each other. The moment when he'd kissed her.

Forget that part, Helen, she commanded herself.

Forget it this instant, she thought. Even as a small, strangled, distinctly nongoverness voice at the back of her mind protested that it had been only a very little kiss.

Their lips had met; their tongues had touched. (So one opened one's lips; one allowed one's tongue . . . She'd always wondered about that.) They'd inclined their heads toward each other; they'd stood among the trees and shrubbery with many inches of space between their bodies. Mouths seeking, mouths finding, nothing more than those happy, busy mouths — unless you counted the way they'd had their fingers linked together.

Such a chaste little kiss. And it had ended so guiltily and abruptly, him pulling so forcefully away from her.

Blushing, stricken, he'd begun to speak in a jerky, stuttering rush of uncompleted sentences, words scattered like buckshot, utterly unlike the fashionable, half-mocking drawl he usually spoke in. "No, this can't be, I do beg your pardon, it's just that, oh, lord, forgive me, Miss Hobart, I shouldn't have, I've no right, I'm an idiot, must tell you . . ." All the while she'd been too astonished to make a sound.

"Come," he'd continued. "We'd better go inside; I'll tell you there." Fingers no longer touching, they'd made their guilty, silent way toward the house.

But perhaps she could permit herself to remember that innocent first kiss after all. (And no, the tongue part wasn't the slightest bit unpleasant; on the contrary. Well, anyway, now she knew.) Perhaps she could have that memory as a sort of keepsake — as if Cinderella had been allowed to keep a glass slipper.

Because really, it was the second kiss she should be trying to forget — the one that had blazed into being on their way back to the house, just before they'd reached the terrace and its bank of brilliant Chinese lanterns.

As though executing a coy, rather droll dance figure, the two of them had stepped into the light for a moment, and then just as quickly stepped back from it into the warm, soft, enveloping darkness of the garden path. Pausing to gaze at each other, they'd moved themselves into a gap in the shrubbery — more enclosed, better hidden from the world. Amid a cracking of twigs, a crushing of leaves, and a scattering of petals, they'd set themselves kissing and clutching among the roses and laurel with an eagerness she was probably doomed to remember for the rest of her life. And which, undeniably, had been every bit as much her doing as his.

He'd put his arms about her waist and she'd put hers about his torso. How well they fit together, she'd thought. For though she was tall, he was taller; and if she was thin with nerves and bones close to the skin, he had all that wonderful, comforting muscle about him. She'd felt herself a vine twining about an oak — before she'd left off the poetical similes and instead remembered the marble Dionysus of the museum. It would have been humorous if it hadn't been thrilling, if it hadn't filled her with a giddy sort of pride to feel him so ardent and excited, rising beneath his belted tunic against her thighs. Hard like marble, but not cold. She could only imagine how warm.

Proud. Excited. Eager. Oh, Lord, and so, so warm. The press of his body, the air heavy with roses, her nostrils pricked with the spice of laurel: Amid the riot of sensation, she could hardly have known what she'd do next. Anything he'd wanted, she supposed — and she wouldn't even try to pretend *she* hadn't wanted it, though she'd be hard-pressed to describe or even imagine the mysterious *it* of her desiring in any of its particulars.

And if *hard-pressed* was a stupid double entendre, so be it. It didn't matter now, did it, sitting here in the kitchen as she was, doing her prim and precise best to protect Mr. Hedges's reputation. Performing her most convincing portrayal of cool, reasonable Miss Hobart, because what did she have besides that version of herself and her hope that no one except Anthony — *Sir* Anthony, she corrected herself — would ever know what a fool Miss Hobart was capable of acting?

Unless he were to tell someone. Did gentlemen at their clubs exchange stories as servants did in their kitchens? She wasn't too awfully worried about the possibility; probably it wouldn't make as good a story as the one Robert the footman would be telling about Mr. Hedges tomorrow.

Because so what if London's adored young Sir Anthony Hedges had kissed a plain governess who'd been stupid enough to let him? What significance if he'd almost seduced her in the shrubbery, at the Withers-Amory ball, less than an hour before he was due to announce his engagement to the fabulously wealthy Lady Isobel Wyatt?

A dull story, really, with an audience of

only one, and that audience probably doomed to tell it to herself forever.

At least she could console herself that she hadn't stayed long enough to hear the engagement publicly announced. Lady Isobel's private announcement — or the portion of it Helen had heard — had been quite enough.

She should be congratulating herself upon her good fortune, her narrow escape. Not a bad night's work, if you considered that she'd also saved the house from being burgled.

The gods, as Mr. Hedges liked to say, must have been with her; it must have been the gods who'd thrust her and Sir Anthony into such a prickly stand of vegetation that she'd been bound to tear the skirt of her gown. Snagged it upon a thorn — the rending of fabric long and loud enough to be heard above his and her breathing and gasping and the cracking of twigs.

She'd pulled herself away from him. Despite her excitement, a lifetime of thrifty mending had produced habits that were evidently difficult to break.

I shall need to stitch it up, she'd told him, *or it'll continue tearing. Up to the knee, perhaps,* she'd added. She and he had exchanged a daring little smile at the shared imagination of how much leg the torn skirt could reveal if left to its own devices.

Yes, of course, he'd replied. *But come back quickly, will you? Please, because I need to . . .*

She supposed that he'd been intending to tell her about it then. It might even have been possible that he'd pulled himself away from her instead of she from him. A shred of decency on his part after all. She wasn't sure she welcomed the fair-minded part of her nature that made her admit it to herself.

"Of course I'll come back." All foolish blissful smiles, she'd been. No logic, no reason, nothing but wanting him and wanting to come back to him as soon as possible. She hadn't even considered what it was he might have wanted to tell her.

But as it had turned out, she hadn't had to hear it from him.

A footman with a very large nose directed her to the rooms where a lady might retire to fix her gowns. She wasn't quite sure what he'd said — he'd seemed to use that nose of his for everything, or at least to look down it at her and speak to her through it at the same time. Trust a servant to know who did and didn't really belong at a grand ball.

But after wandering for a bit in the direction he'd pointed, she discovered there were evidently two withdrawing rooms available.

Two neighboring downstairs bedchambers had been set up for the purpose, and maids fluttered about, ready to help you mend a ripped hem or repair a tumbled coiffure. The larger chamber was quite full, but a second, only slightly smaller one was almost empty, except for some murmuring from two elaborately costumed figures — one tall, one short — seated close together on a sofa set deep in a window alcove.

She didn't see any maids about the second room. But then, she didn't really need one. Scissors, thread, and a bristling pincushion were prominently displayed upon a table. The women in the alcove were too occupied by their conversation to notice her; she certainly wouldn't be disturbing them. Perhaps they'd thought she was a servant — as, of course (she tried to remind herself), a governess really was.

The long rip in the front of her gown went from hem to a few inches below the knee. She could reach it well enough, and she'd be able to sew a straight seam even with her thoughts so full of the sound of his voice — *come back* — while her body was so beguiled by a delicious sort of buzzing beneath her skin.

Come back, come back. It wasn't her best seam or her fastest, but she'd managed nonetheless to tie off the stitching and snip the thread. She'd been just about to take herself back to the garden when she heard the only words that could have penetrated the idiotic haze of happiness she'd been moving about in.

Sir Anthony . . . The words came from the alcove. The shorter lady, perhaps. *Proposal of marriage . . . I'm ready to go downstairs and give him my answer.* The voice wasn't familiar; nor was the heavily painted face below the black Egyptian wig.

But the answer, when it came, came in an unmistakable accent. *You're really sure about that, Isobel?* Helen knew exactly who was speaking, even if she couldn't recognize her. The towering heroine in her elaborate headdress — Queen Boadicea, Helen supposed — was clearly and unmistakably Miss Edith Amory.

Cleopatra must be Lady Isobel Wyatt. *Yes, absolutely sure, dear Edith, and absolutely happy — I'm happy for the first time in my life, I think.*

Helen hadn't known they were friends. But then, why should she? How could she know anything at all about a pair of wealthy young ladies looking for brilliant husbands during the London Season?

Affectionate friends, by the soft, intimate sound of their voices — not competitors after all, no matter what the newspaper gossip said.

How nice for them, she thought dully. How nice to be absolutely sure and happy of something for the first time in one's life. As though there could be any question of one's being absolutely sure and happy, when one had received *his* proposal of marriage.

The dishonest, despicable . . . the bloody lying . . .

But there'd be time — there'd be all her life — to curse him later. What was needed now was to exit as unobtrusively as she'd entered and leave the house before there was any chance of seeing him again.

Astonishing that the footman was able to find her cloak. Perhaps it was because she'd told him the velvet was a little bit frayed about the hem — it must be the only frayed velvet cloak here, she'd thought. And the only one with pockets, for she always sewed pockets into the things she made — why shouldn't women have pockets, anyway? She'd wrapped some coins in a handkerchief this evening before leaving Charlotte Street. She'd tucked them into the pocket: she'd thought she might give them to some servant who helped her, because why shouldn't even a governess do the proper thing?

But instead, of course, she'd had to use the coins for a cab. There wasn't any point even looking for Mr. Hedges. Even if there weren't a Lady Gorham she'd never have found him in this mad crush of people. In any case she'd had no choice but to accept her cloak with its frayed bottom along with the footman's sneer when it became clear to him that he wasn't getting anything in return.

It hadn't been easy to find a cab. Rather belatedly it occurred to her now that she might have put herself in danger by throwing herself in the path of one as she finally had. But she was glad of it nonetheless.

For suppose she'd returned to the house in Bloomsbury a little bit later. Or if the good burglar (as Sydney insisted upon calling him) hadn't been able to talk sense to his reckless colleague.

For the first time since she'd alit from the cab at Charlotte Street, Helen found herself in danger of weeping along with Sydney. Probably it was a sudden overflow of responsibility — a realization that there were too many things to be distressed about, and she couldn't decide which to focus her energies upon. Staring helplessly about her, she probably would have collapsed in tears if Mr. Hedges had not mercifully chosen that moment to show himself at the kitchen door.

His fine new coat had become as rumpled as any of his others; his cravat could hardly be said to be tied at all.

And his face? Odd, the times the family resemblance chose to manifest itself. The expression on his face was strangely familiar. Guilt, she expected — a gentleman out on the town. Guilt had etched the same somber lines on his face as she'd seen on Anthony's earlier tonight.

"Robert has told me what transpired," he said quietly, his voice, his eyes directed to everyone and no one in particular, "and I've taken a quick look around the study. But we won't discuss it further until after we get this child to bed."

For an instant he'd felt himself transported back to that sad, livid dawn at Lake Como. Perhaps, Jasper thought, because of how young and small Sydney looked, with her pale, tearstained face, her little bare feet peeking out beneath her white night rail.

Ought he to have confided any of that to Marina? He'd thought it might be a freeing sort of experience. And perhaps it would have been, he thought now, if he hadn't been summoned so abruptly to a home that had been violated — the study window open and exposed to the world. In such a case, having exposed his deepest thoughts didn't seem a freeing thing at all.

Marina was also the only person in London he'd told about the Aphrodite, locked up in the cabinet the burglars had evidently failed to open. But he'd think about that later. At this moment he was wanted for hugging, soothing, bedside sitting, hand-holding, forgiveness.

"Yes, yes, of course I forgive you for being where you shouldn't have been. We'll speak of it when we're calmer; don't even think of it now."

Everything that had been in the safe was still there. The papers on his desk were still in their neat piles and portfolios. The artifacts on the bookshelves were untouched, and the books as well. If you didn't count Marina's novel, *Parrey,* lying open on his desk.

The child had been reading it. Jasper had told Robert to leave it where it was.

"Let's not move everything," he'd said. "I'll try to get a man from Bow Street to look at it tomorrow — well, today — of

338

course, it's today."

At the moment the important thing was that Sydney hear and believe his re-assurances. He'd be at her side while she slept, he told her once again. No, he wouldn't budge from the armchair by her bed — but she should drink this water that he'd just put those little drops into.

"It's laudanum," he said, because he didn't like to lie to her, "just a very little bit. It'll make you sleep, and sleep's the best thing for you now. You need to sleep."

"And if I dream of the burglars? The bad burglar, you know. Not the good one — I shouldn't mind that so much. But the one with the pistol . . ."

"Then you must also dream of how well and soundly protected you are by myself and Miss Hobart. If the bad burglar comes to you in your sleep, tell him to speak to one of us, because we'll be in your dream with you.

"Or," Jasper continued, "if the blackguard prefers, he'll have to deal with our ship's captain, or the general of our army — just let him try tussling with one of *them.* Though by *then,* you know, we would prob-ably have . . . sailed far . . . far . . . away."

Slowing his voice, he gestured with his chin at the tapestry hanging on the wall fac-

ing her bed. An ancient thing, a bit threadbare and moth-eaten, of a crusade setting
sail to Jerusalem. It had hung for centuries
in the entryway at Wheldon Priory. But
Sydney'd loved its pictures, and so he'd had
it moved to her nursery, and thence to her
bedchamber, in Essex and now here.

Over the years he and she had made up
stories about all the quaint characters
worked into the picture — soldiers, sailors,
musicians playing in celebration of the
expedition getting under way, a lady waving
her handkerchief from a tower. There'd
been a time when telling, repeating, and
embellishing those stories was the only way
to get her to go to sleep.

He took a breath in preparation for mus-
tering the army of imaginary protectors.

Sydney gave a lopsided, slightly nostalgic
smile. "But I'd rather have Anthony protecting me."

"You're quite right," Jasper whispered.

"Anthony" — her voice had become very
slow — "on board the ship with us . . . in
his white . . . tassels."

The laudanum had taken hold. Her long
eyelashes fluttered; the lids trembled and
dropped shut. Jasper turned to smile at Miss
Hobart, who'd been pothering about the
room, but she was engaged — folding the

child's clothing, straightening the articles on the dresser or some other useful thing — and didn't return his glance.

She must be as exhausted as he was. Odd, with the air so warm, that she'd kept her angular frame so tightly swathed in her cloak; perhaps she'd felt the same chill he had at the thought of the danger that had threatened them. Her hair was in disarray, the Grecian knot at her nape undone, a few reddish curls straggling down the dark velvet. Red-gold, rather pretty: He'd never noticed. But the wide mouth that had been so vivacious during the dance looked mournful and dry.

"Mr. Hedges."

"Go to bed, Miss Hobart," he said. "You'll drop of exhaustion in another moment. We all will. The sun is coming up. I'll go to Bow Street tomorrow. If you think of anything else you observed, be sure to tell me in the morning."

She nodded and turned to go.

"Oh, and Miss Hobart."

"Mr. Hedges?"

"Thank you for your tact tonight, and your sound judgment in sending Robert to come and fetch me as you did."

Her face, with its too-prominent cheek-bones, was paler and dryer than ever, her expression blank except for what seemed to be a heavy sadness in her eyes. She must be embarrassed to have been drawn into his affairs. Or simply terrified by the very close thing it had been.

A pity her evening had been spoiled like this. He remembered how surprisingly attractive, how agreeable she'd looked dancing with Anthony. She nodded once more and was gone.

Sydney was fast asleep. She wouldn't wake for some time, Jasper told himself. He could leave if he chose. In a few minutes, he told himself.

Perhaps he'd drowsed. A sooty pink sky showed around the edge of the dimity curtains. An urban sky, he thought, a dangerous sky. He didn't usually think of London — or anywhere in England, for that matter — as dangerous. Nor had he thought it dangerous to store the valuable sculpture here. *Damn.*

Tonight he wasn't so sure what he thought of anything. Tonight — and how very odd, too, that she'd been reading Marina's novel — tonight it was as though a great many things that had been neatly separated were now abruptly jumbled together.

As though the back side of a tapestry — the tangled, not so pretty loops, knots, and hidden connections — had suddenly offered a look at itself.

Odd, uncanny, unsettling, perhaps — for he didn't want to admit to *frightening* — to feel that a boundary had been breeched, though whether of a household or the secrets a household was founded on, Jasper couldn't say.

CHAPTER 19

But there wasn't time the next morning to be afraid. Mortifying enough, rather, to run the gauntlet of the servants' knowing looks at breakfast and on his way out the front door. He'd scrawled a note to Marina, but sent it with a little errand boy from the streets rather than his footman. Silly, perhaps, but his affairs had been exposed to quite enough scrutiny already.

An irony, then, that he, who hated people prying into his affairs, had to bear the slings and arrows of complete inattention at the magistrate's office. For no one here had any interest whatsoever in the burglary that had been attempted against his home and property. The clerk at the desk could barely be bothered. There was other business this morning; Mr. Hedges would have to wait to speak to someone about his case.

Angrily, Jasper took his place on a hard bench against the back wall. A man had evidently smothered to death in his office in the City — chimney plugged up, fumes, something like that. A pity, of course, but why was such a routine occurrence getting so much attention, the magistrate's office full of men bustling about in a hubbub of self-important confusion? Everyone except himself and a few unfortunates who'd been pulled in for petty crimes seemed to be having an entertaining, engaging morning. Doubtless none of them had a terrified child at home, a burglar with a gun who'd promised to return.

Still, Sydney had been feeling better when he'd left her. She was much less afraid in the daylight, and willing to stay with a languid, exhausted Miss Hobart; it was the governess who seemed to need to go back to sleep. But they'd be all right for a while; Miss Hobart would manage, as always.

At least until tonight — for Sydney had asked, in a small voice, whether Uncle might be going out. So much for seeing Marina.

Of course he wouldn't be going out, he'd said stoutly. He'd be guarding the place (if he ever got back there).

A rough-looking man sat down next to him on the bench. Jasper thought to ask him why he was there, thought better of it, and offered the fellow a cheroot.

"Thanks, guv'nor," the man said, and proceeded to tell what he knew about the smothered man in the city, who it seemed had been rather a broker in information. "Bought and sold people's secrets, 'e did. Had business with everybody but Bow Street. They tried to avail theirselves of 'is services once or twice, but 'e refused flat out. Couldn't afford the risk to 'is credibility, see."

Jasper nodded. A terrible thing to deal in secrets, he thought, but interesting to hear about as a way of passing the time.

A vendor from a local public house came by, and Jasper's neighbor sniffed the air appreciatively. Jasper stood him to a meat pie, after which the man allowed that, "they'll probably come 'round to accepting the story that 'e died of a blocked-up chimney and shut the investigation right down. Well, maybe 'e did. But who can say, when a man 'as as many enemies as Rackham, and lots of 'em among the *ton?*

"Still," the man concluded, licking off his suety lips, "I wouldn't expect 'em to get to your case today."

Which was bloody annoying. And then bloody gratifying to prove the fellow wrong when a detective came by some twenty minutes later to announce that he could talk to Mr. Hedges now.

Jasper followed the small, unimpressive detective into a small, unimpressive office — to be told that the man didn't care a whit about his attempted burglary.

"Well, yes, it must've been a shock for the child, but then, you didn't lose any property. Frightfully sorry, Mr. Hedges, but I need to speak to you about something else."

For surely Mr. Hedges knew that his name had been in Mr. Gerrald Rackham's memorandum book.

"Uncle?"

It was ten thirty the next morning. After the disagreeable spell at the magistrate's office — no help there, just more complications — Jasper had gone straight to Anthony's lodgings. But as the boy was out somewhere he'd left a message, asking him to come by Charlotte Street as soon as he could.

Which seemed to be now, for Anthony clearly hadn't been to bed last night.

Drinking? Gambling? Celebrating a betrothal? Wasn't there supposed to be something about a courtship?

Anthony, it seemed, wasn't about to volunteer any useful information about where he'd been since the ball. "I gave the

Albanian costume to the footman, Uncle Jasper. He said he'd have it cleaned and packed away."

"Ah, yes, thanks." For a moment Jasper couldn't think how to begin. Anthony looked increasingly suspicious. Tired, too. His hair was wet, as it had been that day at Eton. He must have only just returned home from wherever he'd been all night, read the letter, taken a cold plunge. He wasn't even dressed with his usual meticulousness. Bless him, he'd taken the seriousness of Jasper's message and hurried over here directly.

Which called for equal directness, then, on Jasper's part. "I need your help, Anthony."

"I . . . beg your pardon, Uncle Jasper?"

"Sit down; I'll tell you about it."

The statue. The attempted burglary. The robber's pointing a pistol at Sydney (Anthony's jaw had worked). The man's promise to return. The lack of assistance from Bow Street.

Everything except the bit the Bow Street detective had told Jasper, about his name — and Marina's — being in Rackham's memorandum book.

Well, Anthony didn't have to know that part.

But by this point they were no longer sitting. Matching their strides, they paced the length of the study, trying to imagine what the burglar had been thinking, how he might have approached the cabinet, tried to open the excellent lock.

"A lovely statue," Anthony murmured.

"Yes, I was damned lucky it was available just when I could afford it."

"After you'd finally paid off those mortgages."

Jasper stared.

"I visited Smythe, the solicitor, you see."

"Ah."

"Don't blame him, Uncle. I needed to be told about the mortgages, the money still owing for the roof. I was thinking of borrowing against the property, you see, but I . . . I didn't. Still, I wish you'd told me more about what bad shape the estate was in for a while."

My responsibility to keep your affairs in order. A man wants to do something for his son, even if he finds himself short of blunt, even if all these years he hasn't known quite how, and most times has made a botch of it. . . .

The problem being that the son had evidently rather needed to feel his own responsibilities to his property. Another

349

botch . . .

"You're quite right. I'm most awfully sorry." Had he ever said *that* before? Odd, it wasn't very difficult to shape the words. Of either sentence.

"Oh. Well. Thanks." They exchanged embarrassed nods.

"I'm told they've done rather a good job." When Jasper continued speaking, his voice was a bit halting. "With the roof, I mean. Excellent tiles and so forth. You'll see what you think when you go inspect the property." He spoke briskly now, confidently; he had to. "Tomorrow. When you take Sydney home. Because I don't want her anywhere around here if the burglar returns."

"No, of course not."

"And I don't want the burglar to think you're taking the sculpture back to Wheldon Priory with you."

Anthony laughed. "No difficulty there. One couldn't think I was carrying anything except myself and Sydney. The phaeton's so small and light, anybody can see there's no room for anything but its passengers."

"But you'll need something small and light with room for three. Sydney's frightened and agitated enough; I don't want her separated from Miss Hobart. Might you be able to borrow something?"

■ ■ ■ ■

Miss Hobart. *Oh, Lord.* Anthony couldn't quite believe that he'd just pledged himself to spending a long day in a small light carriage with the person in the world he least wanted to face, let alone speak to.

Could I tell Uncle Jasper what happened with Miss Hobart? Could he possibly understand?

Astonishing that he was even considering it. An image flashed by his inner eye of Uncle Jasper dancing with Lady Gorham — followed too soon by a parallel and painful image of himself dancing with Miss Hobart. He gazed at his uncle for a moment. The poor fellow hadn't gotten much sleep these past nights. Standing watch over Sydney and the Aphrodite, no doubt. This wasn't the time to tell him about his awful, caddish mess-up with Helen Hobart.

And anyway, what would be the use?

Besides, Anthony chided himself, hadn't he just informed his uncle he wanted responsibility?

All right, then. He was being handed the responsibility for bringing his beloved little sister and her governess safely home to Wheldon Priory, and he would do exactly that. He was good with horses and carriages and his fists, and not a bad shot either. He'd fight burglars, footpads, lions if they should encounter them along the road to Essex. . . .

Forget about lions. The important thing was to get a decent carriage. Because if there was anything he knew about (besides, of course, the endlessly absorbing affair of waistcoats), it was carriages — who drove what, how much each conveyance cost, who might be willing to buy, sell, trade. . . .

"You *can* procure another vehicle?"

In truth, there *did* exist a small curricle — not the best of its sort, but Anthony thought it would serve. Complicated story — debts, rivalries: No point troubling Uncle Jasper with the details. In any case, he thought he could get the carriage. Particularly since he'd managed to win a little last night, pull himself back from the brink of serious fiduciary trouble, at least for the present. He'd been lucky these past thirty-six hours. Desperate, determined not to have to borrow against his estate, but mostly lucky — because Lord knew he wasn't really very good at hazard.

The funny thing was, he wasn't even sure he enjoyed gambling all that much, though he hadn't really considered that until he'd been talking with Helen . . . with Miss

Hobart (*damn!*) out in Lord Withers's gardens. He'd thought he'd enjoyed playing and posing and drinking and larking. What else was he good at, anyway, besides being known and admired?

But really, what *was* the point of acting as a sort of brand mark for someone's gaming establishment? Perhaps if you read your name in the newspapers often enough, you came to think that someone must know what you were like, even if you didn't.

Since that walk in the garden, he'd been coming to wonder if he enjoyed being in the public eye any more than Uncle Jasper did. Quite a surprise, that.

"Anthony, have you been hearing what I've been telling you?"

Lord, how long had he been noodling over his own stupid affairs?

With a start, he turned to his uncle. Poor fellow, he looked pale and strained. A little older. Silly to have imagined that there could have been anything between him and Marina.

"Yes, another vehicle." He said it as firmly as he could. "You can depend on me. Tell . . . tell Miss Hobart to have herself and Sydney ready tomorrow morning at eight."

That was good. He turned to go and then

stopped, his head swiveled over his shoulder. "Oh, and Uncle Jasper," he heard himself saying — though he hadn't intended to.

"Yes, Anthony?"

"Lady Isobel Wyatt refused my proposal of marriage."

"Oh. I *am* sorry."

"Don't be, sir. She was wiser than I. I was lucky, I think, that she refused me. We shouldn't have been happy. I think she loves someone else. There must have been something about the way she phrased her refusal. And I . . ." He shrugged. "Well, I thought I should tell you, anyway."

"Yes, thank you — I'm glad. Well, I'm sorry." Jasper shrugged uncomfortably. "Hell, you know what I mean. I'm . . . Yes, well, you have my gratitude for helping, you know. And my confidence," he added quickly, rather mumbling the last three syllables, but it seemed to him that Anthony had heard them well enough.

They'd shaken hands on it. Anthony had hurried out, exclaiming that he must see about the curricle, glancing in the mirror on his way with an exaggerated shudder of horror at his unkempt appearance.

Jasper supposed that in certain exclusive Corinthian circles one probably couldn't manage a business proposition involving carriages unless one looked one's best.

He should go tell Miss Hobart about the plan to move her and Sydney to Essex. It would be a relief to get them out of harm's way, to concentrate his attention upon the threat at hand. As much of a relief as it had been to learn that, after all, the boy wouldn't be making a cynical marriage.

His mouth twisted at the thought of cynical marriages — and of cynical erotic affairs as well. Of gossip and puffery, of secrets and frightening entanglements. Of the need to feel his family safe and secure — and his fear (remembering what they'd told him at Bow Street) that he may have already compromised it.

CHAPTER 20

When Jasper had hurried off with his footman — it was two nights ago now — Marina'd told her maid they wouldn't be leaving for Calais in the morning after all.

A pity, she'd thought, that the coachman would have to wake up so early, just to bring the horses back to the stable.

A greater pity for herself and any friends of hers — if a public personage like Lady Gorham actually did have friends. She'd supposed she'd find out the answer to that question in the next few days, when the scandal broke, after she hadn't shown up to deliver her "payment" to Rackham.

No matter. She could bear the cuts and sniggers and giggles for a few days. The important thing was not to leave London until she was certain that the burglar hadn't caused any harm to Jasper's niece or the rest of his household.

Though as to what *Jasper* would think of

Rackham's revelations about her . . . well, there she tried not to cherish any illusions. Perhaps she should have insisted upon telling him herself, after the Witherses' ball. But the sad truth was that she hadn't done so because she'd wanted the memory of that last night together to be perfect.

Interrupted by his house being broken into — it hadn't been perfect at all, of course. Still, that was what she'd wanted.

She'd thought herself a great realist. But in the next days, she'd discovered just how many impossible things she *could* want, after all.

While as for what Rackham would have revealed about her . . . In the week before the ball she'd written it all out to post to Jasper when she left for Calais. It had been interesting finally to put into words all the things she'd kept so silent about for so long. Except she hadn't really been keeping entirely silent, had she? Those little sketches about Ireland she'd been writing and then tearing up — when a story wanted to be told, it seemed there was no stopping it.

After Jasper had left her house, she'd put a few drops of laudanum into a glass of water, hoping she'd gotten the dose right; it wasn't something she used very often. Because it would be best to get as much sleep as she could. A day of waiting around for news from Jasper — and then of waiting for scandal to break about her — would be considerably more taxing than a voyage across the channel.

Evidently she hadn't gotten the dose quite right, though, because as she swam back to consciousness her eyes hurt. Brilliant morning sunlight was streaming around the edges of the curtains.

Her maid was shaking her awake — astonished, apologetic, a bit frightened. "My lady, please, my lady." Lady Gorham never woke this late in the morning. "Beg pardon, my lady, are you ill?"

She rubbed her eyes, which felt better. "No, not at all, Molly. I'm quite well." A little bit woozy, but it was really rather pleasant to have gotten more than a few hours of sleep. "What time is it?"

"Half past eight, my lady. Near a quarter to nine."

"How singular. Well, no great harm done. You told everyone we're not leaving today, didn't you?"

"Yes, my lady."

"Good. Ah, well, do you know, Molly, that since I've missed a morning's writing, I believe I'll have an egg for breakfast. Toast. Butter."

"Yes, my lady, but —"

"I know that's rather unusual, but it will be an unusual day, and —"

"My lady?"

"Yes, Molly?"

"Begging your pardon, Lady Gorham, but your solicitor is waiting for you downstairs."

Very singular indeed. She drew on a cap and morning gown and hurried down to her sitting room.

"I hadn't thought I'd be able to stop you from leaving, Lady Gorham." Mr. Williams, the solicitor, rose as she entered.

"But as you see, I've postponed the journey for a few days. A friend . . . might need my assistance in a certain matter. I decided I could wait. But why did *you* care to stop me?"

He stared. "So you haven't read the newspapers yet?"

"I never do until I've done my morning's writing. Why?"

"Well, then you ought to read this."

He handed her the folded newspaper, and she read the short, lurid account quickly before sinking down onto the sofa to tease out what facts were to be found amid the dark innuendo: rumors of the dead man's highly placed enemies, hints that one of them might have hired someone to stop up the chimney. Bow Street, the reporter said, hadn't yet decided whether it was a case of murder or accident.

She raised her eyes. "And *you* knew to come to me," she said to Mr. Williams. "Well, obviously you knew. . . ."

"From all those years of bank drafts, Lady Gorham. Not that I would ever suppose you might have —"

"Paid someone to stop up Mr. Rackham's chimney, Mr. Williams?" She shook her head. "I hated the man, but quite honestly, Mr. Williams, I haven't that sort of imagination." She laughed a little bit wildly. "My imagination, Mr. Williams, tends more to ballrooms and table settings."

"I shouldn't have thought otherwise, my lady, but . . ."

"But it wouldn't have looked so good, would it," she murmured, "to Bow Street, to the polite world, or to London in general, if I'd have left this morning in a tearing hurry."

"No, Lady Gorham."

"Well, you were very good to have come, Mr. Williams, and I'm very grateful — though as you can see, a little too overwhelmed by this news to know exactly how to respond to it."

And so he took his leave of her, after commenting that Bow Street would most likely call it an accident in any event.

How to respond to the news. Well, how *should* she respond to it?

For the next two days, the question tolled like a bell in her ears while the answers multiplied, fragmented.

She should respond to it delightedly: How wonderful to be free of Rackham at last. And without him, who knew what might be possible for her?

Guiltily — for he might have been an evil little toad, but she couldn't help wishing her safety and comfort hadn't come at the cost of his death.

Impatiently — because the only communication she'd received from Jasper was a brief little note written the morning after the attempted burglary. And all it had said was that although nothing had been stolen and no one hurt, things were in some confusion at his home. He'd be going to try to get some help from Bow Street, and he wouldn't be able to see her for a day at least.

Very impatiently indeed — when two days later she still hadn't heard anything further from him.

Trying to put her feelings in order, she paced her rooms in a sort of dream, responding to the news in every possible way in turn and sometimes every way at once.

She was *free,* she told herself. No need to post her letter to Jasper after all — she'd tell him everything there was to tell when next she saw him. For surely he . . . cared enough about her, as she really was, to listen, to understand. She should toss the letter into the fire. But somehow she didn't.

Somehow, instead, she scrawled out another letter. This one wasn't to Jasper: She wrote it in white heat; sealed it before she could stop herself; posted it before the confusion, unbelief, vertigo set in.

Perhaps this reeling, buzzing confusion was what freedom actually felt like.

Well, how could she know? How long since she'd lived without "protection" of some sort, be it from Captain Sprague, Harry Wyatt, or a nasty little toad of an extortioner like Rackham?

Was all of that really finished? Could she simply *live* now?

Simply. Live. Pull a thread from a carefully woven pattern and the pattern threatened to fray into mystery. Sturdy, everyday words like *simply* and *live* began to buzz, shimmer, fragment into multiple meanings.

New clothes might put a stop to all these useless meditations, she decided. A complete ensemble, beginning with a recently purchased corset set with iron grommets for the laces (if anyone required further proof that waists would be getting tighter still). She drew in her breath and bade her maid do her worst. Compared to the riotous anarchy of her feelings these past few days, constraint was simple and comforting.

The chintz gown her maid drew over her head was printed with roses, raspberries, twining green vines. Pretty. Lighthearted. Like summer. Well, it *was* nearly summer. She should ask the cook if there were strawberries in the market yet; the apples she ate in the mornings were growing mealy. She wanted strawberries instead, with clotted yellow Devonshire cream.

She wanted Jasper to tell her she was beautiful in her new print gown and beautiful without it. And then she wanted him to say . . .

But there she was, wanting the impossible again. And the truly awful thing about a little freedom was that suddenly it made you unable to distinguish between what was impossible and what might be possible after all.

A footman knocked on the door of her bedchamber just then, to announce that Mr. Hedges was downstairs to see her.

But Jasper never came here in the daytime.

Nor had he looked so angry since their first night together, when she'd made the mistake of asking about matters he wanted to keep private.

Of course. He'd been to Bow Street. She didn't know exactly what he knew or how he knew it, but she could tell by looking at him that he knew something about Rackham and herself.

She motioned him to sit by her on the sofa. He sat as far away from her as possible, the space between their bodies an impassable gulf.

And all the wild little hopes she'd pretended not to be cherishing began to shrivel as though burned by a night of sudden frost.

She could read it in his face. Not everyone would, she thought. You had to have an eye for how his jaw trembled when he was angry, the way he tried to keep himself from gnawing at his lip. Not everybody would know how to interpret those signals.

"Well," he said, "I haven't gotten much help from the magistrates about my burglary. But I have found out a few things about a certain extortioner."

Spoken contemptuously, coldly, and distantly. His eyes flickering, hands gripping his knees.

She could only be thankful that she hadn't *really* allowed herself to hope.

She suddenly felt very weary, even cross with herself. How stupid, she thought, to have fallen in love with a man while watching him tie a little girl's hair ribbon.

Or had it been the spread of his shoulders when he'd put his hands in the pockets of his rumpled coat?

Perhaps the keen gaze of his eyes through the glitter of his spectacles. Other things too, of course. Thoughts, ideas, flashes of wit, and one need hardly mention the love-making. But, yes, it had been the way he'd looked at her, made her feel some very deep sense of herself. Her selves, perhaps — Maria, Marina — she was seized by a vision of a procession, as though on a marble frieze, of the girls and women she'd made of herself as she'd made her way through a complicated, cruel, dangerous, and (for all that) still beautiful world.

In any case, the damage was done. By making her love him, he'd taught her who she was and what she wanted.

The frightening question was whether he could bear to know it as well.

The answer didn't seem likely to be yes.

She felt something go hard within her. Felt it, heard it: the dull, hollow echo of a gate slamming shut.

Nonsense. She'd heard nothing and she'd say nothing. For what, really, could one say of the foolish fancies she'd been entertaining?

See, the fancies were gone already. She felt nothing at all.

The Season had simply ended a bit earlier than she'd hoped. What was important was that her dignity remained intact. No reason whatsoever why she and Jasper couldn't be civilized about this.

And anyway, she should be grateful to him for having taught her to use language more correctly. Always an important thing if you weren't really a native speaker of the conqueror's English. *Fuck:* Well, she'd certainly learned *that,* in all its varieties.

While as for *love:* Perhaps this experience might help her simulate the emotion more usefully in the future.

"The important thing," he said, "was to ensure the safety of my niece."

"Of course," she said.

"I sent her home to Wheldon Priory. Anthony is driving her and Miss Hobart there this morning, in an uncharacteristically shabby curricle." He laughed rather dryly. "I was surprised he'd allow himself to be seen in it, but he told me it was the best he could get on short notice, and he knew I wanted them away from London as soon as possible. Oh, and you might want to know he's not marrying Lady Isobel. Well, she refused him, actually, but he's not sorry; he said they wouldn't have been happy together, and I think he meant that, that he was beginning to think how to tell the difference."

The calm in his voice felt like a dare, Marina thought, a challenge to respond in kind.

All right, then. "I'm glad of that," she said. "There will be plenty of time for him to find someone to make him happy. Perhaps he'll find a satisfactory way to work out his affairs after all."

While as for us . . . ? The question hovered, unasked and unanswered, in the air above their heads.

"Yes, well," he said uncomfortably — as though someone *had* asked the question.

His eyes had grown suspicious. Uncomfortable, ashamed of himself, she thought, and yet unable to stop.

"They told me at Bow Street," he said, "that my name was in Rackham's memorandum book. New memorandum book, not too many pages filled in. They couldn't find any others of them among his property."

"He probably burned them," she said, "after he transferred the information into his coded ledgers."

He shrugged. "The singular thing was that my name was on a certain page, and so was yours. Oh, and a few other words. *Statue, lock and key.* And a great many question marks."

It seemed he didn't expect a response. "This morning," he said, "Bow Street officially proclaimed his death an accident. Not that the man didn't have enemies — well, *you* know that — but there's no real case. Which is good news for me, anyway, because my detective is now free to help me find out what sort of vicious animal tried to rob my house."

He stopped here. "Because the man who entered my house was armed with a pistol, Marina, and he pointed it at my niece."

She breathed a long, soft *oh.*

He averted his eyes. "So there'll be no investigation from Bow Street, but I'm afraid, Lady Gorham, that I'm going to have to ask you why your name and mine are on the same page of Mr. Rackham's little book. Very few people knew about the statue locked up in my house, but you did. And so I have to ask you . . ."

". . . whether I betrayed you to Rackham?"

Her voice was very low. "Is that what you want to know? Or are you more interested in what Rackham would have betrayed about me, had he lived?"

"You needn't tell me about yourself," he said with a shrug. "It's not what I came to hear." But he winced there, and a hint of a flush spread beneath his sunburned cheeks. She could see that he did care, and she found herself glad of it, and even of his anger. Even if it was only erotic possessiveness on his part that made him care, some stupid, competitive, masculine species of pride. *Mine.*

Hardly yours, darling, she thought. *Not when you're so angry, so disapproving, so very toplofty, and yet so aroused by what you want and also fear.*

"I won't tell you about myself," she said, "because I've already written it out for you, in detail. You can take the paper with you when you leave, which I'm sure will be very soon.

"But as for how you and I got into Rackham's notebook — it may be humiliating to you, but in truth it's probably not very interesting. I should imagine he followed you home from my house one evening, something like that. He knew how to find out all sorts of things. He had sources everywhere — he'd boast about that when I visited him in his office to pay him off every month."

He winced. She could see that he was remembering the day he'd come upon her carriage, stuck in that narrow street, that unlikely neighborhood — *bit of the middle of nowhere,* he'd said. He'd been right about that, and right as well that *nowhere* could *connect to a thousand somewheres.*

She made her voice cold, expressionless. "He hardly needed to learn about you from *me.* What he needed — or wanted — was the spectacle of me betraying you to him. Because yes, there was something he did wish to know about you. Now I wish I'd asked what it was, though only to satisfy your curiosity. Probably it was something about the lock and key to the cabinet in your study. But I didn't ask; I didn't care. There was no way in the world that I would have told him anything about you. A pity you don't know that already. I should have wanted you to *know* that."

He winced again and she continued on.

"I think it would have given Rackham pleasure, great pleasure, if I'd betrayed you to him — perhaps more pleasure than if I'd betrayed myself, which he also wanted."

He gasped a little bit there — though he

bit it back immediately. She had to own that she found the sound oddly satisfying — damn him anyway for suspecting her of betrayal! — even as she marveled that they could be speaking so coldly, so hurtfully.

It was all so needless. Why was trust suddenly so difficult when joy and pleasure had been so effortless?

Sadly, she knew the answer. It was because Jasper and she had both been used — had been betrayed — before, when they'd been young. And nothing was more terrifying to someone who'd been hurt, as each of them had been, than the possibility of being hurt again by someone you knew had the possibility of making you feel . . . as they had made each other feel in their midnights together.

She remembered the bitterness in his voice when he'd told her about Anthony's mother. *I expect it was rather a game for her to seduce me.* Her own experience was different (he could read about it at his leisure), but it had left the same bitter taste.

You built a life around that bitterness. And if, in the course of living your life, it came that you had something to protect — a child, a level of celebrity — you became hard and vicious and ruthless in your effort to protect it, because it was the only thing you *could* do, it being impossible to protect, to recapture, your lost innocence.

She took a folded paper from where it had been tucked into her sleeve.

"It's the story about me," she said, "that Rackham was threatening to tell all of London. You can read it or not, as you like, and whenever you like," she added, "but now you'd better go, because it's late."

Which, of course, it wasn't at all. It was the bright afternoon of a lovely day in June.

But he took it and bowed and turned and was quickly gone. Because even if she hadn't been able to get herself to say it correctly (and she a writer, too), he still knew exactly what she meant.

That it wasn't late. It was simply too late for the two of them.

CHAPTER 21

At least, Sir Anthony thought, they'd gotten off pretty promptly this morning. And as it wouldn't be getting dark until nine or so, perhaps they could get all the way home to Wheldon Priory tonight and not have to stop at an inn.

Anyway, he hoped so, because the possibility of stopping made him distinctly anxious. For the last hour at least, he'd found himself imagining confusions, embarrassments, the unlikeliest of farcical scenarios — an innkeeper mistaking him and Miss Hobart for a married couple, to take one preposterous example.

The most perfect nonsense.

He need only explain that his party required two bedchambers: one for the baronet and the other for the baronet's sister and her governess to share. No question who'd be sharing a room, and there'd be no mistaking anybody's relationship to anybody either. Particularly since today — he sneaked a quick look at her — Miss Hobart had contrived to look the very caricature of a governess, in a long cloak of some limp gray stuff, all creases and travel dust, and buttoned so tight up her neck it threatened to swallow up the big, stiff, awkward bow beneath her chin.

With the deep, dreadful, barrel-shaped affair of a bonnet she'd chosen to wear, you wouldn't know how nice her hair was, or — for that matter — if she had any hair on her head at all.

He wouldn't have known before today. But, then, he'd been too stupid even to look at her, all the many times he could have done so at his ease — the many, many times he'd encountered her indoors, without a cloak or bonnet between them. He'd never taken the slightest notice of the color of her hair, the slope of her neck, the delicate, touchingly valiant set of her shoulders. Not until he'd caught sight of her in rippling muslin, standing half in shadow, half in candlelight, at the edge of a ballroom.

All his fault then, and all the more ridiculous that today he could barely get those images out of his mind — most particularly, it seemed, the knot of curls at her nape. Nor could he quite decide what color those curls were — red or gold or something else entirely. All of which was every bit as ridiculous as his stupid imaginings about stopping at an inn, quite as if the real hazards of travel — the bad food and musty bedsheets — weren't plaguing enough to contemplate.

Bedsheets.

He'd begun getting his thoughts tangled up in bedsheets a few hours back, when Sydney had taken a turn sitting up here next to him and Miss Hobart had retreated to the curricle's little backseat. Sydney'd been telling him how, on a certain trip to Bath, Miss Hobart had persuaded (though *terrorized* might have been a better word) a particularly slatternly innkeeper into taking a hot flatiron to the damp bed linen, until the sheets were suitable for the family to sleep on.

Sydney often liked to natter on about what a marvel of capability and virtue her governess was. And although, over the years, Anthony had tended to retreat into his own thoughts when his sister got on that hobbyhorse of hers, this morning he hadn't. On the contrary, this morning he'd encouraged her, listening avidly, asking for details — particularly about what a comfort Miss Hobart could be when one was ill. Yes, he supposed he could see that — though *he,* of course, had never been ill — and Sydney had been happy to oblige with as many stories as he wanted. For it seemed to please her to make a sort of useful household saint of her governess, if only to assure herself that *she* needn't try to emulate such a superior model of behavior, quite out of reach of human copying.

Superior people seemed to have that use, Anthony reflected. *But no, Syd,* he thought. *You're wrong. She's* not *a saint.*

Nor a goddess, for all that she'd looked like one that night. She's a living, moving, breathing, desiring human being.

Desiring — well, it had seemed so anyway.

Desirable.

Desired. He risked another glance, now that she was back beside him.

Yes. He knew she was there beneath the cloak and bonnet. The person he'd seen. Touched. Kissed. No forgetting her any more than he could ignore the palpable and potentially embarrassing results of his remembering. The fact of the matter was that he was getting his thoughts in a stew of bedsheets and bedchambers because he'd managed to conjure some shadowy, hazy, gauzily draped bedchamber of the imagination with her in its midst, draped in a tangle

— a tumble — of gauzy bedsheets.

Or — now — was she undraped, untangled?

But definitely tumbled.

Nothing to be done about it. One's imagination went where it would; one's body had no choice but to follow. In Anthony's hitherto cheerful experience of these matters, one could keep better control if one faced facts, took it in good-humored stride. He'd simply have to turn his hips a little bit away from her for the remainder of this bouncing, jolting ride home to Wheldon.

Which was turning out a far worse ride than he'd expected. For, as long as he was being honest with himself, he might as well admit that the curricle he'd procured for them was really pretty dreadful. Embarrassing that he hadn't found anything better. His back, his thighs and haunches, would be starting to ache even if she *weren't* here beside him.

When they stopped to change horses (which they'd have to, pretty soon), he hoped he'd be able to get some advice about the vehicle's right wheel, that sort of wobble he was feeling — well, that unevenness, anyway. One probably wouldn't call it a *wobble;* it wasn't really *that* bad. Was it? How long had it been going on, while he'd been attending to his own, um, condition?

But now that she was seated next to him once more, with Sydney in the back, he rather thought he wouldn't mention the wheel to Miss Hobart. Helen, he'd called her, his voice muffled against her neck, his senses clotted with the smell of roses, of laurel, of *her.* Perhaps — he could only hope so, anyway — she hadn't heard him when he'd whispered her name.

They'd barely spoken to each other since setting out this morning. Uncle Jasper had looked pale, solemn, as if he hadn't gotten much sleep. Neither Anthony nor Miss Hobart had wished to burden him any further. Nice, at least, to pretend that there might have been *that* understanding between them.

Anthony had felt himself oddly reassured by the possibility of that small complicity between them, as they'd set out with Sydney in the little backseat and a small basket of sandwiches in Miss Hobart's lap, a clear eight inches of space between the nearest potential point of contact between Anthony's right thigh and Miss Hobart's left. Maybe it would get better, he'd told himself. Maybe he could think of a way to beg her pardon and they'd find a way to be friends.

He'd allowed himself to hope so until

they'd gotten past the Pentonville Road, when she'd asked in an icy voice whether he could stop driving for a moment so that she could exchange places with Sydney — sit in the back, farther away from him.

Well, she hadn't exactly *said* she wished to be farther away from him. Any more than when he'd warned her that she'd be terribly cramped in the little seat, she'd retorted that she'd rather bear the discomfort, the cramps, her feet going all pins and needles, than sit anywhere in proximity to him.

She hadn't had to say any of it. He could feel it radiate from her like mist drifting off an icicle, while she repeated (slowly, patiently, and loudly — as though he were more of an idiot even than Uncle Jasper had thought him) that she wished to exchange seats with Sydney. Whenever Sir Anthony found it convenient: She wouldn't impose her wishes upon him; he might stop whenever he chose — which had, of course, obliged him to stop the horses immediately to effect the change of position.

After which — and it had been most of the day, for it was now well into the afternoon — she'd ridden cooped up in a seat entirely unsuited to her tall figure, refusing to allow him to hand her in or out. When they'd stopped to change horses, she'd levered herself out to hobble about most pathetically. He'd watched helplessly, guiltily, as she'd forced her limping steps to become slow and deliberate, working the cramps out of her feet and legs. The last time she'd sunk down on a low bench, one willowy leg crossed at the knee. Massaging a long, graceful foot with her fingers, she'd quizzed Sydney in a worried voice about where her handkerchief had gone to and when she'd begun sneezing.

And now she was up front again, having effected the rearrangement without a word to him, and not uttering a word since. Surreptitiously, he checked his pocket watch. Almost an hour of perfect, maddening silence. Fifty-eight minutes.

Ah, she'd cleared her throat. As though it pained her to have to speak.

"I came up here from the backseat, Sir Anthony, solely because I wanted to feel that bump in the right wheel from this position. I think something's gone wrong with it. I don't suppose *you* might have noticed."

"Of course I noticed." Need he have snapped at her? He softened his voice. As though in a drawing room, he tried the beginnings of a smile, but she wouldn't have it. "Nothing to worry about," he said. "It's not so bad as it seems. Happens often with

carriages of this sort." He hoped it did —
the truth was he usually rode in better carriages. Not that he was about to tell her
that. He'd messed things up enough already.

They went on in silence for another fifteen
or so minutes until the wheel had not only
gotten bumpier but had begun to make a
sort of grinding sound.

"It *is* that bad," she said. "And you're a
fool as well as the cad you proved to be the
other night." She paused for a moment.
"Fool enough to endanger me and your
sister because you won't admit how bad it
is, or even stop to examine the problem.
There's some sort of mechanical implement
in the backseat where Sydney is, you know."

He didn't know. He hadn't inspected the
vehicle carefully. It had been the only one
he could get on such short notice — its
owner had condescended to let him have it
in exchange for the phaeton, and to forgive
some rather serious gambling debts into the
bargain, so it had seemed a reasonable thing
at the time.

Hardly reasonable, though, if it left them
in a ditch at the side of the road.

She was probably thinking something
similar. He was glad he could barely see her
face within that horror of a bonnet. "I think
we should check the wheel," she said now.

"Can't one tighten things up or something like that?"

Something like that. He should have paid more attention when he'd chatted with the man who took care of his phaeton. The business of springs and axles and how things were bolted together was a fascinating thing but a greasy one — he'd always meant to get beneath the carriage himself, but he'd never been dressed for it. Still, they had had a few interesting conversations — if he could only remember them.

"Was the object you saw a spanner?" he asked.

She shrugged impatiently. "Perhaps it was," she said. "I wouldn't know what such a thing is called. But once my papa's gig had a bad wheel, and I remember that he went to the shed where we kept such things, and he did something with one of those flat iron bars with a sort of notched square hole, like a large eye of a needle, at the end, and the gig seemed to draw a little better after that."

He remembered how easily, out in the Witherses' garden, they'd spoken about ordinary things. He'd liked that about her — it wasn't like flirting or being elegant; it had simply been . . . *talking,* being with someone who had, after all, grown up in

382

the same neighborhood.

Though in rather different circumstances, he reflected, as she now was taking pains to remind him. "Of course, the living my father got from yours wasn't very large, so even as a gentleman and a minister in the Church of England, Papa had to do things for himself, like attend to the wheels of his gig. Unlike a gentleman like *you,* all set to marry a lady with forty thousand . . ."

"It's called a spanner," he said, and stopped the horses.

Because she was right. If not about his marrying forty thousand pounds, then certainly about his being a cad. And more important, at least at this moment, about his being a fool for not stopping before the wheel had begun that hellish grinding.

Though she *might* have told him earlier about the spanner.

They had to wake Sydney, who was sneezing and a bit fractious. "Go back to sleep, dear," Miss Hobart said. "I'm sorry we needed to disturb you; I'm going to wrap this shawl around your throat to keep the breeze away. We'll soon be moving again, though. Sir Anthony has things well in hand."

He expected that even Sydney could hear the mockery in her voice. *Well in hand.*

Lord, she could be annoying, even if he *was,* in fact, a cad, a fool, and what ever else she might call him.

But at the moment the problem was to remember how the man had held the tool, which he *thought* was called a spanner, and how to turn the little screws at the end to make it usable for different size bolts, and which way you needed to twist a bolt to tighten it. He was *pretty* sure those things were called bolts, but perhaps they weren't.

And how to get himself underneath the axle without mucking up his coat and trousers. Not to speak of his boots — and the possibility of the horse kicking him with its back leg. Of course it *would* be the more skittish of the two horses, the one on the right side, closer to the wheel, no doubt as maddened and vexed by the jolting and the grinding noise as any of the curricle's passengers.

"I'll calm the horse," she said, in a voice that had just a touch of drollery about it now. Even if he could hardly see her face, her bonnet seemed to have the effect of a sort of pipe organ, amplifying her amusement at his discomfiture.

Still, she *was* doing an excellent job with the horse. He watched her tapering hands slide over the creature's nose, stroke a velvety ear, her fingers long, slim, and light in the coarse black mane. She made her voice low and melodious while she took off her bonnet to bring her head closer to the gelding's muscular neck.

She could ride; he remembered that now. Odd how you forgot things, only to remember them when it was too late for them to do you any good. He'd seen her riding out to the village once, a long time ago, on a little cob. Not the best of horses — but he could remember the set of her hips, the ease with which she guided the animal.

"Easy, easy, my dear . . ." The sound of her voice called him back to the present, to the sight of her hair, even pulled back so severely over her ears as it was, shining bright against the smooth expanse of chestnut brown.

Red? Gold? Yes, well, he couldn't stand here debating the color while little green-veined white butterflies flitted about in the sunlight.

Though it would have been nice to do so.

Also nice to have a shawl or a blanket — something, anyway — between himself and the dirt of the road. But Sydney was still sniffling. She needed the shawl more than he did. Wincing, he took off his coat, spread it on the ground, unbuttoned his waistcoat, and swung himself beneath the carriage.

Interesting how it all fit together down here. A pity he hadn't gotten beneath the beautiful phaeton while he'd still owned it. He'd have to pay more attention next time he had a good vehicle. But even with this dreadful piece of engineering, and even though he'd pinched his finger with the screw part of the spanner, he was beginning to understand how it worked, how you could fit it around the larger and the smaller bolts. It seemed that they tightened if you turned them in the direction a clock ran; he'd found that out after he'd taken one off by mistake and had to roll about on the ground to find it in a little pile of gravel, trying to ignore the pretty sound of, "Yessss, ooh, what a handsome fellow it is, oh, yes, my biiiig, my handsome . . ."

He had it now. He tightened each in a row along some sort of strip of metal that seemed to have something to do with a spring, until . . .

"One's gone missing. We've lost it."

"What? I can't hear you. Oh, don't mind *him,* my dear, my beauty; we're very well. . . ."

Must she continue that infernal crooning? He pushed himself out from under the clumsy little carriage, tearing the elbow of his shirt in the process.

Her upper lip was a bit moist, her eyes calmer than hitherto. And she'd unbuttoned her cloak. How fragile her rib cage had been against his chest. What a beautiful line her clavicle made.

"We've lost a bolt. Or one of those square things that tightens around it. Or both, I'm not sure. It's my fault."

"Well, it is *that.* We should have stopped long ago. If you hadn't been so intent on proving you knew what you were doing."

"Or if *you* had mentioned we had a *tool* that I might have used to work with."

Tool. As though he hadn't enough problems, he thought, without every word coming out of his lips having a slippery, provocative meaning of its own.

She glared at him. A bit of her hair had come loose about her cheek. Whatever damn color it was.

"And if *you* hadn't insisted on cherishing your resentment of me," he continued, "sitting so silent and superior, brooding on how I'd wronged you, fairly praying that I'd make an ass of myself by getting us into this fix."

He'd be awarded no prizes for logic with *that* one, he thought — not to speak of rhetoric. Not that he'd ever wanted to win a school prize — he'd wanted to be like his papa, not Uncle Jasper, whom the fusty old dons at college still talked about with awe and reverence.

Still, it was true. She *had* been silent and superior; she *had* cherished her resentment of him.

It was true, and he could see that she knew it too.

She shrugged her shoulders. "Well," she said, "can you blame me for wanting to see you make a botch of things? Could anyone blame me?"

"I can't. I am an ass. And a cad too, even if I'm *not* marrying forty thousand pounds."

"I'm sure I don't care *what* you're marrying," she said. "Or whom. What I do care about is that Sydney's safe — and that we get her into bed, because she's sniffling. She's prone to the catarrh, you see, and it won't be good if her ears get blocked up."

"I could go try to find the bit of metal that we lost," he said, "or we can try to continue on without it. For I did tighten all the other ones — and I did remember not to tighten them too hard, because you can shear them off if you do, you see, mess up the threads."

Embarrassing to have called attention to the very little bit of mechanical knowledge

388

he did have. And more embarrassing that he welcomed the brief nod she gave him of something distantly resembling approval.

"Do you think," he asked, "that we should try to go on as we are?"

She nodded again. "Let's try it. For a little bit, anyway; we'll see how much it bumps and whether it's still making that noise. Perhaps it won't be too dreadful."

A breeze picked up the wisp of hair that had curved down the slant of her cheekbone to her wide mouth. You weren't supposed to find such a mouth attractive. Illustrations in the newspapers and the fashion plates in magazines were all of sweet little rosebuds.

The sound wasn't as bad as it had been, and the wobble seemed quite a bit better. He told her that he thought there was an inn in a few miles.

She nodded. "I think so too. And at least Sydney's sleeping. Yes, let's go on as we are."

For he *had* done a good job, she thought rather grudgingly, and the next minutes passed sedately and without incident.

Silently too.

How lovely his hands were on the reins, she thought. How well he managed the horses. How often she'd wished she could be riding next to him as she was now.

Though in her wishing, she'd rather imagined them speaking to each other.

How strange, contrary, and really rather infuriating that the only way they'd known how to speak to each other all day was about a wobbly wheel. The only words that had passed between them had been an argument about whose fault it was that they might be stopped on the road.

He grunted something she couldn't make out and transferred the reins from one hand to the other while he tried to pull some sort of burr out of the sleeve of his coat. It seemed he couldn't manage it. The burr stuck fast.

"Here," she said, "let me take the reins for a moment so you can attend to that."

Again the grunt — incomprehensible, though clearly angry and resentful. How entirely unfair, when it was so obvious she was the injured party. *How dare* he *be angry at* me, Helen thought. And wasn't it absolutely typical of him to act so childishly just because he'd messed up his coat?

Or might it have something to do with what he'd said before? About her resentment?

"I'll take the reins now, thank you."

She handed them back. Must he be so curt, so short-tempered? She'd gotten a lot more response from the horse.

Though perhaps he was right about that much, at least. For probably they shouldn't be speaking to each other at all. Yes, she'd been foolish to let down her guard. The important thing was to get Sydney home, or perhaps even into bed before they got home. Perhaps at the first good inn . . . Well, she'd see when they stopped. Assuming they *got* to an inn before the wheel got worse. Or before they were stopped on their way by a thief too stupid to see that they couldn't possibly have the statue with them.

A bit frightening to imagine being accosted on the highway. And rather exciting that Anthony — *Sir* Anthony, she reminded herself — had put a loaded pistol in a little pocket affixed to the inside of the carriage, near his left boot.

He *was* a good shot. She knew it because the only time these past years that he came to Wheldon was to hunt, both on foot and on horseback. He was a good horseman too; from her upstairs window she'd sometimes watched him galloping up the drive to the front of the house, swinging himself down to the ground, coattails flaring away from his thighs. It had been as thrilling and agonizing to watch him those times as it had been to see him asleep on the riverbank

391

last autumn.

But today was most agonizing of all. Because today — though he doubtless wouldn't believe it — he was handsomer, with his clothes all torn and dusty, than she'd ever seen him. He hadn't bothered putting his hat back on; his hair had bits of stuff in it — pieces of twig, she thought, and something else too. Oh, dear, something was moving. It was really rather sweet, a tiny caterpillar. Too bad, she thought, that she couldn't reach a finger into that forest of bright, waving hair, rescue the bewildered little creature, set it down on a leaf.

He'd probably take offense if she asked permission to do so.

Or perhaps he wouldn't. The cheerful, straightforward young man she'd danced with the other night would have found it amusing.

But *that* young man had been a sham — the one sitting beside her was a liar, a cheat. Except perhaps insofar as today he'd had the wit to point out how she'd been stubborn, resentful — how *she'd* contributed to the fix they were in. And he *had* gotten the carriage moving again, even if neither of them knew for how long it would last. And figured out how to use the *tool* . . .

Troublesome word — she'd encountered

it once in that coarse meaning in her father's library. In a translation of one of Juvenal's *Satires,* a Roman senator's *tool* was held up to ridicule for its length, or the lack of it. She'd blushed, laughed, and never told a soul. Well, whom could she have told? Certainly no one nowadays, when she was bound to act as a model for Sydney. No, not Sydney, she reminded herself. Soon enough it would be a pair of American young ladies in Boston.

Well, the spanner, then, and she *should* have told him about it earlier — he was right about that.

But she was right too — that no one possibly could blame her for being resentful, thoroughly and utterly furious at him for kissing her as he had when he'd proposed marriage to someone else.

And no matter what he might say, "marrying forty thousand pounds" was a perfectly accurate description of his intentions. At least from a rhetorical standpoint — *synecdoche,* taking the part for the whole — "forty thousand" was an excellent way to describe the young woman he'd proposed to. And just because *he'd* probably dozed through that part of his university education, she'd be damned if she'd apologize for her erudition. Damn him for making her feel that she should, for making her feel so plain, so desirous of his beauty, so horribly envious of the girl with forty thousand. . . .

Wait a minute.

Unless he'd meant something else entirely. Unless he'd meant he *wasn't* marrying Lady Isobel.

I'm ready to go downstairs, the young woman had said, *and give him my answer.* But as to what that answer had been . . . ? Still, he *had* proposed. A moral principle was a moral principle. It didn't matter what the earl's sister's answer had been.

Oh, yes, it did matter — she had to admit it to herself. It mattered terribly, and principles would simply have to wait while she thought this out.

She'd better put her bonnet back on, she thought. The wind was picking up; her hair was probably a fright. Besides, with her bonnet shading her face she'd be able to stare at him from its deep recesses without his being able to stare back at her.

Because at the moment she didn't want him to stare back. She wanted to be alone with her thoughts, and with wanting him, with wishing and wondering. If she only had another few weeks in England — for certainly Mr. Hedges would straighten out the business of the statue soon enough and then she'd be off — she was going to look at him for as long as she could, unbearably beautiful with leaves in his hair, dust on his boots, and the dirt of the road on his coat, the tiny caterpillar inching its way down his collar, his shoulder, his sleeve . . . as though to measure the tiniest details of the picture he made. Under blowing clouds, a high, hot afternoon sun moved slowly across the sky. *Move more slowly,* she commanded it. Because if she couldn't have him forever, she'd make *right now* feel like it would never end.

Which was why, she expected, she'd seen the very smallest movement of shadows in the brush during the instant before the horseman burst out upon the road. And why she'd heard the cracking of twigs and perhaps even the horse's snort the same moment — or even the moment before — the highwayman in the bushes had spurred his mount forward.

And why she was able to speak so calmly and clearly. "Anthony. Someone. In the bushes."

Calmly enough not to startle him. He remained alert and quickly handed her the reins. Time *was* passing slowly; it felt possible to accomplish a great deal between each breath you took. They weren't going at much of a pace, and so the horses simply continued their plodding, while he reached in the pocket at the side of the carriage, brought the pistol forward, cocked it, and took aim.

He knocked the man's hat off with the first shot, and got him in the leg, it looked like, with the second, knocking him from his horse. The horse galloped away; the man seemed to be in a ditch. She couldn't see him from where she sat, but he probably still had his pistol — was there anything to stop him from shooting at them? She'd been just about to speed their own horses forward when Anthony had jumped from the carriage to run over to the side of the road.

She heard scuffling, angry shouts. Something about . . . Oh, Lord, he wasn't really trying to find out if their attacker had been after the statue? What did it matter?

He'll be killed. I should have been quicker to whip the horses on.

She stopped the horses, jumped out of the carriage, put her arms around Sydney in the backseat — the child was half-asleep, bewildered, and — *oh, dear* — feverish.

And waited. Probably, she was to think later, she'd waited no longer than ten minutes, though it felt like several hours until he walked back, a pistol in each hand but missing his neckcloth.

"He was after whatever money we have. He doesn't know anything about a sculpture," he said. "I'm really pretty —"

Certain of that, he was going to say, for that was what he did say later, as well as that the leg wound didn't look very bad; the highwayman could probably bandage himself with the neckcloth in a while, and, anyway, when they stopped they could send someone to see to him. But at that moment he didn't have a chance to say anything, because she'd pulled him to her. Knocking her bonnet completely off her head, she'd kissed him so hard as to make the other night's adventure in the shrubbery seemed like child's play.

She sobbed and clutched at him and kissed his face and lips and especially his bare throat. She could feel his pulse against her lips, or perhaps that was just her own fists beating at his chest as she wept that he must never, *never* again run off like such a fool, for the sake of an old marble statue, "just because your uncle cares about it, Anthony; you're a damned fool."

She sobbed that it didn't matter who was at fault for the wheel; didn't he understand that what was important was *him?*

"And that what's important" — this in some raving Fury's voice that was also her

397

own — "is *me.* Even if you're going to marry the rich girl, you simply have — you had — no right to terrify me by risking your life for some stupid lump of stone and going off and leaving me and making me wait so long — do you hear me, Anthony?"

He must have. Because he was kissing her back, and laughing and comforting her and telling her that of course he wasn't going to marry the rich girl, and then he was kissing her again. Which might have gone on a great deal longer if Sydney hadn't sneezed so loudly in the midst of a torrent of aghast, astonished giggles to see them so. And which brought on a new awareness of their responsibilities, and how they'd have to be bringing her to an inn and putting her to bed and calling a doctor before they'd be able either to sort any of this out or to throw themselves at each other again.

But for the meantime — and for perhaps a great deal of time to come — it seemed as though they'd be all right if they simply went on as they were.

CHAPTER 22

The end of June. The Season drawing near its close. Brilliant for some, satisfactory for others, and then there were the unfortunate few — debutantes wearing too-tight smiles on their faces; penniless, rejected younger sons — who'd simply have to wait a year and try again.

At least there were no more debts to be paid to a certain party in an airless office in the City, no more of the nagging fears and anxieties that had plagued so many for so long. And in consequence, fewer unpleasant, unreasonable demands relayed belowstairs — not so many complaints about an overdone roast or a badly decanted bottle of port.

Had Rackham finally made too dangerous an enemy? Or had he simply been a victim of his own meanness, the filth accumulated in pipes and chimney finally choking off his overheated rooms? He'd kept so many secrets about so many other people; perhaps now someone was keeping one about him. Or perhaps the secret was simply that there wasn't one to be known.

Impatient with all this philosophizing, polite London shrugged its well-tailored shoulders and turned back to the business of a Season's pleasure.

A pity, though, that Sir Anthony wasn't to be seen these days. Had himself a run of luck at hazard, it seemed, and paid some debts. The *on-dits* speculated that he'd run off to the country — quite singular, it being well before hunting season. People wondered if the young baronet had gotten his heart broken by the rich young lady who'd also decamped — and quite abruptly too — for a tour of Wales with her friend the American heiress. Others insisted the heart-breaking must have gone the other way, with Sir Anthony withdrawing his attentions and Lady Isobel the one in need of consolation.

But everyone agreed what a perfect shame it was for the Rotten Row suddenly to be missing one of its most decorative fixtures, to be replaced, these long summer afternoons, by a dull gentleman in a bad waistcoat driving that beautiful phaeton through the park.

At least Lady Gorham still adorned the

paths, laughing and lovelier than ever. But even so, one felt a heaviness in the air, of ennui setting in. Fashionable shops, caterers, and confectioners were beginning to let go their seasonal employees. The laws of political economy were strict, predictable: For those on the underside of a Season's tapestry, less work meant less money. The languid months of high summer were a time for sealing marriage contracts, toting up wins and losses in the stakes for dowry or dynasty. After these necessary but tiresome few weeks, the polite world would be glad to move on to Brighton for a whiff of sea air.

Dependable hostesses like Lady Gorham might still give their dinner parties: In fact, these short evenings she stayed later at balls and receptions (she flirted more too; the young beaux were happy about *that,* and so were the *on-dits*). But even she was beginning to pack up her house. She'd puff her novel at Brighton, tie up the Season's tapestry at the water's edge.

And now she was gone.

Jasper put aside the newspaper. Two newspapers, actually, both of which agreed she'd left for the seashore.

But the burglar would be back; he was

sure of that. There wasn't much he could do but wait, so he'd buried himself in his study and tried not to think too hard about certain things. Had he really sounded so priggish, that last meeting? But had she really needed to wake him from his silly, cozy dream of her?

Late at night, he still pored over the letter she'd handed him.

Probably better that it had ended so abruptly. The gap between them was too broad to bridge.

Too late. Let it go. Polishing his spectacles and now jamming them back onto his nose, he forced his mind back to antiquity, a world where he was an authority on *something,* at least. Scowling, he set himself to writing as quickly as he could, with not a thought to the condition of his shirt cuffs. When he absolutely had to rest — to stretch out his fingers, crack his knuckles, and work out the cramp in his wrist — he allowed himself to reread the post that had arrived from Anthony in Essex.

Two letters in one week with the hunting dog on their seal. What wouldn't he have done for that once? And it was really rather touching the way Anthony had tried to be gentle about the fever Sydney had suffered, carefully assuring Uncle Jasper that she was recovering — from it and from the shock of the attempted burglary too. She'd been very brave when the doctor had lanced her ears — "each of us squeezed one of her hands, tightly as we could" — and since then she'd been mending rapidly. It was getting more difficult to keep her in bed, even with the housekeeper at Wheldon spoiling her with custards and blancmanges.

The roof was all fixed, and it seemed the men had done a good job on it. Quite unexpectedly, Anthony thanked his uncle for having taken care of the property all these years. The writing became a bit difficult to decipher there, the handwriting gone shaky, prose halting and unclear — the boy was no writer under the best of circumstances. Still, the message seemed heartfelt. Anthony hoped to be taking care of the estate himself, he said. Perhaps, he said, he might begin *his* improvements with the kitchen, which was really awfully antiquated. He and Miss Hobart had been asking the housekeeper's advice about what was needed, and were working together on some drawings.

There was a blackened-out word just before *Miss Hobart.* Jasper peered at it sharply, with eyes accustomed to teasing out an artifact's secrets. Could the name

Helen be buried below all that ink? Could the letter be hiding the best news of all? It was possible. They were young, without mistakes to brood upon, pasts to weigh them down.

The kitchen's awfully antiquated . . .

. . . And so, I expect, am I, Jasper thought. More comfortable making pronouncements about the far-off glories of the past.

He turned back to the manuscript on his desk. He could add a few sentences, draw a few more distinctions, sharpen up the knife-edged ones he already had — particularly in the chapter treating certain comic and embarrassing misapprehensions fashionable collectors were wont to make. The one about a recent purchase of a sculpture with the wrong head restored was particularly, wickedly amusing — he'd made hay of it for Lord Kellingsley's amusement. But the not entirely cheering truth was that the book he was writing was finished, and his work on Kellingsley's collection and library very nearly so as well.

He need only add the engravings he wanted Colburn to include, and Mowbrey could pack up the manuscript with string and brown paper and send it off.

What was he going to do with his time now? If he weren't careful he'd lose himself in dangerous, seductive thoughts, his mind wandering places he didn't want it to go, Odysseus sailing past the Sirens.

In the letter she'd handed him, there'd been an oddly angry postscript. Not about herself, the hard life she'd lived as a girl, the insults to her dignity, the vain, vicious, traitorous father she still seemed to weep over. All that stuff had been bad enough, and made him feel stupid for not understanding who she was and who she'd always been beneath the grace, the wit, and the finery — had let him know how entirely inadequate he'd been to the formidable task of loving her, if it hadn't been too late for that anyway.

The postscript, though, was more formal and abstract: couched as a little lecture to gentlemen like himself, a warning against the dangers of imagining themselves and their nation heir to the glories of long ago and far away. It might make an interesting experiment, she'd written, for such a worthy gentleman to take a closer look at the day-to-day business of keeping order in a troublesome little island just west of a choppy green sea — to forgo the glories of past and future empire and instead to look to today and what empire had cost the men (and particularly the women) who were its victims.

Stern stuff. He hadn't known she had it in her.

Just one of the many things he hadn't known of her.

He pushed the finished manuscript to a corner of his desk, reached down to a locked drawer, and pulled out a portfolio. The oldest pages were yellowed. A piece of work he'd put away years ago — fascinated, perplexed, and even angered by it. A love story, in Greek, from the second century after Christ. He'd been noodling away at the translation for years, on and off without thinking about it very much, sometimes instead of his monographs.

A pity, he thought before he could stop himself, that he'd never shown it to Marina.

There were a few of these old prose works. "Novels," one would have to call them, they were about very little except lovers separated and reunited. Inferior productions: In classical times one wrote about the important subjects — war and empire — in verse. The one he'd been trying to translate, *Daphnis and Chloe,* was a simple pastoral, lots of kisses stolen in field and forest. But most of the ancient novels were full of adventures — shipwrecks, slavery, pirate raids, lovers parted under duress. Sometimes the lovers' benighted parents even sent them off to sea — as though to ensure that events would have every opportunity to separate them.

It was laughable, in its way, how the writers contrived that their characters endure every misfortune the ancient world could provide, forced them to bear every possible trial — except age and cynicism, perhaps, a lifetime of bruising experience, pride, and stubbornness.

She might have enjoyed these manuscripts. He could almost imagine her looking over his shoulder — like Anthony and Miss Hobart . . . Helen — working together on some drawings for a kitchen.

Stupid. When would there have been time? The late-night hours were too short; there'd been so much else to do, more immediately urgent matters to attend to. One needed to have the days as well. One needed time. A lifetime, a life . . .

A shared life. For a moment — before he reminded himself that he and she didn't share anything anymore — a shared life seemed the most thrilling and dangerous adventure of all. Shrugging ruefully, he turned back to his ancient, pastoral love story . . .

■ ■ ■ ■

. . . at approximately the same time that, some fifty miles away, Sir Anthony Hedges woke up from a most pleasant nap in a leafy glade at the edge of the forest of Wheldon Priory.

It would be the last of these outings for some time. For tomorrow, at long last, the doctor would be letting Sydney out of bed. In truth, Anthony thought, she was probably prowling about the house in her dressing gown at this moment — unless the housekeeper had chased her back to her bedchamber. Nice that the housekeeper and Helen seemed to be on such good terms — the old lady had given the closest thing to a broad wink this morning when she'd told him that he should take himself and Miss Hobart for a ramble, get themselves out of the stuffy house in this close summer weather, before the storm blew in from the east.

Looking up at the sky, he tightened his arms about the young woman — still sleeping? yes, it seemed so — in his arms. Yes, there would be rain. In an hour, he expected.

Tomorrow he and Helen would have to

embark upon a painful regimen of chastity — until they could bring his all-too-clever and inquisitive little sister back to Uncle Jasper in London, and inform him of their plans to marry.

To make an honest woman of her, he'd joked, and she'd joked back that she hoped she could keep her honesty, with what they'd be paying to fix up the kitchen and then . . . hmm, perhaps the tower bedchamber. Oh, yes, the tower bedchamber, widen the windows, so they could have the outdoor country that they both loved indoors with them.

The clouds were flying more swiftly overhead; she was beginning to stir in his arms. Leafshadow dappled the hollows beneath her wide cheekbones, above a mouth too wide and fleshy ever to be fashionable. She was too thin, delicate hands like migrating birds, legs too long to be believed, tapering down below the too-prominent lines of her hips. Her shift had fallen over one elegantly molded shoulder to expose the small slope of a breast below the swoop of her clavicle. He swept his lips over the nipple. It rose to meet his tongue; her mouth curved; her eyelashes fluttered. In the light of the sun, they were the same elusive color as her hair.

Her hair was pretty, but really it was only

her eyes, the bronzy green of ripening pears, that might generally be accounted beautiful. As she opened them now, he saw the reflected clouds flying by, and he felt the ache of how lovely he found her. Perhaps at some other time, in some other place, people would be able to see what he saw in her elusive, wood-nymph slenderness.

Or perhaps not. And then, perhaps, it was better that they didn't — because something in him hoped that no one would ever suspect the other ways in which she had proved herself to be *fearsomely excellent.* No, all of that would just have to be his secret, and all the better that way.

Even if no one but he ever found her beautiful, Sir Anthony Hedges — handsome, pleasant, likable young London Corinthian, soon to settle into his ancestral home as a comfortable, companionable country squire alongside his practical, competent, surprisingly ordinary-looking wife — saw something rare and wonderful in the face and body beneath his.

And although he wasn't generally considered a young gentleman of profound intelligence, he was in every way intelligent enough to cherish what he had.

"Is it late? Is it time to go back?" she whispered.

"Not late at all," he whispered back. "We have plenty of time," he said, just before he covered her mouth with his mouth, her body with his, as overhead the leaves of beeches and poplars shuddered in anticipation of summer rain.

CHAPTER 23

Jasper had taken to reading the newspapers with terrifying speed and selectivity. Where once he might impatiently have scanned a page of dense type for news of battles won by Greek emancipationists, these days he reserved his keenest eye for notes of dinners, routs, and receptions at Brighton, the most overwrought and extravagant of them presided over by an increasingly overweight and exhausted George IV.

She'd appeared once in these accounts, arm in arm with some blond lordling wearing those ridiculous, newly fashionable side-whiskers. But not since then. Which *might* mean . . . well, any number of things — no point trying to think what.

There was no way he could be sure.

And given that it was over now, what did it matter?

What mattered was guarding the statue from harm, protecting the security of his home from further violation.

There was a soft rapping against his study door. He looked up to see Mr. Bright, his little Bow Street investigator, standing small and pale against the footman's imposing bulk. Rackham was still their most likely path to the burglars, but thus far Bright hadn't been able to come up with much beyond what Marina had already surmised.

And today, it seemed, was no exception.

"The watchman near Brook Street saw the fellow once or twice, loitering about late at night. Told him to move on, of course, but the watch can't be everywhere. Rackham could've seen you go in o' a midnight, or out sometime later."

Tactfully, Bright had turned his gaze away from Jasper, letting his eyes come to rest somewhere near the upper bookshelves, the little terra-cotta temple offerings. "As stealthy as you no doubt were, Mr. Hedges."

Jasper nodded curtly. "She wouldn't have needed to tell him anything about me. He could have learned the truth easily enough by simply keeping a sharp eye out; he'd probably found out about the Aphrodite from the workmen who'd delivered it to me. But haven't you found out anything yet about the people who were paying him to pass the information along?"

The little detective shrugged. "I'll ask around some more, but so far all people have been willing to tell me was some stuff about what Rackham was like in his own personal conversations, the few times he left his office to have a drink with someone."

Jasper couldn't imagine why he should care, or why he should keep paying the man's expenses. But he didn't know what else to do; the burglar had promised to come back. And until this mess was cleared up he couldn't bring Sydney back to London.

He nodded. "Carry on then, Mr. Bright." He rose from his desk to see the man out.

"A half week's more expenses," he added, and the detective's face shone to match his name at the sound of that. He knew an easy job when he saw one.

"Strange bird, Rackham," he told Jasper as they came to the entryway. "Didn't mix much, no wife nor family. Someone thought he might have had a girl in his past, perhaps when he was in the army. Mary, or something like — broke his heart that she'd never look at him, he said. A man I talked to said Rackham wept about her once, when he was in his cups."

Or something like.

Jasper nodded, his face blank behind his

spectacles, his inner vision dazzled by a sudden image of something opening, revealing itself. It wasn't the solution to his own mystery; it was the solution to Rackham's. But still, it ought to count for something.

He bade the man from Bow Street good afternoon and stood in the dim entryway, the sound of the heavy front door closing and reclosing in his ears while his mind kept opening to let in the light.

He felt a pang of loneliness. Clean and orderly, the house seemed all echo and shadow without Sydney.

Get used to it, he told himself. She ought to be going to school. She needed more than a loving, eccentric uncle in her life — more, even, than the best of governesses. Before any of them knew it she'd be a young lady. Jasper had hidden her — and himself too — from the world for too long.

Wandering back down the hallway to his study, he took himself to task for not having dismissed the detective. Bright wasn't likely to get any further, and it wasn't as though Jasper could afford the few extra days of the man's expenses. But somehow it seemed fairer to let Sam Bright have the money in recompense for the truth he'd just unwittingly revealed.

Mary, or something like. Something like

Maria. Marina. The poor sod had drunk himself into a fatal stupor brooding about his Mary, Maria, Marina, while the fire smoked and the furnace stopped up and the air turned to poison.

Somebody ought to know it, to mourn and . . . well, just to know it. Someone had to understand that Rackham had led her to believe he hated her because . . . well, because a man had *some* pride, hadn't he? Sam Bright had told him that Rackham made his "clients" come to him every month to pay. Jasper could see her — back rising straight from the sweep of her skirts, heavy-lidded eyes all disdain. Clearly as he could imagine Rackham, ears pricked for her step on the stairway, her knock at the door. Because a spiteful visit, a monthly exchange of insults, was better than not seeing her at all.

What sad, grotesque shapes passion sometimes twisted itself into. Like it or not, love wasn't all a matter of Eros and Aphrodite.

I'll keep your secret for you, Rackham, he thought — keep it sadly and respectfully, an offering for poor Rackham's unhappy soul, wandering in its dark grove in Hades.

While as for the twists and turns of his own soul? He walked slowly back to his study. He'd deal with his own soul later.

Idly, his eye fell upon the newspaper neatly folded on his desk. Even now, this late in the Season, there were announcements of exhibitions, lectures. At the home of Lord and Lady Eccles, Mr. Ayleston-Jones would be speaking on the provenance of a sculpture of a Greek athlete, recently restored, in Lord Eccles' collection.

Jasper allowed himself a sneer. He'd seen the collection. The restoration was all wrong — the angle of attachment of head to torso absurd, the head itself at best a poor copy. Too bad his book wasn't coming out sooner. It would make hay of Eccles' stupid restored athlete. For one of the engravings Jasper had insisted that Colburn's artist copy for inclusion in his book showed quite clearly the logic of the sculptors of that place and period. The engraving was one of the most precious in his collection. He'd bought it at auction in Rome many years back; it had once belonged to a Renaissance pope.

Jasper smiled wryly. For now that he thought back on it, he could remember that Ayleston-Jones had also wanted that particular engraving. Lord knew why, since he'd learn nothing from it — but Jasper had taken particular pleasure in securing the thing for himself, even if it had meant spending more than he could afford.

He wondered whether Ayleston-Jones also remembered the engraving. He must not, Jasper reminded himself, or he wouldn't be opening himself up to savaging for such an obvious error.

High time, he thought, to get the engravings out of the portfolio, which remained on the shelf of the locked cabinet, above the Aphrodite statue.

His thoughts strayed back to the night of the burglary. How panic-stricken he'd been. He'd hurried into this room to make sure the Aphrodite was still there, leaf through his portfolios, count the irreplaceable engravings.

He'd counted them twice — all present and accounted for — and then he'd locked everything back up and run up the stairs — two of them at a time — to get back to Sydney.

Counted them. Leafed through the sections of the portfolio. Hurried.

He found that he was once again in a very great hurry. That he'd sprung up and out of his chair, across the room to the cabinet. His thoughts were turning themselves about while his fingers turned the key. It was as though he could feel — could *see* — the fine levers and tumblers falling into line within the lock.

How quickly a locked-up mind could spring itself open once it had rid itself of a few preconceptions. And how many times had he said that very thing in the course of making some fine distinction, some clever bit of antiquarian deduction, to fix the date or time or creator of an artifact?

And so he found that he wasn't surprised in the slightest, upon opening the portfolio, to discover that the engraving . . . that it *wasn't* the engraving. That what he found in the portfolio wasn't an engraving at all, but a recent pen-and-ink drawing standing in for it, not as good as Miss Hobart would have done but better than Sydney could have. Done on old paper — the man had been careful there; the paper had fooled Jasper's fingertips as he'd counted. Twice.

The engraving itself was gone. Destroyed, perhaps. This thing left in its stead was useless — it could have sprung from his own fantasies, no proof of anything.

He corrected himself. The pen-and-ink drawing — and the theft of the original — were proof, in case he needed it, of how far a man would go to be thought right about something. Climb into a window, wave a pistol in the direction of an innocent child, destroy evidence.

The burglar — clearly Ayleston-Jones,

with the help of someone who could pick a Bramah lock — had never wanted the Aphrodite. He'd wanted the engraving, and he'd gotten it. The plan had always been to make the job look like a failure — open the safe, substitute the false engraving for the original, lock everything back up neat as you please, leave it looking completely undisturbed. Nice touch as well, the loud cart or wheelbarrow they'd brought with no intention of using: the sound of it rattling over the cobbles couldn't help but suggest that they'd intended to carry away the statue in it.

And nice quick thinking, Jasper had to admit, to exploit the unexpected event of finding Sydney asleep at his desk. Clever to wake her up, wave a pistol in her face, tell her to "tell your uncle . . ." All of which had made the "failed burglary" more convincing and distressing. Mr. Ayleston-Jones might not be much of an art authority, but in this event his native dishonesty had stood him well.

For a moment Jasper allowed himself to feel himself robbed of a valuable engraving, cheated of the opportunity to make a solid professional point, infuriated that Sydney had been endangered. For the next moment — more wryly — he allowed himself a moment of amusement at how neatly he'd been deceived. He could put away the stupid pistol he'd been carrying. No one would be coming back to get anything. He could do whatever he wanted with the statue. What was more to the point right now was that without the engraving, his chapter on a certain kind of bad reconstruction would be worthless.

Good that he hadn't sent it off to Colburn. He'd have to write about something in its stead. Perhaps, for a concluding chapter, something a little different. He looked up at the little carvings atop his bookshelf. Not even of marble — they were terra cotta, baked earth — crude carvings of eyes, hands, knees, breasts. Offerings to the gods from imperfect, mortal humans, for healing.

And he thought again of his little translations — the old Greek romance stories, written after the Athenians, the Spartans, the Macedonians had lost their greatness, when the business of empire had fallen to the Romans, and Greece no more than a sort of pleasure garden for Romans on holiday.

Unlike the triumphant builders of the Parthenon, the authors of these old romances weren't the masters of the Mediterranean.

In the face of their own private passions, it was as much as they could do to try to master their own feelings, to write in the spirit of devotional offering.

The author of *Daphnis and Chloe* had written to remind those who'd loved — and to teach those who hadn't — what love felt like. He'd made art out of the mixed, impure, everyday business of desire and satisfaction, separation and reconciliation.

I've written a book about great, important, public and triumphal art, Jasper thought. *I've done my best to trace its provenance, to make sharp, fine distinctions between what is authentic and what isn't.* But he'd finish it in a humbler mode, in homage to something less grand. He'd write about a comfort that he felt deeply in need of.

Well, he'd do it as soon as he'd written to Anthony and Sydney, to call them back to London. Because time was hurtling by — one could see it just by looking at Sydney, how tall she'd grown this year, by reading Anthony's letter with attention. Jasper had lost too much time already. He wanted those he loved with him when he could have them, what ever he could have of them.

CHAPTER 24

Happy as she was to be seeing her uncle again, Sydney had to own herself disappointed by the plan he'd devised for punishing the man who'd taken the engraving. Particularly in light of Anthony's stirring and inspiring set-to with the highwayman, Uncle Jasper's notion seemed just a trifle dull-spirited.

Not that she'd exactly witnessed much of what had gone on out there on the road to Essex. In truth what she mostly remembered was being hot and dizzy, half-blinded and nearly smothered by the scratchy shawl about her neck and mouth and Miss Hobart's arms squeezing the breath out of her. (Though, of course, she wasn't Miss Hobart anymore. She was *Helen* now, and it was lovely to think that they'd be sisters, doubtless to enjoy many good times together, after Helen and Anthony had gotten over their understandable but in truth rather irritating compulsion to spend nearly every waking hour in each other's company.)

But even if she hadn't really seen Anthony go after the highwayman, Sydney felt as though she had. For she'd heard so much from Helen about Anthony's gallant, impulsive bravery — not to speak of Anthony's repeated avowals that he could never have done it without Helen's marvelous clear-sightedness — that she'd built herself a highly satisfactory substitute memory of the incident.

The thief who'd broken into their house on Charlotte Street deserved to be similarly punished. Uncle Jasper ought to go after the blackguard with his own pistol, she thought, or perhaps even his fists.

Despite her protestations, however, her uncle remained adamant and, as it had turned out, absolutely correct. She'd become convinced of the wisdom of his plan the moment she and he (and Anthony and Helen too) walked briskly down to the first row of seats set up in Lady Eccles' conservatory in Richmond.

There'd been some question at first of how to get them invited to the lecture. Uncle had had to ask favors from sympathetic art collectors, but eventually they'd managed it. Fortunately, Lady Eccles wasn't entirely au courant in the world of antiquities and its controversies. And so, upon urging, she was happy enough to invite the eminent scholar Mr. Hedges, in the company of the highly decorative Sir Anthony, just suddenly back from the country.

They'd arrived early, all of them looking their best after a lovely morning sailing down the Thames, Helen valiantly endeavoring to appear comfortable in the costume her new modiste had made for her and not to mind the stares that Sir Anthony's fiancée must draw. Anthony, of course, could always be depended upon to turn heads, and so they let him take the lead, the other three of them filing after him into the front row of little gilt chairs, silently taking their seats to listen, polite and stony-faced, to the vile man's drivel. They'd even applauded at the end — which had been fun — in the obvious, minimal way people applaud when something is palpably dreadful.

Just to make him understand — and he did understand, you could tell, from the way his voice had quavered and Lady Eccles had looked embarrassed for him — that they'd made him ashamed of himself.

They'd let know him that *they* knew the truth about the statue and the engraving, and that they also knew what sort of a man would threaten and endanger a child in order to hide a truth. And a further consolation was the gossip Anthony'd picked up, that Mr. Ayleston-Jones had had his own house burgled recently, and that he'd been neatly deceived by some woman into the bargain. Not that he'd lost anything as valuable as an old engraving. Just some silver plate — but it served him right.

Most important, though, they were secure in the hope that Mr. Ayleston-Jones would be proven wrong when new evidence came to bear. Because there was still loads of stuff to be discovered; if Uncle Jasper's Greek scholar friends had anything to do with it, good new information *would* surface, and the modern world would know more and more about the ancient past.

More, but not everything, he'd added quietly. You could never know everything about the past; there were times when you could hardly be sure of the present — which was rather a new and confusing sort of thing for him to say, especially as he'd gotten a look in his eye that was stern and oddly vague at the same time, which Sydney had found equally confusing. For they'd had such a lovely day, and she'd felt herself comforted to know that the man who'd frightened her so cruelly hadn't gotten away with quite everything after all. And yet if she were honest she'd have to admit that her uncle hadn't appeared so triumphant as she would have expected.

Perhaps it was merely a matter of too many decisions to be made, details to attend to. There were proofs of his book to correct, and a new commission too: Another London gentleman wanted his library looked at. Uncle was looking forward to Dr. Mavrotis's visit as well, and the triumph of sending the Aphrodite to her home in Athens. Not to speak of the upcoming wedding, and all their own family's resettling and reshuffling. After Anthony and Helen married and returned to Wheldon, Sydney and Uncle would be taking a much prettier dwelling in Hampstead, where they could take long walks in fresh air, and be near the young ladies' school where Sydney would be beginning in October.

After which time, Sydney hoped, she might be turning again to her novel, which seemed oddly stuck.

Or not so oddly. Perhaps there was simply too much about love that she didn't understand — for she could hardly pretend not to have been utterly taken by surprise by the business between Anthony and Helen. And it continued to irk her that she couldn't understand Uncle Jasper's occasional spells of dejection, despite his evident delight at Anthony's engagement and what good friends he and Anthony had become at long last.

Sometimes she was able to cheer him up when one of those spells descended. But sometimes she wondered if she was the right person for the job. Because sometimes, oddly, she'd find herself disagreeing with him even when she really didn't, just to give vent to certain mysterious feelings of her own.

Where did these sudden storms of emotion come from? Sometimes she was frightened of going to school, and ashamed to tell anyone for appearing a baby, and sometimes she couldn't wait to be among girls of her own age. Girls or young ladies? Some days she wasn't even sure what to call them. Or herself. Her dresses didn't seem to fit as well as they had a few months ago, and they seemed just a little . . . childish? Perhaps there was a better way to wear her hair than tied with ribbons. At Wheldon, once again, she'd spent an awful lot of time brooding over that family portrait and her jowly and truculent baby self.

Still, every day wasn't quite so tempestuous. Lessons with Uncle Jasper were fun, especially when he allowed her to build an argument of her own, to see how far her own thoughts would take her. And it was fun as well when the two of them walked around older, sometimes shabbier parts of town and talked about what they saw.

For with the polite world decamping in large numbers, the west side of the city became emptier every day. It was rather like being on a boat, Sydney thought, whose passengers had all run to starboard, leaving you on the port side lifting out of the water, feeling that you might capsize. Fortunately, on the east side of Regent Street, in Bloomsbury and Holburn and Ludgate Hill, where common working people went about their tasks quite as always, things remained more normal and homelike.

If she'd still been writing, Marina thought, she might quite have relished the quiet outside her window. But as it was, she would have preferred the cries of errand boys and the creak and rattle of carriages to the rustle of her own thoughts as she supervised the servants who were packing up the house.

She'd be seeing Henry Colburn in a few days to tell him he might do what he liked with the novel about the fatuous twin. She wouldn't be puffing it. Well, she'd hardly be able to do so from a small, plain village in County Wexford. The gossip writers wouldn't be following her there, at least, when at long last she'd be going to visit the sister she'd left behind so long ago.

Written in response to that impetuous note she'd scrawled out in that dazed period after Rackham's death, her sister's letter had reached her in Brighton, sent along by Merton. Its stiff, formal, very few words were written in a hand clearly more accustomed to kneading, washing, and mending than to wielding a pen. And yet there'd been a tight-jawed eloquence about it. Perhaps her sister ought to have been the writer, Marina thought: Utterly removed in tone from the overwrought felicities of fashionable style, the spare little communication was nonetheless utterly and furiously effective.

Far more so than she'd expected. After so many years of silence, she hadn't even expected an acknowledgment of her communication. And in truth, what she'd received had been grudging enough acknowledgment: The burden of the message was her sister Margaret allowing that yes, she could use a little cash. Things were hard at home — the next sentence quickly adding that it could hardly be a surprise, things

430

had always been hard *for most of us.*

The letter hadn't bothered to enumerate the ones it hadn't been so hard for. Not only Maria — the prettier of the two sisters — but the vain, handsome, and traitorous father. Not only had he informed to the British about rebels hiding in the countryside, he'd tried to sell Maria to a brutal English officer: she'd had no choice but to run away with Sprague instead. Yes, there'd been the drunken evenings, the tabletop dancing in his library — but at least he hadn't beaten her, as the man her father wanted for her would surely have done.

And at least there'd been books for her to read, days when Captain Sprague had been out soldiering.

It wasn't so easy for me either, Margaret. Still — and Marina couldn't deny it — there was hard and there was *hard.* Reaching up a hand to move the curtain away from her window at the hotel at Brighton, a large, square-cut emerald on her index finger had picked up a ray of sunlight, in the event she might need the truth pointed out any more crudely. Peering down upon the gay promenade, what she saw instead was a bare, narrow street with two small Irish girls walking down it, giggling like to burst at something; she couldn't remember what anymore.

What different destinies each of the Conroy girls had grown up to. It must have been dreadful for Margaret when Maria had gone to live her debauched life with the captain. Speak of gossip — all of Henry Colburn's magazines combined wouldn't equal the rivers of talk that had flowed through that plain little village. A wonder that any decent man had been willing to marry Margaret; a miracle that — or so Marina had heard — he'd been a good and kind one too.

Now there's a story, the renowned Society novelist thought, *that might be worth telling.* Margaret's letter said he was dead now, with no details of how or when. But the general sense of the thing was that if Maria were to come to her door (with some money in hand), she wouldn't be turned away.

And so that was where she — Marina, Maria, these days she hardly knew which — was going. Not forever, but for long enough to settle some money on Margaret and whatever family she had — she hoped there were children — and to try to see if they could get through an afternoon or an evening without bitterness. To walk the streets and roam the hills and try to remember how it had all been and perhaps to find her way forward from there.

She was frightened. Which was why she'd

have to do it quickly, as soon as the house was properly packed up, furniture in holland covers. In two days the gentleman who'd bought the Lawrence portrait would be coming to fetch it away. There was still Colburn to attend to. After which she need only wait until Madame Gabri had finished some new, very austere gowns and cloaks for her — because she certainly wasn't going to descend upon the village as the widow of an English peer, *my lady* in a blaze of sartorial glory.

The modiste had had a splendid season. It was good of her, Marina thought, to take the time out to make the new, plain little wardrobe, in the midst of the difficult job she was having making a wedding dress for that not very promising young lady who'd surprised everyone, plain *pauvre petite.* Madame had looked up knowingly, and Marina had returned her glance with a meaningful smile, though in truth she hadn't the faintest notion what this was about, for she'd stopped reading the *on-dits* and hadn't taken a walk in Hyde Park since her return from Brighton. At least her corsets laced up as well as they needed to; sadly, she hadn't much of an appetite these days.

But since her errand had brought her to

Bloomsbury, and since she wasn't sure when she'd be returning to London . . . Well, all right, it *was* stupid, but she wanted a last walk around the comforting sprawl of objects — the ancient, the beautiful, the curious, and the mysterious.

Even if it meant chancing a meeting. Chancing it, or stupidly, recklessly putting herself in the way of it — since, as he'd said more than once, they lived so close to the institution that it was rather like their own drawing room.

Unsure, she paused on the threshold of the gallery, trying not to think too hard about her intentions or anything else. Except for her certainty, now that she'd caught sight of the pair of them, that both he and the girl appeared taller than she remembered. Of course, girls of that age did rather begin to shoot up in height at about the same time they began to develop troublesome imaginations (for she could remember some of the things that she and Margaret had ignorantly, innocently giggled about). While in his case the added height was merely the effect of the proper coat and neat trousers he wore.

At least she'd done that much for him.

The girl was arguing — a bit more audibly this time — about whether there might be a different interpretation for the frieze. King Something, the sacrifice of his daughter — Marina couldn't catch the names. The child's erudition was like to make her head throb. Jasper stood facing away from the door to the gallery, but the set of his shoulders was unmistakable — avid, alert. The set of his features would, of course, be skeptical — to try to mask his delight.

She took an abashed step backward. Foolish for her to come: She hadn't discovered anything she didn't already know. At least she was lucky that his attention was so entirely engaged. She could simply drift back into the neighboring gallery.

Except it seemed that she couldn't. For the backward step she'd taken had brought Marina perilously close to bumping into a stout lady and her companion coming up directly behind. She begged their pardon in a voice that unfortunately hadn't proved quiet enough to escape notice. Damn this barnlike room; it could pick up echoes, and this time it had.

Best to be polite then. Smiling, shrugging her shoulders, she came forward to greet them. He was smiling too, if you could call the rictus he'd composed his features into a smile. Marina wondered if her own countenance was doing something equally ghastly with itself and decided it probably was.

Nod, smile, how do you do. It wasn't taking very long. The girl already appeared peeved to share her uncle's attention. Quite as she had a few months — *only* a few months — ago, when she'd looked more a child, when she hadn't gotten that touching, leggy awkwardness about her.

"Lady Gorham, may I present my niece, Miss Hedges."

But how surprised the girl looked, even as she murmured and bowed politely. How odd — for Marina could see a sort of admiration in the too-transparent blue eyes. Surely this erudite young person didn't read novels. And yet Marina had seen the expression before — the gratitude for pleasure given, curiosity about the giver, the polite effort not to stare.

And in this case something else as well. *Syd's devilish clever,* Anthony had once told her. And while Marina, Jasper, and his niece had exchanged pleasantries, the girl had kept a part of her attention trained upon her uncle, who was, it had to be admitted, gazing at Marina in some confusion.

Yes, well. She was glad of *that,* in any case — even if the confusion wasn't going to do anybody any good. Brightly, a bit abruptly, she glanced at her pocket watch. My word, look at the time, a pity to miss the marbles today, and with such delicious sunlight pouring through the skylight too.

The farewells were quick, cordial, confused. Sadly, she realized, as she turned away, she hadn't thought to ask after Sir Anthony. No time to do anything but turn back through the adjoining gallery, down the corridor, through the courtyard, and into her carriage, waiting on Great Russell Street.

So much for *that.*

And so much for the Lawrence portrait that went out the door the next day. One didn't need a gorgeous striver of a younger self looking over one's shoulder every time one greeted a guest. No more brand marks. When she returned to Mayfair, she thought, she'd greet her guests as whatever self she happened to be. She hoped she'd know that, after Ireland.

But it seemed she'd have to do without the brand marks sooner than she'd reckoned. Right now, in fact. For her footman was announcing a Miss — yes, he'd said *Miss,* though her heart had leaped for a moment when she though she'd heard *Mr.* — Hedges.

It hadn't been all that difficult to get here.

Sydney'd been plotting it since yesterday at the museum, when it had become uncomfortably apparent . . . Well, *something* had become uncomfortably apparent, even if Sydney didn't know quite what.

But she *had,* after all, just spent a week in the country with a newly engaged couple. And stupid as she might be about such matters — and as scrupulously circumspect as Anthony and Helen had been in her presence — there were a few things it seemed she'd learned from being around them.

Her memories drifted to a magnetized piece of iron Uncle Jasper had given her when she'd been five or six, and how she used to like to get a pile of iron filings to line up when she waved the magnet over them. Yes, *that* was what she'd been reminded of, those dinner times with Anthony and Helen at Wheldon Priory, when the air in the room had seemed to waver and then to take shape, moments when one of them had asked the other for the salt or the wine or even the turnips.

She hadn't remembered the toy magnet then, but it was impossible to forget it now. Since yesterday, anyway, since she'd seen Uncle Jasper and the beautiful lady exchanging looks as they had. The same beautiful lady who was so confident on the page, so formidably witty and knowing — and so likely to break Sydney's good, plain, retiring scholar of an uncle's heart if Sydney didn't take things in hand herself.

Lady Gorham might be Sydney's favorite author, but it was impossible that she could be anything more. She must remain an Olympian presence only, with as little to do with ordinary, everyday people as the gods in their thrones on the Parthenon frieze — bigger, more serenely composed, sharing the architectural space but blissfully unaware of the fraught little human dramas around them. And certainly not exchanging such confused but charged glances as Lady Gorham and Uncle Jasper had been.

It hadn't been difficult to get permission to go to Bond Street to shop for a wedding present for Anthony. She'd been saving her pocket money; he needed a new watch fob, and now that he and Helen were so eager to fix up Wheldon Priory, he didn't buy himself things so easily. She knew the geography of the streets: When they'd first come to London, Miss Hobart had posted Greenwood's Map on the wall of her schoolroom. Of course, it was also a lucky thing that Lady Gorham was so well-known as to have a sobriquet. At least one knew where to go to find the Beautiful Bluestocking of

Brook Street.

Beautiful as the mama Sydney could never hope to equal. Not that she'd ever thought about Uncle Jasper caring about beautiful women — or women at all, for that matter. It was what was most simple and comforting about him at a moment in her life when the last thing needed was further complication.

Nor had it been difficult, once they'd come out from the jeweler's, and once the fob was tucked safely in Robert's pocket, to slip around a corner, lose herself in the flow of passersby, and get herself to Brook Street.

It might have been difficult to find the individual house, though. She'd expected she'd have to ask, which made her rather afraid. Fortunately there were a few women walking alone, housemaids and chars on errands, by the look of them. Sydney had just screwed up her courage to ask a girl not much older than herself, in a clean checkered apron, where she might find Lady Gorham's house, when she spied two workmen carrying a painting in a heavy gold frame out of a neat brick house with black shutters.

Sunlight bounced off the surface of the oil paint, but by squinting she was able to make out the image of the lady herself. Congratulating herself on her luck, she smoothed her skirt and bonnet and walked quickly up the front steps.

No turning back now — much as she wanted to, much as she'd begun to consider what a worry she'd created for Robert and for Uncle Jasper. Perhaps she ought simply to hail a cab — which would mean knowing how to do so, not to speak of where a cabstand was, and whether a driver would even give a girl her age a ride. Girl or young lady — she wasn't sure which would be the worse thing to be, in the difficult situation she'd put herself in.

But she'd already grasped the large brass knocker. Shaped like a lion's head, it was her favorite sort of doorknocker. The house was pretty, too — well, of course, she reminded herself, just imagine how fabulously wealthy someone who wrote *Parrey,* and *Farringdon,* and all the rest of them must be. Which was why, among the other hundred or so reasons Sydney had compiled, the lady must realize that she wasn't a proper match for Uncle Jasper, who had simple, austere, intellectual tastes.

Rapping politely, she rehearsed the chief of these reasons in her mind as she hoped to present them to Lady Gorham. Not too bad, she told herself — perhaps she could go through it another time. Perhaps, she thought hopefully, it would take them a long time to answer the door. It wasn't so bad just standing here; she felt much safer than she had out on the pavement.

But, as it happened, she didn't even have to knock twice.

CHAPTER 25

"Do sit down, Miss Hedges."

Most of the drawing room furniture was in covers. *Oh, dear,* Sydney thought. Lady Gorham wasn't even going to be in town much longer. It had been an excessively foolish idea to come here.

But then Lady Gorham smiled in what she might have intended to be a questioning, encouraging fashion, but which seemed to Sydney to have a edge of mockery about it. And the mockery playing about the curve of the lady's beautiful lips reminded Sydney of how the lady had looked at Uncle Jasper in the museum — both times! — and how Uncle Jasper had looked back. And suddenly her errand didn't seem so foolish after all.

"Thank you, Lady Gorham. I . . . I was merely passing by between shopping and the park, and I thought I might . . ."

"But how very kind of you."

Merely passing by. It was difficult — in the midst of what felt like a riot of contending emotions — not to be charmed by that *merely.*

But where, Marina wondered, was the governess? Come to think of it, she hadn't noticed that lanky young person yesterday at the museum either. Got a better position, she expected; quite possibly they hadn't hired a new one yet. Marina was hardly an authority on nursery matters, but it was her general impression that people in Society complained quite a lot about governesses coming and going.

All of which left her with the immediate problem of how to speak to the coltish creature on her sofa, all flushed cheeks, dusty shoes, and good frock grown slightly too short for her — had Jasper noticed?

And did girls this age really go out shopping by themselves in London? There must at least be a footman holding her packages, loitering outside the house on the hot pavement.

"Should you like a cup of tea?" she asked, rather helplessly. "I fear it's a bit dusty here with all my packing. Not quite as bad as out-of-doors, I expect. But I was thinking I might like something to drink myself."

"Thank you, Lady Gorham. A cup of tea would be very —"

"Or orange water?"

"Oh, yes. Orange water, thank you."

Marina nodded to her butler. "And, Merton, do invite Miss Hedges's footman into the kitchen and give him a drink as well. He must be awfully parched."

The girl's cheeks flushed even darker, her gloved hands twisting about each other.

"Beg pardon, Lady Gorham."

"Yes, Miss Hedges?"

"But I don't have a footman outside, my lady. I . . . I came alone to speak to you."

"By carriage?" But Jasper didn't keep a carriage.

"No, ma'am. On foot."

"Ah, quite. Well, just the orange water, Merton."

He bowed and retreated after having caught the covert signal in her glance. Good that he'd caught it, she thought. *Let's hope he knows what to do with it. . . .*

She turned back to the girl. "Well, then, Miss Hedges, it must be a matter of some urgency."

"It is, ma'am." The large blue eyes were touchingly transparent. Marina felt herself torn between an ungovernable rush of sympathy and something a good deal less worthy. Envy, she supposed, of someone who could be sure of seeing him at the breakfast table every morning.

"Well, then." She allowed herself a brittle laugh, one woman of the world to another. Let the little beast do with it what she might, she thought — after which she felt rather a beast herself for having thought such a thing.

Her voice softened. "Well, having gotten yourself here alone and on foot — most enterprising of you, I must say — you might want to let me know your purpose for coming."

Rather as Jasper might, the girl squared her chin. After which she took a breath and then a quick glance at the ceiling, as if to consult some hidden text secreted up there.

"Thank you, Lady Gorham." Text, it seemed, firmly in mind, she continued more confidently. "Well, the thing I've come to say, ma'am, is that it would be a very bad thing if my uncle, Mr. Hedges, were to fall in love with you, as it has come to my attention that he's in danger of doing. And so I must ask you to promise to make sure that he doesn't, which promise might possibly necessitate your avoiding his company."

Evidently astonished that the sky had not

fallen from the weight of her pronounce-
ment, she paused to look about herself.

Marina found herself equally astonished.
"Pray, do continue," she said softly.

"Because, Your Ladyship, I've known him
all my life, and he's not a gentleman for
witty, elegant society or the brittle sort of
heartbreaking that goes on there. I mean,
he's very clever —"

"I shouldn't doubt it."

"But in a different way from you."

"I shouldn't doubt that either, though I
can't help wonder how *you've* arrived at
your evaluation of my cleverness, or my
character, for that matter."

"Oh. Forgive me; I should have told you
how much I've learned from reading *Parrey,*
and *Farringdon,* and *The Verge of Indiscretion,* and *A Gentleman of Reputation,* and —"

"I see. I'm honored."

"Oh, yes — they're wonderful, and so
instructive too. I've read as many of them
as I've been able; they're each of them so
excellent. I try to copy . . . well, to learn
from them, in my own little efforts — and
so I've come to feel that I know . . ."

Except that as the girl pronounced the
words, her blue gaze turned abruptly inward, revealing to Marina a certain doubt
as to how much she actually knew after all.

447

Curious how very like him she is in some ways. Keen. Skeptical. Only more sensible, for all her youth. Or perhaps that's because she's a woman — or will be.

And she reads — even tries to copy — my books. Difficult not to take some pleasure in that last detail — even if, as Marina hastened to remind herself, it was hardly to the point.

Her guest gulped another large breath of air and was hurtling on apace. "In any event, I do feel I've gained a considerable acquaintance with the polite world and the sorts of things people say and do in Society. I've learned from you how important wit and style are, what power they can afford. And if it weren't my own uncle in question, and in a way myself . . . Well, I expect what I'm trying to say, Lady Gorham, is that although my uncle is a great and learned gentleman, and my family a reasonably distinguished one, I've learned this Season that we're not of London's *haut ton* by inclination."

Marina raised her eyebrows as she tried not to feel too brutally cut by that careless *we.*

"But certainly," the girl added anxiously, "you must see what I mean, at least since Anthony's engagement to Helen."

"Helen . . . ?"

"I know that people are gossiping about him falling over head and ears with a governess." The voice grew wistful. "And I wish they wouldn't, though Anthony says it doesn't matter. But you must get my meaning, even if you *are* smiling. . . ."

With surprise and delight, and at the memory of her own part in helping him ask the "very superior person" to dance. For her young guest's sake, though, Marina forced her features to fall into more respectful, serious lines.

"Anyway," the girl continued, "though I'd like to write novels, I know I shouldn't want my life — and certainly not Uncle Jasper's — to be like what I read about or what I see and hear on the Rotten Row. And so, to be perfectly and precisely honest . . . and in conclusion" — she gave a little nod of satisfaction and relief — "I hope you can see how I shouldn't want to lose Uncle Jasper to you, if only for a Season."

Marina could see it all too clearly. "Especially when it must feel like you've lost a brother and a good, kind governess all at once — to each other."

"Perhaps." A bit truculently. "I expect so."

And Marina could also see — dimly, hazily, and for the first time, it seemed — a few other things. "Of course," she offered, "your uncle won't be having *you* about him for all that many more years. Have you thought of how solitary his life might be when you're gone?"

Miss Hedges could only shrug. And indeed, Marina thought, the assertion might appear a bit far-fetched, given how slowly time moved when one was . . . what, twelve? Thirteen?

"Not, mind you," she added, "that I'm saying you must marry. I suppose you're lucky enough to have some property of your own."

A careless nod.

"You've an intellect, you seem willing to make an effort toward a vocation, and it's evident that you have a feeling for language, logic, expression. . . ."

A widening of the eyes, a half-abashed, half-delighted parting of the lips, and a lightning flash of beauty to come. All of which appeared and disappeared so quickly that Marina couldn't quite be sure she'd seen it.

But at the moment there were more important matters to be considered. Which would be easier to address, she thought, if she didn't find herself plagued by a distant sense that she'd already had this conversation somewhere.

"While as for your uncle and myself and the promise you wish me to make . . ." She spoke haltingly, still bothered by the lingering familiarity of it. Or if not this precise conversation, something very like it, with someone else exceedingly interested in imposing her own will over . . .

Ah, but she had it. And now that she did have it, she couldn't stop herself from laughing — no matter how likely that was to nettle the imperious young person on her sofa. Impossible amidst her gasps and giggles and even a few tears not to say in a wondering and halfway delighted tone of voice, "But it's Lady Catherine de Bourgh."

The girl turned her head to see who might have entered the room. Whereupon, seeing nobody, she could only stammer that she didn't know to whom Lady Gorham could be referring. "Certainly not myself. For *my* papa, as you know, was only a baronet."

Marina dabbed at the corner of her eye with a napkin. "My dear, do you really not take my reference to the literary personage you so vividly bring to mind?"

The girl shook her head.

"Really," Marina said. "But you surprise me there, Miss Hedges. So erudite a young woman not yet to have encountered a novel

451

called *Pride and Prejudice*?"

"I . . . I read your books at a friend's home, and in Uncle Jasper's study, in secret. We don't have a great many novels — actually, we have none except yours, which we must have gotten by mistake. My uncle and my governess don't read them, and —"

"Your uncle and your governess have sadly neglected your education, and their own too, in their ignorance of the few really good novels. But then, Miss Austen never had a Henry Colburn to puff her work. So I expect it's no surprise, even if it is a scandal, that more people have read me."

So this was the child he'd been protecting so zealously. From everything that seemed to him dangerous and corrupt. From *his* mistakes, and the world's too.

One must want to do so when one loved a child; one must want to do it even if it were impossible. One must want to build walls between the pure and the impure, draw the strictest lines of demarcation between innocence (as a very strange but favorite poet had had it) and experience.

Only one couldn't. One could only look for wisdom and honesty to pass along, to help the child make her own way through the necessary, perilous middle ground of building a life.

While as for one's own — childless — self? For it had quickly become clear that while Jasper had been protecting his niece, the person Marina had been endeavoring to protect was herself. But wasn't that an equally impossible and quixotic endeavor?

And what good, she wondered, had she done herself by shying away from the possibility of a rejection too painful to be risked? To what end had she forbidden herself from telling him the single most important thing?

"I doubt, Miss Hedges, that you need worry about your uncle being in love with me. I'm quite sure I've already succeeded quite well in obviating that occurrence. And yet I must inform you that I'm unable to comply with your wishes: I can't and so I won't promise to, um, stay away from him, as you put it. Not yet anyway. Because there's one thing I haven't told him, one secret that still needs to be disclosed."

She'd been looking everywhere but into the wondering, transparent depths of the eyes she felt fixed upon her.

Afraid of drowning? But one couldn't be afraid when one needed to be an example — at the very least of a sort of honesty.

And so she took her own large breath of air, acknowledged her caller's gaze with a gentle yet implacable one of her own, and spoke very softly. "I'm afraid that I must see him one more time to tell him that I love him. No matter what he may say, do, or think about that information. Or about me."

She rose out of her chair. "My butler has sent some footmen out looking for him to tell him where you are. You really oughtn't to have frightened him, you know, as you most assuredly did by going off by yourself. In truth, you oughtn't even to have frightened your own footman — it wasn't fair. But if Mr. Hedges doesn't come soon for you, we'll send you back home in my carriage.

"Come along to the library," she added. "We'll find you something to read while you wait."

In truth she'd rather cherished the hope he'd have already arrived. Because the easiest way for her to cope with this muddle of feeling would have been if he'd appeared in the doorway in time to overhear her confess her love for him to Sydney. There would have been a quick, economical closure about it, a sprightly suddenness — not to speak of relieving her of the challenge of having to say it all over again directly to his face. A good enough effect, if a slightly cheap one: It was probably how Lady Gorham (who was no Miss Austen) would have written it.

But in this case it wasn't how events (which have their own rhythms, speeds, and complications) unfolded.

For upon being told of Sydney's disappearance Jasper had gone to Bow Street. And so, consequently, it had taken Marina's footman some time to catch up with him, leaving Marina wondering all the while at the anxiety Jasper must be feeling.

Was this what it was like when you raised a beloved child? she asked herself. How strange. How awful. How really rather splendid to care for someone in this way.

How frightened he must have been by Sydney's blithely setting off as she had. What a short memory a loved and cherished child had, even so soon after a pistol had been pointed at her.

But this wasn't the time to think about any of that, Marina reminded herself — or to dwell on the memory of another, less loved child, her memories more sharply, painfully etched. This was the time to share his relief as he entered her house — long limbed, rumpled, apologetic, his jaw still taut from the scare he'd gotten. Marina led him into the library. Sydney wrenched guilty eyes away from the amused and amusing Miss Elizabeth Bennet — not handsome enough to tempt Mr. Darcy, indeed! Marina retreated back to the drawing room.

To wait for what seemed like a terribly long time. Though what did she know about what one said to a headstrong child — who'd been trying to protect her uncle as foolishly and lovingly as he'd been trying to protect her?

But here they finally were at the door, side by side, and each of them so solemn and also so alike in their expression that she had to be amused despite her agitation.

Each of them, it seemed, with something to say to her.

CHAPTER 26

Jasper began by thanking her. "For sending for me so expeditiously. For attending to my niece. For allowing us to disturb you so shamefully this afternoon when it's evident you're exceedingly busy, and so we shan't be taking more . . ."

Sydney glanced meaningfully at him, and he corrected himself. ". . . *much* more of your time."

To which Sydney appended her apologies and a curtsy. "I have been very glad of the opportunity to speak to you, Lady Gorham, and to get to know you a little. And I wonder . . ."

This time it was her uncle sending the reproving glance. Which, however, did not cause Sydney to correct herself, but only to continue with what it seemed to Marina she'd been intending to say from the first. "I wonder whether I may avail myself of the loan of your carriage, as you offered, in order that my uncle might take as much time as he might possibly need to hear what you have to say to him. And also . . ."

Marina hardly had to look down at the volume still in the girl's hand — which was probably just as well, for her head was beginning to swim, and she found that she needed to attend to keeping her balance. "Of course you may borrow the book, to read in the carriage and at home tonight, and as long as it will take you to find out how it all comes out.

"And I have been very glad to get to know you a little as well, Sydney," she managed to add, before Merton led the girl away and they were alone together in her sitting room.

Jasper closed the double doors and stood with his back to them. "Well," he said.

"I love you," she replied. Because if she didn't say it now she would never say it. And which turned out to be far easier to say than she would have imagined, even if she did rather mumble it, being half turned away from him and having retreated into the window alcove.

It was also a very quick thing to say. Which wasn't such a surprise, or shouldn't have been — because it wasn't very many syllables nor a very complicated idea. But having never voiced the phrase before, she'd somehow fancied it a very great and grand utterance — as though, when one gave breath and timbre to it, *I love you* would issue forth from one's lips amid fanfare and flourishes.

As, of course, it hadn't. It had sat on her tongue, vibrated upon the air for a second. And now it was gone. Hardly worth the trouble of getting the carriage for Sydney, she thought rather distractedly — when a second later he was standing by her side, his arms very tight about her as he gathered her to himself, and time and the world seemed to reshape themselves about their linked bodies. The sound of hooves on cobblestone and of a carriage rumbling down the street became oddly distant, as did everything outside the little bubble of time and space surrounding him and her, their hands and mouths, her breasts crushed against his chest.

The only real measure of time, it seemed, being the beat of their pulses and the swell and stream of their breath.

"I love *you*." He murmured it into her neck. "I *trust* you. Forgive me that once I didn't know how to." He breathed it into her ear. "I want to be with you. Every day. I want to marry you." His lips were on hers now. As though he'd said the essential things. As though there was nothing left to say.

But, of course, there was a very great deal to say. They'd said so little to each other up until now. The midnight meetings had never been long enough. He was right, she thought: They did need the daytimes.

A lifetime of days with someone you loved seemed like so very much to ask.

She moved her face away from his; she leaned back in his arms and tried to look solemn and serious.

"And it doesn't matter to you," she asked, "that there still might be talk? Rackham might have left hidden papers, you know, and not every man at Bow Street is as honest as we like to think. Information gets around; you hate spiteful publicity. Who knows if next year I'll get my voucher . . . ?"

Evidently it didn't matter in the slightest. And when she pulled away from the next kiss, she didn't lean back quite so far. One could discuss these things, it seemed, at very close range.

"And you must take into account as well," she said, "how the gossip that follows me will affect your family. Because one of these days you'll be looking for a husband for Sydney, and . . ."

He kissed the tip of her nose. "In order to

find someone singular enough to marry the woman Sydney bids fair to be . . ."

She nipped his chin. "Yes," she said, "I take your point. You've brought her up to be so very much herself that he'll have to be willing to contend with a great deal already."

"As I shall, Marina, if I try to bring her up any further without your help. As I did so dreadfully with Anthony . . ."

"You didn't do so badly. Shall you ever tell him?"

"I don't think so. He loved the man he thought was his father. I won't make that more confusing for him. I think I've learned to offer thanks for what I do have, the odd mixture of it, the way he's turned out to be what he is, and his sister . . . well, we shall simply have to see who *she'll* be, won't we? And if I may have you, in all your miraculous singularity, in the mixture . . ."

"I think I pushed myself into the mixture, as you call it, before you were ready, when I felt myself too old to be his lover . . ."

"Thank the gods for that."

". . . and found I wanted to be . . . well, not quite a mother; you know I can't have children. . . ."

He kissed her cheeks, her eyelids, her chin — he ran his lips over the moist tips of her eyelashes and made her shudder and grasp

461

him tighter around the waist.

"One way or another," he said, "I think we've found our family in the shifts of fortune and affection. It seems to me you found Anthony before I did." He grinned at her. "And if not a mother, you *could* — you *can* — be an aunt. Well, Sydney will have to call you something, won't she?"

"I expect she will."

"And you won't really be giving her *too* many novels to read, will you?"

"Only the very best ones. So I'm to be *Aunt Marina,* then. Sounds very proper. Hmmm, perhaps you'd like me to wear a cap?"

Evidently not, because he'd begun taking the pins out of her hair. Slowly, so he could watch and she could feel it tumble down about her shoulders. And when he finished, and after she'd shaken out the wild little curls, he held her again while she undid the knot of his cravat.

She supposed there was still a great deal more to discuss.

Where would they live? *How* would they live? How did one combine the thick, bright pleasures they already shared with the everyday miracles of care and responsibility?

Would he come with her to Ireland? Yes,

of course. She wanted to bring him there, because he, and other Englishmen, needed to understand about this troublesome, most unexotic western edge of the empire they took such pride in.

But for her first visit back in pursuit of her past, she thought she'd better go herself and then come back to him.

And then she thought that she'd thought enough for one day.

Because there'd be other days, the mortal procession of shared days and nights, the wonder of living together within the limits of precious human time.

Enough right now to feel it in each other's arms as they made their way first to the sofa and now down to the rug. To see it in the slant of summer sunlight creeping around the edge of the curtain, spilling over the sprawl of their bodies. To taste it on each other's tongues. To know for the first time that there was enough time, that the tides of passion and empire had brought them home.

CHAPTER 27

It had been exciting, Sydney thought, to see the Aphrodite's little crate loaded into the hold at Falmouth. Uncle's friend Dr. Mavrotis would be accompanying the goddess home to Athens; the reverence he'd shown for his errand was most gratifying. Sydney had wanted to stay and watch the ship set sail, but there were still so many miles to travel before they could send another goddess home, as Uncle had put it — because, of course, the packet boats to Ireland embarked from Holyhead and Milford, in Wales, at the western end of the island.

"Hardly a goddess," the lady in question had cautioned him, and they'd all three laughed as the late-summer landscape flew by the windows of the post chaise.

There wasn't time for a call upon Lady Isobel Wyatt and Miss Amory — for the two young ladies had determined to live together as companions and had set themselves up in a Welsh cottage. "Perhaps on my journey back," Lady Gorham had said; it seemed she'd received an affectionate letter of invitation from her stepdaughter. But Sydney must have missed some of the conversation here — there'd been something she hadn't quite caught about Lady Isobel's inheritance from her father. Or perhaps it was that she'd been so eager to work through the quirky complications of *Mansfield Park* with such an astute reader of novels as Lady Gorham had proved to be. Uncle Jasper affected to doze during these discussions, but Sydney could see he had an ear cocked and would probably ask to borrow the volume after Lady Gorham had sailed.

Lady Gorham. For although Miss Hobart had immediately become Helen, even before she and Anthony had married, Sydney had determined to begin calling this lady *Aunt Marina* only when the syllables came easily to her — and certainly not before the wedding in October. It had been agreeable to make her own decision about this. She'd announced it a week ago on the way home from a highly satisfactory visit to Madame Gabri (who wasn't at all fazed, it seemed, by the demands of a new young customer growing an inch taller every week), and

Lady Gorham had agreed it seemed the best way.

The discussion in the carriage had been stimulating. Of course, it helped that Sydney and her aunt-to-be were bound by ties of mutual vocation, but Sydney wasn't so naive as to overlook the care the lady and Uncle Jasper took not to make her feel *de trop* when the three of them were together. Much more tactful than Anthony and Helen, but then, you'd expect it of a couple who were so much older and wiser. Visits home from school would be quite comfortable. No need to worry about it, as she had at first.

Still, once they'd gotten to the dock, Sydney could see that they wanted a private moment before the packet boat left. Which was a good opportunity for her, in truth. Because although the novel about Lady Philippa was still in its doldrums, Sydney had decided to take Lady Gorham's excellent advice and observe ordinary people, to see what stories she could make of *their* lives, taking note of interesting faces and turns of phrase.

Like "we shall be helping my new husband's mam to pack up — yes, she sold the cottage in Ireland for a few pounds — and then we'll be bringing her to America with us. We did quite well with what we got off *him,* payment for that strange job where they didn't take nothing much, *and* then the silver plate we got too." A giggle here. "But the biggest adventure is learning to call myself *Missus.* I don't think I ever expected to be so happy, and thanks for the wedding congratulations."

All of which would have been interesting enough (for in a little corner of her mind Sydney continued to regret the lost opportunity to visit Cincinnati, Ohio), if all the happy chatter weren't tumbling so effusively from the lips of such a pretty woman, dressed so elegantly in gray lavender silk twill.

And how much more interesting when the woman linked her arm confidingly into that of the handsomest man Sydney had ever seen — quite putting Anthony in the shade, he was so tall, strong, romantic, and just a little bit dangerous-seeming, with such sly, glittering . . . *familiar* dark blue eyes.

Don't be a fool, and stop scaring the child by pointing a pistol at her.

She mustn't stare. Even if it seemed to her that Uncle Jasper had cast the lady in lavender a quick glance, and the lady had almost smiled in the way of fluttering her eyelashes in the direction of Uncle Jasper and Lady Gorham, and Lady Gorham had stood very straight and elegant, drooping her eyelids and smiling in the way that was always sure to discombobulate Uncle Jasper.

Even if in all the flurry and confusion, Sydney had been *sure,* absolutely certain, that the handsome, dangerous, and yet good (she was sure of that as well) man with the dark blue eyes had winked at *her.*

Very quickly, before turning to his beautiful bride to lead her on board, quite as Uncle Jasper was handing his bride-to-be on board the packet boat at the same moment.

So many stories: They seemed separate and yet not so; perhaps they were waiting for Sydney to weave them together — like Lady Gorham, like Odysseus's Penelope and the goddess of the Parthenon who had invented weaving. Perhaps the stories were waiting for Sydney to weave herself into the picture one day as well.

And now everyone was waving, to the tinny but celebratory sound of a little band of street musicians. Uncle and Sydney each gave them a coin before waving their last giddy waves, calling out their love and farewells and bon voyages, throwing kiss

after kiss as the packet boat caught the tide
and left the shore.

AFTERWORD AND ACKNOWLEDGMENTS

If the portrait that hangs in the Countess of Gorham's sitting room might have seemed familiar to any readers, it's because I had a real portrait in mind: Sir Thomas Lawrence's famous painting of Margaret, Countess of Blessington, a detail of which adorns the lovely cover of my prior novel, *The Slightest Provocation.*

So thanks are due to the Penguin Group art department, not only for a widely admired book cover, but for sparking my curiosity about the woman behind that portrait, and suggesting a model for the heroine of this historical romance novel. I drew upon many elements of Margaret's life for Marina — her youth in Ireland, her marriage, her career as a novelist, and her friendship with the famous dandy the Comte d'Orsay. Margaret's story can be found in *Last of the Dandies,* by Nick Foulkes. In *The Edge of Impropriety,* I recombine these elements with a free hand, and give my heroine, Marina, a far happier ending.

Marina's publisher, Henry Colburn, was also Margaret's. And, as in my novel, Colburn was an energetic figure in the London publishing world. Among the hundreds of books he published was *Vivian Grey,* by a feverishly ambitious young Benjamin Disraeli — who in 1834 did at last get his subscription to Almack's. More about Colburn, Disraeli, and society (or silver-fork) novels of the period can be found in Ellen Moers's *The Dandy: Brummell to Beerbohm.*

Jasper Hedges isn't modeled on anyone, but I did do a lot of reading about the British interest in classical sculpture during the Regency period, and about the ongoing controversy over possible repatriation of the Elgin — or Parthenon — Marbles (you'll call them one thing or the other, depending on what side you're on). Early nineteenth-century arguments for sending the sculptures home weren't as uncommon as one might think: The source for Jasper's disparaging dinner-table comments about Lord Elgin is Christopher Hitchens's *Imperial Spoils: The Curious Case of the Elgin Marbles.* A wealth of excellent general information on the subject may be found in William St.

Clair's *Lord Elgin and the Marbles.*

About the Parthenon, the sculptures, and the British Museum, the most concise, clear, and delightfully written source I encountered was Mary Beard's small book, *The Parthenon.* Anne Carson's *Eros the Bittersweet* is an indispensable beginning point for anyone who wants to think about how the ancient Greeks shaped (can I say invented?) this powerful concept, and also about the second-century A.D. Greek romance novels. Translations of the novels have been collected and edited by B. P. Reardon: *Collected Ancient Greek Novels.* As for Jasper's thoughts about love and death, gods and mortals: The idea of gods as big, mischievous children is one I've always liked; while writing this book my imagination was particularly sparked by the comments (much richer and darker than mine or Jasper's) in J. M. Coetzee's novel *Elizabeth Costello.*

An embarrassing number — perhaps the majority — of these sources were introduced to me by my research partner and constant source of love, strength, and inspiration: my husband, Michael Rosenthal, who's my most astute reader in every sense of the word. I'm grateful as well for forthright and useful criticism from Penni Kimmel, Ellie

473

Ely, and my editor, Laura Cifelli — and hope I did justice to the help I was offered.

Thanks also for encouragement and ideas from Ellen Jacobson; Doreen deSalvo; Bella Andre; Candice Hern; William de Soria; my agent, Helen Breitwieser; and my romance-writing partner in crime, Janet Mullany.

During its writing, I was fortunate to have the opportunity to think about this book online, in my posts to historyhoydens .blogspot.com and thespicedteaparty .blogspot.com. Thanks to everybody who shared their thoughts during those conversations, to my fellow hoydens, and to the other "crumpet strumpets" at the tea party.

And thanks again to the Penguin Group's art department, for a cover (on this one) that just may have outdone the last one.

ABOUT THE AUTHOR

Pam Rosenthal is a native New Yorker who currently lives in San Francisco with her husband. She loves to hear from readers at www.pamrosenthal.com.

The employees of Thorndike Press hope you have enjoyed this Large Print book. All our Thorndike, Wheeler, and Kennebec Large Print titles are designed for easy reading, and all our books are made to last. Other Thorndike Press Large Print books are available at your library, through selected bookstores, or directly from us.

For information about titles, please call:
  (800) 223-1244

or visit our Web site at:
  http://gale.cengage.com/thorndike

To share your comments, please write:
  Publisher
  Thorndike Press
  295 Kennedy Memorial Drive
  Waterville, ME 04901